Chasing Shadows

Margaret Alty

Published 2019 by arima publishing

www.arimapublishing.com

ISBN 978 1 84549 740 8
© Margaret Alty 2019

Printed and bound in the United Kingdom

Typeset in Garamond

Swirl is an imprint of arima publishing.

arima publishing
ASK House, Northgate Avenue
Bury St Edmunds, Suffolk IP32 6BB
t: (+44) 01284 700321

www.arimapublishing.com

Chapter One

It was late on Friday afternoon when Claire picked up the keys to Tulip Cottage. She had been delayed leaving London by a couple of last-minute phone calls and the journey down to the New Forest took longer than it should have done due to roadworks on the motorway and a further hold-up at the exit junction for the A35. The cottage was on the outskirts of Upper Nettles, a small market town a few miles south of Lyndhurst. She had only been there once before when she had viewed the property a couple of weeks ago, but remembered Upper Nettles had been signposted immediately after driving through Lyndhurst and joining the A337; a narrower and quieter road, taking her into the centre of the town.

Apart from the delays, and after she had left the London suburbs, it had been a pleasant drive and now, as she pulled up outside Tulip Cottage, she felt she had made the right decision to come here. Well-meaning friends, including Dan, her agent, had warned she might find the rural life claustrophobic, but she hadn't agreed with them. As she told them, it wasn't as if she was going to turn herself into a hermit by choosing to live in the country and besides, she would have to make regular trips back to London. No, she decided, slipping the key into the lock and opening the front door of the cottage, it did feel right; a life without Tom it was true, but the final breakup of their relationship had, she now acknowledged, been inevitable.

There were still times when she experienced again the deep hurt of his deception, a bitter reminder that she had never really known him at all, wondering how much longer it would have taken to find out he'd been two-timing her. It had been pure chance she had seen him with another woman when he should have been in Paris attending a business conference as he had told her. Exactly one month ago, and she had been in a taxi going back to the flat in Great Russell Street and, having stopped at a set of traffic lights in The Strand, couldn't miss seeing them walking across the road directly in front of her. They were so deep in conversation it was doubtful whether they even noticed the taxi, far less seen the woman passenger leaning forward in her seat to make sure she wasn't hallucinating, but it had been Tom alright and what she had witnessed had been like a physical blow, the deception, if anything, made worse by his denial later, insisting he had been in Paris and not in London, saying she had been letting her vivid imagination run away with her. That had been the final insult and she could tell by the closed-in expression on his face, that as far as he was concerned, the subject was closed, paradoxically making it easier for her to sever her ties with him.

She hadn't wasted any time, refusing to allow him to spend another night in the flat and had watched silently as he had packed his suit carrier, untidily cramming the few items he had acquired over the last three years they had been together, into another bag and the final way he had zipped it close, told her everything; he had no regrets in leaving her, relieved perhaps she was making it easy for him.

She heard a week later he had moved in with one of his colleagues from the office, presumably a temporary measure until he got himself sorted out. But, as far as she was concerned Tom and she were now history; ironically, it hadn't been seeing him with the woman, it had been the fact of him lying to her, which had strengthened her resolve; in other words, she could no longer trust him.

Tulip Cottage had few neighbours, the nearest being about two or three hundred yards away; she could make out the red-tiled rooftop from her lounge window, but the main part of the house was shielded from view by a tall beech hedge.

It was so incredibly quiet; she hadn't passed any vehicles on the way out of Upper Nettles, but this was what she had been looking forward to, right from the moment she had made up her mind to come here. Dan had been visibly stunned when she'd told him, not by her decision to move out of London, but why to somewhere hardly anyone had ever heard of buried away in the middle of the New Forest.

"For God's sake, Claire, of all the places in the south of England, why choose there?" he'd asked.

"I think it was more Upper Nettles choosing me, than the other way around, Dan." she'd told him.

"Explain. Please."

"I'd already decided it was time to make a change, but I really had no idea of where I wanted to go until I saw a photograph of Tulip Cottage; this was in an estate agent's window in Regent Street. I thought it looked idyllic and when I went in to enquire they told me exactly where it was in the New Forest."

"You're not chasing rainbows, I hope, Claire; I don't need to tell you that the word idyllic is something of a misnomer in these far from idyllic times."

"I believe I could be happy there, Dan," she'd said simply, "also, I think it will be conducive to my writing."

"That's alright, then." he'd grinned. Dan Philips had been her agent for years, ever since the publication of her first book and they understood each other. She had once introduced him to Tom, but she got the strong vibes that the two of them hadn't taken to each other. Tom had never said anything and she hadn't seen any point in asking what he thought of Dan, realising from that moment it was probably best to keep her professional life separate.

The interior of the cottage had been completely renovated and bore little resemblance to what it must have looked like originally: the wooden beams and the stone-built fireplace were still intact, but the ground floor was now open-plan; cream-painted walls; shelving, acting as a division between the living and dining areas; chintzy-covered sofas and chairs in muted shades of mustard, pale green and lemon, a long marquetry-inlaid coffee table, book cases running the length of one of the walls and at the far end of the room adjoining the kitchen, floor-to-ceiling glass sliding doors leading out on to a paved terrace; there were no pictures or ornaments, but her own would be arriving the following day, together with her other personal possessions.

The bedroom, almost as large as the lounge, faced the front of the property and from here she could see more of the house across the road; traditionally built, although probably not as old as Tulip Cottage. There were two cars parked on the gravel drive outside the front door and although most of the windows were open there appeared to be no-one around.

Apart from the bathroom, there was only one other room, this one leading off from the bedroom and which Carol Black from the Agency had described as a dressing-room, possibly because of the built-in cupboards and full-length wall mirror, but she had already decided it would be ideal for her study and, as with the dining area and the kitchen, overlooked the terrace, but from this height, gave her a much clearer view of the green lushness of the New Forest, also of its sheer vastness; a stream meandered over to her right, the slim trunks and branches of what she reckoned could be alders, shakily reflected in the water; further along, a narrow wooden bridge and, at the water's edge, two ponies, heads lowered in unison, drinking from the stream. On the other side of the stream and further up from the bridge, a single-storey building, stone-built like Tulip Cottage, but perhaps not quite so old; a conservatory had been added, with narrow steps leading down to the water's edge. So, she thought, going back downstairs to the kitchen, she wasn't as isolated as she had first thought when Carol had shown her round the week before.

She had brought a bottle of wine with her, and after unpacking and arranging her computer and papers in the study, took it with her out on to the terrace, turning her chair round to face the last rays of the sun, when her mobile rang.

'Claire,' Tom's voice, strident and unwelcome to her, 'don't ring off.'

'Yes?' sorely tempted to do just that.

'Where are you?'

'I don't see that's any concern of yours, Tom.'

'Look, Claire, we need to talk. I gave Dan Philips a ring, but all he told me was that you were now living in Hampshire.'

'I have no wish to talk to you; I thought I made that clear the last time I saw you; we're no longer together, Tom.'

'I know, I know,' impatiently, 'but I want to explain; persuade you to change your mind.'

'That will never happen; goodbye, Tom.' cutting him off, fully expecting him to call back, but he didn't. She sat quite still for a moment, trying to re-capture her former sense of peace, her wine remaining untouched. She couldn't understand his persistence; he had destroyed the love she once believed she had for him and no amount of talking would rekindle that. Sighing, she leaned forward for her glass and took a long contemplative sip of her wine.

*** *

She was on the edge of sleep when she was disturbed by the sound of breaking glass; it must have been after midnight, but she didn't switch on the bedside lamp to find out; instead, throwing back the duvet, she padded bare-foot across to the window in time to see a white saloon car emerge from her neighbour's drive and, with a revving of the engine, speed off in the direction of Upper Nettles. Most of the house was in darkness, except for a room on the ground floor; the French windows wide open and light streaming out, illuminating the lawn. Someone was playing a guitar; strains of "Blue Moon" reaching her clearly, but she couldn't see anyone and no sign of the broken glass. Perhaps, she thought, going back to bed, country living wasn't so quiet after all.

The carriers arrived shortly after ten in the morning and by midday she had completed most of the unpacking; already the cottage looked more lived in with her collection of crystal and china, her books, many of which she'd had for years, and her pictures, but she would need to find someone to hang them for her, never having tackled that task before and lacking the confidence to try. She had already planned to take the day off, much preferring to keep to her old routine of morning and afternoon sessions; mornings working on her current book and afternoons spent checking through the draft and usually finishing the day by catching up on any paperwork and phone calls. She needed to stock-up the freezer and purchase anything else she might need, also to place an advert, possibly at the newsagents, for a daily help, but first she would call in at "The Hunters Arms" for a lunchtime drink and something to eat. It could be a good opportunity to meet some of the local people; that way, find out more about the town, at the same time discover just how friendly they were to someone they may very well label as an 'outsider'.

There were a number of pubs and restaurants in Upper Nettles, but she thought "The Hunters Arms" looked the most inviting and could have been a stopping-off place for parties of the New Forest hunters centuries ago, imagining when horses would have been tethered to posts outside the inn; not as it was today with cars lining the street, each of them displaying the obligatory parking ticket. With buildings like these still remaining, she felt a sense of timelessness where the modern bustle survived side by side with a much slower pace of life and somehow didn't detract from what the people of the New Forest wanted to achieve; no wonder, she thought, it was now one of England's National Parks.

Parking was permitted outside "The Hunters Arms", although there were no free spaces, but she remembered seeing a car park at the rear of "The Nettles Hotel" at the approach to the town and she left the car there, walking the short distance back into the High Street. The front door of the pub was open and, stepping down the shallow steps, she went inside. Unlike Tulip Cottage, she doubted whether many changes had been made over the centuries: low-beamed ceilings, dark wood panelling, a stone-flagged floor and an enormous fireplace; another reminder of bygone days long before smokeless zones.

There were several customers waiting to be served, but it didn't take long for the woman behind the bar to deal with their order and within a couple of minutes it was her turn.

'I'd like a white wine, please.'

'Any preference?'

'Chardonnay, if you have it.'

'We certainly do,' she smiled, taking a bottle of Chardonnay down from the shelf, 'are you on holiday?'

'No, although I must admit it does feel like it; I only moved in yesterday, so everything is very new to me.'

'I know what you mean,' she said, opening the bottle and pouring out the wine, 'but you'll soon settle down. We're a friendly lot in Upper Nettles.' she added.

'I'm Claire Walters, by the way.' Claire told her.

'And I'm Deidre Portman and that's Chris my husband over there.' pointing to the tall grey-haired man serving at the other end of the bar.

'You have a really lovely place here, Deidre; terrific atmosphere.'

'Thank you; it takes a bit of looking after, but we think it's worth it, also we're lucky in having the patio at the back which can be a real sun trap when the weather is like it has been these last few weeks.' and then with an apologetic smile moved away to serve another customer.

'Good morning, Trevor,' Claire heard her say, 'your usual?'

'Please, Deidre.' he answered in an accent which she couldn't place, 'What a morning! I don't think I've ever had so many customers in the gallery at the same time; mind you,' he drawled, 'none of them bought anything.'

'That's a shame, Trevor; maybe you'll have a better afternoon.'

'I sincerely hope so; something to do with our economy, I suppose. I trust we're not in for another recession; that's what Maurice thinks anyway and he could very well be right.'

He was only a few feet away from her and seemed unaware of her close scrutiny, allowing her to indulge in her favourite past-time of people-watching when she tried to piece together the various facets of anyone whom she found interesting. Deidre had called him Trevor and perhaps the gallery he mentioned could be for both exhibiting and selling works of art. He was, she reckoned, in his early fifties, more plump than stocky, light brown hair, brushed back from a high forehead; neatly, if somewhat flamboyantly, dressed: pale blue linen trousers and matching jacket with a royal-blue and white polka dot cravat tied loosely into the open-neck of a white shirt. And who was Maurice, Claire wondered.

Deidre's attention was, once more, taken up with attending to some more customers and perhaps looking for someone else to talk to, he turned to where she was standing.

'On holiday?' he asked, making her think this was how people in Upper Nettles struck up a conversation with someone they had never seen before and as she had with Deidre, told him she had only arrived yesterday.

'Are you Claire Walters, the writer?' he asked as soon as she mentioned her name.

'I am, yes.'

'I have to say I haven't read any of your books, but Maurice has and I recognised you from your photograph on the back cover.'

'Maurice?'

'Maurice is my partner, Claire.' he said looking at her closely as though gauging her reaction, but she was going to disappoint him, Claire held no firm views on another person's sexual inclinations and if the pair of them were living together, that was their business and didn't concern her. She had spent too many years working among people who had elected to live unconventionally, to be either shocked or judgemental.

'He is obvious a reader, then.' was all she said.

'Oh, he is; he'll be quite thrilled when I tell him you're living in the same town as us.' going on to tell her about the art gallery they had set up twelve months ago, having returned to England after spending some time in Australia. As soon as he mentioned Australia, she recognised a faint Australian accent in his voice where there was a slight rise in cadence at the end of each sentence.

Claire noticed the woman coming over towards them before he did and couldn't stop herself smiling at the dramatic way he re-acted when she tapped him lightly on the shoulder.

'Hello, Trevor.' she said.

'Sylvia!' twirling round to face her, 'How lovely to see you!' kissing her on both cheeks, 'How are you?'

'I'm fine, but I'm sorry; I'm interrupting you.'

'No, not at all; Claire,' he said, 'allow me to introduce you to a dear friend of mine, Sylvia Crossman; Sylvia,' dragging out the introduction, 'this is Claire Walters, Upper Nettles' brand new resident.'

'Hello, Claire,' she said, shaking hands with her, 'welcome to Upper Nettles; I hope you'll be very happy living here.'

'I'm sure I shall.' she smiled, wondering where she fitted into what appeared to be the social hub of the town. Sylvia Crossman was probably about ten years older than herself, she guessed; an attractive woman with a remarkably smooth skin and a natural blonde; her hair shoulder-length and framing an oval-shaped face.

'So, Claire,' she asked, 'where are you staying?'

'At Tulip Tree Cottage, just on the edge of the town.'

'Tulip Tree Cottage,' she repeated, 'I know it well; it's a lovely house and such a beautiful setting.'

'Isn't that near where Johnnie Wall lives?' Trevor put in quickly.

'Yes, that's right, Trevor,' and Claire could tell by the careful way she answered him she was reluctant to say anything further; intrigued, remembering the disturbance in the early hours, she waited, hoping to learn more about her neighbour, 'I suppose you could say, Claire,' she explained, but not with any enthusiasm, 'that we have a well known celebrity living in our midst, albeit, at the risk of being uncharitable, Johnnie is no longer as famous in the music business as he was fifteen or twenty years ago.'

'In other words,' Trevor piped up, displaying the catty side of his nature, 'he's a has-been.'

'I don't want to sound totally ignorant, but who is Johnnie Wall?'

'Have you heard of the "Bandanas"?' Sylvia asked her.

'I think so, but it must have been a long time ago.'

'It probably was,' she nodded, 'although, apparently, they are still doing the occasional tour, but mostly in Europe these days. Johnny,' she went on to explain, 'is their bass guitarist; there's another three in the group and most of them have been with him right from the beginning, back in the early nineteen-eighties.'

'Does he come into the town or keep himself to himself?'

'Surprisingly perhaps, especially in a town as small as this, I haven't seen him; what about you Trevor?'

'Two or three times only, I would say; I've heard people say he's a bit of a loner, although Pete Carr, the group's saxophonist, comes in here fairly regularly whenever he's visiting. I never told you this, Sylvia, but Maurice and I once went to one of their concerts when they were performing in Sydney.'

'Really.' making it plain she wasn't too keen on the group and, as if homing into what she was thinking, gave a rueful little smile, 'I expect you're wondering why I'm being so negative about them, Claire, but the truth is, I have a great abhorrence of anyone who takes drugs and Johnnie Wall has a history of a number of drug offences, even served a prison sentence in Germany when they were touring there a few years ago.'

'I see; as it happens I share your views, Sylvia.'

'All too common these days,' Trevor said, 'especially in the music business.'

'Sadly, that's all too true, but it's no excuse,' she said, 'and when you consider the majority of their fans are young people, it's even worse. Anyway,' she went on, 'let's drop this subject, shall we; far too depressing. I haven't asked you, Claire, what sort of work do you do, unless you're a lady of leisure?'

'I'm a writer and that's really why I've been able to make the move down here, because I work from home and don't have the precarious task of looking for a job.'

'Are you really; I don't believe I've ever met a writer before. What sort of books do you write?'

'Crime fiction mainly.'

'How very interesting. Have you ever met a writer before, Trevor?' she asked him.

'No, I haven't, Sylvia.' and going on to tell her how he had recognised Claire from one of his partner's books. Claire couldn't help noticing how he frequently brought Maurice's name into the conversation but, by the bland expression on Sylvia's face, it would seem she was used to him.'

'Goodness, is it that time already?' Sylvia said, glancing at her watch, 'I have a hair-dressing appointment at two.'

'Glamorous Glenda's, I presume.' Trevor said, fluttering his eyelashes.

'Now, Trevor,' making a half-hearted attempt to remonstrate with him, 'don't be unkind. Glenda runs an excellent salon; Upper Nettles is lucky to have someone so highly trained.'

'I'm sure.' he drawled, obviously determined to have the last word.

The expression on Trevor's face was so outrageously camp, Claire had some difficulty in stifling a spontaneous burst of laughter.

'Claire,' pointedly ignoring him, 'we must meet for a coffee sometime.'

'I'd like that.' and not for the first time experiencing the awkwardness of saying she did work a fairly full day and, apart from lunchtimes, didn't normally take a break, but Sylvia hadn't specified any particular time, meaning she was spared for the moment of making any explanation to her.

Trevor also made the excuse of having to get back to the gallery and they both left together. Once they had gone, Claire picked up one of the menus from the bar and ordering another wine from Deidre, took it with her over to one of the tables by the window. She hadn't realised socialising with people she had never met before could be so draining. Trevor, in particular, was hard work, although, not so with Sylvia; Claire had liked her open frankness; Sylvia was what she would describe as a no-nonsense type of woman and looked forward to getting to know her. Unlike Trevor, she had obviously spent a number of years in Upper Nettles and would be familiar with its residents' various foibles, as she had been with Johnnie Wall and perhaps it was characteristic of her not to try and disguise her dislike of him, especially considering the fact she was aware he was her immediate neighbour. Claire hadn't even seen the man yet, but she was fairly certain, he had been the one playing the guitar last night, but so very late. Surely, that in itself, indicated he must live quite differently to most other people. *Normal* people, she thought, didn't continue playing their guitar while glass was being broken on their premises and someone, whether a guest or not remained to be seen, drove off at a great speed in the early hours of the morning. It could be, as obviously Sylvia believed, that Johnny Wall was a drug addict and this unnatural behaviour was the result of his addiction, or he was merely an eccentric, oblivious to what was going on around him.

As soon as she was seated and even before she had a chance to look at the menu, her mobile rang and preparing herself for another call from Tom, she pressed the button, much relieved to hear Dan's voice.

'I trust you have settled into your new abode, Claire.'

'More or less, Dan; just a few things left to do. I've been spending the last hour talking to a couple of local residents, also, meeting the landlady of a quaint pub in the town.'

'Good,' he said briskly; a man of few words, and waited for him to tell her why he'd called, certain it wouldn't just be to ask after her welfare,

'Claire,' he went on, 'I've got a book-signing arranged for next Wednesday at Waterstones in The Strand. Usual time, eleven.'

'That's no problem, Dan; I'll be there.'

'That's fine.' he said, ringing off.

The remainder of the afternoon passed quickly: stocking up with enough food and provisions to last for a couple of weeks; Upper Nettles' only supermarket, although not large, carried a wide range of goods, with she noticed as she reached the check-out, a board displaying small adverts, presumably placed there by the shoppers, offering a variety of services, including one which immediately caught her attention: "Part-time cleaner available. If interested, please call Mrs Maud Green on 023 8028 4123", and jotting down the number, joined the end of the queue to pay for her shopping.

So far so good, Claire thought, not displeased at the way the day was turning out; she had met a few people, had begun to familiarise herself with the town's various amenities, perhaps found herself a home help which would free her from day to day cleaning and, the proverbial icing on the cake, the book-signing on Wednesday; an event she always enjoyed, plus the not-knowing of how successful the outcome would be.

There was a message on her answering machine when she returned to Tulip Cottage and knowing it couldn't be for her as so far she hadn't given anyone the number, she waited until she had unpacked the carrier bags and found a place for everything, before she switched it on. A woman's voice broke the silence in the hall: 'Johnnie, I need to talk to Pete; he's not answering his mobile, so will you *please* tell him to call me. Thanks.' Weird; must be crossed wires, but never having experienced it before. The woman hadn't given her name, no doubt had taken for granted he would have recognised her. Could he be the Johnnie Wall Sylvia and Trevor had been talking about, Claire wondered, and Pete, remembering the band's saxophonist was called Pete and, hoping this was a one-off incident, put it to the back of her mind.

Maud Green answered the phone on the first ring; she sounded a pleasant woman with the distinct Hampshire accent Claire had heard several times since arriving in Upper Nettles and was quick to tell her she had worked for the last people who had Tulip Cottage and would be only too happy to come in three mornings a week, even going so far as to provide her with the name of the vicar's wife at Saint Martin's Church as a character reference, adding she had been working at the vicarage every Monday and Saturday mornings for the last ten years.

***

Claire awoke with a start by repeated tapping at the front door. It was still dark and, as the night before, she couldn't make out the time on her travelling alarm clock. She heard it again, this time more urgently, when abruptly it stopped, followed by voices; this was becoming a habit, she thought, not knowing whether to be concerned or not. It had previously not occurred to her that living in a relatively isolated place, even although the town was no more than a mile away, that she could be vulnerable; in her naivety, believing that country life bore no resemblance to being constantly made aware of city muggings, bag snatchings and teenage gangs, hell-bent in stealing what they could from you, she had allowed herself to become complacent.

She was on the point of going over to the window to see who was out there when she heard someone crying, not loudly, but sobbing, accompanied by convulsive gasps as whoever it was, struggled to catch their breath. At the window now, but keeping well back not wanting to be seen, she looked down, but she couldn't see anyone. As she did so, she noticed a light flickering further up the road, but was distracted by two figures emerging from the deep shadows immediately below the window, watching as they walked a few yards away before stopping abruptly half-way across the road; she was unable to hear what they were saying, but by the aggressive way one of them was standing, vigorously shaking the woman's shoulders, whatever it was, only increased her distress. Claire couldn't remember ever feeling so helpless; what she was witnessing could simply be a lover's tiff and, of course, none of her business, but it didn't alter the fact she felt sorry for her. Another sound suddenly caught her attention; someone else was out there, hearing a man's voice, harsh and discordant, calling out to them, one arm raised, beckoning them over to where he was standing, but the woman was resisting, trying to pull away, but he was too strong for her, and grabbing her by the arm, dragged her with him to the open gates. Claire stood where she was, watching as the three of them walked up the drive to what she now knew to be Johnnie Wall's house, to the moment when they reached the front door and went inside. Unpleasant, she thought, closing the curtain, and going back to bed. She wondered about the light she'd seen, realising now that it could have been from a bicycle lamp; it hadn't been all that far away but it hadn't passed during the time the people were out there, meaning whoever it had been must have stopped; she knew there were no other properties nearby.

She had difficulty in getting back to sleep; her mind too active, puzzling over what she'd seen. It had grown stuffy in the room and for the second time that night got up to open the window slightly. After some more tossing and turning trying to find a comfortable position, she felt herself drifting off to sleep when she heard the sound of a vehicle turning on to the road from Johnnie Wall's house, the lights from the headlamps shining briefly through the curtains, to be followed only minutes later by another car driving along the road in the direction of Upper Nettles. Fighting sleep, she tried to fathom out what was going on, but proving too much for her she must have fallen asleep, a deep sleep this time and didn't wake up until after eight the following morning with the sound of the wood pigeons under the eaves of the cottage.

There was another car outside Johnnie Wall's house the next morning, but this time, early though it was, there were signs of activity; a tall, thin guy who could have been the one she had seen with the woman, was leaning against the bonnet of one of the cars, listening to what the other two were saying, one of them now and again gesticulating wildly, waving his arms in the air before turning his back on them and striding away around the side of the house. Shortly afterwards, the thin one, pulled himself upright, and went back inside. As though aware of being watched, the other man looked up at the bedroom window and for a fraction of a second their eyes locked. He had seen her. Affecting an indifference she didn't feel, Claire moved away, to where she didn't think he would able to see her. He remained where he was for several seconds, not taking his eyes away from the window and then, as if losing interest on whether they'd had an audience, walked away, not where the other two had gone, but up the drive towards the gate. A shiver of apprehension ran through her sensing that he was coming over and having no idea how she would be able to handle the situation. She waited, holding her breath, expecting the front door bell to ring, but nothing. Throughout the morning, as she pottered about in the kitchen arranging and re-arranging the various pots and pans and cooking utensils which had arrived yesterday, she couldn't put out of her mind what she had witnessed the night before, finding it impossible to merely forget the incident, casually dismissing it as unimportant. It certainly had seemed important enough to the woman; her obvious distress was real alright.

Around midday she saw two of the cars driving away from the house, certain from where she was standing at the lounge window, there was no woman in either of them. She recognised the three men she'd seen earlier; the one who'd been waving his arms about was on his own and drove away first, closely followed by the other two. How many were actually living there, she wondered. She had got the impression yesterday from Trevor that Johnnie Wall was something of a recluse; a "bit of a loner" as he'd described him. For someone who preferred his own company he appeared to surround himself with quite an entourage.

Later, she questioned herself why she had decided to go across to the house, but at the time, her sole intention was to find out whether the woman was there or not. She may have left hours ago, remembering the car she'd heard in the early hours, but on the other hand she may still be in there. She supposed she just wanted to know whether she was alright. It was an impulsive decision, but Claire disliked loose ends, excusing this trait in her nature as being the result of writing for a living and having too vivid an imagination. She had lost count of the number of times Tom had accused her of letting her imagination run away with her, although in the early days of their relationship he hadn't found it irritating; more proof, not that she needed it, that what Tom and she once had together had finally run its course.

The walk up the drive seemed to take an inordinate length of time, shrugging off the uncomfortable impression of being watched, but the front door was closed and there were no windows open on the ground floor. Taking advantage of the silence, she walked round to the back of the property, following the path the two men had taken, until she reached the glass door of a conservatory. She didn't get any further when she heard footsteps on the path behind her.

'Can I help you?' the same voice she had heard last night called out to her.

'Sorry,' swivelling round to face him, 'I don't mean to intrude, but I've just moved into Tulip Cottage across the road and thought it would be neighbourly to come over and introduce myself.'

He was stocky, broad-shouldered and certainly didn't look like a rock star, not that she had a great deal of experience in what to expect, never having met one before, but there was one thing; he was not pleased to see her and apparently incapable of hiding his annoyance. Lacking in social graces, she thought cynically, regretting the impulse to do her own bit of amateur sleuthing.

'There's nobody at home,' he said, 'so, lady, you've had a wasted journey.'

'That's too bad;' wanting now to get away, 'perhaps I'll call another time.'

'I shouldn't bother.'

She didn't say anything further, but giving him what she hoped was a withering look, retraced her steps back to the gate. All the way she was aware of his eyes searing into her; she didn't turn round, there was need to; she knew he remained standing there until she had crossed the road and opened the gate of Tulip Cottage.

Chapter Two

'I don't see we have much choice.'

'One always has a choice, Clive.'

'Well, in this instance, I don't think so; he's over-stepped the limit.'

'Presumably you mean the limit we set him.'

'Of course that's what I mean. To a certain degree, David,' Clive Robinson said, stifling a yawn; he had been up for most of the night repeatedly going over figures which had continued to make little sense to him and this early meeting with David was draining him of what little energy he had, 'you have to admit, we had to trust the man, but we've also got to face facts, unpalatable though they are, that he has made a grave error; mostly to himself, in abusing that trust, all of which means we have to take steps to dispense with his services, otherwise our association with him could have unfortunate repercussions.'

'And how do you propose to achieve that; he's not likely to give up without a fight.'

'Don't I know it, David, but in the end he'll have no option but to sever his ties with us.'

'Just like that?' David asked, raising his eyebrows as he was in the habit of doing when he was exercising restraint; a silent, but eloquent signal that he had his own views about Tom Jackson's business techniques and was only waiting for the opportunity to say so. David and he had been in partnership for almost fifteen years and they worked well together, both of them having been with the same merchant bank in the City and on reaching a stage in their professions when they felt the need to make radical changes, had agreed to combine their knowledge and resources to form the management firm, trading under their names, Robinson & Waterman, Financial Investment Consultants. It had been a gamble, but after a shaky start in the early years, it had succeeded. They were now administering a number of hedge funds, occupying a prestigious suite of offices in London's West End; their clients being either accredited individuals or institutional investors, all having significant assets. As with many other hedge fund managers, they would from time to time invest their own money in a fund, which assisted in swelling their own interests along with those of the investors. As he solemnly faced David across the boardroom table, he was questioning the wisdom of including Tom Jackson into the business even although it couldn't be disputed his substantial infusion of liquid assets, the source of which neither David nor himself had chosen to query, working on the premise it was better not to know, had considerably enhanced their joint finances, but this 'head in the sands' attitude had, he was now realising, been foolhardy, giving them no option but to deal with the situation before it was too late.

'I can tell by your expression, David, you're anxious to make your point, so fire ahead.'

'There isn't a great deal I can add, actually,' he said quietly, 'and not to put too fine a point on it, there really is no doubt that Tom has, probably for some time, been siphoning off a certain percentage of the returns, money which should have been calculated fairly instead of going into his back pocket, but regrettably we haven't any substantial proof, have we?'

'No,' Clive admitted slowly, agreeing with everything he was saying, 'we haven't, except those figures I was checking through last night do show up a certain pattern, which indicate quite strongly that he could be hoodwinking us.'

'Yes?'

'Tom Jackson is smart, David, perhaps even clever, but I don't believe he's clever enough; in other words, he's become greedy; over the last six months or so, there's been a steady increase in the percentage of what, in essence, he's describing as commission.'

'And it has taken us until now to discover this discrepancy. Oh, I know,' David added, 'we've had our suspicions about how he's been arriving at some of his figures, but it's never been all that significant.'

'Until now, David.'

'Until now.' he repeated grimly, his mouth set in a thin straight line. 'So, he has to go.'

'Afraid so; it will mean of course that we're unable to include his last infusion for the Hanley Account, that will have to be topped up by ourselves, but so be it. It is a small price to pay perhaps in order to pre-empt any future problems which I believe would be inevitable should we continue to have him with us.'

'At least he's nothing to do with our new account.'

'From what you've been telling me about Gregory Thornton, it sounds pretty solid, no need for us to do any topping-up there, although I have to say, David, he is somewhat unorthodox in his methods of transferring funds, especially of such a substantial amount.'

'Oh, I suppose you mean, his apparent reluctance to meet with us personally, but if you think about it, Clive, given the type of business he's in, not all that surprising, and certainly no way unique either.'

'That wasn't exactly what I meant, but his reluctance to make the transaction through the banks.'

'True,' David accepted, nodding his head in agreement, 'the man's into land development, Clive, inevitably money changes hands, and literally, the right hand doesn't *want* to know what the left one is up to, if you get my drift.'

'I get your drift alright; all the same, the amount of cash money being transferred does carry certain risks.'

'I don't deny that, but I don't think you need concern yourself on that score, Clive; I'll be taking delivery of it on Wednesday afternoon.'

'I'd be a lot happier if it could have been sooner, like tomorrow for instance; I don't like delays, David, especially when it comes to money transactions, cash or otherwise. Obviously you trust the person you're using.'

'I trust her alright,' David answered, 'I met with her briefly on Saturday on my way back to London, and, as you know, this isn't the first time we've used her services; she gets a fair percentage for her trouble.'

'So does Tom Jackson.' making no attempt to conceal his cynicism.

'Okay, I've taken on board what you're saying Clive, but going back to Tom, have you any other reason for wanting to dispense with his services?'

'Astute as ever,' Clive smiled for the first time since they came into the conference room, 'and you're right, I do. You see,' he explained, 'there have been a number of what are really no more than murmurings, that some of the 'big boys' at his bank, are not too happy about the performance on some of his customers' investments, and quite frankly, David, I find that worrying.'

'Well, it is, and once they decide to look closely at those accounts, there could be more to discover –'

'– which could link him with us.' Clive finished for him.

'He's been with them for a while, hasn't he?'

'Yes, about ten years; I remember when we first met Tom he said he'd joined the bank more or less immediately he returned from his time in Hong Kong.'

'He could have become complacent.' David commented dryly.

'More than likely.'

'How do you propose we approach this severance, then?'

'That's a bit tricky, but I don't think we should mention any suggestion of what I've been hearing in the City.'

'We could simply say we're cutting back, the impending recession, that sort of thing, therefore a temporary change in our policy is going to be necessary.'

'I couldn't have phrased it better myself, David.'

'There's something else, Clive, which may not have occurred to you, but it's concerning any records of those transactions between us over the last five years; he must have them stored somewhere and I wouldn't have thought he'd have them on his system in the office.'

'That's a valid point,' Clive said, mentally kicking himself for not considering the importance of such sensitive documentation, 'and you're right I'm sure, they won't be at the bank, therefore he must have them at home, either on his computer there or filed away separately.'

'That would certainly be the safest.'

'We have to get hold of them, David before someone else does and you can be damn sure if the bank already have their suspicions about his activities, anything of that nature would be the first evidence they would look for.'

'This could prove difficult.'

'I realise that, but not insurmountable; we know where he lives, it would then be a question of waiting until we can gain access to the apartment. Mind you, I don't know how we would achieve this, but there must be a way; wait until he and his girlfriend were out I suppose -'

'- that's just it, Clive;' he interrupted, 'he and Claire are no longer together.'

'Oh.' momentarily taken aback, 'That's news to me; how did you find out?'

'He told me; it was about a couple of weeks ago. I was having a drink in "The Sherlock Holmes" when he came in. He looked a bit down so I asked him what was up and he said she'd thrown him out.'

'Thrown him out; just like that?'

'He didn't elaborate and quite honestly, I didn't really want to know about any domestic problems he might be having.'

'I don't suppose he mentioned where he was living now?'

'Only that he was staying with one of his colleagues until he found somewhere more permanent.'

'I see what you mean now by it being difficult. Any ideas, David?'

'Not really, except he'd need to find a secure place, away from anyone taking it into their heads to have a snoop around amongst whatever possessions he took with him.'

'That's given me an idea, only an idea mind you, but from what you've said it sounds as though his departure from Claire's place must have been quite sudden -'

'- you mean he may have left them there until such time as he could go back and pick them up?'

'Yes, that's what I was thinking. So,' he went on, more confidently now, 'as we have the address, we could still think of a way of getting into the apartment.'

'Well,' David grinned, 'how about one of us going along there and having a look at the apartment block, see just how penetrable – or impenetrable it is.'

'Alright, that makes sense. Mind you,' he added, 'if there is a concierge in evidence I reckon we can forget it.'

'This is all very much a wild goose chase, wouldn't you say.'

'You know what they say, David' he was quick to react, 'desperate times, desperate measures.'

'And you believe these are desperate times, Clive.'

'They could be.'

***

Tom Jackson had spent most of Saturday trying to discover where Claire had gone; it had been a waste of time calling her po-faced agent expecting to get any change out of him and he didn't believe him for one minute when he said he didn't have her new address, only that she'd moved to Hampshire. Of course he bloody had it! It was just one big conspiracy, even that friend of hers, Sophie Bingham, had been no help. He couldn't think of anyone else he could speak to, and even if he did, no doubt he would get the same treatment. As far as he knew, Claire hadn't known anyone who lived outside London; also she had never given any hint of wanting to move away, wondering for the first time just how well he had known her. She had been damn quick to react the way she had, as though she wanted out of their relationship. Had she been waiting for an excuse? She hadn't even given him a chance to explain the other day, realising, by doing so, he would have had to admit he hadn't been in Paris, not forgetting the woman she'd seen him with, meaning he would have to continue lying, something at which he had over the years become quite adept. There was another thing; how had she been able to find somewhere else so quickly? Presumably she was renting, which she must have seen advertised. Claire wasn't the type of woman to answer advertisements, she was far too careful, therefore she must have dealt through an estate agent, but which one; the enormity of the task bordered on the ridiculous. Recalling those agencies she would normally pass on a daily basis, he began to mentally dismiss each one as being unlikely for the simple reason from what he could remember, they only handled properties in London and the Home Counties, not as far afield as Hampshire. Even if they were computer networked, which was more than probable with the larger ones; they wouldn't necessarily display their photographs where Claire may have seen them. By late Saturday afternoon Tom had had enough of literally going round in circles and achieving zilch, deciding to make one final stab at finding her and wondering, as he dialled the number of the first agency from the Yellow Pages, why he hadn't thought of doing this before. At the fourth attempt and on the point of abandoning what was proving to be a useless exercise, he was told by Baxter & Partners in High Holborn that their branch in Regent Street had recently started to promote sales in the provinces as part of a current promotional campaign, although the woman he spoke to wasn't sure whether this included lettings. There was only way to find out he decided; he would go along there and see for himself.

Baxter & Partners, tucked neatly between one of London's long-established gents' outfitters and a shipping office, was at the lower end of Regent Street, although disappointingly their window was only displaying glossy photographs of West End properties. There was nothing for it, he would have to go in and fabricate some sort of reason for his interest, but he would have to make up his mind quickly with, he noticed from the sign on the glass door, only another fifteen minutes before they closed.

Apart from the bored-looking girl behind the desk whose expression scarcely altered when he went in, he was their only customer, which was hardly surprising he thought cynically, considering the extortionate prices of the properties he had seen on offer so far.

'Can I help you?' she asked, her voice lacking even a modicum of interest.

'I'm not sure,' hoping his smile would bring some animation to her face, 'but I'm looking for a property out of London; to rent.' he added quickly.

'Where were you thinking of exactly, sir?'

'Have you any in Hampshire?'

'I'll have a look, but most of our properties are for sale,' lightly touching the keyboard of her computer and scrolling down the screen, 'we do have quite a few in Hampshire, but they are all for sale.'

'That's too bad. A friend was telling me he had seen one advertised here recently, but perhaps he was mistaken.'

'He might not have been,' she said, her manner showing a minimal sign of improvement, 'we did have a special out-of-town window display about two or three weeks ago, but it may very well have gone by now.' returning to the computer, 'Yes,' she nodded her blonde head, which could be interpreted as a token of apology, 'I think this might have been the one your friend saw; Tulip Cottage,' she read out to him, 'Upper Nettles, Hampshire, a charming completely renovated eighteen century one-bedroom cottage on the outskirts of Upper Nettles in Hampshire's New Forest. Let agreed.' she finished, this time managing a smile, whether of sympathy or satisfaction in finding what he'd asked for, he couldn't tell.

Of course he could be well off-beam, but somehow he didn't think he was, but either way, he had to check it out. Upper Nettles, he thought, making his way back up Regent Street towards Piccadilly, it sounded a back-water sort of place to him and in the New Forest, probably miles away from anywhere civilised. Tom's knowledge of that part of the country was sketchy; he was a Londoner and felt more comfortable in cities, not for him the questionable cosiness of a neighbourly existence where no doubt everyone knew everyone else and if they didn't, they would do their utmost to find out. Claire had been different, he realised that now, although when they had first met he had considered her to be a city girl. How wrong can one be? Even if she wasn't in this Upper Nettles place, she must be somewhere equally remote, at least, as far as he was concerned.

It had now become imperative to move quickly; he couldn't explain this sudden urgency to get those discs back. Claire finishing with him in such an abrupt way had literally thrown him off-balance; too much had been happening, he'd had no time to consider what he should do next, whereabouts in London he should choose to live being of some importance, he couldn't stay with Ben indefinitely; he was already getting the vibes from his girlfriend that she didn't like the idea of a lodger, even if only a temporary one. And there was Clive Robinson. Tom wasn't entirely impervious to the way, albeit subtly, his manner had changed

towards him over the last few weeks, though God knows why it should
have; neither he nor David had anything to complain about. He was the
one taking the risks; he was the one walking on the proverbial tightrope.
But, first things first: find where Claire had gone, retrieve those discs,
make inroads to finding a flat and then put some serious thought into
what was bugging Clive.

His mobile rang as he reached the door of "The King's Head", and,
deciding to take the call before going in, he pressed the on-button.

'Tom, it's Jilly.'

'Hi, I was hoping you'd ring. Where are you?'

'Shaftesbury Avenue,' she said, 'I've been shopping.'

'I take it you're free, then?'

'Yes, for hours probably; David's spending the evening with clients, at
the Savoy, no less.' she laughed.

'How does "The King's Head" in Piccadilly sound, not so grant, it's
true, but -'

'- but me, no buts! Sounds great to me. I'll be there in about ten
minutes or so.'

'Okay, I should be able to get us a table at this time of the evening.'

It was good to hear her voice, more especially when it was unexpected.
He had known Jilly Waterman for five years, but it was only recently
when what they had considered was no more than a friendship between
two people sharing similar interests, had developed into something more
meaningful. At the beginning, he had experienced pangs of guilt in
deceiving Claire, but he hadn't let them interfere with his growing
relationship with Jilly. He was aware that eventually he would have to
decide between the two women, but up to when Claire finished with him,
he hadn't placed a time limit on exactly when that would be. Jilly and he
had never discussed any possible future they may have together, not to
any degree that is. Her marriage was something she scarcely ever
mentioned; he wasn't even sure whether she actually preferred to remain
married rather than embark on another one, and one which could end up
in the same way. In many respects, they were well suited; they lived life
on the surface, seldom planning and enjoying moments of solitude,

introspection even, in the way did Claire did. He was honest enough to recognise his meanness of spirit when he was making these comparisons between them, but Claire's ability to switch off, the way her expression would change, how her eyes almost out of focus would look past him, never failed to irritate. The fact, or the excuse, that it meant she was thinking through what she had either written, or was about to write, made no difference. Tom had always felt excluded at moments like that; as though she had completely forgotten he was in the same room. Jilly was the exact opposite: she enjoyed being with other people, always the first to laugh when anyone said anything remotely amusing; she was never still and certainly, except when asleep, never silent. Not for the first time he speculated about her marriage to David, remembering the adage that opposites attract. Certainly in their case that must be true. David Waterman, in Tom's view was dull; predictable, undeniably elegant, an elegance only money could provide, and what sense of humour he had, measured out meagrely and, perhaps conversely when least expected and invariably surprising him. It was seldom he met either Clive or David socially, apart from the odd business dinner, but nothing as intimate where wives or girlfriends would have been included, which, fortuitously the way everything had turned out, Claire had never met either of them or Jilly, except for when she saw them together on the day he should have been in Paris and had immediately, rightly as it happened, jumped to conclusions which promulgated in the big heave-ho.

Chapter Three

Claire spent the afternoon working, now and again glancing out at the tranquil scene below the study window; there were more wild ponies by the stream this afternoon and a few feet away from them on the grassy bank, deer and their young were placidly grazing, the three baby fawns keeping close to their mothers, their legs thin and spindly as they tried to keep their balance on the slope. Apart from a party of cyclists earlier on one of the bridle paths she had seen no-one else to remind her she was less than a mile away from the town, then, just before six, she heard church bells melodiously breaking the late afternoon's silence, assuming they must be from the church in Upper Nettles, the one which Maud Green had mentioned. She smiled as she remembered what Dan had said in the caustic tone he sometimes adopted, that he hoped she wasn't chasing rainbows, but perhaps he had been right; perhaps that was exactly what she was doing. It could be she was asking too much; expecting to be accepted into what was to her a totally different world. Time would tell, she thought, switching off the computer and clipping the printed notes together, took them downstairs with her.

The ringing of the front door bell as she reached the hall made her jump and for a fraction of a second she hesitated before opening the door, the unpleasant encounter of the morning still too fresh in her mind, but annoyed with herself for allowing something which was no more than a blip in an otherwise pleasant weekend, to produce such an unreasonable nervousness. Common sense prevailed, and taking a deep breath, she walked purposefully over to the door. The last person she expected to see was Jack Andrews standing on the step, clutching a huge bunch of roses and wearing a diffident expression.

'Jack!'

'Hello, Claire,' he smiled broadly, whether at her stunned reaction she wasn't sure, 'I would have phoned, but although I did have your mobile number, it seems to have gone astray over the years.'

'Come in, Jack. It's really great to see you. How did you know I was here; I only moved in on Friday?'

'It's no great mystery,' he said, coming into the hall, 'but I was in "The Hunters Arms" at lunchtime and Deidre Portman told me.'

'Oh,' still not quite understanding, 'but in Upper Nettles; you're not living here as well, are you?'

'Yes,' he laughed, following her into the kitchen, 'like you probably, I felt in the need of a change, somewhere not too far from London, but where I could hear myself think, although I must admit it is a coincidence both of us choosing the same place which is little more than a village and virtually unknown to anyone not familiar with this part of the country.'

'This surely calls for a drink;' she smiled, taking a bottle of wine from the fridge, ' afraid I can't offer you any beer, though.'

'Doesn't matter, wine will be great.'

Taking the bottle and a couple of glasses they went out on to the terrace. She was trying to remember when she had last seen him; it must have been at least six years ago, although she had known Jack Andrews years before then, back to when she had been working for the publishing firm in South West London; there had been a crowd of them, all still in their twenties, young, ambitious and free from any serious commitments. They used to meet up for a drink after they'd finished work at the end of the week, always in the same pub which invariably had been packed and to find a seat practically impossible, but it didn't matter to them. Later, some of them would walk along to Charlie Chang's "Lucky House" and consume as much Chinese food as they could manage. Often Jack had been with them, but once he became engaged to Caroline they saw less and less of him and as often happened, most of them having moved on, they had lost touch. She had heard what happened to Caroline, but although Claire felt she should have sent her condolences at the time, she felt it would have been intruding. That last time, she'd just started going with Tom, therefore it must have been, as she had thought, six years ago.

'I wanted to write to you, Jack, when I heard about Caroline, but I didn't want to intrude. I'm sorry.'

'There's no need to be,' he assured her, 'really.'

'It must have been dreadful for you; I can't even begin to imagine what you must have gone through.'

'It was,' he said quietly, 'but somehow I managed.'

'Was that the reason you decided to leave London,' she asked, 'too many memories?'

'I wanted to, Claire, at the beginning, but I stuck it out. I think I realised if I did leave then I wouldn't be able to go back there; if you know what I mean.'

'I think so.'

'It's four years since she died and looking back over that time, I believe remaining in London being surrounded with everything I had always been used to, long before I met Caroline, helped me to come to terms with losing her.'

'That's good.' she said simply, realising there was not much else she could say to him.

'And what about you, Claire?' he smiled, raising his glass, 'I've seen your books, so I knew you were still writing, but Tom, am I right in saying he's no longer around? Sorry,' he added, 'that sounded a bit impertinent of me.'

'No, I don't mind at all; Tom and I broke up about a month ago. I realise now that the relationship would never have lasted much longer, and I suppose you could say that when I found out he'd been cheating on me, also insisting in denying it, I broke it off.'

'What a cad!'

'A good old-fashioned description,' she laughed, 'and most appropriate!'

'So,' he asked, what are your impressions of Upper Nettles?'

'They're still very much first impressions, but I like it here.'

'Different to what you're used to?'

'Very.' smiling, 'I haven't asked you yet, but whereabouts are you living?'

'Over there.' the grey eyes twinkling as he pointed to the house I had already noticed by the stream.'

'Never!'

'Yes,' he grinned at her disbelieving expression, 'I bought the cottage a couple of years ago; it was in a bit of a dilapidated state, but once the renovations had been done, including the extension for a studio, I moved in.'

'What a coincidence; it's incredible that someone I've known for more than fifteen years, and haven't seen for ages, should suddenly appear, having chosen to live right across the stream from me in the heart of the New Forest! Amazing!'

'Life does indeed move in mysterious ways.' He smiled broadly.

'And are you still working for the same newspaper?'

'No, they weren't happy about my suggestion to continue working for them when I wasn't actually living in London, although I could have still been able to deliver my weekly columns just as easily from practically anywhere else in the south of England, so they gave me no alternative but to break away from them and go freelance, something I had been meaning to do for quite a while.'

'It must have been a big step though.'

'A gamble, Claire, but it paid off I'm happy to say; it's certainly given me more flexibility.' 'I suppose really you could say that people like you and me are fortunate in the type of work we do. The only person I had to appease was my agent. At first, when I told him I'd decided to move here, he couldn't believe it; he made it plain he considered the New Forest as another country entirely! Anyway, he's calmed down since then, no doubt realises it isn't all that far away from London.'

'I received similar reactions, but I think some of my old friends, although they would never admit it, are secretly envious.

'I know what you mean.'

'Jack, what do you know about the people who live across the road from here?' she asked him, curious to find out more about them.

'Not a great deal; only that the place is owned by Johnnie Wall and he's frequently visited by the other members of his rock group.'

'I was introduced to Sylvia Crossman yesterday in "The Hunters Arms" and she mentioned them, but I got the distinct impression she wasn't all that keen on Johnnie Wall; she didn't say much about the others.'

'Probably because of his drug offences, I expect. There's certainly something of a stigma attached to them, which won't do their image much good. It's a pity, because Johnnie is a damn good guitarist, although a little bit too mournful for my liking, but there's no denying he has talent.'

'I think it must have been him I heard playing late on Friday night.' deciding to mention the disturbances to him, mostly because for some reason she wanted to discuss something which had been niggling her, although she couldn't exactly explain why it should have done, 'I don't suppose you would have heard him from where you are.'

'I did hear him, actually, and I would say it was Johnnie alright; he has a very distinctive sound, not dissimilar to Eric Clapton.'

'I did think it strange though, because he didn't seem to be too concerned in what was going on outside his house.'

'In what way?'

'The sound of breaking glass, it was probably what woke me up and then this was followed by a car screeching away from the driveway and heading off towards Upper Nettles, but all the time he continued playing.'

'Odd, even for him. I heard the tyres, but not the glass; probably for reasons best known to himself, he considered it didn't concern him.'

'There was something else, Jack,' she went on, wondering what he would make of what she was about to tell him, 'this happened last night; again, very late; it must have been well after midnight, but somebody, a woman I think, was knocking at my front door -'

'- what?' shocked, '- now, that *is* odd, Claire; what happened next?'

'She was crying, quite uncontrollably in fact, then I heard a man's voice. I looked out of the window, and by this time she was outside on the road with him; they appeared to be arguing, at least he was, she was still crying and then someone else appeared at the gate, Johnnie Wall's gate, I mean, and beckoned them over, which he did, practically dragging her along with him.'

'I wonder what that was all about.'

'I don't know, but this morning I couldn't keep thinking about it and went across to the house with the excuse of introducing myself, but really I wanted to know whether she was alright. Oh, I don't know, a bit pointless I suppose, but the incident concerned me.'

'That's understandable; did you see anyone?'

'Yes, an unpleasant character,' describing him, 'he made it quite plain I was not welcome.'

'That sounds like Gerry Steele; by all accounts from what people have been saying he's Johnnie Wall's 'minder'.

'Minder?'

'Sounds somewhat dramatic,' he smiled, 'but I'm sure you'll soon discover that Upper Nettles being such a small town where nothing very exciting ever happens, people tend to latch on to anyone or anything which is even slightly unusual and fabricate; mind you,' he went on, 'there are times when they are not entirely wrong, but not often. As far as Gerry Steele is concerned, they can hardly be blamed for labelling him in such a way; as you've seen for yourself he does behave like one: protecting his employer, that sort of thing.'

'Arthur Daley in the television series has a lot to answer for.'

'You're right; it's perhaps unfortunate that the locals latched on to the description for Gerry Steele; ever since that series, the word minder has conjured up an image with certain criminal connotations.'

***

It rained heavily during the night, with spasmodic flashes of lightning followed by rolls of thunder as the storm passed over Upper Nettles and surrounding forest, making its ponderous way towards Lymington and the Solent, but by first light, the only signs of the downfall was the steady dripping from the lower branches of the oak trees lining the road into the town.

Sara Blakeman, hair stylist at "Scissors" in the High Street, arrived for work at the usual time, shortly before nine on Monday morning, surprised to find Glenda hadn't fastened back the shutters, but having a key she was able to open the salon. The first thing she did once she was inside was to check the appointment diary, noting that her first booking was for nine-thirty and Glenda's one hour later. The town hall clock was chiming nine at the same time as their new apprentice, Pru Carter, arrived.

'Sorry I'm late, Sara.' she apologised.

'That's alright, Pru; we've half an hour before Mrs Struthers' appointment, so if you could make sure the shampoo and conditioner dispensers are full, I'll deal with the shutters.'

'Isn't Miss Nicholson here yet?' Pru asked, pulling on her overall.

'Not yet,' uncertain whether she should be concerned or not, but in the six years she had been working for Glenda, she couldn't remember her not being in the salon before her in the mornings and when, an hour later, she still hadn't arrived and there had been no call from her, she began to worry. They had a relatively easy day ahead of them and she wouldn't have any trouble coping with those bookings they had already taken, although handling any additional clients could prove to be a problem. By one o'clock, she managed to take a short lunch break, deciding to call Glenda on her mobile, but only to find the line was dead. There could, she realised, be a simple explanation for this, but it didn't alter the fact she had no other way of knowing how to contact her. She knew Glenda's address in Lyndhurst, but it would be impossible to make it there and back in time for her next booking at two-fifteen. Somehow, she and Pru would have to cope with the remaining appointments up until they closed the salon at six and then, if she still hadn't heard anything, she would have no choice but to drive over there and find out what was wrong, but if, as she was beginning to suspect, Glenda had been taken ill, she would have to re-arrange the bookings they had taken for the next few days, realising she couldn't possibly manage otherwise.

The day finally came to an end and they were able to lock up, by this time she was seriously concerned; it wasn't like Glenda not to have called, even if she was ill, she would surely have got someone else to do it for her. Although Pru didn't say anything, it was obvious by her worried expression as she folded a fresh batch of towels from the dryer, she was wondering what must have happened, and presumably felt it wasn't her place as having only been with the salon for a few weeks and from what Sara had noticed, very much in awe of Glenda. Must be like treading on eggs for the poor girl, Sara thought sympathetically, remembering when she had been the same age and starting work for the first time, where everybody around her appeared super-confident which had only made her feel more of a novice than ever.

***

Number six Willow Crescent, a secluded cul-de-sac close to Lyndhurst High Street, was one of a dozen semi-detached houses and, parking in front of the gate, Sara walked up the gravel path to the front door and rang the bell. She waited a few seconds before trying again and when there continued to be no answer, went around to the back of the building. The whole place had a deserted air, realising she was wasting her time; for the fourth of fifth time that day she tried to phone Glenda, but as before, nothing.

'Excuse me,' a woman's voice called out to her, 'but I don't think Miss Nicholson is at home.' her head and shoulders gradually appearing from the other side of the hedge.

'She didn't turn up for work this morning,' Sara started to explain, 'and I was beginning to think she must be ill, also,' she added, 'she hasn't been answering her mobile.'

'I don't think she's ill, although of course she may be, but I saw her about six on Saturday evening and she looked fine. She wasn't around yesterday either,' she added, 'which was a bit odd when I come to think of it because some friends of hers called and they were surprised to find she wasn't in, especially as apparently she'd invited them for lunch.'

'I suppose she could have been called away suddenly; a relative taken sick, or something.' Sara suggested weakly, but not really believing what she was saying; she was quite simply thinking of any reason, however unlikely, to explain where Glenda could be. Sara knew virtually nothing about her employer; they seldom met socially, except for the occasional drink after they'd closed the salon. Glenda was the sort of woman who didn't talk about her private life; it was almost as though she used her outward appearance of flamboyancy in the way she dressed as a foil to prevent people seeing through to the real Glenda, but none of these pointless speculations, Sara though as she made her way back to the car, were going to help in solving the problem.

She was on the point of pulling away from the kerb when her mobile rang and switching off the engine, she answered it, fully expecting to hear Glenda's voice, but it was Don wanting to know where she was.

'I've been worried about you, darling,' he said, recognising his concern, 'I was so sure you would be home by now.'

'Sorry, Don, I should have phoned you, but I thought you would be still at your meeting.'

'It finished early,' he explained, 'so I thought we could eat out this evening. Anyway, where are you, not still at the salon?'

'No, I'm in Lyndhurst,' quickly going on to tell him about Glenda, 'but I'm no further forward; she just seems to have vanished into the blue beyond, Don and quite frankly, I don't know what I should do.'

'She could turn up tomorrow of course,' he suggested, 'but then maybe not, and obviously you can't carry on indefinitely in the salon without her.'

'I know; it wasn't too bad today, but as I've often told you Mondays are usually quiet.'

'Tricky; when does a person become a missing person, I wonder.'

'A very good question, Don. Her neighbour has just told me that some friends of hers called round yesterday, Glenda had invited them for lunch, but she wasn't there.'

'Alright, Sara, I'll tell you what we'll do. It isn't right that you should be carrying this responsibility on your own, but why don't we have a word with Peter Gale, or I should say Inspector Gale to give him his full title, I've known him for years, he'll know what to do.'

'It would certainly be a weight off my mind.'

'Good. So, I'll wait at the flat until you get home and we'll walk along to the police station together. Afterwards,' and she could tell he was smiling, 'we can have a meal in "The Hunters". How does that sound?'

'Sounds okay to me.'

***

Upper Nettles police station as "The Hunters Arms" and several other buildings in and around the High Street, dated back to the early sixteenth century; mostly single-storeyed, the low-hanging thatched roofs replaced years ago by red tiles which had now blended in quietly with the ancient stone, mellowing to a warm russet hue. Inside, except for the uniformed desk sergeant, it bore little resemblance to what was traditionally expected of a police station. Even the sepia-coloured prints lining the walls depicting Upper Nettles and surrounding heath and woodland in the days when hunting deer was a royal pastime, created a convivial, almost welcoming, atmosphere. The general office took up a good part of the reception area, with the offices used by Chief Inspector Richard Cavendish and Inspector Peter Gale on the first floor, including both the interview and conference rooms. It had been a quiet and uneventful day, allowing Peter and his superior to catch up with a backlog of paperwork which had accumulated over the last few days and now, at almost seven-thirty, Richard was preparing to finish work for the day, having switched off the computer and closed the window, when Peter appeared in the open doorway.

'Something rather strange has turned up, sir,' he said, 'which could mean we have a missing person on our hands.'

'Not another teenager running off to seek his fortune elsewhere?' recalling the last incident about seven or eight months ago when a pair of seventeen-year-olds took it into their heads to leave home only to turn up a month later having run out of money.

'Not this time, no. She's called Glenda Nicholson and although she doesn't live in Upper Nettles but in Lyndhurst, she owns the hairdressing salon here; "Scissors" it's called. Her assistant, Sara Blakeman has just been in to say that Miss Nicholson didn't turn up at the salon this morning.'

'Presumably, she's been trying to get in touch with her throughout the day?'

'Yes, that's right. No luck on the mobile; sounds as though it's out of action, but there could be a number of reasons for that. Anyway, she drove over to Glenda Nicholson's house in Lyndhurst after she closed the salon this afternoon, but there was no sign of her there.'

'Could have been taken ill.' Richard suggested.

'That's what she thought, but then she spoke to the neighbour who said she'd seen her on Saturday evening, but perhaps more telling was that some friends turned up for lunch yesterday, only to find an empty house.'

'They must have been invited, then; they wouldn't have turned up unexpectedly.'

'No, they told the neighbour they'd been invited alright; this is the reason, sir,' Peter explained, 'I considered we should look into it, but the main problem is, Sara knows precious little about her employer.'

'Someone must.'

'True.'

'However, Peter, I agree with you, we should make a few enquiries; have a word with the neighbour, that would be a start. What sort of age is Glenda Nicholson? I take it she lives on her own and what about boyfriends?'

'As to age, Sara thought about forty, but she wasn't certain. The neighbour should be able to tell us if anyone lives with her or not, and as to any boyfriend, so far we've no idea.'

'Alright, Peter. Incidentally, do we know how long she's had the business?'

'Six years apparently, but Sara didn't know where she worked before, only that she thought she came from London.'

'It doesn't exactly narrow the field.' Richard said caustically.

'It doesn't, does it? I think I should wait until the morning before seeing the neighbour just in the event she may turn up.'

'That's best. What about the salon, Peter; can Sara manage without her?'

'She says that with a bit of juggling with appointments, she could, but obviously not indefinitely. They have an apprentice who's only been there for a few weeks, therefore she won't be qualified.

'She's bound to be a help though, fetching and carrying, that sort of thing and if the salon can be kept open for the time being it would give us a little leeway; we don't want to press any alarm buttons in case there is something sinister behind all of this.'

***

Glenda Nicholson's neighbour was called Barbara Freeman and once she recovered from her initial apprehension when Peter introduced himself, she didn't hesitate to invite him in, taking him through to the kitchen; a bright sunny room facing the square of lawn at the back of the house.

'I do hope nothing has happened to Miss Nicholson.'

'We've no reason to think so, Mrs Freeman, but we have to do our best to make sure there's no call for alarm. I understand you told Miss Blakeman yesterday that you last saw your neighbour on Saturday evening around six.'

'Yes, it would have been about then; in fact, she usually returns home at that time.'

'Did you speak to her?'

'Only to say hello.'

'How did she appear to you?'

'Just as she always did, Inspector; no different.'

'Could you describe the people who called the following day?'

'Oh, dear, I'm afraid I'm not very good at remembering faces, but I'll try.' she smiled apologetically.

'Just a rough outline will do,' helping her, 'there were two of them, I believe.'

'Yes, that's right; a man and a woman; in their early to mid-forties, I would say. He was tall, he must have been about six foot and she was about my height, five foot-three.' she added.

'Their appearance, Mrs Freeman, hair colouring, perhaps.'

'He had dark brown hair, short, and she had really lovely hair, a deep auburn and she wore it tied back in what they used to call a chignon, very sophisticated she was.'

'Did you happen to hear either of their names mentioned?'

'Only hers; he referred to her as Lillian, but I don't know what his was. Sorry.'

'No, that's alright. Quite a good description actually. Were you able to see their car, presumably they drove here?'

'Oh, yes; a silver-grey BMW.'

'And you didn't see or hear Miss Nicholson at any time on the Sunday?'

'No, nothing, but I knew she couldn't be there.'

'Why?'

'Because her car wasn't parked in the driveway; that's where she always leaves it even although she has a garage; probably because she finds it more convenient.'

'It could be,' he nodded, 'I mentioned the Sunday,' he went on, 'but what about after you saw her on the Saturday, didn't you hear her driving off sometime during that evening as presumably she must have done if her car wasn't there the following morning?'

'I didn't hear her, but – and I'd almost forgotten this until you mentioned the car, but I had to drive into Brockenhurst later that evening to pick up my husband at the station; he'd been in London all week.' she explained, 'And when we were on our way back home and driving through Upper Nettles I noticed it parked outside "The Hunters Arms".'

'What time would this have been, can you remember?'

'It must have been about nine-thirty, Inspector; the London train was on time and it only takes fifteen minutes at the most to reach Upper Nettles.'

'When did you leave for the station, Mrs Freeman?'

'About quarter to seven, Inspector; my sister lives in Brockenhurst, you see, and I called in to have a coffee with her before driving on to the station.'

'Can you remember whether Miss Nicholson's car was still outside her house then?'

'Now you come to mention it,' she said, her expression thoughtful, 'no, it wasn't there.'

'And you didn't hear her return at any time during Saturday night, or even the early hours of Sunday morning?'

'Not a thing, no, but I'm sure she didn't come back because around midnight, I went upstairs to close the landing window and her car wasn't there then.'

'It would seem,' Peter said, 'that she lived on her own, but no doubt she had friends, perhaps someone who called regularly?'

'You mean men friends, I suppose?'

'Not necessarily, Mrs Freeman. You see, at this stage we know very little about Miss Nicholson and anything you can tell us about her could be helpful in building up her background.'

'Oh, I see what you mean,' nodding her head thoughtfully, 'but I don't think there is much more I can add that you probably don't know already. She bought the house about six years ago; this was shortly after we moved in here. She told me about the hairdressing business she had in Upper Nettles, and that she had been living and working in London before then, somewhere in Bloomsbury, I think she said, I'm trying to remember exactly where because she did say and as I know that part of London quite well, I was interested.'

'Presumably in the same line of business?'

'Yes, that's right,' she answered, but absently, as though still trying to remember what she'd been told, 'it was near Russell Square, that's right, I remember now, Brunswick Place, that's where it was. I don't know whether she actually owned the salon there, she didn't say.'

'She may have kept in touch with any friends she had around that time.'

'You were asking whether many people visited her, Inspector.'

'Yes?'

'Well, at first when she moved in, there were quite a few, they could have been from her London days, helping her to settle in, that sort of thing maybe, but weeks, even months, might go by when I didn't notice anyone calling next door, until about a year ago I think it was.'

He wanted to prompt her, but decided not to, hoping she would eventually come to the point, getting the distinct familiar vibes that perhaps what she was going to say next was the link they might be looking for.

'I would say he was a few years older than her, but I would often see him driving up and then the two of them would go off in his car together, usually at the weekends.'

'Can you remember the last time you saw him.'

'It must have been a couple of weeks ago.'

'You say he looked older than Miss Nicholson?'

'Yes, by a good ten years I would say. He had one of those 'lived-in' faces if you know what I mean, Inspector, which could have meant he was actually younger than he appeared. He was tall, a lot taller than her, lanky in fact and I often wondered whether he was an artist, really because of the casual way he was dressed, I never saw him in a suit and never with a collar and tie.'

'Not your conventional business man, then?'

'Oh, no, not in the least.' she smiled for the first time.

'What sort of car was he driving?'

'It wasn't always the same one; when I first saw him, he had a white Peugeot, then after that, he always had a Volkswagen convertible, bright red.' she added.

'I don't suppose you would have seen the registration number?' he asked, but not really expecting her to have noticed it, far less remember the number.

'Sorry, Inspector, but I didn't. All I do know though,' she went on quickly, as though suddenly remembering, 'the first car, the Peugeot, was a left-hand drive.'

'Did he look English to you, Mrs Freeman?'

'I *suppose* he did,' frowning, 'I never thought otherwise, and I never heard him speak so I've no idea where he could have come from.'

'Don't worry, Mrs Freeman, you've been very helpful and I'm grateful for you taking the time to talk to me.'

'That's alright, Inspector, it's the least I can do; Miss Nicholson is a good neighbour and I do hope she's alright.'

On the way back to Upper Nettles, Pete pulled up in front of "The Hunters Arms". He had meant what he'd said to her; Barbara Freeman had been helpful and not for the first time in his career, marvelled at just how observant neighbours could be, although no doubt some would describe them as nosy busy bodies, but where, he thought wryly switching off the engine, would we be without them in this business.

The pub had only been open for about ten or fifteen minutes and Chris Portman was adding a final polish to the brass optics.

'Good morning, Peter,' he greeted him, 'a lager?'

'Make it a half please, Chris; I've a feeling I have a long day ahead of me.'

'Sounds ominous.' Chris said, giving him a rueful smile, reaching up for a glass from the shelf above his head.

'Could be, but I hope not. Apart from whetting my thirst with your fine ale, Chris, I wanted to ask you a couple of questions before your lunchtime trade gets under way.'

'Fire ahead, Peter.' passing his lager to him.

'It's about one of your customers, Glenda Nicholson.'

'Yes?' a surprised expression appearing on his face.

'Would you say she was one of your regular customers?'

'Fairly, yes; sometimes she comes in after she's closed the salon, but she's in most weekends.'

'I believe she was here on Saturday evening?'

'She was, yes, but she didn't stop for long.'

'Was she with anyone?'

'No, she was on her own.'

'You say she wasn't in for long; was this usual for her.'

'It depends who she's with I suppose, and she probably would have had a second drink on Saturday; it was still early, well before ten, but she took a call on her mobile and as soon as she'd finished her drink she left.'

'Any chance you may have overheard who'd called her.'

'Afraid not,' shaking his head, 'I was at the other end of the bar when her mobile rang, but Christine may have done, Peter; I remember now, she was serving close to where Glenda was standing.'

'Is Christine on duty this evening?'

'Yes, she should be here around six-thirty; do you want me to ask her when she comes in?'

'No, it's alright, thanks Chris; I'll have a word with her later this evening, if that's alright with you.'

'Of course.'

'Incidentally, was Glenda parked outside that evening?' remembering what Barbara Freeman had told him.'

'Yes, she was.'

'When she left, did you notice whether she drove away in the direction of Lyndhurst which I understand is where she lives?'

'I didn't; we were beginning to get busy by then, although possibly Deidre may have done. She was clearing the tables when Glenda left and she would have seen her leave.'

'I'll ask her in a minute, Chris; is she around?'

'Yes, she's in the kitchen preparing the lunches. Peter,' he asked tentatively, has something happened to Glenda.'

'I hope not, Chris, but she hasn't been seen since Saturday evening and as she didn't turn up at the salon yesterday morning, we're implementing an initial enquiry into where she could have gone.'

'Oh, dear, this doesn't sound good.'

'It's early days yet,' Peter said, 'and she may very well turn up at any time, but we have to make sure all the same.'

'Of course.'

'So far, Chris,' he went on, 'it's not generally known; Sara Blakeman is continuing to manage the salon in her absence, so rather than start a spate of rumours which as you probably know can spread in this town at an alarming rate, we're trying to conduct this enquiry as discreetly as possible.'

'I understand, Peter, of course I do, and I think you know me well enough to realise I won't say anything.'

'Thanks, Chris, that's appreciated.'

Before he left the pub, he had a quick word with Deidre and, as Chris had thought, she had seen Glenda Nicholson leave on Saturday evening, also that she drove off in the direction of Lymington. Deidre didn't ask him any questions, but by her serious expression he could tell she realised there was something wrong.

The few spaces in front of the police station of what technically was allocated parking were occupied, forcing him to park in the yard at the rear of the building, but before doing this, he had to move a bicycle someone had placed obtusely against the brick wall and, using the back door, made his way upstairs to his office.

By one o'clock, having written-up his notes in preparation for his meeting later in the afternoon with Richard, Peter took a call from the desk sergeant to tell him that a lady called Mrs Maud Green was in reception and had asked specifically to talk to him.

'She says it's about her son, Inspector;' Sergeant Colin Baker said, 'apparently, he's missing; he went out on Saturday evening and hasn't returned home.'

Chapter Four

Normally, no-one in Upper Nettles police station would have taken the disappearance of Jamie Green seriously; it hadn't been the first time he had left home only to turn up a few days later, having run out of money and missing his mother's cooking, therefore Sergeant Colin Baker could be excused for attempting to treat this as a matter of routine, but the insistence of Maud Green left him with no option but to comply with her wishes, although not understanding why she would particularly want to report directly to the Inspector when she must have realised he would feel exactly as everyone else did at the station. Jamie Green, now in his early twenties had been in and out of trouble since the age of eleven, starting off with petty thieving from the local supermarket and tobacconists and progressing to short-lived joy riding, stealing cars which drivers had inadvertently left unlocked, but never managing to get very far due to the fact he hadn't yet learned to drive, resulting in him being forced to abandon the vehicle, miraculously without causing any damage, either to himself or to the car. Jamie was an opportunist, destined eventually, Colin felt certain, to end up inside, surprised he hadn't done so already. The more charitable in Upper Nettles made half-hearted excuses for him, blaming his unruliness on losing his father before reaching his teens, most of them agreeing that Maud Green was far too indulgent with him, this being evident in the woman's distressed state when she came into the Station and in many respects, he was relieved when Inspector Gale had taken the woman off his hands.

'I hope you didn't mind me asking to speak to you personally, Inspector Gale,' Maud Green said as soon as Colin, unceremoniously, had ushered her into his office and she had settled her thin frame into the high-backed chair in front of his desk, 'but as you have already met Jamie, well -' floundering, the frown deepening as she struggled to explain, 'well, I thought -' this time giving up altogether, the tired eyes pleading for his understanding.

'It's alright, Mrs Green,' coming to her rescue, otherwise he thought, they could be there all afternoon, 'it's clear to me you're very worried about Jamie, but I don't need to remind you he has gone off before and has always returned home more or less safe and sound.'

'I know,' she nodded, 'but that was when he was younger, Inspector. He's matured a lot since those days, besides,' she went on, more confidently, 'even if he had decided at the last moment to stay with one of his friends in Brockenhurst over the weekend, he would have been back by now because, you see, he had an interview this morning and he told me he really wanted the job.'

As unlikely as that sounded, Peter had to go along with her, but the inescapable fact remained; two people closely connected with Upper Nettles had disappeared at the same time. As most police officers, he did not trust coincidences, having learned when he first joined the force, it was a rare case which was solved by placing any reliance or credence on them; it just didn't happen.

'Alright, Mrs Green,' he said, pulling his notepad towards him, 'I'll take a few notes which should assist us in trying to find him.'

She didn't say anything, merely remained sitting upright, a look of hope replacing the earlier one of despair.

'First of all,' Peter said, 'what time did Jamie leave home on Saturday?'

'About seven, Inspector.'

'Did he say where he was going?'

'He did, yes, he said he was meeting some friends of his in Brockenhurst for a drink.'

'Did he mention the pub they were going to?'

'No, but it would probably have been "The King's Head", he's often mentioned it, telling me that's where they all meet on Saturday nights.'

'And how did he get there, Mrs Green; by bus?'

'Oh, no, he had his bike, Inspector.'

'Right,' jotting down the few salient points, 'and were you worried when he didn't come back that night?'

'I didn't realise it until the next day because I was in bed well before eleven, but I wasn't all that worried; sometimes he stayed over with one of his friends and had another session on the Sunday lunchtime before coming back.'

'I see. And yesterday, when he still hadn't turned up, what did you think?'

'Well, I was working at the council offices all morning and I always start there very early, eight o'clock, in fact. I did a bit of shopping before going on to my next job; Mondays are busy days for me.' she added, 'And when I eventually got home and he still wasn't there, I kept thinking he would come back later in the evening, but of course he didn't.'

'So, by this morning, you decided to report him missing.'

'That's right; I would have come earlier, but I had another cleaning job first thing this morning and as I've only started working for the lady, I didn't want to ask for time off, therefore I came along here as soon as I'd finished.'

'I have to ask you this, Mrs Green,' he said tentatively, not sure how she would react, 'but what was Jamie wearing when he went out on Saturday evening?'

'Oh, dear,' placing her fingers nervously on her lips.

'It's just a routine question.' trying to reassure her.

'I see, well, his jeans, but then he always wore jeans, a checked shirt, red and white, with short sleeves and he took his denim jacket with him.'

'That's good enough,' Peter nodded, adding the notes to his list, 'you said he cycled there.'

'Yes, he went everywhere on his bike.'

'Do you know the make, Mrs Green?'

'I think it's a Raleigh, yes, I'm sure it is.'

'And the colour?'

'Dark blue.'

'Finally, Mrs Green, did Jamie tell you where he was going for the interview?'

'At Conway's Nurseries on Lyndhurst Road, Inspector, it was for a summer job.'

The bicycle was still in the yard when he returned from Conway's Nurseries, noticing that beneath the grime the faded enamel had once been a dark, almost navy blue and on a closer inspection he saw for the first time that the front wheel was slightly buckled, also there were shreds of damp green moss caught up in the spokes of both wheels. Giving it one more glance before going up the back steps to the Station, he walked through to the reception area; Colin Blake was still on duty at the desk and looked up in surprise to see him, obviously not expecting him to come in that way.

'Do you know anything about that bike out there, Colin?'

'I haven't seen it myself, sir,' he said, 'but it must have been the one Sergeant Jones booked in before I came on duty this morning. Apparently, it was found earlier by a man walking his dog; I'll just check what the sergeant wrote down.' pulling that day's report sheet towards him. 'Yes, here we are,' he said, pointing to an entry made at ten forty-five, 'Terry Edwards he's called, sir, lives at number thirteen Lyndhurst Road, telephone number 023 8028 5732; he spotted the bike amongst a clump of gorse bushes in that area everyone calls Nettles Hollow, it's only a few yards away from the road.'

'I know where it is, Colin; thanks, and if you jot down the telephone number for me, I'll give the man a ring.'

Walking up the stairs to his office he felt sure the bike must belong to Jamie Green and if he was right, it didn't bode well for the lad, stifling a feeling of foreboding and one he had been trying to ignore from when he'd heard about Glenda Nicholson. The whole area would have to be searched of course, and as far as footprints or tyre marks were concerned they were going to be hampered now because of the heavy rain on Sunday night. Ironic really, he thought, when people had been complaining for days about the long dry spell, the weather should choose this weekend to change, not that there was anything anyone could do about the situation.

Before taking off his jacket, Peter lifted the receiver and dialled the number Colin had given him. The woman who answered told him her husband was not expected home from work until around six-thirty and once Peter explained why he was calling, said she knew about him finding the bike and that she would get him to call the police station as soon as he came in.

***

Later, towards the end of the week, no-one in Upper Nettles could remember when the rumours first began to circulate, or from where they originated, but on Tuesday evening a small group of regulars in "The Hunters Arms" were discussing in some depth what they were describing as the mysterious disappearance of Glenda Nicholson. Not one of them seriously considered or even tentatively suggested she may have been called away suddenly. It was as if they wanted a drama in their midst, albeit one of their own making. It could have been that one of Glenda's customers made it known how her appointment time had been altered and instead of Glenda attending to her as usual, she had been replaced by her assistant, or it could have been from a number of sources. Certainly Sara Blakeman was making no secret of running the business practically single-handedly and she had no intention of inventing any reason and, surprisingly perhaps, no-one asked her why Glenda wasn't in the salon. Even Pru had said nothing, quietly accepting that despite her employer not being there, business was continuing more or less as usual.

Trevor Wheatley was among "The Hunters Arms" first regulars, explaining to anyone who cared to listen, that tonight Maurice was cooking them both a meal to surpass all meals, reminding them of his partner's culinary skills.

'Sounds delicious, Trevor.' Deirdre smiled diplomatically, having lost count of how many times Trevor had told them in minute detail of the various dishes his partner had concocted, hoping he wasn't going to regale them with the startling range of herbs and spices Maurice appeared to favour.

'It will be, Deidre, believe me, but I thought I would leave him to it, not that I'm much help in the kitchen. Is it true,' he went on without pausing to take a breath, 'that Glenda Nicholson has done a disappearing act?'

'Honestly, Trevor,' Deidre said, trying to keep her face straight; the man was outrageous and probably without realising just how funny he was. Camp wasn't in it, she thought, shaking her head, 'I'm sure you're wrong. I expect she's just gone away for a few days.'

'Hmmph!' affecting exasperation and looking round as though seeking a more receptive audience and one who would be more conducive to enhancing his growing belief there was something sinister behind why no-one he'd spoken to had seen Glenda'.

'You could be right, you know, Trevor,' Charlie Oakes, Upper Nettles' postman, a notorious gossip and known for taking a keen interest in each item of mail he delivered, in particular the post cards, seeming to derive considerable pleasure in reading them first, 'if you ask me,' he went on, making a poor attempt to lower his voice as though about to impart something of high importance, 'something's happened to her.'

'Oh, really?'

'Yes, you see,' nodding his head and reminding Trevor of one of those felt dogs often to be seen in the rear windows of cars, 'this morning I had a registered package for her only to be told by Sara Blakeman she didn't think Miss Nicholson would be coming into the salon for the next few days and that was all she said, giving me the distinct impression she had no idea when Miss Nicholson would be back.'

'Well, Charlie, perhaps she doesn't know.' disappointed; he'd been expecting something far more informative than that and not for the first time thought old Charlie was a bag of wind.

'Course she does, she was hiding something that one, probably got too big for her boots now she's in full charge, expect she hopes her boss never comes back.'

'Charlie Oakes; that's a dreadful thing to say!'

'Oh, hello, Sylvia, I didn't see you there.'

'Well, I am, and I couldn't help overhearing; don't you think there are enough rumours flying around at the moment without you adding to them?'

'They might not be rumours,' Charlie retaliated, looking indignant, 'anyway, 'that package looked important, quite bulky it was too.'

'I give up.' Sylvia Crossman said, raising her eyes heavenwards and walking round to his other side to order a drink.

'What do you think, Sylvia?' Trevor asked her when a disgruntled

Charlie had moved away further along the bar.

'I don't know what to think, Trevor,' she said quietly, 'she could have personal problems; she didn't look too happy when I saw her on Saturday which wasn't like Glenda, but I'm sure whatever they are, she'll sort them out.'

'Perhaps not.'

'Trevor; don't you start! I absolutely refuse to indulge in gossip. I see Christine is on duty this evening.' adroitly changing the subject and smiling over towards Christine Tomlinson whom she noticed was replenishing Charlie Oakes' glass.

'Deidre and Chris must expect to be busy.' he answered abstractedly, dissatisfied with the way the conversation was going. Trevor liked nothing better than some second-hand excitement in his otherwise uneventful life; since Maurice and he had returned from Australia he had frequently admitted, but only to himself, they had been a lot happier in Sydney where there was always something going on, but here, each week was very much the same as any other and now, when it looked as if something with a bit of spice to it had turned up, he couldn't find anyone prepared to discuss with him the ins and outs of what could have happened to the town's leading hair stylist and the fact she was a flamboyant creature only whetted his appetite for anything which could turn out to be a scandal and at the same time, as far as he was concerned, shake the town out of its permanent state of complacency. Look at them all, he thought cynically, their whole lives trudging drearily along the same old treadmill: work for those willing and able, except for the retired, of which there were many in Upper Nettles; dinner each evening which most of them called tea, half an hour spent engrossed in some soap opera or other, followed by a couple of beers in their local and for the remainder of the evening discussing the weather or football. Yes, he decided, Maurice and he had made one big mistake coming here, making up his mind it was time he owned up to him that he was quite frankly fed up and wanted them to find somewhere else before they became too old and decrepit to care, or worse still, ran out of energy.

'She's our next-door neighbour, you know.' the man standing

immediately to the right of him said; Trevor had seen him in the pub several times but didn't think he lived in the town.

'Who is?'

'The woman you've been talking about, Glenda Nicholson.'

'Oh, really.' not sure he wanted to get into conversation with him. Trevor was an inverted snob, in spite of his apparent garrulous manner, he was very selective on whom he spent his time talking to, even mere acquaintances, people he was never likely to see again, came under the same category and there was something about the man he couldn't take to, although unable to actually say what it was; perhaps it was his over-familiarity which jarred, but Trevor's eagerness to pick up any snippet of information about Glenda over-ruled his self-imposed prejudices.

'Yes, she moved into her house about the same time as my wife and I bought ours, about six years ago this autumn it would have been; I'm Bob Freeman, by the way.' adding as an afterthought, formally shaking Trevor's hand, giving him no alternative but to exchange the gesture.

'I believe Glenda lives in Lyndhurst.' not knowing what else to say; he wasn't even certain Glenda did live there; he only remembered vaguely Sylvia mentioning it some time ago, but he hadn't been paying much attention, not being interested in the woman who had apparently mesmerized half the females in Upper Nettles.

'That's right; she's our next-door neighbour, that's in Willow Crescent, just off the High Street.' he added unnecessarily. 'Anyway, it's true what people have been saying,' he went on, his brown eyes shining behind the heavy frames of his glasses, reminding Trevor incongruously of a conjurer about to pull out a rabbit from his hat, 'because someone must have reported her as missing because my wife had a visit this morning from an Inspector Gale asking her when she had last seen Glenda.'

'And when was this?'

'Saturday evening,' appearing not to mind the direct question, but already Trevor was too intrigued to make any attempt to curb his mounting interest, 'but she must have gone out again because we both saw her car outside here later on when we were driving past.'

'And I take it she didn't come back home?'

'You take it right, my friend and if you want my opinion, I think there is something very wrong here, very wrong indeed. Also, some friends of hers called to visit her on Sunday, they'd been invited, so they told Barbara, that's my wife,' he added, again unnecessarily, 'but of course Glenda wasn't in. Strange, wouldn't you say?'

'It does sound odd, yes.' reluctant to encourage him.

'The Inspector asked for a description of the couple who called there, you know.'

'I suppose they would have to, police routine, that sort of thing.'

'Barbara has a good memory for faces, so she was able to tell him what they looked like, but I was more interested in their car; very flashy and expensive, probably the pair of them are worth a bob or two to be able to afford a motor like that.'

'Yes?'

'BMW it was and not only was it the latest model but had its own personal registration number and they don't come cheap either.' he added knowledgably.

'There's quite a few expensive cars in the area.' rapidly losing interest, sure he wasn't going to learn anything further.

'Perhaps there are.' he admitted reluctantly, taking a deep sip of his beer.

Taking advantage of what was probably only a brief lull in what else he may have to impart, Trevor finished off the rest of his drink and made his excuses to leave, hoping as he walked across to the door, that this Bob Freeman didn't intend making a habit of frequenting what Trevor guarded jealously as his local; after all, he grumbled to himself, he was a resident of some standing in Upper Nettles, wishing now he hadn't allowed himself to get into conversation with him.

He stepped out on to the pavement as Claire pulled up and giving her a wave, carried on up the street to "The Gallery" where Maurice would be waiting for him and eager to hear what he had managed to glean about Glenda Nicholson, looking forward to his excited reaction when he told him the police had already started making enquiries. Perhaps, he thought, the euphoric effects of two large glasses of red wine giving him a more philosophical view, life in upper Nettles may not be so dull after all.

***

'Hello, Claire,' Sylvia greeted her as soon as she came in, 'how are you settling in?'

'Fine, thanks, and I actually managed to get some work done today which always makes me feel better within myself, if that makes any sense.' she smiled, not missing the puzzled expression on Sylvia's face.

'I suppose I do,' Sylvia said slowly, 'but writing, for a living I mean, must take a dreadful amount of concentration.'

'I don't know so much about concentration; I would say, at least with me, it is more a question of discipline; it's all too easy to stop and have a cup of tea or, as I've found already here, allow my mind to drift off as I look out of my study window.'

'I'll take your word for it;' Sylvia laughed, 'anyway, Claire, what would you like to drink?'

Saying she would like a white wine, Claire noticed for the first time, there was someone else behind the bar.'

'You won't have met Christine yet, of course,' Sylvia said, following her glance, 'she's only here part-time but as her husband works in the Middle East, she's always available to come in when Chris and Deidre are busier than usual, as they are this evening.'

'They are, aren't they,' looking round at the crowded bar, 'and it's only Tuesday.'

'And I have a very good idea why that is;' Sylvia commented dryly, 'you'll find out, Claire, that as soon as anything evenly remotely out of the ordinary occurs in Upper Nettles, it immediately sets people's tongues wagging and what better place than your local.'

'It sounds as though I've missed something.'

'I doubt it,' her cynical tone unchanging, 'but most of these people have convinced themselves there is something sinister in Glenda Nicholson not turning up at the salon yesterday morning.'

'She's your hairdresser, isn't she; you mentioned her on Saturday.'

'That's right; poor woman, just because she's probably decided to have a couple of days off, everyone appears to be jumping to the same conclusion.'

'Rather extreme.'

'I would say so, Claire, but that, I'm afraid, is what it can be like here. They're good people really; their only fault is this awful habit of gossiping. Mind you,' she went on relentlessly, 'sometimes it's difficult not to become embroiled in it all and before you know where you are, you're just as guilty of rumour-making as the rest of them!'

'You mean it's catching.'

'Yes;' she laughed, 'rather like measles and chickenpox, I suppose. If you stand too close to anyone contagious, you're bound to catch it!'

'I'd better stand well back, then.'

Deidre came over to serve them at that point, Sylvia ordering two glasses of Chardonnay, and as she watched her opening a new bottle, Claire thought over what Sylvia had been saying. Although she had made light of what seemed to be the local tendency to tittle-tattle, it was obvious she disapproved and wondering whether she had stronger reasons. Perhaps at one time she'd had first-hand experience of being the centre of such rumours, especially if they had been unfounded. It was possible. Once again, she was being reminded of the marked contrast between city and country life. Here, Claire realised, people took a keen interest in their neighbours; whereas in London, although she had been living in her apartment for seven or eight years, she had not even known the names of her immediate neighbours. If someone had asked her at that moment which she preferred, she didn't believe she would be able to give them an honest answer. It wasn't that she was beginning to regret already moving away from the city, although she wished she could rid herself of this impression of feeling apart from what was going on around her. Give it time, Claire, she told herself; common sense telling her she couldn't possibly expect to be immediately absorbed into this new and more than a little strange environment, deciding to ask Jack the next time she saw him what his reactions had been when he first arrived.

'Shall we move away from the bar, Claire,' Sylvia suggested, 'it's getting a bit cramped for space around here.'

Taking their drinks with them they walked over to one of the alcoves where it was quieter, but having to practically push their way through. A man's voice, louder than the others, reached them as they moved away: 'When you're ready, Christine;' he called, 'four pints of your Best Bitter.'

'Alright, John, coming up.'

As soon as she spoke, Claire knew where she had heard her voice before, and looked over at the woman behind the bar; she was an attractive woman, light brown hair with copper glints and cut short, high cheekbones and slightly slanted deep blue eyes, probably, Claire reckoned, in her late thirties. So, she concluded, following Sylvia over to the alcove, she was the person who had been trying to get in touch with someone called Pete. Pete Carr, Johnnie Wall's saxophonist? More than likely. Sylvia had mentioned a husband, fairly or unfairly, the old saying "when the cat's away, the mice do play" jumped into her mind.

'What happened to your car, Christine?' the same man's voice, following her.

'Trust you to notice, John.'

'Couldn't help it; you'll have to get a complete rear light, you know. Anyway, you haven't said; how did it happen?' obviously not giving up and seeming not to care, or notice, he was embarrassing her.

'Oh, some idiot pranged into me in the car park ....' unable to hear anymore, but as she sat down beside Sylvia, she had worked out exactly how it must have happened: Christine, she didn't know her surname yet, had been across the road at Johnnie Wall's house on Friday night, there had possibly been an argument and she'd stormed off, probably backing into some obstacle as she left the property, before driving back to Upper Nettles. One mystery solved, Claire thought, and how many more to go?

Chapter Five

Claire first noticed the police in the small copse on the other side of the stream when she drew back the kitchen curtains shortly after seven the following morning. There were five of them, recognisable by their regulation blue shirts and dark trousers, as they slowly and systematically pushed their way through the thick mass of brambles and gorse. Close by, half a dozen wild ponies grazed, the incongruity of the scene not lost on her as she stood there wondering what could be going on. The tiny flutter of apprehension persisted as she filled the cafetière and put a couple of slices of bread into the toaster. They were obviously searching for something. Or someone. Whatever the reason for justifying five members of the police force being out there, it must be considered sufficiently serious. Beyond that, she refused to speculate; it would be all too easy to jump to conclusions, remembering what Sylvia had said the day before about rumour-making being contagious.

She had already made up her mind to take the train into London rather than drive and have the added problem of parking, having learned that the Intercity service from Bournemouth to London called at Brockenhurst. To Claire, watching the Hampshire countryside roll by, it felt very much a novelty, although realising if she had to make the journey regularly, she would soon think differently and would no doubt end up looking like many of the other passengers she'd seen that morning; faces pale and drawn as they stoically made their way to work with the inescapable knowledge they would have to go through the same procedure in reverse at the end of the day.

She took the tube from Waterloo to Charing Cross and walked the short distance to Trafalgar Square. Waterstones, prominently positioned under the arches of Grand Building and overlooked by Nelson's Column, never failed to give her that feel-good factor as soon as she went inside, the sound of the constant stream of traffic in the Strand hardly audible once she had closed the door behind her.

She still had plenty of time until midday and after introducing herself to the supervisor responsible for organizing events such as today's book-signing, walked upstairs to the coffee shop on the first floor. She had never known "Costas" not to be busy; a pleasant oasis where office workers, barristers and lawyers with the inevitable smattering of students, amicably shared tables and, remarkably, never seeming to encroach on each other's space. She queued at the counter for a coffee and was fortunate to find a seat at the exact moment when Dan emerged from the lift; not for him using stairs when he didn't have to.

'Good morning, Claire,' he said, walking over to her, 'you're early.'

'I know,' she smiled, 'courtesy of British Rail.'

'Very wise.' he nodded, 'What did you think of the window display?'

'Eye-catching, Dan; you've worked hard to promote "No Cover-up".'

'Your book's worth it, Claire.'

Praise indeed, she thought: Dan Philips wasn't given to handing out compliments, his words acting as a fillip, metaphorically keeping her fingers crossed that sales today would justify his efforts.

'How's your current book going, Claire; not too many distractions I trust in Upper Nettles?'

'Reasonably well,' she said, not all that surprised he should be asking her, although wishing he wouldn't; Claire had a deep-rooted superstition of discussing any book she was working on, especially in the early stages.'

'The reason I'm asking, Claire,' he went on as though reading her mind which, after all these years he probably was, 'is that I've had substantial interest from your readers for a sequel to "Tomorrow Never Comes". What do you think?'

'My goodness; I wrote that about seven or eight years ago.'

'Seven, Claire; the book went 'live' on the 1st June 2003.'

'Oh.'

'I can see by your expression, I've taken you by surprise; anyway,' giving her one of his dry chuckles, 'I'll leave the idea with you, Claire. Not that I need to remind you, but you do have a large appreciative readership out there, so -' leaving her to add her own opinions, knowing full well, she wouldn't disagree with him.

'- keep the punters happy, eh?' she laughed.

'Claire Walters you are becoming a cynic!'

'Must be living in the country, Dan; all that fresh air!'

The book-signing went well with a steady flow of customers many of them stopping at the table which had been allocated to her and buying a copy, and actually waiting for her to add her signature. On occasions like this, where she came face to face with the people who were sufficiently interested to part with their money to want to read what she had written, she felt quite humble. More reason she supposed that when given the chance she should listen to what her readers wanted. It wouldn't be too arduous a task to pick up from where she left off with the book Dan had mentioned, sections of the plot slipping into her mind and realising with a jolt it had mostly been set in a small town now all that dissimilar to Upper Nettles. *Déjà vu?* Perhaps.

By four-thirty, she was able to start packing up, not dissatisfied with the way the afternoon had gone.

'Hello, Claire.'

'Jack!' looking across the desk at him, 'You do seem to be in the habit of popping up these days!'

'I do, don't I;' he grinned, 'but I knew you would be here.'

'You did?'

'It's quite simple,' he explained, 'I had to be in London today, a meeting I couldn't get out of, and saw your books displayed in the window as I walked past earlier, also the notice saying you would be having a book-signing, so,' he added, smiling broadly and reminding her of how he used to look years ago, 'here I am! I thought we might go for a drink somewhere, that is if you've nothing else planned'

'That's a brilliant idea; where shall we go?'

'"The Moon"?'

'Sounds good to me, it shouldn't be too busy at this time.'

"The Lord Moon of the Mall", one of the West End's oldest and probably the most popular pubs; she had been there dozens of times, sometimes with Tom, but more often with Sophie. Claire had known Sophie Bingham for more than twenty years, long before Tom and even before she'd met Dan. In the early days, still in their teens, they had both worked for "The Daily Telegraph" in the advertising section, Sophie staying on with them and progressing to editorial, while she had joined the publishing firm, but they had continued to meet, spending hours over numerous glasses of wine, discussing work, boyfriends and practically anything else which was happening around them during those carefree years when neither of them really had any serious commitments, but this had changed significantly when Sophie, having only been married a year, lost the baby, followed almost immediately by her husband, unable to handle the situation, walked out on her. It had taken Sophie a long time to pick up the threads of her life again and although they hadn't met so often then, their friendship had survived. Claire had phoned her on Monday to tell her how she was settling in and about Jack living in Upper Nettles. Sophie's reaction had been surprising, remembering what she'd said: "Life certainly moves in a very strange way, wouldn't you say?"

"I suppose it does." she'd answered slowly, reluctant to admit there was anything so insubstantial as preordained in Jack electing to live in the same place as herself, much preferring to put it down to coincidence.

"You always liked Jack, didn't you, Claire?"

"If I didn't know you better, Sophie Bingham, I would think you were match-making!"

"He's a nice guy; steady, reliable and - "pausing for a second, "available."

"What makes you so sure he's available?"

"Well," and she could tell by her voice she was smiling, "he'd hardly have turned up on your doorstep wanting to see you, if he'd married again, or had a steady girlfriend, would he?"

"Alright, Marjorie Proops, we'll leave it like that, shall we."

"Okay, point taken, but seriously, Claire, I'm glad he's there, someone you know in your hide-away in the New Forest and if Tom should turn up, Jack could be just the person to call on if you needed any protection."

"What do you mean by protection; an odd word to use, even for you, Sophie."

"I don't know so much; I wasn't going to mention this, but Tom phoned on Saturday asking for your address which naturally I didn't give him, but it was his manner which concerned me."

"I suppose he was a bit miffed when you didn't tell him."

"It was more than that, actually; he sounded – well, I wouldn't say *desperate* exactly, more determined than anything else, he said it was important to know where you were living."

"Don't worry about him, Sophie," she reassured her, disguising her annoyance with Tom; he should have known better than to phone Sophie, he'd always known she hadn't thought much of him. On the rare occasions when they were ever in each other's company, neither of them had made any attempt to hide their mutual dislike, "he's probably frustrated, for some inexplicable reason, not to get what he wants, though goodness knows why he's so eager to know where I'm living. He phoned me as well; this was on Friday, not long after I'd moved into Tulip Cottage, making a big pretence of wanting to see me as he wanted a chance to make me change my mind."

"He doesn't let up, does he?"

"No, but he's wasting his time, Sophie; eventually he'll give up."

"Perhaps his pride has been hurt, being rejected, I mean."

"You could be right." although not really believing that was the reason for Tom's persistence, remembering the look of relief on his face that last time she'd seen him.

"He sounded terribly intense, Claire; anyway," she'd concluded, "as I've just said, it's good to know you have Jack there on the spot if Tom should take it into his head, if and when he does manage to find out where you are, to pay you a visit."

"Okay, Sophie, so you think Jack could be my knight in shining armour if the occasion should arise when I need to be rescued."

"You're being flippant, Claire, but I meant it. There's something I don't trust about Tom; don't ask me what it is, just put it down to my adverse chemical reaction to his so-called charming personality."

"He'd no right to bother you; he should have realised you wouldn't have told him."

Claire was reminded again of Sophie's words as she and Jack waited at the set of traffic lights in front of Waterstones to cross the road, ironically the same lights where she'd seen Tom, realising now what

Sophie had meant when she'd said there was something about him which she didn't trust. The incident, similar to a brief flashback, lasting no more than seconds, was almost a replica of another time, about a year ago. Claire had completely forgotten about it until now, but she'd arranged to meet Tom in "The Sherlock Holmes" after he'd finished work. The pub had been packed and unable to find a seat, she remained at the bar to wait for him. There were a number of customers blocking the doorway, but she spotted him right away, surprised to see he was with someone, but when he came over to her he was on his own; she had immediately thought she'd been mistaken and didn't even mention it to him, but the woman had been the same one she'd seen him with over a month ago. Why on earth, she wondered, had it taken her so long to remember, to realise that he had been with her outside "The Sherlock Holmes" that evening and that the pair of them had come in at the same time. She had been so sure at the time she'd been mistaken, she hadn't even thought to look round the packed bar to see where she'd gone. How blind she had been, but Sophie, although she hadn't been there, had recognised that particular weakness in his character which told her he wasn't to be trusted! Perhaps, she concluded, that was what the old proverb, 'love is blind' meant.

Claire waited until they were in "The Moon", and Jack had brought over a couple of drinks to their table, before saying anything about the police she'd seen earlier.

'I didn't notice them,' he said, 'but that was probably because I had left it a bit fine to catch the train; I'm afraid I'm not usually an early riser.'

'They were still there when I left, although by that time they'd moved further over.'

'It doesn't sound too good, does it?' raising his glass before taking a sip of his beer.

'I honestly didn't know what to think.'

'You say they were in the copse at the other side of my place?'

'Yes.'

'The locals call that area Nettles Hollow; it's very much overgrown, therefore it's a quiet spot, even the animals are not interested, not much grazing there for them.'

'No doubt we'll find out when we get back.'

'Too right,' giving her a rueful smile, 'I expect the tongues in Upper Nettles have been wagging all day!'

'Sinister.' giving an involuntary shudder.

'I expect you're beginning to wonder what you've let yourself in for, moving into such a rural part in the county, what with the odd behaviour from across the road.'

'I suppose so.' she said, trying not to put too much importance on the weekend events making a conscious effort to curb her over-active imagination.

'There might be a simple explanation for why the police were there, Claire, breaking into her thoughts, 'although I have to admit at the moment I can't think of one.'

'Neither can I? I'm not normally a nervous type of person, but well; these last couple of days have been strange to say the least.'

'Listen, Claire,' his expression serious as he looked at her, 'I've given you my mobile number, so if you're worried at any time, it doesn't matter what time, please give me a ring. Will you?' he added when she didn't answer straight away, but once again she was thinking of what Sophie had said.

'Thank you, Jack.' she said at last, taking another sip of her wine.

They had another drink before leaving, agreeing they might then avoid the peak-time rush at Waterloo. By the time they finally arrived back in Brockenhurst it was still light and would be for at least a couple of hours and Jack suggested as they walked across the station car park to collect their cars, that they call into "The Hunters' Arms".

'And catch up on the latest news.' she said lightly.

'Well, yes,' he smiled, 'I'm sure we'll find someone more than willing to tell us what's been going on today!'

Jack hadn't been exaggerating. The discovery of a woman's body on the outskirts of Upper Nettles had been on the six o'clock television news, but by then, as he and Claire learned as soon as they entered "The Hunters' Arms", it would appear that practically everyone in the town and surrounding district had either seen or been told about the police search earlier in the day and, although the name of the victim hadn't been released, many of them had convinced themselves that she had been Glenda Nicholson and had not been slow in voicing their opinion.

'My word, what a hubbub,' Jack remarked as they manoeuvred their way towards the bar, 'I've never seen the place so packed; we'll be lucky to get a table.'

'There's one over there,' she said, 'it looks as though everyone wants to stay around the bar.' she added.

'True,' he nodded, 'anyway, I'll try and get us a couple of drinks; what would you like, Claire?'

'A white wine, please,' she said, walking over to the table. She'd spotted Sylvia at the far end of the bar and waved to her; Trevor Wheatley, was also there, talking to a couple of people she remembered seeing before, but he hadn't seen her.

As on Sunday when she'd been in, she overheard snippets of conversation as she weaved her way through:

'There can't be any doubt about who she was ….......'

'….. I always thought there was something a bit mysterious about her, didn't you?'

'Well,' this remark from a middle-aged grey-haired woman clutching a glass of Guinness to her broad chest as though she was concerned someone would spill the contents, 'she was a *foreigner*, wasn't she?'

'Even so, Molly, she didn't deserve to be murdered.'

'Nobody *deserves* to be murdered, Jim,' she retorted to the man squashed up next to her, 'but all the same …..'

'….. but we don't know for sure, though, Molly, that it was Glenda Nicholson ….'

'….of course it was,' she interrupted sharply, 'it stands to reason if you think about it….'

Whatever the woman called Molly said in reply was drowned out by another surge of customers coming in and by this time she had reached the table. So much for Deidre saying they were a friendly lot in Upper Nettles, Claire thought cynically. She couldn't help feeling slightly disillusioned, let-down even; she had truly believed people in such a small community would have been more charitable to anyone who hadn't spent all their lives in the town. She certainly had a lot to learn about small-town living.

'You look thoughtful.' Jack said coming up and putting the drinks on the table.

'Oh, it's just that I couldn't help hearing what people are saying; they sounded as though they knew without any doubt who the dead woman was, but it was more than that, Jack; it was the implications beneath what they were saying; what I mean is they firmly believe she was Glenda Nicholson and the fact she hadn't originated from Upper Nettles somehow reduces the awfulness of her murder, it was as though they weren't even surprised. Do you know what I mean?'

'Of course I do, Claire. I've only been living here for three years but, like you, it didn't take me long to pick up on their wariness of strangers.'

'Even although they've lived here for quite a few years and, in Glenda Nicholson's case, set up business in the town, from which I'm sure many of those women who were born and bred here are more than pleased about; meaning they don't have to traipse into Lymington or further afield.'

'They probably are,' Jack agreed, taking a sip of his lager, giving her the impression there was more he wanted to say, but perhaps reluctant to voice what he was actually thinking, 'but, Claire, I don't want to pass my cynicism on to you; it wouldn't be fair, you need time to absorb yourself into the general atmosphere of the town, meet more people and find out what makes them tick.'

'We've known each other a long time, Jack,' she said slowly, unnecessarily, 'and I think we can afford to speak frankly. Actually,' smiling and playing with the stem of her glass, 'I would quite like the benefit of your cynicism.'

'You're sure?'

'I'm sure.'

'Well,' he said slowly, putting his glass back down on the table, 'perhaps cynicism is too strong a word to describe my personal view of the good people of Upper Nettles; as I've said, it didn't take long to suss them out, or I should say to suss out the infra-structure which no doubt goes back hundreds of years. Who knows; I'm no historian, but all I do realise is that this wariness you mentioned, while it certainly exists, is on three levels.'

'You're intriguing me, go on.'

'These are only my opinions,' he warned, 'but it's concerning acceptance, there are those who describe anyone who comes to live in what they consider *their* town as newcomers. They are the polite kind. Secondly, there are others, the not so polite others, who label them as outsiders, and finally, the downright rude folk, who call them foreigners.'

'Not to their faces, surely?'

'I have heard some of them, yes.'

'How unkind.'

'I don't honestly believe they mean to be unkind, you know; it's the way they think and what they believe. Call it a deep-rooted prejudice against anyone who doesn't *belong*,' he emphasised, 'they don't intentionally use the description in a derogatory sense; I'm sure of it. Basically, they're good honest folk, most of them have worked hard all their lives and I think any newcomer who arrives in their midst is seen as some kind of threat; in other words, especially the older generation, they don't like change of any kind, not all that far removed in fact from their medieval forbears.'

'Wow!'

'Too heavy for you?' he grinned, his eyes crinkling in amusement at her startled expression.

'No, not in the least. Anyway,' she laughed, 'I suppose I asked for it!'

'I don't want to put you off coming to Upper Nettles, Claire. I mean that, you know,' he said, placing a hand gently on her arm, 'I never thought I'd see you again and when I heard that by some incredible coincidence you were here, I just couldn't believe it. Well,' smiling, 'what more can I say.'

'You don't need to say anymore, Jack, because I understand, also I feel exactly the same. As my young niece would say, gob-smacked!'

'Very descriptive. Seriously though, I should have asked you on Sunday whether you needed any help, hang some of your pictures, or something useful like that, perhaps?'

'Obviously you saw them leaning against the wall when you came into the bungalow,' she gave a rueful grin, 'and, I might add, they are still there, but if you're sure you wouldn't mind, I really would appreciate it if you could, Jack. I've kept putting off the task, in case I made a mess of it.'

***

The onerous task of identifying the body, in the absence of any next of kin, fell on Sara Blakeman, but, having mentally prepared herself, she carried it out calmly and did not, as she had feared, pass out when the cover was pulled back to reveal the face of the woman for whom she had worked for the last six years. 'I felt completely numb, Don,' she told her boyfriend afterwards, 'it was a strange feeling, you know. While I realised it was Glenda lying there, it was as if I was looking at – nothing, she really had gone. Do you know what I mean?'

'I think so, my love,' he'd smiled sympathetically, 'you've been through a lot these last few days and it couldn't have been easy for you in there. What about the salon, Sara; are you going to keep it open?'

'I've been thinking about that. When Inspector Gale told me the news, my first instinct was to close, but I've decided to carry on, at least until I know what's going to happen with the business. The problem seems to be that nobody knew anything about Glenda, only that she arrived here six years ago from London, bought both her house in Lyndhurst and the business at the same time.'

'Strange.'

'I know; as far as I can remember, she never had many personal calls, or visitors either.'

'Peter Gale will fathom everything out, I'm sure, Sara, so try not to worry too much.'

***

While not exactly worried, Peter Gale was concerned, even puzzled, that it had been Glenda Nicholson's body they had found in the copse, only yards away from where Jamie Green's bike had been, but no sign of him, cursing again the heavy downpour on Sunday night, resulting mainly to a lack of any evidence; no flattened shrubs or broken branches to show there had been a struggle, no footprints, not even a scrap of torn clothing. The pathologist, Jim Stevens, had confirmed the approximate time of death as being between midnight on Saturday and one the following morning, explaining it had been impossible to be more precise due to the adverse weather conditions. There had been considerable bruising to one side of the head, although the cause of death was by strangulation; shreds of silk, possibly from a scarf, were caught up in one of the victim's earrings; she may have been wearing a scarf but there was no sign of one, but if she hadn't been, Peter thought, it could indicate the murder had been premeditated, and may even not have taken place at the copse, there was no way of telling.

So far, they had very little to go on: Glenda Nicholson had last been seen by Deidre Portman driving away from "The Hunters' Arms" between nine and ten on Saturday evening, possibly as a result from a call on her mobile and going, not towards Lyndhurst where she lived, but in the opposite direction. There had been no sign of any handbag on or near the body, although as Sara Blakeman had given them the spare set of keys which Glenda had always kept in the salon, they would be able to make a search of her property in Lyndhurst, a task which needed to be carried out as soon as possible in the event there was anything which could give them some information on what little they knew about the woman. Presumably her mobile would have been in the handbag which was a major drawback as they could have indicated who had made the call to her, especially as it was unlikely she would have taken the time to clear it, therefore, trying to discover where she could have gone after she left "The Hunters" was anyone's guess, he grumbled to himself, although there was perhaps one indication she hadn't been going all that far away from Upper Nettles if, as he was beginning to suspect, Jamie Green's disappearance was connected in some way with what happened to her. Somewhere, he reasoned, Jamie fitted into all of this, otherwise the fact his bike was abandoned so close to where the body was found, also his subsequent disappearance, just didn't add up. Terry Edwards, when he'd spoken to him yesterday, was positive the bike hadn't been there on Friday evening when he'd walked past the copse, therefore it could safely be assumed that this must have happened sometime over the weekend. His talk with the landlord at "The King's Head" in Brockenhurst confirmed that Jamie Green and his friends had been in there on Saturday evening and didn't leave the pub until last orders were called which would have been shortly after eleven, and that he hadn't been in the following day; all of which pointed to Jamie making his return to Upper Nettles that night. It would have taken him no more than thirty minutes to reach the outskirts of Upper Nettles, the road from Brockenhurst being a straight one and at that time very little traffic. He should have then reached home by midnight, but he didn't. Something occurred to prevent him finishing his journey. He had already noted where Jamie and his mother lived and knew to reach the council estate, he would have had to pass Nettles Hollow. Had he seen something – or someone – along that final stretch of road? And, if he had, where the heck was he now? Too many imponderables, Peter concluded, deciding it was time to go over these latest findings with Richard.

It was only a matter of hours before news leaked out that an official identification had been carried out confirming that the victim, as most of the people in Upper Nettles had already decided, had been Glenda Nicholson, a woman many of them knew personally, if not actually to talk to, but used to seeing more or less on a daily basis.

This official knowledge did nothing to assuage what could only be described as a growing unease in the community, a grim reminder that Glenda Nicholson had been murdered and, although less vociferous, those prone to speculating, were assuming her killer must be someone local. No-one was heard to suggest it may have been a random killing committed by an outsider, therefore, although more low-key, the rumours continued, creating an intangible but disturbing atmosphere around the town.

It was perhaps unfortunate, but inevitable, that on the following day,

"The Gazette", Upper Nettles' weekly newspaper, treated the murder as front-page news, which resulted in emphasising what was rapidly developing into a fascinating interest in the stark reality of a murder taking place in their home town. The journalist, Phil Berry, lived in neighbouring Lyndhurst and it was apparent he had done his homework, using his own local contacts in the town where Glenda Nicholson had lived, together with what he had been able to glean from in and around Upper Nettles. The surprising mention of Jamie Green's name within the context of his column only added further fuel to the rumours.

"The scenic tranquillity of Hampshire's New Forest," he had written, "was abruptly and shockingly disturbed on Wednesday morning with the macabre discovery of a woman's body partially concealed amongst a tangle of brambles and gorse in the area called Nettles Hollow on the outskirts of Upper Nettles, one of the Forest's many ancient villages. The victim has now been identified as that of Glenda Nicholson. Miss Nicholson lived in Lyndhurst, six miles away from Upper Nettles; a small town, considered to be the 'capital' of the New Forest', its historical background dating from the eighteenth century when the surrounding area of the town was established as a royal hunting preserve. On speaking to Miss Nicholson's neighbours, it was clear they were visibly stunned to hear of her death, but no more so than among the residents of Upper Nettles where she had owned the hairdressing salon since arriving from London six years earlier. It would appear there is considerable mystery surrounding the murder, and up to the time of this paper going to press, the police authorities have made no announcements as to who may have been responsible for the crime. It is to be hoped, for the sake of the residents' peace of mind in and around Upper Nettles there will be no delay in solving the case.

It may or may not be of any significance, but the writer has it on good authority that the disappearance of Jamie Green, a young resident of Upper Nettles, is causing some concern. Jamie spent Saturday evening with friends in Brockenhurst as he is in the habit of doing, but he has not been seen since. One, perhaps, should ask oneself whether Jamie's disappearance occurring on the same night that Miss Nicholson was murdered, should be considered as something other than coincidence, but this could be part of the mystery yet to be unravelled by the authorities."

'There it is, Peter,' Richard said, slapping his copy of the Gazette back on the desk, 'in black and white.'

'He's certainly spelling it out, isn't he?'

'You could say that,' he said wryly, 'but you can't fault Phil Berry, though; he knows where to draw the line, although it's a pity he had to bring in Jamie Green's name.'

'He's right about it all being a mystery.' Peter commented, 'It is sluggish though, sir; what we need is a breakthrough. Going back to Glenda Nicholson, her life, certainly her former life, does appear to be shrouded in mystery.'

'You're right, Peter and this is what we're faced with, unravelling the mystery, as Phil Berry so aptly wrote. Mind you, I'm not altogether certain if by trawling back into her past will necessarily explain why she met her end the way she did.'

'It would help if we knew who she was friendly with, wouldn't it? For instance, sir, there's the couple who turned up for lunch on Sunday. I'm thinking it might be a good idea to have another word with the neighbour. So far, we've only spoken to the wife, but it's possible her husband could add to what she's told us; the couple's car for instance, Barbara Freeman only told us it was a silver-grey BMW, he may have been more observant; I suppose it's too much to hope he'd have noticed and made a mental note of the number, but you never know, he may have done.'

'It's worth a shot, Peter.' he nodded, 'Also, that boyfriend, and it does sound as though he was Glenda Nicholson's boyfriend; according to Barbara Freeman, the first car he'd been driving had been a left-hand drive one. Whether or not that has any bearing on the case remains to be seen, but the description she gave you of the man is interesting; she was fairly descriptive too. I think we should have a word with some of the other neighbours, hear what they may come up with. I know it's all a bit weak, but at the moment we're very much clutching at straws.'

'I know,' Peter agreed, 'and talking about cars, sir, what's happened to Glenda's?'

'A good question, Peter, what has happened to it. We've got the log book now, so unlike the BMW, we're not stymied there; cars are not exactly easy to dispose of though.'

'Neither are fingerprints, sir, if it should turn up.'

'Exactly, therefore it would be reasonable to suggest it's being kept undercover somewhere, but, another question, where?'

'The murderer has had at least a head start of three days; it could by now be miles away from here.'

'Has it occurred to you, Peter,' Richard asked, 'that there could be more than one person involved in her death?'

'It hadn't, sir, but now you come to mention it, it does seem feasible. Certainly,' he went on thoughtfully, 'in respect to the disposal of the car, decidedly less risky than if one person had the task of driving it away and presumably needing transport to return here, that is if we are talking about the killer living locally.'

'It may still be in the vicinity of where she left it on Saturday night. Bearing this in mind, Peter, I think we should try to resurrect, if we can, those last movements of not only Glenda Nicholson, but of Jamie Green.'

'You believe there's a connection?'

'I'm certain there must be,' Richard answered, pulling his notepad towards him, 'look at it this way, Peter,' drawing a straight line down the centre of a clean sheet, 'here we have the road from Upper Nettles at the bottom, leading out of the town, in the direction of Brockenhurst. For the moment we won't take it any further, mainly because of the timing involved, in that Glenda left "The Hunters' Arms" between nine and ten on Saturday night, let's call it approximately nine-thirty, and Jim confirmed the time of death as being between midnight and one the following morning. If, for the purpose of this exercise, Peter, we call it two and a half hours if we say she was killed around midnight; Jamie left "The King's Head" in Brockenhurst at about eleven-fifteen and, as far as we know, started to cycle back to Upper Nettles then. Perhaps we should speak to those friends of his, in the event, it was after that time. However, and this is where it gets somewhat obscure, but if Jamie had been in the vicinity of Nettles Hollow at the same time as the killer was depositing the body, he could have seen this, but as his bike had been thrown into the shrubs and there's been no sign of him, it could be argued he was seen by the killer. We're unable to take it any further than that as we don't know whether Jamie was apprehended by the killer or made a run for it, but for the present, the bottom line being, Peter, if you work on this theory, it does seem feasible, dare I say it, to assume there is a connection, albeit a rather tenuous one. What's your opinion, do you consider it too farfetched?'

'No, I don't, but I've been thinking sir.'

'Yes?'

'While it could have happened like that, Jamie may have seen something amiss before then -'

' - go on; this is what we need, throw as many possibilities into this particularly murky fish pond.'

'Well,' he began hesitatingly, 'I was wondering why the killer should choose the copse, why there? Whether she was murdered there or elsewhere, what was he, or they, doing there in the first place? Sorry, sir, a bit garbled, I'm afraid.'

'No, Peter, not in the least, carry on.'

'If he'd killed her some distance away, but still within the forest area, he had plenty of available places he could have chosen, which does suggest he may have come from somewhere nearby; not necessarily in Upper Nettles and I would think Brockenhurst would be too far away, but on the outskirts of Upper Nettles, presumably, if our first theory is correct, along the road or not far from it, between Upper Nettles and Brockenhurst. And, if he had, it's possible, I realise a remote possibility, but Jamie may have seen him acting suspiciously before he reached the copse as he was cycling along the road.'

'You have made a very interesting point, you know. It's a fairly quiet stretch of road, but not entirely uninhabited; there are quite a few properties scattered along there and some of them do face the road. How good is your memory, Peter?' he smiled, picking up his pencil again.

Chapter Six

Johnnie Wall seldom read newspapers or listened to the news. He had no interest in what was happening in what he considered to be an alien world; his one and only consuming passion was music and anything else, even relationships with the opposite sex which at the most he found a temporary, although questionable, pleasure, were of little consequence to him. It's doubtful whether he even knew of "The Gazette's" existence and if someone hadn't left a copy on the hall table he may have remained in ignorance for a little longer why he hadn't heard from Glenda as he'd expected after Saturday's debacle. It was the headline on the front page which caught his eye: "BODY OF WOMAN FOUND IN UPPER NETTLES NOW IDENTIFIED"; he read on, and reaching the end, remained where he was, as though transfixed, incapable of believing what he'd read, until gradually the implication filtered into his brain. Glenda was dead; strangled, it had said.

Unaware he was still holding the newspaper, he walked slowly into the lounge and over to the open windows, but not seeing the recently raked gravel of the drive or the well-manicured lawns, even oblivious to the sprinkler which the gardener had placed in the centre earlier, the widening arc of spray sparkling in the late morning sunshine. Instead, he was forcing his fuddled memory back to Saturday night, but it was hopeless; he'd been as high as a bloody kite, had been for most of that afternoon, acknowledging that total recall or even partial recall would be practically impossible although he could remember with surprising clarity how indignant Glenda had been, but as to exactly why, his memory was hazy. Resembling a smudged CD, the mental pictures he was getting were spasmodic and disjointed with a good part of the dialogue missing. He had a vague recollection of phoning Glenda on her mobile, something about a party, then, a space of time, he had no idea how long, because the next 'clip' was when Glenda appeared

"I thought you said you were having a party, but I don't see any of the guests, Johnnie. Where are they all?" her voice unnaturally loud to his ears as she had approached the French windows, and then his own voice:

"They didn't turn up, darling'; there's only me and, waiting in the wings, a faithful and very frustrated, Gerry."

"You're talking in riddles; I think I should go."

"Don't be a party pooper, Glenda; just relax, help yourself to a drink or something stronger, there's plenty, and enjoy the moment."

"But," had she been trying to humour him? "there is no party."

"That's where you're wrong," and unsteadily, aware of a sudden surge of adrenalin, he had stood up, carefully propping his guitar up against the chair, "Gerry and I have this desire to be entertained and this is where you come in."

"If you mean what I think you do, Johnnie, you can forget it; what you and I do when we are alone together isn't something I want to share with anyone else, especially that thug!"

"Tut. Tut. Don't let Gerry hear you say that; he's a good-looking guy, with a normal guy's appetite."

"I'm going, Johnnie. You disgust me!' here, there was a break; the film had frozen: Glenda remained where she was, framed in the open window, then with a silent hiccup, the clip resumed, not from where it had left off, but some indeterminate time later; it could have been only minutes, he was outside in the middle of the road with her and dragging her back to the house. Gerry had been there, he remembered he was at the gate, calling over to him, but he couldn't hear what he was saying. Again, there was a pause, a longer one this time, and they were back in the lounge, Gerry had been with them and this was when Glenda became hysterical, throwing herself against him, pounding her fists against his chest. He must have passed out at this point, but in the fraction of a second before he lost consciousness, he heard Gerry say he would take her home. After that, nothing, it must have been around six, as it was becoming light, when he surfaced; he was lying on the sofa covered by his duvet which Gerry must have brought downstairs for him sometime during the night. His head had been pounding and in those first waking moments he had absolutely no recollection of the night before. Shrugging off the duvet, he pulled himself upright and using the arm of the sofa for support, tentatively and painfully got to his feet and made his way upstairs; Passing the open door to the kitchen he could hear voices; Pete's and Eddie's, they seemed to be arguing, but he neither had the strength or the inclination to go in there; instead he'd carried on, and taking one step at a time, went upstairs and along the corridor to his bedroom. He had dropped heavily on to the bed and it must have been within seconds he was asleep, this time, a deep and dreamless sleep and not waking until around eleven, the sun streaming relentlessly through the window. The blinding headache had receded, but leaving in its wake, as it always did, a euphoric emptiness, but at least he felt he could face the day and after a shower and a change of clothing, went back downstairs. The front door had been wide open; Pete and Eddie had been outside and while not exactly arguing, neither of them looked too happy.

"What's up with you two?" he'd asked them, leaning against Pete's car, and waiting for some sort of explanation.

"Nothing much, Johnnie." Pete had replied.

"It didn't sound like nothing to me."

"Pete's got all the answers!" Eddie had said, throwing his hands up in the air and, swivelling round on his heels walked off round to the back of the house.

"Well?"

"Nothing for you to worry about, Johnnie; just Eddie getting irate about something Gerry said; it's not important."

"It sounded as though it's important to Eddie."

"You know, Eddie, Johnnie; always inclined to get things out of proportion."

"Are you going to enlighten me or not," he'd asked him, although the way he had been feeling, not too concerned whether he was going to or not, "otherwise," he'd gone on, but only half-heartedly, "I'll be thinking this is some sort of conspiracy."

"It's nothing like that; it's about last night, that's all."

"What about last night?"

"I'd already got back and was in bed, when Eddie turned up; this was apparently about three in the morning and he'd no sooner pulled up outside here, when Gerry walked up the drive. He refused to tell him where he'd been, said he couldn't sleep and had gone out for a walk."

"And I take it, Eddie didn't believe him."

"You're damn right he didn't!"

"Why not?"

"Why not?"

"Yes, why didn't he believe Gerry? Sounds quite feasible to me."

"Do you remember *anything* about last night, Johnnie?" he'd asked.

"Not much."

"I didn't think so; you were out for the count when I came in, flat out in fact. I didn't disturb you, thought it best to leave you there, so I put your duvet over you in case it got chilly during the night."

"Thanks."

"Don't mention it, mate." grinning.

And that was that. Eddie had left around midday, saying he wanted to get back to London that afternoon and that he would give him a ring later about the trip he was making to Amsterdam later in the week, and Pete and he had left at the same time, deciding to have lunch at "The Montagu Arms Hotel" in Beaulieu. They'd asked Gerry if he wanted to come with them, but he'd not been interested, saying he preferred to stay here. He had been in one of his uncommunicative moods for most of that day, although he did mention at some point about the woman who had moved into the cottage across the road, said he'd found her snooping around outside, and hadn't believed her when she told him she only wanted to introduce herself, Gerry was like that; definitely lacking in any social graces and it was typical he hadn't recognised what was no more than a friendly neighbourly gesture, immediately interpreting her appearance as suspicious.

Johnnie had enough on his mind without concerning himself with Gerry's paranoia, looking again at the newspaper article and, sure enough, towards the end it mentioned that Glenda had been murdered on the Saturday night and who was this Jamie Green? He had been so shocked to hear about Glenda he had glossed over what they were calling the added mystery of his disappearance. It didn't make sense. In fact, nothing made sense. Gerry would have driven her home and then come straight back here. Wouldn't he?

Johnnie had known Gerry Steele for years, right back to the early days when Gerry had been working as a bouncer for Ted Warren at his nightclub in London's West End. Pete and he used to frequent "Ted's Revue Bar" often round about that time; revue being something of a misnomer, when strip club would have been more apt. But Gerry's career as bouncer ended abruptly when Ted Warren was shot dead one night in a particularly nasty brawl involving members of the Metropolitan police force. And now this, he thought, tossing the paper on to one of the chairs, what the hell was he supposed to think? Was Gerry a killer? Good question. How well did anyone know anyone else, the cynical half-answer slipping uninvited into his brain, struggling to make itself heard amongst the rest of the stored-up garbage? One thing for sure; somebody killed her. He would have to talk to Gerry of course, but the unpalatable fact remained; whatever the final outcome he, personally, would be involved, his name once again dragged through the media mud and the inevitable aftermath, culminating in the final destruction of his so-called reputation. A background of drug abuse seemed pretty tame compared with being tainted with suspicions of murder, however tenuous they may be.

It wasn't until the middle of the afternoon when Johnnie first realised Gerry wasn't around. He'd said at breakfast, he was going to drive into Lymington to stock up on provisions, this being part of his weekly routine, but usually he would have been back around midday, perhaps a little later if he'd decided to stop off and have a beer and a bite to eat, but he should have been back by now. Ever since he'd read that damn article he had been on edge, unable to concentrate on the musical score he had been planning to include in their next tour, but any inspiration had vanished, leaving him superstitiously reluctant to reach out for his guitar and escape into the solace he needed, in case he wouldn't be able to. There were other ways, quicker, more fool proof, but it would be too easy to pick up the whisky bottle or resort to his other, equally effective narcotic, but they weren't the answer, not this time. What he needed was company, somebody he could talk to, but Pete was in London and the other two, Spike and Eddie wouldn't be back from Amsterdam until the weekend, but there was someone, hesitating only momentarily before picking up the receiver and dialling her number.

***

Peter had drawn a blank at most of the houses he'd been to in Willow Crescent, the responses he'd received being almost identical; he was fast coming to the realisation that the residents of this undoubtedly prestigiously sought-after area of the town had fine-tuned the questionable art of keeping themselves to themselves. None of them had so much as shown a flicker of interest, or sympathy if it came to that, when he had mentioned Glenda Nicholson's name. Without exception, they had displayed an open reluctance to even acknowledge that the murdered woman had been one of their neighbours and while, presumably, they would have seen her regularly during the months and years she had lived in such close proximity, it was abundantly obvious to Peter they just didn't want to know. He had intentionally left number seven until the last in the hope that Barbara Freeman's husband would be back from work but before going along there, rang the doorbell of the remaining property, the one on the other side of Glenda Nicholson's.

The woman who came to the door was different to those others he'd seen that afternoon in that she didn't visibly recoil when he showed her his identity card, instead, she smiled sadly.

'Poor Glenda; what a dreadful thing to happen to her, Inspector.'

'It was, yes;' immediately heartened by her reaction, 'and we're doing our utmost to find the person responsible. What I'm trying to achieve at the moment, madam,' he went on, 'is to establish her background, by that I mean her personal background. We know very little about her, only that she owned the hairdressing establishment in Upper Nettles and had done so for the past six years after arriving in the area from London, but we know little about her social life, any friends she may have had and it's for this reason we have to depend on people who, like yourself, lived near her and perhaps had seen her on a daily basis.'

'I understand, but I'm not sure I will be able to help you, Inspector. I'll try of course, but Glenda wasn't what I would describe as a gregarious type of person. She was friendly, but although my husband and I have lived next door to her since she moved in, we didn't mix socially you understand. She was some years younger than us, that could have been the reason, also,' she added, 'she had her business which must have kept her fully occupied and she was away most weekends.'

'I don't wish to take up much more of your time,' Peter said, feeling slightly encouraged by what she'd said, 'but there are a couple of questions I would like to ask you.'

'That's alright, Inspector; perhaps it would be better if you were to come in rather for us standing out here on the doorstep. It should stop the twitching of curtains if you did.'

'Neighbourly interest.' he commented.

'I'm not so sure,' she answered, leading him across the hall and into the kitchen, 'although we've lived here for ten years now, I still miss the anonymity of being in a city. I'm sure Glenda must have thought the same, but she never said.'

'Did she ever tell you about her life in London, Mrs -'

'- Coleman,' she supplied, 'Rosemary Coleman. And, no, Inspector, all I remember her saying, and this was not long after she'd moved in, was that she'd worked in Bloomsbury, not far from Russell Square. Apparently, she owned a small hairdressing salon there and when the lease expired decided to move out of London. I remember asking her why she'd chosen to come to the New Forest, but she'd been a bit vague; perhaps she hadn't wanted to elaborate for some reason or other.'

'Did she have many visitors, Mrs Coleman?' hoping he was going to learn more than he had from Barbara Freeman.

'Not really, except for one friend she had; he used to visit quite often.'

'Did she ever mention his name?'

'No, but then she didn't have to, Inspector; I'd already recognised him.'

'Really?' was this the first lead they'd had in this enquiry so far, he wondered, waiting for her to elaborate.'

'Mind you,' she smiled, 'my husband didn't believe me, but I wasn't wrong; he was Bernie Croft.'

'Bernie Croft?'

'Sorry, Inspector, you may not have heard of him; he was a guitarist with "The Bandanas", but he left the group around 2000 I think it must have been. I was a big fan of the group; this was years ago, of course, when I was still in my teens. Bernie Croft was with them from when they first started but his appearance hadn't changed all that much. He has one of these 'lived-in' faces, a bit like Keith Richards actually.'

'Did you ever mention to Miss Nicholson you recognised him?'

'Oh, no, Inspector; middle-aged women are not supposed to rake up their adolescent crushes, besides, Alan, that's my husband, said I'd better not as I would look foolish if it turned out I was wrong.'

'But you don't think you were?'

'No, I don't.'

'Have you any idea why he left "The Bandanas", I was wondering where he was living now.'

'I see what you mean,' she nodded, 'well, as to why he broke away from them, I think there was some kind of scandal; I never knew the details. He could have fallen out with Johnnie; it was about the time Johnnie was convicted of drug offences, this was when they were on one of their European tours.'

'He shouldn't be too difficult to trace. Can you remember the last time you saw him, Mrs Coleman?'

'I didn't actually see him, Inspector, but he was here the Sunday before last; Alan and I were on our way back from the morning church service and his car was parked outside Glenda's house then.'

'You've been very helpful, Mrs Coleman; there's only one other question I want to ask and it's concerning the couple who I've been told called to see Miss Nicholson last Sunday. Did you see them?'

'No, I didn't; we spent the day with our daughter and her family, but Barbara Freeman, I don't know whether you've talked to her yet, told me about them.'

'I believe Miss Nicholson had invited them for lunch.'

'Yes, that's what Barbara said, but that was a bit odd, you know, Inspector.'

'Why do you say that?'

'Because when I spoke to Glenda during the week, I think it was Thursday evening, she mentioned that she had booked herself in to the new Health & Fitness Spa in Bournemouth.'

'And this would have been for the Sunday?'

'That's right, but,' she said thoughtfully, 'it's possible she may have changed her mind.'

While it was perfectly feasible in what Rosemary Coleman had suggested, Peter couldn't dismiss the possibility of the couple's visit being irrelevant. As he walked along the pavement to the Freeman's house, he made a quick recap of what he'd been able to cover that afternoon: While the majority of the neighbours he'd spoken to had admitted, albeit reluctantly, that they had noticed the BMW outside Glenda's house, they were all unanimous they had never seen the car or the couple in their crescent before. This, in itself, was neither significant or even noticeably helpful to their enquiry, except to illustrate those two people could provide some much-needed light on the somewhat sketchy background of Glenda Nicholson; hopefully, he thought, ringing the Freeman's door bell, he was about to learn more about the BMW, if not about the two people purporting to be her friends, sufficiently so to have been invited for lunch.

Bob Freeman came to the door, promptly introducing himself.

'Barbara was wondering whether you would be returning, Inspector Gale.' he said, opening the door wider and gesturing for him to come in and as in an action replay, taking him into their kitchen.

Barbara Freeman, who had been at the sink rinsing through a couple of mugs, quickly dried her hands on a tea towel: 'What dreadful news this is, Inspector. I simply cannot believe what's happened to poor Glenda. Simply dreadful.'

'It certainly is, Mrs Freeman.' Peter said, shaking hands with her. At least her reaction to the murder didn't correspond to the majority of Willow Crescent's other residents.

'How can we help you, Inspector?' Bob Freeman put in, his dark brown eyes reflecting his wife's distress. 'As Barbara has just said, this is a shocking business. Shocking. I was having a pint in "The Hunters' Arms" the other evening and everyone I spoke to were already fearing the worse; I think seeing your officers searching in Nettles Hollow convinced them, but now, after what's been written in "The Gazette". Well, what more can I say?'

'All very unpleasant;' Peter said, waiting for an opening, already recognising that Bob Freeman was one of those men who gave garrulous a new dimension, 'one of the reasons I'm here, Mr Freeman,' he went on quickly before the man took the chance to continue his flow, 'is to try and fill in a few gaps which have appeared so far in our enquiry; the main one, as far as you and your wife are concerned, being the couple who called to see Miss Nicholson last Sunday, in particular, the car they were driving. Your wife has already told me the make of the vehicle and that it bore a personal number plate.'

'Yes, that's absolutely correct. A very nice new motor, and an *expensive* one, I might add.'

'Can you remember the number, sir?'

'Not the number, Inspector, but I did see the name of where he must have bought the car; it was on one of those sales stickers on the rear window, very neatly placed it was, but I noticed it alright, that was when they drove off.'

'That could be helpful to us, Mr Freeman.'

'I'm sure it will be,' he nodded smugly, the owl-like glasses moving in unison, obviously making the most of what he probably considered as keeping him in suspense for as long as possible, 'I'd actually heard of the company and that they only deal with top of the range vehicles, way beyond my modest means of course, more's the pity.'

'And the name of the company, sir?' prompting him; talk about extracting blood from a stone, he thought impatiently.

'Knights of Kensington they're called, Inspector.'

'Right, I'll just jot that down.' Peter said, flicking over to a fresh sheet in his notebook, although realising without the registration number it could prove difficult to trace, 'You mentioned that it was a new model, Mr Freeman, have you any idea of just how new?'

'Well, if you want my opinion, Inspector, I would say it was brand new, definitely this year's model.'

'Thank you, also for your time.'

'Don't mention it,' this time making no attempt to conceal his look of self-satisfaction, 'only too pleased to assist the local constabulary.'

Peter drove slowly back to Upper Nettles, going over what he had managed to find out and not dissatisfied; Rosemary Coleman had been particularly helpful in respect to the man who had apparently been a regular visitor, the last time being the weekend before Glenda was murdered. Although he couldn't remember ever having heard of Bernie Croft, he knew of the rock group, but only because someone had told him when their lead guitarist had bought the old Grange in Lymington Road, therefore, provided there was no real animosity remaining between them from when he split from the group, presumably Johnnie Wall would be agreeable to giving him some idea what the ex-member of his band was doing now and they could then take it from there; Peter couldn't help feeling that Bernie Croft fitted into this enquiry. It was always possible he and Glenda hadn't met more recently, if not at the house, somewhere else. Immediately this idea came to him, he thought again of the Saturday night; when he'd spoken to Barbara Freeman on Tuesday, she'd given him the time of when Glenda returned home from the salon and the time she and her husband had seen her car parked outside "The Hunters". Chris Portman confirmed that Glenda left the pub before ten and had only been in long enough to have one drink, but there was another time he'd overlooked. Barbara had been sure that when she left to pick up her husband at the station, Glenda's car hadn't been outside her house and that this had been at quarter to seven. She hadn't heard the car leaving, otherwise she would have said; it could have been practically any time between shortly after six and before six forty-five. So, where had she gone? The space of time between, say six-thirty and around nine when she arrived at "The Hunters", indicated wherever it had been must have been in close proximity to Upper Nettles, but where? In Upper Nettles itself? It's anyone's guess, he thought wryly, by now approaching the town and the beginning of the High Street, the first building on his right, the attractive Georgian mansion with the low gable roofs of "Nettles Hotel", and slowing down, allowing the car behind him to overtake, he pulled over and drove into the hotel's car park.

The lounge bar, in keeping with the ancient architecture, overlooked by a minstrel's gallery, dark wood panelling, gilt-framed mirrors and paintings of former owners, glittering chandeliers and windows opening out to a walled garden and terrace, was warmly welcoming and creating a subdued ambience of another era. A pianist was playing softly in the adjoining restaurant and he could hear the chink of glasses and cutlery as the waiters prepared the tables for the evening meal. There were only half a dozen customers in the bar: an elderly couple sharing a half bottle of wine; two men in business suits, heads close together, examining columns of figures and two women; one of them middle-aged and overweight, wearing a long voluminous dress in Hermit-the-frog green, treble strings of multi-coloured glass beads resting on her massive bosom and on surprisingly small feet, matching green high-heeled sandals; the other woman in stark contrast, was about thirty, long dark hair tied back loosely with a black and white chiffon scarf, reminding him of Victoria Beckham but without the pout; slim to the point of thinness and wearing a simple, sleeveless black shift, her only jewellery, a single string of pearls. There was an open brief case on the floor beside her feet and she was writing in a spiral notebook, similar to the ones he used, but she didn't look up as he walked past her on the way to the bar.

Peter had been in the hotel a number of times, but not for some months, surprised to see that Jim Head was still there; Jim had been the hotel's head barman for years, he could remember seeing him on his first visit and had thought at the time he looked too old to be working, but nudging forty himself, and looking back he could remember thinking that most people who were probably younger than he was now, had seemed old! The passage of time, he thought wryly.

'Good evening, sir, how are you?'

'Busy.' Peter smiled, ordering half a lager.

'I expect you are, sir,' shaking his head sadly, 'this murder is a dreadful business; poor woman, I read about it this morning in "The Gazette", he added, passing Peter his beer.

'I thought you may have done, Jim,' taking an appreciative sip, 'I'm assisting the Chief Inspector with the enquiry and what we're trying to do is recreate as far as we can Glenda Nicholson's movements on the night she was murdered. We know she was in "The Hunters' Arms" for part of the evening, from around nine o'clock on Saturday, but she was only there for less than an hour, so what we have to do is find out where she was before nine and from when she left "The Hunters" -'

' - the lady was in here earlier, sir,' he interrupted quickly, 'it was about quarter to seven until just before nine.'

'It had occurred to me that she may have been; did you speak to her?'

'Only to say good evening; the gentleman she was meeting was already here, sitting over there,' indicating by a slight movement of his head to one of the tables by the open window, next to where the two businessmen were sitting, 'and she went straight over to him.'

'I see,' Peter nodded, 'and had you seen him before?'

'No, I'm sure I hadn't.'

'Do you know whether he was staying here, Jim?'

'I'm not sure; although,' he added, 'he paid for their drinks by cash; usually guests add their drinks, and meals of course, to their hotel bill and then settle by credit card when they leave.'

'I can check at reception, but perhaps you would be good enough to give me a description of him, just a rough outline will do, Jim.'

'Well,' stroking his chin as he remembered, 'he was in his forties, mid-forties, I would say, about my height, five-eight, clean shaven, light brown hair, cut fairly short, fairly average I suppose you would say. Afraid it's not much of a description.'

'No, that's fine; hopefully it will give us something to go on. You say she left around nine?'

'Yes, that's right; I don't know about the exact time, but I think it must have been slightly before then as we had a party of twelve arrive at nine and she'd gone by then.'

'And her companion.'

'Oh, he remained, finished his drink and then went into the restaurant.'

'Thanks a lot, Jim; you've been very helpful; at least now we know where she was prior to arriving at "The Hunters".

The girl on the reception desk was equally as helpful; she'd been on duty on Saturday night and with the description Jim had given him, she remembered seeing him arrive and walking through to the bar although she wasn't sure about the time, but Jim had said it had been about seven, she also confirmed that he wasn't a guest and she'd never seen him before. Presumably he would have been driving, but as he would have had to park at the rear of the hotel, she wouldn't have seen his car and as the hotel didn't employ a parking attendant, there was no-one he could ask. As an after-thought, Peter decided to have a word with the head waiter in the restaurant, remembering that one of the windows actually overlooked the hotel's car park. One of the restaurant staff may have noticed the man who'd been with Glenda walk back to his car. It was a possibility, although only slight, but worth asking.

The pianist was playing the opening chords of "Chariots of Fire" when he reached the restaurant, the haunting melody softly unfolding and merging into the background. Peter stood for a few seconds in the open glass doorway, waiting until Joseph, another of "The Nettles" older members of staff, had finishing talking to one of the waitresses. Joseph had already indicated he'd seen him by a slight nod of recognition.

'Inspector Gale,' he said, striding towards him, his hand outstretched in greeting, 'good evening.'

'Good evening, Joseph;' Peter smiled, not for the first time appreciating the advantages of having always lived in the area; there was seldom any need for him to introduce himself, 'I won't take up too much of your time, but I've just been talking to Jim Head.'

'I noticed you talking to him; I expect you're here about what's been happening recently? A murder in Upper Nettles; dreadful, really dreadful.' he added, lowering his voice.

'It is, Joseph and that's why we're making every endeavour to discover who was responsible. I understand that the victim, Miss Nicholson, was in the lounge bar on Saturday evening and it's her companion we are interested in locating, this being for elimination purposes, as we have to do with any murder enquiry of course.'

'I understand, Inspector. I didn't see the lady myself, but Jim told me she'd been in on Saturday, this was after we'd read the piece in "The Gazette" today, and presumably he has told you that her companion came into the restaurant for a meal.'

'That's right, he did. There are only a few questions I need to ask you,' Peter explained, 'the first one is how he settled the bill for his meal, by cash or did he use a credit card?'

'He paid by credit card, Inspector.'

'Did you happen to see his name on the card, Joseph?'

'I can't remember his initials, but his surname was Waterman.'

'You've a good memory.' he complimented him.

'Normally, I don't, Inspector,' he smiled, 'but my wife recently bought me a Waterman pen for my birthday, so that was why.'

'I see, and my second question is whether you, or perhaps one of your staff, noticed whether he went into the hotel car park when he left the restaurant, and if so, and I know this is a long shot, if they did, whether they happened to see his car?'

'Oh, dear, that is a difficult one. I'm sorry, but I didn't notice, Inspector. The last I saw of him was when he left the restaurant and walked through the lounge bar to the front door of the hotel, but if you don't mind waiting for a couple of minutes while I ask the waiters who were on duty on Saturday night.' excusing himself and walking to the other side of the room to where two waitresses were putting the finishing touches to the tables, returned almost as quickly with one of them.

'This is Penelope, Inspector,' he said, ushering the girl forward, 'she did happen to see the gentleman in the car park.'

'Hello, Penelope,' in an attempt to put the girl at her ease; she was young, no more than seventeen and obviously nervous, probably never having spoken to a police officer in her life before, 'nothing to worry about, all I would like to know is whether you saw the car he got into.'

'I can't remember the registration number,' she said apologetically, 'except it wasn't a local number.'

'Alright, I didn't really expect you to remember, not many people would have, you know, but what was the make of the car; that could be a help?'

'It was a BMW sports car, dark red with an open top. I'm sure about the make, Inspector, because my uncle has one the same, although his is white.'

He thanked her and with a brief nervous smile, she went back to what she had been doing, no doubt relieved her ordeal was over.

'A pity she didn't get the number, Inspector.' Joseph commented, but not too harshly. Peter had meant what he'd said, very few people would have made any attempt to remember a car registration number, but what little she had told him, wouldn't be wasted. It wouldn't necessarily help them to find the man, but it was better than nothing. The fact that she did meet someone that evening must have meant something, although whether it had any significance to the murder enquiry remained to be seen.

***

Earlier, when Peter was wrapping up his final interview in Lyndhurst, Richard, having called into "The King's Head" in Brockenhurst, was gratified to find that two of the early evening customers had been with Jamie Green the previous Saturday. They would be about the same age as Jamie, in their early twenties, but unlike him they both appeared to be employed, if the red tee-shirts with the name of a local building firm printed on the front of them, was anything to go by. Neither of them had seen a copy of "The Gazette", therefore were unaware that the police were treating him as a missing person.

'How long have you known Jamie?' Richard asked them once he'd explained that Jamie hadn't returned home on Saturday night.

'Two or three years, it would have been.' one of them, who'd told Richard he was called Jason Graham, answered, 'That would be about right, wouldn't it, Trev?'

'Nearer three, I think;' Trev was quick to correct him, 'it was when we were working on that big conversation in Mill Lane; Jamie was taken on as a labourer right at the beginning of the project.' he added for Richard's benefit.

'I see, Richard nodded, 'but I'm told he's not been employed recently.'

'That's true, although he was telling us on Saturday when he was in here, that he had an interview for a summer job at the nurseries in Upper Nettles.'

'He's not had much luck with jobs.' Jason put in, 'Not altogether his fault, just that he finds it difficult to stick a job for long.'

'When you left here on Saturday, did he say he was going straight home.'

'He didn't actually say he was going back, but we saw him cycle off in that direction.'

'And was that when you last saw him?'

'Yes, that's right,' the one called Trev, answered this time, 'none of us expected to see him until this Saturday.'

'Do you know whether he was in the habit of going anywhere else for a drink?'

'I don't think so,' Jason said, 'he never said, but it's doubtful; Jamie's never exactly flushed, being unemployed.'

'What we're trying to do,' Richard explained, 'is to find out if he had other friends, some-one he may have gone to that night, a girlfriend perhaps.'

'He doesn't have a girlfriend; he's not gay,' Jason added quickly, 'he's had girlfriends, but I think they soon get fed up with him, not having a job I mean; girls round here like you to spend money on them.'

'Do you think something's happened to him?' Trev asked Richard.

'That is a possibility,' Richard answered carefully, 'but, apart from his bike having been found on the outskirts of Upper Nettles, we've no evidence to support that; we're not even able to confirm that he did in fact return to Upper Nettles on Saturday night; he may have done and, for whatever reason, the bike had been abandoned, alternatively, he never cycled back and the bike had been taken by someone else to where it was later found.

'I don't understand, sir,' Jason frowned, 'if he'd been involved in an accident, surely he would have been taken to hospital, or -'

'- if he'd been killed,' Trev finished for him, 'his body would have been found – like his bike.'

While there was a certain logic in their thinking, it was apparent to Richard that neither of them was aware of the murder of Glenda Nicholson or, if they were, either hadn't realised she had been killed on Saturday night or hadn't made any connection, unlike most of the residents of Upper Nettles, most of whom would have read the news in "The Gazette" by this time.

Driving back to Upper Nettles and although it was now almost seven-thirty and time to finish for the day, he decided to make a couple of random calls as a start in forming some sort of re-construction of when Jamie would presumably have been cycling along the same stretch of road. There were, as Peter and he had agreed, a few properties between Brockenhurst and the approach to Nettles Hollow, but with only one or two exceptions, they were too far back from the road for anyone to have seen or heard anything untoward, wondering as he drew closer to the outskirts of Upper Nettles whether he could be wasting his time, especially as they didn't really know what they expected to hear. Miracles never happened in what was no more than one long hard slog in sifting through the most miniscule of leads in any murder enquiry, and more so perhaps in this one. The disappointing fact remained, it was now Thursday evening, almost a week since Glenda Nicholson was murdered, and they had precious little to show for their combined efforts.

He was now driving past the high hedges of "The Grange", the home of the rock star, Johnnie Wall. Richard had never been one of "The Bandanas'" greatest fans, mainly because he found their music too soulful for his liking, therefore hadn't shared the local stir of interest when Johnnie Wall had decided to make his home virtually on their doorstep, although rather suspecting this wave of suppressed excitement, especially by the younger generation of Upper Nettles, was due more to the group's debatable illustrious history. Instead of turning left into the driveway of "The Grange", he pulled on to the grass verge and, switching off the engine, walked across the road to Tulip Cottage. This action hadn't been a sudden change of mind; he would call on Johnnie Wall and whoever else shared the house with him, but having seen two cars parked outside the cottage, it had reassured him that someone must be at home.

***

'There's something not quite right about the balance of this one, Claire.' Jack said, stepping back from where he'd hung the last picture. There had been twelve pictures altogether and it hadn't taken him long, once she'd told him exactly where she would like them to go.

'There isn't, is there,' she agreed, 'I wonder why.'

'You've had no problem with it before?' taking the picture down again, and as he did so, both heard a faint rattle from inside the frame and shaking the picture slightly, he felt the slight movement as if something had shifted.

'Can I take the back off?' he asked.'

'Of course you can; do you need a knife to prise it off?'

'I don't think that will be necessary; look at this, Claire,' he added, 'it's only held in place by cellotape.'

'That's not right is it; none of the others are.'

'I would say, judging by the quality of the frame itself, it's definitely not right.' watching him as he gently, and easily, peeled the strip of tape away and levering the back away from the wooden frame.'

'My God,' she gasped, 'how the heck did that get in there?' looking in astonishment at the computer disc Jack was now holding, but she guessed, instinctively she knew who'd placed the disc in there. There was only one person it could have been. She'd had the picture for years, long before she'd known Tom; Sophie and Neil, the man Sophie had been married to, had given it to her when she moved into the flat in London, and they had both watched Neil as he had hung it on her lounge wall; a task which only took seconds and he got it right first time, there'd been no need to fiddle around to get it straight.

'It must have been Tom; no-one else would have done it, Jack. I'm positive about that. What do you think we should do with the thing?' she added, looking in distaste at the disc in the palm of his hand.

'Don't look so worried,' he smiled, 'you're finding it offensive, aren't

95

you; I can understand, you know. Somehow, it must seem to you the reversal of a theft, instead of someone removing one of your belongings, they have placed something you don't want in one of them.'

'That's exactly how I feel, I just want to get rid of it, but -' not really knowing what she wanted to do.

'You could always do that, of course, and it's your prerogative, Claire, although once that's done, it would be tantamount to forgetting it, that is if you could, but then there would be no way of finding out why it was in there in the first place.'

'You're right. I'm finding it rather difficult to be practical. It's so, so unpleasant.'

'I know. If you're right, and I'm sure you are,' he said slowly, 'and that it was Tom, I can only think of one reason why he should have done that.'

'Obviously to hide it.'

'Yes, probably not wanting to leave the disc where someone else could find it, which makes me believe whatever the content might be, he didn't need to have immediate access.'

'I can't help thinking there is something dishonest, even illegal about it all; I feel tainted somehow.'

'That's understandable.' his smile sympathetic.

'Perhaps we should read what's on it.'

'If you're sure?'

'Yes, Jack; I'm beginning to recover from the initial surprise, unpleasant as it was, and what I'm feeling now is anger at him taking such a liberty.'

'That's a healthy reaction.' he grinned. 'I tell you what, if you've got some tape I'll finish hanging the picture, it should be alright now, and then we can find out.'

'It could be in code.'

'You *have* recovered!'

'I've been thinking,' she said on their way upstairs to her study.

'Yes?'

'I didn't mention to you that Tom phoned me last Friday not long after

I'd arrived to ask me where I was living, saying he wanted to explain in the hope I'd change my mind about finishing with him.'

'Did you believe him?' Jack asked.

'Not really, but I couldn't think why my whereabouts should be so important to him; he'd actually phoned my agent and Sophie, but he didn't get any change out of either of them.'

'And now,' he prompted, 'you know why?'

'Yes, I think so; he wanted to get his disc back. You see, when he left I didn't give him any time, I just wanted him to go, so he quickly packed up his clothes, some books and other things, and went. He probably planned to return for it, but then, when he discovered I'd moved away, he wasn't able to. It makes sense doesn't it?'

'It makes a lot of sense. So, shall we see what he's so eager to get his hands on.'

'Right, here goes,' slipping the disc into the drawer of the computer.

At first glance, it didn't make a great deal of sense, it may just as well have been in code, but scrolling down the screen, what had appeared to be random and disjointed notes became more formulated, the text resembling a diary dating back to 2005, five years earlier, followed by names, including telephone numbers. Scrolling down further, many of the names were repeated, below which, like a mini-spreadsheet, amounts of money in US dollars had been entered followed by a number of calculations being a percentage of the main amounts, and extended to form the totals. There was very little more text, not sufficient to give them a clear idea of what it all meant, except various words were often repeated: long positions; short positions; leverage. The last entry had been made three months earlier on 10th April this year, against which had been keyed-in two names, names which had not been included in any of the previous ones: Robinson & Waterman, meeting at their offices to discuss further injection to the Clarkson account.

'What do you think it all means, Jack,' Claire asked him when she'd reached the end.

'I would say it's to do with stocks and shares, out of my sphere of knowledge, I'm afraid; I only have a layman's understanding of the workings of the stock market and a pretty limited one at that, I might add.'

'Me too; I've always thought it very much a risky type of business; I don't think my nerves would be up to all the speculation which must go on; shares rising and then just as quickly falling, knowing when to sell or buy. Even if I had what people so glibly describe as a financial adviser, I would still feel uneasy.'

'Could you trust them, though?'

'That's right.'

'Reading that,' he said, pointing to the screen, 'it would seem there's a bit of underhand manipulating going on, wouldn't you?'

'Very much so. It doesn't solve the problem though, does it, Jack; what do we do with it?'

'We're in a bit of a cleft stick here,' he said thoughtfully, and she could tell he was trying to come up with a solution, 'if you hold on to it or if you destroyed it, it puts you in rather a vulnerable position and that worries me, Claire.'

'You feel as strongly as that?'

'I do,' he answered, placing a hand on her arm, 'look, these last few days seeing you again and realising by some act of fate we happened to make an almost identical decision in leaving London and moving to, of all places, a small town in the New Forest, well, I don't want to do or say anything which might presume on our friendship, but I do care about you, very much in fact. There, I've said it.' leaning back in the chair and giving her an apologetic grin.

'Oh, Jack,' she sighed, 'I understand how you feel, I'd be a fool not to, but it so happens, I feel the same.'

She was prevented from hearing what he was going to say next by the ringing of the front door bell.

'I'd better answer it.' she said, standing up, inordinately grateful he was with her, Sophie's words of warning coming back to her.

'I'll come down with you.'

The man standing on the doorstep with the rather attractive grey/blue eyes and the rugged Harrison Ford features didn't look menacing and, more importantly, bore no resemblance to any of the characters she'd seen from across the road; any feelings of apprehension were quickly dispelled when he showed her his identity card.

'I apologise for disturbing you so late in the day,' he said, 'but I'm conducting an enquiry into the death of a local woman whose body was discovered near here.'

'How do you think I can be of any help?' Claire asked him.

'You may not be able to, madam, but by talking to people in this area, it's possible someone may have seen or heard something on Saturday night which could have some relevance.'

'I see; perhaps you would like to come in, Chief Inspector.' she suggested, realising she would have no choice but to tell him about the disturbance on Saturday night; it would then be up to the police to take it any further, but she was in no doubt that they would.

She took him through to the kitchen and introduced him to Jack who had been standing in the open doorway to the terrace. He may have heard what the Chief Inspector had been saying, but there was no change in his expression as the two men formally shook hands.

'I believe I've seen you before,' the chief inspector was saying, 'last summer at the village's cricket match, you presented the trophy to our local team, didn't you?'

'That's right; I was somewhat surprised to be asked to do that, you know,' Jack smiled ruefully, 'especially as I was a virtual newcomer to Upper Nettles.'

'Obviously word must have got around that you were a keen cricketer yourself.'

'Could be.'

'However,' the Chief Inspector, giving the impression he was reluctant to return to the reason for calling, although Claire wasn't taken in for a minute by his matter-of-fact manner nor by the informal open-necked sports shirt and soft leather moccasins, certain they belied the tough interior of the man, 'as I was explaining to Miss - '

'- Walters, Claire Walters.' Claire told him.

'- to Miss Walters,' accompanied by a quick smile in her direction, 'I'm trying to speak to anyone who lives in this area of Upper Nettles, in the hope that they may have noticed anything untoward late on Saturday night. We have made a little headway since the discovery of the woman's body on Wednesday, but we need more to enable us to trace her movements from when she was last seen in Upper Nettles shortly before ten on Saturday night up to the estimated time of her death around midnight. We have reason to understand she was driving along this stretch of road in front of your property, Miss Walters, in the direction of Lymington, but we don't believe she went as far as that, perhaps no further than Brockenhurst, and as her body was discovered in Nettles Hollow, a relatively short distance away from here, we think it's feasible she was murdered somewhere in-between.'

'Have you identified the body yet?' Jack asked.

'Obviously you haven't seen this week's "Gazette", Mr Andrews;' another rueful smile making its appearance, 'otherwise you would have known, but yes, a formal identification was carried out on Wednesday, confirming that the victim was a Miss Glenda Nicholson.'

'The name doesn't sound familiar,' Jack said, 'did she come from Upper Nettles?'

'No, she lived in Lyndhurst, but had a business in the town here.'

'The hairdresser?' Claire asked, remembering Sylvia mention her hairdresser's name on Saturday.

'That's right; did you know her, Miss Walters?'

'No, I didn't, but I heard her name mentioned by someone I was introduced to on Saturday. You see, Chief Inspector, I'm quite new to Upper Nettles; I only arrived on Friday, so I haven't had time to meet many people.'

'I see.' but it was clear by his bemused expression and by the quick glance he gave Jack he didn't see at all.

'Claire and I have known each other for over fifteen years,' Jack on cue, as if reading her mind, 'and I suppose you could say it was one of life's strange coincidences that we should find ourselves living in the same part of the country.'

'As you say, a coincidence. And do you, Mr Andrews,' he asked, his lips in what she could swear was the beginning of a smile; what a weird conversation this is, she thought, 'by another coincidence live nearby.'

'Yes,' and as he did on Sunday, pointed across the stream to his cottage, the early evening sun casting long irregular shadows across the grass, 'over there, that's my place.'

'Hmmph,' for the first time noncommittal, 'fairly far back from the road though, but did you hear anything on Saturday?'

'I can't say that I did,' Jack answered, 'the occasional car, yes, but only faintly, but that's normal.'

'And you, Miss Walters? Did you hear anything you considered to be out of the usual, I do realise of course that Saturday would only have been your second night here.'

'There was a disturbance, actually,' taking a deep breath before continuing, not altogether sure just how much she should say and wishing she'd had time to discuss this with Jack, 'I don't know the exact time; I went to bed around eleven and must have fallen asleep quite quickly, but I was woken by the sound of someone knocking on the front door. I wouldn't have gone to the door of course, not so late, but I did get up and have a look from my bedroom window.'

'Weren't you afraid?'

He genuinely wanted to know; grateful he wasn't putting any pressure on her to finish what she had to say.

'Not really. I suppose I should have been, but I think it was because I had this preconceived idea that living in the country would be relatively safe, compared to city life, that is. I've always lived in London.' she added.

'Regrettably, we're not immune to crime, although not on the scale of cities, of course. When you looked out,' he went on, 'were you able to see the person who'd been at your door?'

'It was a woman, Chief Inspector, but as it was so dark, and as she had her back to me, I didn't see her features; I reckon she would have been about my height, slim, with long hair, that's all, I'm afraid.'

'You say she had her back to you?'

'Yes, by the time I got to the window she was in the road.'

'Alone?'

'No, there was a man with her.'

'Before we go any further, Miss Walters, I want to reassure you that everything you tell me will be treated with discretion; what I mean is, I don't want you to concern yourself with repercussions should you mention anything which may lead us to reveal the person or persons responsible for the murder of Glenda Nicholson. I'm not suggesting at this stage that the woman you saw outside had been her. The man you've mentioned; can you describe him?'

'Only that he was tall, thin, longish hair, and I think it could have been light-coloured, but I'm not sure. Sorry, but that's the best I can do.'

'Do you think you would recognise him again?'

'I don't think so.'

'So, what were they doing?'

'They seemed to be arguing, but that's not exactly right, he was doing all the talking and he was trying to drag her across the road with him, but she didn't want to go.'

'Was there a car parked out there, by the side of the road, I mean?'

'No, there wasn't.'

'What happened then, did she go across the road with him?'

'After a few minutes; she didn't have much choice, he was a lot stronger than she was.'

'Did you see anyone else, or was it just the two of them?'

'There was another man,' although she had disliked the man Jack had told her was probably Gerry Oakes, it was like telling tales out of school, but she couldn't stop now, 'he'd been standing in the gateway of the house across the road, and they joined him.'

'Did you see in which direction they went?'

'Yes. I really dislike having to tell you this, Chief Inspector.'

'I understand how you must be feeling.'

'Anyway,' taking another deep breath, 'they walked up the drive to the house.'

'I appreciate your frankness, Miss Walters, if it's any consolation you've been considerable help to us, even if what you witnessed on Saturday transpires to be nothing but what is often described as 'a domestic'. Finally, is there anything else you can remember?'

'I don't think so, except the light I saw during the time the man and woman walked over to the gate; I thought afterwards it could have been a bicycle light, it definitely wasn't a vehicle's.'

'From which direction was this?'

'From the right, from Brockenhurst.'

Chapter Seven

Sylvia replaced the receiver, but even after the call she continued to hear his voice, that distinctive cadence which hadn't diminished over the years and sounded just as she remembered.

She had only been eighteen when she first met Johnnie Wall; theirs had been a brief courtship, followed by an equally brief marriage. Both her parents had strongly opposed the relationship, insisting she was far too young and refusing to believe that Johnnie had any future in the music business, all their dire warnings coming to fruition when she confessed to them she was divorcing him for adultery. Thanks to her father's money and influence, plus an expensive lawyer Johnnie would never have been able to afford, the divorce went through quickly, but leaving her, as young as she was, with a void which took years to fill because she had loved him, had been mesmerised by him, never, in her naivety, thinking she wouldn't have been enough for him, because apart from the other women in his life, his one and only true passion was his music. He'd married again, more than once, but she'd forcibly put him out of her mind and she didn't learn any more about him until some years later she read in one of the nationals that he was serving a prison sentence in Germany for drug offences, because by that time she had moved out of London and lost touch with the old crowd she used to mix with. She had no idea when he'd started taking drugs, he hadn't been on them during the time they were together, she was certain of that; it could have been around the time he formed "The Bandanas". Sylvia had never met any of the other members of the group and hadn't been all that happy when she heard he'd moved into the area and bought "The Grange", but by then he was well and truly out of her system; a phase in her life she preferred to forget. Hearing from him this afternoon had come as a complete surprise, leaving her with mixed feelings and still not knowing why he'd phoned. He had given her no explanation and she hadn't pressed him. Why hadn't she? The perversity of human nature, she supposed, walking over to the window and looking down into the High Street, gratified to see that everything appeared as it normally did out there: a warm sunny afternoon in the middle of June; holidaymakers, strolling along the cobbled pavement, pausing now and again to look in the bow windows of the newly-opened craft and gift shop and, a few doors further along, the minimalistic window display in Trevor and Maurice's "Gallery"; several of them going into "The Boiling Kettle" tea rooms and the intermittent flow of traffic, drivers conscious of the many speed bumps, recent acquisitions in the town. She had intended to drive into Lyndhurst and see an old friend of hers, but talking to Johnnie again after such a long time had unsettled her, making her feel restless, going over again what they'd said to each other.

"I hope you didn't object to me phoning you, Sylvia?" he had asked, without any preamble.

"Why should I, Johnnie; I can't say it's not a surprise to hear from you, because of course it is." automatically going on the defensive.

"I suppose you knew I'd bought "The Grange"?"

"I'd heard."

"I did think of phoning you when I first moved in, you know, but somehow didn't get round to it."

"You knew I was living here then?" not giving him an inch and determined not to play games with him, wishing he would either say why he'd phoned or make some excuse and get off the line.

"Yes, Pete told me; he said he'd seen you in "The Hunters' Arms" one evening."

"I presume you mean Pete Carr?"

"Yes, that's right, but then of course you never knew him, did you?"

"No, I didn't. Anyway, Johnnie, are you going to tell me why you've called?"

"I needed to talk to someone, someone impartial."

"And you think an ex-wife, a woman you haven't seen for over thirty years, fits the bill?"

"I would like to think so, Sylvia."

"Really, apart from this being a ridiculous conversation, quite frankly I would rather you hadn't phoned me; thirty years is a long time, but then I shouldn't have to remind you of that. We don't even know each other anymore, that is, if we ever did. The past is the past, as far as I'm concerned and that is exactly where I want it to remain. It sounds as though you have something on your mind, something you're reluctant to discuss with one of your friends; if it's a shrink you're looking for, you have picked on the wrong person and," she added caustically, "if you are in some sort of trouble and have this wild notion of unburdening it on to me, you would be wasting your time, Johnnie; I do not want to know."

"You never used to be so hard, Sylvia."

"I really don't think that deserves any comment, Johnnie."

"I've obviously misjudged you; perhaps that's the story of my life, not understanding other people, not even understanding myself."

"I think we should bring this call to a close, Johnnie." wondering just how sober he was, or whether he was, as she'd heard it described, 'high'; whatever, he wasn't making much sense.

He didn't stay on the line for much longer, having presumably come to the conclusion he'd made a mistake attempting to get in touch with her.

"See you around, then; it's been good talking to you again, Sylvia." were his final banal words before he rang off, leaving her with the silent receiver in her hand.

What a strange day this is turning out to be, she thought, walking restlessly into the kitchen and going through the automatic motions of filling the cafetière and taking a mug from the cupboard above the work top. First, meeting up with an old friend from the past and while she had been delighted to see Clive again, she couldn't rid herself of a feeling of unease in his company today which had intensified when Trevor had appeared on the scene. Clive had obviously not been pleased when Trevor mentioned he'd heard him asking about Claire Walters in the "Gallery", although he'd done his best to cover up his annoyance. She was becoming as guilty as everyone else in this town, she decided; too quick to suspect hidden meanings behind what was no more than a polite exchange between two men who scarcely knew each other. But, then, remembering back to when she used to see Clive quite often in the pub they all used to frequent at the weekends, he had been rather secretive about his private life, always quick to ward off any personal questions, however well-meaning they may have been; that could be the simple explanation for his reaction. If he was reluctant to mention how well he knew Claire that was entirely his concern; there was no reason why he shouldn't want to look her up; as he'd said, he was in the area and being so close to Upper Nettles thought it was too good an opportunity to miss. What could be more natural than that? Even so, the niggle of uncertainty persisted, it still didn't explain the tenseness in his manner right from the first moment they'd met in "The Hunters" this lunchtime.

And, now, another reminder of what she always thought of as her previous life, the call from Johnnie. What she needed, Sylvia decided spooning sugar into her coffee, was a change of scenery for a few days. Too much had been happening recently to disturb the smooth equilibrium she had worked so hard to achieve since leaving London and making a new home for herself in what she had truly believed would be a peaceful and uneventful village in the heart of Hampshire's New Forest, wondering how Claire must be feeling. She'd enjoyed her company the other evening, although with all the background noise in the pub it had made any worthwhile conversation practically impossible, deciding to invite her for coffee the following morning and, taking out the card Claire had given her, dialled her number.

***

Probably for the first time in "The Gazette's" history they were ahead of the national press in that the local people of Upper Nettles and surrounding district had learned of the identity of the woman's body in Nettles Hollow in advance of anyone who happened to see the piece slipped unobtrusively inside the pages of the 'nationals' on Friday morning. Possibly the reason for the scanty coverage could be explained by the relatively long time which had elapsed since the body had been found, but more realistically it could have been due to the fact that most people had little or no knowledge of where Upper Nettles was placed geographically in relation to the rest of the country and subsequently, almost as soon as the news had faded from the television screens on Wednesday evening, had been forgotten. It was even questionable whether there would be any further interest in the case by the media, thereby reassuring those residents they would be spared the unwelcome appearance in their town of reporters eager for any morsel they could glean, anything to pad out what meagre information they had of the murder.

Chris Portman had no fixed views either way; whether they were left alone by the press or not, although he had freely admitted to Deidre that if they did arrive this could only be good for business.

'I suppose so, Chris, but I can't help feeling there's something ghoulish in all this continual talk and speculation about the poor woman, positively unhealthy.'

'Unhealthy it might be, my dear,' he grinned, albeit shamefacedly, 'but you have to agree we've never been so busy.'

'Yes,' her lips tightening in displeasure, 'everyone seems to have become extremely thirsty this week.'

'Well, all I can say is, it's a good thing we have Christine to help out, keeps her occupied while Steven's in the Gulf.'

'She doesn't look too happy these days, probably missing him; it can't be easy having a husband who works overseas for months on end.'

'I don't think that young lady is missing her husband, Deidre,' he said, lowering his voice and looking over to where Christine was serving a group of people who'd just come in.'

'Don't you, Chris?'

'No, I don't; okay, she's a good barmaid, great with the customers, I can't fault her, but you'd have to be blind not to notice what's been going on recently.'

'You've lost me, Chris; this sounds very much like village tittle-tattle to me.'

'Hold your horses, my good woman; I'm only going to mention what yours truly has seen with his own eyes.'

'No doubt you're going to enlighten me.' she sighed, picking up a glass and polishing it unnecessarily.

He knew the signs; Deidre, although she was in the pub business and the recipient of endless gossip, had over the years built up a barrier against joining in, maintaining a front of polite interest, but remaining non-committal, and he respected her for it. It wasn't that she didn't have her own opinions, because she did and very strong ones at that, but she only discussed those with him and never while they were working. He remembered seeing the old wartime posters warning the people to be verbally discreet: "Walls have ears"; well, he thought philosophically, so do pubs and in his experience, there was nothing wrong with any of his customers' hearing! As it happened he was prevented from explaining to Deidre what he'd meant by another surge of customers and it wasn't until after they'd closed and were in their sitting room in their flat upstairs, he had the chance to talk to her on her own again.

***

When Glenda hadn't turned up in the lounge bar of the Hotel Russell at four o'clock on Wednesday afternoon as they'd agreed, David hadn't been too concerned, assuming she'd been held up in traffic; it wasn't until there hadn't been any call from her he began to feel uneasy and when he tried without any success to get through to her on her mobile this only intensified. He didn't consider for one minute she'd double-crossed him, he knew her too well to believe that, the only alternative was to think something had happened to prevent her making the journey into London. As he sat there, a half-drunk glass of lager on the table in front of him, he tried to rationalise. She may very well still be on her way to meet him and had been delayed and then found, for some reason or other, she couldn't get in touch with him on her mobile; the simple explanation could be she'd neglected to recharge the thing, although in David's experience, invariably there *was* no simple explanation for anything which occurred out of the ordinary; it was firmly embedded in his pessimistic brain to look on the negative, that way, as he'd often justified to himself, the chances of being faced with the unexpected were minimised. He tried her mobile later, but there was still no connection; he didn't have her home number, although it would be easy enough get the number of the salon in Upper Nettles through Directory of Enquiries, but he could do that in the morning if it was necessary.

He found it impossible to sleep that night and, in order not to disturb Jilly, but mostly to avoid having to make any explanations for his restlessness, spent the hours until dawn lying full-length on the sofa; by then too exhausted to make even a feeble attempt to curb his rising panic; he must have dozed off at some time, because when he finally opened his eyes, the early morning light was streaming through the lounge windows. It was only six o'clock, hours yet before he could call anyone, but more for something to do than anything else, he padded bare-foot into the hall and dialled the number for Directory of Enquiries; in less than five minutes he'd been given the number of "Scissors", Glenda's hairdressing salon. It was still only seven o'clock when he'd finished his coffee, making it last as long as possible; he could have made himself some toast, that being the limit of his culinary skills, but he had no appetite, realising that sooner or later Clive would have to be told about this latest hiccup in what had been a fairly clear run in their business for a number of years, knowing in advance what his reaction would be. It had always been accepted right from the start of their relationship that he and Clive worked in a different way, meaning they never encroached on each other's handling of clients' accounts and this mutual trust had always worked in the past and David could see no reason why it couldn't continue to do so. It would seem now, if as he was beginning to suspect, they were going to lose Gregory Thornton's account on top of the current problem with Tom, they could have even more to cope with. As far as Tom Watson was concerned, he and Clive were no closer to finding out where his ex-girlfriend was living. Clive had only said the day before they couldn't afford to hold off for much longer in issuing the ultimatum to Tom; at least that would be him out of the way, but it wasn't a comforting feeling to know that the taped evidence of their involvement with him was ever-present. As Clive had said in his characteristically caustic way, "The woman must be somewhere, for God's sake; she couldn't have simply vanished, leaving no trace; bloody impossible, David! If we find her, I'm convinced we'll find the tape! If you think about it, logically I mean, as I'm sure you do, where else can it be, he wouldn't have destroyed it. Also," he'd gone on, an unfathomable expression on his face, "I have a sneaking feeling that as soon as we give him the push, he won't hesitate to use it, all of which quite frankly disturbs me a great deal." Remembering what he'd said again as he sat in the familiar surroundings of his own kitchen, looking out towards the contemporary decking he'd recently had installed and the expensive garden furniture arranged artistically by Jilly, he experienced an involuntary shiver. Apprehension? No, much more than that. What he'd just experienced, although only lasting seconds was a feeling of foreboding. It wasn't only the finding of the tape which was crucial to them, to their business and to their future; it was Tom himself. He was the pivot. By dispensing with his services, and getting hold of the tape, he would still be there. He could, David was sure, compile a replacement one. On the other hand, if they did nothing; merely dismissed the importance of this damning evidence and continued with Tom's services, the unpalatable fact remained, they would be in a vulnerable position if, as Clive suggested, the bank was becoming suspicious of Tom's performance. Was he arriving, in a circuitous route, at the meaning behind Clive's manner yesterday? David had always recognised there was more than a hint of ruthlessness in his partner's character which he had chosen ostrich-fashion to ignore. Clive Robinson was a tough realist, with a strong streak of self-interest. Apart from the business they had built up together, the two of them had very little in common and although each of them was motivated by money, as far as David was concerned, although honesty didn't always come into their handling of investments, that was as far as he was prepared to venture beyond certain legal boundaries.

David was a pacifist; he wouldn't have been able to have lived with Jilly for so long if he hadn't been, when literally turning a blind eye to her numerous indiscretions had become second nature to him. Being married to a woman of her elegance and social graces suited him; she was decorative and undeniably an asset on those occasions when he had to entertain clients, excelling in small talk, her mercurial personality acting as a perfect foil for his serious and unbending persona.

He'd showered and dressed and was on his way downstairs when the telephone rang and certain it would only be for him at that time of the morning, he jumped down the remaining stairs to the hall to answer it before Jilly had time to pick up the receiver of the extension by her side of the bed, but he was too late, she had beaten him to it. Expecting to hear Clive's voice, it took him a couple of seconds, to realise it was Tom and that the call wasn't for him after all.

' - I know it's early, Jilly,' he was saying, 'I hope I didn't wake you.'

'You did, actually,' she answered, 'what time is it anyway?'

'Almost eight,' Tom replied, 'are you free to talk?'

'Yes; I think David must have left for work.'

'Good; it's about tomorrow, Jilly, I'm taking the day off, and wondered if you would like a drive into the country.'

'The country?' making it sound as though it was some foreign place, completely beyond her ken.

'Yes, the New Forest.'

'That's in Hampshire somewhere, isn't't?'

'Yes, that's right, not far from Bournemouth actually.'

'I've never been there, Bournemouth I mean, Tom, but I'm afraid I won't be able to make it. I've been invited to an engagement luncheon at "The Savoy"; if you'd been going there today, I'd loved to have gone with you.'

'That's too bad, I would have been glad of your company, darling.' the endearment making him cringe, but David remained where he was by the hall table and continued to listen to what the pair of them were saying.

'Sorry.' not really sounding as though she meant it, David decided, or perhaps more truthfully, deluding himself into believing she wasn't particularly concerned whether she accompanied him or not, 'But,' she was going on, 'what's this sudden attraction to The New Forest?'

'Oh,' he replied, 'there's something I have to collect there and afterwards, which shouldn't take long, I thought we could have some lunch; Upper Nettles will, I presume, have a reasonable restaurant.'

'Upper Nettles,' she repeated, 'what a quaint name; have you been there before?'

'No, I haven't.' David immediately sensing he was reluctant to say any more; his brain trying to fathom out what surely must be a coincidence.

But if it wasn't a coincidence, why the hell should Tom be going there, to the same place, not much more than a village, where he'd been himself only a few days ago. But, quietly replacing the receiver before the call came to end, not wanting Jilly to discover he was still there, he collected his jacket and briefcase and quietly let himself out of the house to walk the short distance to St. John's Wood Underground Station.

All the way to the West End and even after he'd reached Bond Street and made his way to the office and taken the lift up to the third floor, his mind had been focusing solely on the conversation he was fast beginning to regret he'd listened to and how best he could handle the implications it could generate; it wasn't only the possible inference of Tom's link with Upper Nettles which concerned him, but the more personal one of facing up to the fact of his relationship with Jilly. He had no illusions about her, his mind working along the lines that what he didn't actually know was no more than conjecture on his part and being unfounded, didn't exist, but for the first time he was being forced to accept she was being unfaithful to him. As the lift came to a halt, he had concluded that this alone wasn't what irked him; it was having to admit to Clive the circumstances of how he'd learned about Tom Watson's proposed visit to Upper Nettles, because he would have to, and taking a deep steadying breath, opened the door to the main office.

Pippa, their new receptionist, greeted him automatically, her lacklustre manner jarring on his nerves and not for the first time he wondered why these girls bothered to get jobs which so obviously bored them to distraction; he had long lost count of how many of them had come and gone since they'd opened their offices in South Molten Street, no doubt lured by the mistaken belief of working in London's West End and making a mental guess of how long she would stay with them. And what sort of name is that anyway, he muttered under his breath, Pippa!

Clive's door was open as he walked past on the way to his own office, giving him no chance to put his thoughts into some semblance of order.

'Good morning, Clive.'

'Morning, David, have you a minute; I've had some further feedback from the bank.' he said, looking up from his desk, 'Is everything alright,' he added, looking at him more closely as he went into the room, closing the door behind him, 'you look a trifle put out this morning.'

'I am, but I didn't realise it was so noticeable.' and sitting down heavily in front of the desk loosened his tie; it was warmer than ever today, although Clive had opened both windows and tilted the slatted blinds to shield the room from direct sunlight, also to reduce the continuous sound of traffic.

'Look,' he said quickly, surprised to see the look of genuine concern on his face, 'whatever is worrying you, it can't be that bad, surely.'

'It depends on how you view what I'm going to tell you, Clive. Anyway,' making a positive effort to pull himself together, 'first of all, -'

'- I'll organise some coffee for us,' he interrupted, pressing the intercom on his desk, 'the task shouldn't be beyond Pippa's capabilities.'

'Don't count on it!' David smiled for the first time; his partner's knack of lessening the tension was contagious, wishing he could be more sanguine, but a bit too late in the day to change his inherent pessimistic nature.

In a surprisingly short time the coffee was brought in and with, even more surprisingly, a plate of "Walkers" shortbread biscuits.

'Thank you, Pippa,' Clive said to the girl and was rewarded by a wide smile.

'Well, well,' David remarked, 'I didn't think she was capable.'

'Of supplying us with refreshments?'

'No, being able to smile naturally!'

'She's not so bad, David;' he said, 'these days in London you have to take what the Agency provides, but in many respects, things haven't altered all that much since we first started work; these Sloanies are only filling in their time until they find a husband who will meet with Mummy and Daddy's approval.'

They both sipped their coffee in silence for a moment, David wondering where best to start. As serious though Glenda's non-appearance might be, he couldn't help thinking there was a sense of urgency in what he'd overheard earlier, although if pressed, he wouldn't have been able to explain. What was fogging his brain, idly watching the dust mites floating between the open spaces in the window blind, was the strange phenomenon of the possibility, however remote, of Tom's connection.

'I'm finding it difficult to know where to start,' he said at last, replacing his cup on the saucer in front of him and pushing it to one side, 'but, perhaps you will be able to make some sense out of it all, because I'm damned if I can.'

'I'll try; you know what they say: two heads are better than one, or I should say two brains, so fire ahead, David, I'm listening.'

'Well, and this could be the more worrying, Glenda didn't keep our appointment yesterday. I've been trying to ring her, but her mobile appears to be out of action. I've got the number of her hairdressing salon and I'll try that this morning, but other than doing that, I can't think of any other way of finding out what could have happened.'

'I take it you haven't been in touch with Gregory Thornton?'

'No, not yet; I'll have to of course, but the reason I've held back is because I don't want to alarm him unnecessarily if there is a perfectly reasonable explanation for her silence.'

'Well,' he said philosophically, 'if there isn't and she's reneged on her agreement with us, we'll deal with that in due course. It won't exactly be the end of the world for us, David; I'm not dismissing Gregory Thornton's reaction of course. To put it mildly, he isn't going to be pleased, but as I said to you on Sunday, I wasn't too happy about the way he's been going about the transaction; there's always a risk in that sort of arrangement and he, of all people, should realise that.'

'You're right of course, Clive, but I wouldn't have thought it of Glenda.'

'Dare I say it, David,' he gave him a rueful smile, 'but everyone has his – or her – price.'

'*Touché!*'

'So, what's really bugging you, then?'

'Something which could be a further development in this business concerning Tom Jackson.'

'Yes?'

'I overheard a telephone conversation this morning,' David said, carefully selecting his words, and trying to over-ride his discomfort of having to include his wife's name in his explanation, 'this was at home, just before I left, and when the phone rang I was so sure it would be for me, I made to answer it, but Jilly got there first. This is the embarrassing part, Clive, but it was for her -'

'- it was Tom wasn't it, David?' he interrupted.

'Yes, it was; how did you guess?'

'Not really a guess, old boy, he was the only person I could think of, that's all; you'd already made it clear it was something to do with the business.'

'You knew about – about their relationship?'

'I didn't really know; let's say I had begun to suspect they might be having an affair.'

'How?' intrigued, momentarily forgetting their joint concern about Tom Watson.

'I'd seen them together a few times, that's all, David; nothing particularly clandestine in that you might say, but, well, it was just their manner towards each other, difficult to explain exactly, but you probably know what I mean. Sorry, David.'

'Don't be, Clive; I should have realised, but then, another old saying, the husband is the last to know.'

'Probably a truism. However, back to business, obviously what you heard must have some bearing on our current concerns over his questionable dealings with us?'

'As to that, I'm not sure but, if anything, what he did say was more puzzling than anything else. You see, he'd phoned Jilly to ask her if she would like to accompany him to Upper Nettles -'

' - what!'

'Exactly.'

'Did he say why?'

'Said he had to collect something from there, and that's all; I put down the receiver then, but I don't think he was about to elaborate any further.'

'No wonder you're puzzled, David. What the hell is the man up to?'

'I wish I knew.'

'Let me think for a minute, David,' he said, doodling abstractedly on the pad in front of him, 'we may be able to ignore any suggestion that this has anything to do with Glenda and the meeting she may or may not have had with Gregory Thornton on Sunday, and think along a totally different line.'

'Which is?'

'To treat the re-occurrence of Upper Nettles as one of life's coincidences and come up with some suggestion of why Tom should want to visit the place and what did he have to collect. Any ideas.'

'Sorry, but I haven't.'

'Perhaps I have a slight advantage over you here, David, apropos what I wanted to talk to you about when you first came in.'

'Yes?'

'I heard last night from the person who mentioned the other day about the bank having certain reservations about Tom's dealings with a number of their clients' accounts and, apparently,' Clive went on, clasping his hands together as he explained, 'one of those clients has since died and his chief beneficiary, his oldest son, no less, has been looking into his father's affairs and, being in the banking business himself, it didn't take him long to discover several discrepancies which he promptly brought to the attention of the authorities -'

'- the authorities,' David interrupted, 'you mean the police?'

'No, at least not yet, he's lodged his findings with an ombudsman, naming his father's bank, who naturally in the course of their investigations were informed. You won't be surprised to hear that the account was among those in Tom Watson's portfolio.'

'That sounds pretty damning.'

'For Tom, yes, but it could also be for us, David if they should learn of our involvement.'

'Did this contact of yours actually give you the name of the client?'

'Yes; Hanley Clarkson.'

'The name rings a bell,' David frowned, mentally running through the names of their various clients, 'yes, I remember, he was among the first investors Tom passed to us, it must be at least four or five years ago.'

'You're right, September 15th, 2005 to be exact.'

'Is Tom aware they're on to him, Clive?'

'He might have a pretty good idea; I'm not sure whether they've said anything to him yet, although he must be aware they've been looking through his portfolio of clients, but apparently he's no knowledge of the emergency meeting of the shareholders which has been called for tomorrow morning.'

'Surely he'll have to be informed?'

'Presumably, but it strikes me the bank are keeping this very low-key at the moment, no doubt trying to work out how best they can avoid any adverse publicity; they won't want any mud slung at them, and if they, as a body, can avert any scandal of that nature, all to the good.'

'When they do approach him, he'd have to come up with a credible explanation, although God knows what.'

'They may not give him the opportunity, you know. No matter which way you look at this, David, he's in a tight spot and quite frankly, it makes me exceedingly nervous.'

'Well, when that time comes, it will be up to Tom, won't it; he's a slick talker, but I'm beginning to see where you're coming from now, Clive; it's that blasted tape, or whatever it is he's got his dealings with us recorded on, you're thinking about.'

'Too right I am.' Clive nodded, the doodling transforming itself into the recognisable outline of the hangman's noose. 'I would make a stab at saying, that if he's beginning to get negative vibes from his people, he may be particularly anxious to retrieve what is undoubtedly a crucial piece of insurance for him if the outcome should go awry. What do you think?'

'I would say it's an educated guess; we've certainly had no luck in trying to locate his ex-girlfriend, but perhaps he has.'

'Mind you,' Clive pointed out, putting an instant dampener on their conjectures, 'he may already have the tape.'

'That's true, but it doesn't explain why he's planning a visit to Upper Nettles. He's up to something, Clive, I'm sure of it.'

'In other words,' Clive said soberly, 'whichever way you look at it, it puts us in a vulnerable position. If they 'throw the book' at him, he's bound to do his utmost to extricate himself and whatever avoidance tactics he might use, it's inevitable we would be implicated. In fact, I would say it was out of his character *not* to retaliate and that, as far as I can see, is the only weapon he has in order to alleviate some of the blame.'

'He could do that, Clive, with or without the tape.'

'That unpalatable fact has not escaped me, David. If we work on the premise that Tom isn't aware of this morning's meeting, provided the bank don't move too speedily, it might give us a head start if we manage to get our hands on the tape as soon as possible, we would be in a position then to confront him before he's called for an explanation.'

'Do you honestly believe that will make any difference?'

'It might. The outcome of the meeting cannot bode well for him; they are his employers, David, they have the upper hand, meaning it is more than likely they'll fire him, and if that happens his banking career will come to an abrupt end, he may consider it would be more prudent to keep in with us.'

'A reasonable assumption, I suppose,' David said thoughtfully, but not altogether convinced he shared his partner's hypothesis, logical though it may sound. In theory, given Tom Watson's egoism, he may very well consider that as a financial route, but considering the breakdown of their trust in him, was it feasible, 'but if we did decide to continue with his services, could he continue to provide us with the calibre of investors he has been doing?'

'As to that, David,' Clive answered, 'I would say he would; Tom Watson is a personable character, not yet forty, but with a wealth of background knowledge of those people who move in a more affluent society than us. He's a good brain and an equally good memory; in fact, one could describe him as 'switched on', both in computer technology and in the stock market. He knows his way around, David.'

'I don't disagree, you know, and above all, he's a survivor.'

'Yes, of course, but initially, when he finds himself quite literally without a job and nothing looming on the horizon to match the salary he must currently be earning, I would say he would be eager to maintain the status quo, with a few significant provisions, naturally.'

'Such as?'

'Such as implementing a watertight scrutiny on everything he passes on to us, and not only in a monitory nature, David, but a full and concise profile on every one of those investors.'

'Can we trust him, Clive?'

'To a certain extent, we can, but this time we make absolutely certain we are covered. I'm sure you'll agree, David, what he's provided over the years has been substantially beneficial to the firm and,' he added, 'to us personally.'

'Okay,' David sighed, 'I'll go along with that.'

'Fine. Now, Upper Nettles; you've been there, how would you describe it?'

'Well,' having a fair idea of what was in his mind, 'to Londoners like you and me, Clive, we would call Upper Nettles a village, but to be more accurate, I would describe it as a small town which probably hasn't changed all that much over the centuries; there are few modern buildings and most of them much-restored giving one a pretty good idea of how they would have looked in days of yore, but all a bit twee for my taste. There's a church, a town hall, one main street, called inevitably the High Street, with a hotel at one end and half-way along, "The Hunters' Inn", ye olde coaching house, and from what I could see when I called in for a pint on Saturday is the meeting place for locals and holidaymakers alike.'

'Where, apart from the holidaymakers, everybody probably knows everybody else?'

'I would say that describes it pretty well, parochial living at its best, or at its worse, depending on your point of view.'

'That could be to our advantage.'

'In what way?' rapidly losing his drift.

'Well, if Tom's ex-girlfriend has moved there, she would naturally be labelled as a newcomer, wouldn't she, and it sounds if she wanted to socialise she wouldn't have a great deal of choice? Folk will have bound to have noticed her, and you'll always find someone willing to have a chat. Probably don't have much else to interest them.'

'I take it you're planning on going there, then, Clive. Mind you,' David pointed out, 'you'd be a stranger in their midst as well, but I see what you're getting at.'

'That's the whole point, nobody will know me and if I was to mention her name, on some pretext or other, to any of the locals, well, if she is living there, I might strike lucky; it's worth a stab though, wouldn't you say?'

'At least you won't bump into Tom.'

'That *would* put the wind up him; also, it just *might* have enabled me to kill two birds with one stone!'

He had to hand it to Clive, he thought, walking along the corridor to his own office. David had long ago realised and accepted that his partner had the edge on logical thinking; no wavering at the edge of indecision for him, possessing the ability to surge forward, appearing to brush aside the pros and cons of a tricky situation, and once, having made that decision, didn't hesitate in carrying it through to its conclusion. He also believed in hunches, an area in which he resolutely shied away from; hunches were too insubstantial for his pragmatism to take seriously and certainly to trust, although he had to admit, albeit reluctantly, Clive's positive approach to the various problems they'd encountered since they started the business had been more than a contributing factor in them reaching a solution. And David could think of no reason not to think he wouldn't succeed this time.

He tried Glenda's mobile number again, but as before, without any success. He next dialled the number of the salon, letting it ring for several seconds, but as he made to replace the receiver, a woman answered.

'Good morning, "Scissors" Hairdressing Salon.'

'Good morning, could I speak to Miss Nicholson please?' David asked her.

'I'm sorry, -' an imperceptible pause, made more pronounced by the unexpected silence on the line, '- but,' she continued awkwardly, 'Miss Nicholson is unavailable.'

'It is important,' David pressed on, 'but if she's with a client, would you mind very much telling her I'd like a quick word with her?' This time, the silence lasted longer before she answered him, during which time he sensed there was something wrong; this was no hunch, the vibes he was getting at that precise moment were instinctive; Glenda was not in that salon and the woman was finding it difficult to say anything further.

'Are you a friend of Miss Nicholson?'

'An old friend, yes.' his mind now on alert and characteristically fearing the worse.

'I'm sorry to tell you, but – oh, dear,' her distress now apparent, 'you obviously don't know, but Miss Nicholson was -' this time unable to go on, forcing him to say more than he intended.

' - is she ill?'

'No, I'm afraid it's far worse than that, Miss Nicholson's body was discovered yesterday; she'd been murdered.'

'My God! This is dreadful news; when did it happen, do you know?'

'The police are saying it was on Saturday night.'

Shocked, he brought the call to a close, thankful as he did so, she hadn't asked for his name. All the forebodings of the previous evening had returned, realising now that he'd sensed there had to be a strong reason for being unable to get hold of Glenda, but never in a thousand years, had he thought it was because she'd been killed. And now, when he'd recovered from the initial shock, he couldn't fully absorb what he'd heard. As his brain cleared and he was able to think more clearly, he was still unable to understand why it had happened. The woman had mentioned Saturday night, although it had taken four days for her body to have been found; she had been murdered on Saturday, the day before Gregory would have been handing over the cash to her, which presumably ruled out robbery as being the motive. Quickly following on from what the woman had told him, his natural thought process led him to question why Gregory hadn't called when, presumably, Glenda hadn't been at home on the Sunday waiting for him as they'd arranged, meaning he had no alternative, but to phone him. Using the office phone, David dialled the mobile number Gregory had given him.

'I've been expecting you to call, David;' were almost his first words when he answered, 'I take it the package arrived safely?'

'Sorry, Gregory;' his concern with having to break the news of Glenda's death immediately replaced by one of confusion, 'but do you mean you've actually mailed the cash to us instead of what we agreed?'

'We seem to be at cross-purposes here, David,' he said, his voice crackling with static, 'I apologise for the bad line, but I'm at Orly Airport, Lilian and I are flying on to Hong Kong this morning, so I'll make this as brief as possible; we didn't see Glenda on Sunday for the simple reason she wasn't at home, in fact her neighbour told us she hadn't seen her since she came back from work on Saturday; also, there was no sign of her car, so as Lilian and I were leaving for Paris first thing on Monday morning, I posted the cash to her by registered mail before setting off for the airport.'

'To her home, Gregory?'

'No, to her business address, I assumed as it was registered she would be in the salon when it was delivered.'

'I've got bad news for you, Gregory;' dreading his response and taking a deep breath before continuing, 'I only learned about ten minutes ago that Glenda was murdered on Saturday night. Sorry, but I don't know any more than that, only that her body wasn't found until yesterday.'

'Christ!'

Chapter Eight

Clive Robinson arrived in Upper Nettles around eleven-thirty, having left London immediately he'd finished talking to David. He hadn't worked out any form of the strategy he should adopt to find out whether his gut feeling was right or not in that Claire Walters had chosen such an out of the way place to live, although Clive, even with his cosmopolitan background, had to admit there could be certain attractions in wanting to escape the ceaseless frenzied activity of city life, but as he covered the last few miles, once leaving the motorway, and the green density of the New Forest encroached on either side of the road, he couldn't think of one single reason why he ever could make that kind of radical decision. Certainly not for him, he thought irritably, finding it impossible to overtake the mud-encrusted tractor lumbering along in the centre of the road in front of him because of being constantly thwarted from overtaking by a stream of approaching vehicles. It wasn't until he'd driven through Lyndhurst and negotiated the complicated one-way system he was able to put his foot down until he reached the branch-off for Upper Nettles.

His first impressions as he drove into the High Street of what David had described as a small town were that Upper Nettles bore no resemblance to any small town he'd ever been in. This place, which, to him, seemed to be just one long street with a plethora of tea-shops and gift shops, was little more than a village. As David had said, it bore the recognised landmarks of a town, but in Clive's cynical view it was still a village, and a rural one at that, despite the many holidaymakers thronging the cobbled pavements.

He found an empty space in front of what appeared to be the one and only pub. "The Hunters' Arms", according to the weathered wooden sign above the door, looked every inch of what it was either purporting to be or what it had once been God knows how many centuries ago. Claustrophobic wasn't in it, he thought, stooping to peer through thick mullioned windows into the dark interior; not all that inviting, but definitely not to be ignored. It was still too early, he reckoned, for any of the regulars to be in there, feeling sure, as with any other country pub he'd been in, there would be a hard core of them, and a possible source for local gossip, where at least one person would be eager to impress with his local knowledge of people's comings and goings, which, hopefully, would include any newcomer who'd arrived recently. Instead, he carried on up the street, passing first, a flower shop; plastic pails crammed full with bunches of roses and chrysanthemums, alongside pots of geraniums, had been placed outside the door, making walking along the narrow pavement even more difficult; next door, another craft shop; an ancient spinning wheel taking up most of the window display alongside glazed pottery and other examples of locally produced impractical artefacts especially for the tourist trade; a restaurant and tea-room came next with a chalk-board outside proclaiming that they sold the best cream teas in the New Forest. He was on the point of turning back, finding the extent of what Upper Nettles had to offer in the way of anything remotely interesting utterly depressing, when he came to a small gallery which, despite the ancient architectural structure identical to its neighbours, appeared totally out of place in a parochial setting such as Upper Nettles. It had to be the window display, Clive decided, or more accurately, the lack of it, which singled this one out from the others. Where their windows were crammed full with what they were hoping to attract unsuspecting customers, presumably most of them holidaymakers, looking for a memento to take back home with them, the gallery's display of only one painting, framed in light oak, of a stretch of white sand, unpopulated and unblemished, with the variegating blues of the ocean stretching out as far as the horizon, was understated and certainly Clive thought, more in keeping with any gallery he'd seen in Bond Street. Intrigued, almost forgetting the purpose behind his visit, he turned the brass handle and went inside. He wasn't disappointed: the interior, apart from a wide stone archway leading to what seemed to be a studio, had been transformed to resemble a miniature art gallery, exhibiting different styles and categories of artwork; oils and watercolours, both traditional and abstract, hung comfortably next to crayon and pen and ink sketches. The overall effect was quite striking, so much so, it was some minutes before Clive became aware of the tall man with a shock of white hair and a goatee beard standing in the archway silently studying him.

'You look like someone who appreciates art.' he said, stepping forward into the gallery.

'I am, yes and I must say I'm very impressed. I never expected to come across such a fine display in Upper Nettles.' realising as soon as he'd finished speaking how pompous that must have sounded, but he needn't have concerned himself, as to his astonishment, he threw back his head and laughed.

'No need to apologise,' he said, 'you're not the first person to have made that comment since we opened our gallery, and no doubt you won't be the last. Perhaps you would like one of our catalogues to take with you; it isn't our policy to put pressure on anyone who comes in here,' he added, 'so please feel free to spend us much time as you would like.'

'Thank you,' Clive said, taking one of the catalogues from him, 'normally,' he went on, 'I would enjoy having a closer look, but unfortunately my time is rather limited; I'm trying to locate a friend of mine,' Clive fabricated, at the same time working out how best to phrase in a roundabout sort of way exactly what he wanted to know, 'and as I'd heard she'd moved into the area, I was hoping I'd catch up with her. A bit of a wild goose chase, really,' he added, 'but as I was passing through the New Forest this morning, I thought it would be too good an opportunity to miss.'

'It's possible I might be able to help you;' he said, 'although Trevor and I haven't lived here for long we still don't know many of the locals, but it's a smallish place, therefore it's always possible either of us may know your friend.'

'That's kind of you,' wondering if this off the cuff visit to the gallery would provide what he was looking for. Too good to be true, he thought, but then, you never knew, 'her name is Claire Walters and I understand from what I've been told, has only very recently moved here.'

'My goodness me!' holding both hands palm upwards in exaggerated surprise, confirming what he'd already thought. Like many modern-thinking men of his generation, Clive had no prejudices against those who'd chosen a less conventional path. So long as they weren't completely over the top in their behaviour and, while the gallery owner, or as he'd already implied the co-owner, was verging on the dramatic, he'd met a lot worse.

'You know her?'

'Well, I don't actually *know* her,' he emphasised, his pale eyes peering short-sightedly through rimless spectacles, 'it would be more accurate to say that I know *of* her! You see, Trevor met her the other day and straightaway he recognised her from the back cover of one of her books. It was "Tomorrow Never Comes", an excellent novel; I just couldn't put it down. I am one of the lady's greatest fans in fact. Sorry,' no doubt sensing the impatience he was doing his best to hide, wishing he would get to the point, but not wanting to sound too eager. Not that it mattered, he supposed; as soon as he got the information he wanted, he didn't plan to return and it was extremely unlikely he would see him again, but all the same, he was erring on the cautious. Too many years literally watching his back meant he couldn't be any different, 'I'm straying away from the point, aren't I,' he was going on more quickly, 'but Trevor told me she'd only arrived in Upper Nettles last Friday, that was the day before he met her in "The Hunters" and had been really tickled pink when she told him she'd moved into Tulip Cottage; a well-known writer practically living on our doorstep, so to speak.'

Just like that, Clive thought. Claire Walters, Tom's ex-girlfriend *was* living here, so his hunch had been right. Spot on, in fact, allowing himself to feel a certain complacency.

'Is the cottage far from here?'

'Oh, less than a mile I would say, it's on the outskirts of the village on the Lymington road. You can't miss it; Tulip Cottage is immediately across the road from the old "Grange".'

'I should be able to find it alright then, thanks a lot for your help.'

'Don't mention it.'

All the time he had been talking, Clive was planning his next move. Up to now, his aim had been to find out where Claire Walters was living, and beyond that, he hadn't decided on what sort of approach he would make, but somehow, he had to gain access to the property. It wasn't as if he was naïve enough to believe what he was looking for would be in full view; that was a ludicrous thought. He could, of course, act as though he was unaware that she and Tom were no longer together, by explaining he had fully expected him to be there but rejected that idea almost immediately; it could only lead to complications; she would have wanted to know how he'd found out where she'd moved to, and of course, would ask for his name, giving her a false one wouldn't, he felt sure, convince her he was genuine. He would have to come up with something far more plausible. There was one advantage, Clive thought, walking back to the pub; although Tom may have mentioned him to her, they had never met each other. It was always possible that she did know about Tom's involvement with David and himself, although he rather doubted it; Tom Jackson was too smart to indulge in any confidences which could place him in a vulnerable position in the event their relationship should come to an end, which in fact it had. He had to work on the premise that Claire knew nothing about any of his business activities outside the bank, therefore would be unaware of the existence of anything, as incriminating as a tape or computer disc, which because of its importance to Tom, and to anyone else sufficiently interested, had had to be kept somewhere safe. He had given up trying to fathom out a likely hiding place, where only Tom could lay his hands on it if and when it became necessary. It sounded as if his departure from the flat he'd shared with her had been a sudden one, therefore perhaps he would have had no opportunity to take the tape with him, especially as he rather suspected that departure, instigated apparently by her, had been conducted in her presence, this further indicated by him now wanting to pay this visit to Upper Nettles. In many respects, it was all beginning to tie up: his bank calling the emergency meeting, with or without his knowledge, although Clive would have been surprised if Tom hadn't had some inkling they were looking into his files, all of which gave some credence to him planning to come here.

As he stepped out on to the pavement again, he remembered he hadn't switched on his mobile and immediately he'd done this, it rang, the lilting strains of "Green Sleeves" turning a few disapproving heads in his direction.

'Clive, it's David, I've been trying to get hold of you.'

'Sorry, I've just this minute remembered I hadn't switched the damn thing on.' he apologised, at the same time out-staring a sour-faced woman who had had the cheek to stop to listen to him. Nosy old cow, he muttered under his breath.

'I thought so; anyway, Clive, thought you should know, especially as you're now presumably in Upper Nettles, but I phoned Glenda's salon after you left and spoke to her assistant; it's not good, I'm afraid, but Glenda's been murdered. On Saturday night.' he added.

'What!'

'Told you it wasn't good.'

'What happened, David?'

'The girl didn't go into details, but apparently she'd reported to the police when Glenda didn't turn up for work on Monday morning -'

'- but this is Thursday! Why has it taken all this time?'

'Because her body wasn't found until yesterday, that's why.'

'Bloody Hell!'

'Exactly.'

'So, what about the money? I presume Gregory Thornton still has it?'

'I was coming to that,' David explained, 'I called him, he was at Orly Airport in Paris and presumably he and Lilian will be on their way to Hong Kong as we speak. Anyway,' continuing, 'when he turned up at Glenda's house on Sunday and found she wasn't there, he decided to send the cash by registered mail to her at the salon.'

'When did he do this, David; did he say?'

'Before they left for Paris on Monday morning.'

'Presumably it would have arrived at the salon by the following day.'

'I would say so.'

'You know what this means don't you, David; that cash will now be in the hands of the police and it could mean trouble for us.'

'Not necessarily, Clive; I would think it could mean trouble for Gregory Thornton. He's the one who sent it after all.'

'I wish I could share your confidence, but you're probably right. We just act dumb, is that what you're suggesting?'

'I'm not suggesting anything, Clive,' he answered quickly, wearing his cautious hat, 'there's no need at the moment to believe we should concern ourselves unduly. If the authorities should link our name with this transaction, it doesn't infer we are acting illegally, but they might be interested in how Gregory Thornton acquired such a large amount of cash; of course they will immediately jump to the conclusion that he's either into money-laundering or avoiding tax; both offences carry very heavy penalties. No, Clive, he's the one who should be panicking, not us.'

'You're right, of course, David. What we don't see, we don't know, eh?'

'Exactly.'

David *was* right, he thought, bringing the call to a close, he had over re-acted although he had to admit that this latest problem on top of everything else which was happening at the moment, did add to the stress. But, the reason for him being in Upper Nettles today had nothing to do with the diminishing Thornton account, but with the real and serious issue of being more than one step ahead of the law if and when Tom Jackson decided to squeal.

By the time he'd reached "The Hunters' Arms" and ordered a beer from the woman behind the bar, he was no further forward in what he could do next in respect to finding the tape or disc. The last he wanted to do was drive up to Tulip Cottage, with a hastily cobbled-together reason for him being there, and probably making a complete hash of it; whatever he came up with, had to sound plausible, not only to him, but to Claire Walters; he needed time to think. He had, after all, the rest of the afternoon, there was no immediate rush. Clive Robinson was tenacious by nature and used to taking risks, if it meant waiting until she was out, confident he would be able, with the variable skills his partner knew nothing about, to gain entry into the property, he would do just that. He reckoned, it wouldn't take him long to search the property, the task surely made easier by the fact she had only just moved in and working on the assumption she knew nothing about the tape, there couldn't be many hiding places; it would have to be concealed in something she had brought with her and hadn't needed to look in. Tom had been living with her for some time, about six years he'd remembered David telling him once, therefore it was feasible he could have left something behind when he left the flat, some item perhaps which she hadn't even noticed in the move to Upper Nettles. Pure guesswork of course, but what else did he have to go on? He was loathe to return to London empty-handed, and if he did, it wouldn't have been without making a damn good attempt.

More customers were arriving, and he watched them as they struggled to make up their minds where they were going to sit, such obvious indecision immediately indicating they had to be visitors. Some seconds elapsed before one of them came over to the bar to order drinks, leaving them to finally settle on a table to their liking. Just as well they're not in a London pub, he thought cynically; they wouldn't last two minutes! Losing interest, he picked up his glass to take another sip, when he saw Sylvia Crossman silhouetted in the open doorway, looking exactly as she had done the last time he'd seen her; the same elfin face with the thick glossy ash-blonde hair, the vivid blue eyes and the curving mouth betraying her French ancestry. She had seen him, the expressive eyes widening in astonishment, as she walked quickly towards him.

'Clive! How extraordinary! After all this time!' she said, kissing him lightly on both cheeks.

'I couldn't believe it when I saw you standing there; truly a vision from the past! And how fantastic you look.' he added.

'You haven't changed, Clive;' she smiled teasingly, exactly as he remembered, 'you look pretty cool yourself.'

He had genuinely meant the compliment; she really did look fantastic, but then Sylvia had always possessed that uniquely understated glamour of a typical Parisian, although as far as he knew, she had always lived in England, her French mother having moved there on her marriage to one of the English aristocracy. It's doubtful whether he would have ever met her if his girlfriend at that time hadn't introduced them. This had been back in the nineteen eighties, years before he and David had set up the partnership; Patsy and Sylvia had both been working for the same dance studios in London's West End and while he normally shied away from pubs and nightclubs predominantly frequented by the theatrical crowd, Patsy had insisted and, wanting to please her, he'd gone along. Sylvia, Patsy had been quick to tell him had been married to Johnnie Wall, the lead guitarist of "The Bandanas" who round about then were beginning to make a name for themselves on London's music scene.

"They were only married for a couple of years, Clive," she'd said, "but when she found out he was cheating on her, that was too much for her; she just couldn't take it, so -" she'd shrugged, "end of marriage!"

For the next year or two, while Patsy and he were still together, he was often in Sylvia's company although he couldn't remember ever actually having any real conversation with her, but that's what it had been like then; they were all young, still in their twenties, life was easy, jobs for most of them were plentiful and nobody ever appeared to be short of cash. After Patsy and he split up, he never went back to any of the places they'd gone together and after a couple more girlfriends, none of them in show business, he'd seldom given those earlier years a thought - until now. Seeing Sylvia again was like un-locking a secret door, one he hadn't known existed, to find old memories caught up in some sort of frozen tableau. Weird. Clive had never considered himself to be in the least bit fanciful, not even imaginative, and wasn't too sure whether he liked the experience.

'What would you like to drink, Sylvia?' he asked, breaking the spell, and moving to one side of the bar to make room for her.

'I'd love a white wine please, Clive.'

She had no sooner taken a sip when they were interrupted; he was an odd-looking character, at least for such a parochial setting as here in Upper Nettles; the overall effect of his expensively tailored linen suit, in pale blue of all colours, set off with a blue and white spotted cravat tucked loosely below a double chin, was so effete he didn't seem real; even in the pubs he frequented in London, the man would have been out of place.

'Hello, Sylvia, darling;' he enthused, air-kissing her on either cheek, 'aren't are you going to introduce me to your friend?'

What a poser, Clive thought, inwardly cringing, but taking a quick glance at Sylvia, saw that she appeared neither surprised nor amused, presumably used to him.

'Of course I am, Trevor,' she smiled, 'this is Clive Robinson and is in fact a very old friend, from the days of my youth.' she added, a twinkle this time in those cat-like eyes.

'Hello, Clive,' he said, formally shaking hands with him, 'is this your first visit to Upper Nettles?'

'It is, yes and very picturesque it is too.'

'Aha,' he exclaimed, half-raising his hand, 'I recognise your voice, you were in our gallery a short while ago, weren't you?'

'That's right, I was.' beginning to regret coming into the pub, having neglected to take into account that as he had at first thought this place was a village, where everyone presumably, if they didn't know what you were doing, would do their damnedest to find out.

'I thought so; I wasn't eavesdropping, you understand,' he went on garrulously, appearing oblivious to his reluctance to elaborate, 'but I was in the studio, you may have noticed it, and I overheard you asking my partner about our new resident, Claire Walters.'

'Yes, and he was very helpful.' wondering how he could shut the man up, he quite obviously wanted to know more, but was going to be disappointed, and at the risk of snubbing him, he briefly repeated what he had already told his partner, that as he was in the neighbourhood he thought it would be too good an opportunity to find out where she lived.

There was silence for a few seconds as the man Sylvia had called Trevor peered at him over the rim of his glasses, a speculative gleam in his dark button eyes and as though sensing his own discomfort, Sylvia adroitly changed the subject, but Clive could see he wasn't satisfied and made no attempt to conceal his frustration; no doubt disappointed in not gleaning some snippet of information which he could pass on to the first receptive listener. Somehow, Clive decided cynically, looking round the bar and noticing areas of open interest in his presence, it wouldn't take him long.

'Have you seen "The Gazette" this morning, Sylvia?' he asked, turning to her and appearing to lose interest in him.

'I have, Trevor, and very grim reading it makes too.'

'Grim it certainly is, my dear Sylvia,' he pattered on, pretending to lower his voice and failing miserably, 'but Glenda's sad demise was hardly news; *everyone*,' he emphasised, ' since Monday in fact, have been thinking the worse.'

'No doubt you're right, Trevor,' she answered him quietly, but Clive couldn't miss seeing the way her lips tightened slightly in what he could only think was disapproval, 'but as I've said to you before, I don't like gossip, the whole sad business is nothing to do with us, therefore we should say or suggest as little as possible; it's the only way to keep the rumours at bay.'

'Hmmph!' was Trevor's only reply and huffily, after a brief farewell, moved along the bar to talk to someone else.

'Don't mind Trevor,' Sylvia commented when he was out of earshot 'there's no real malice in him, he takes a keen interest in everything which goes on in the village.'

'I must say you're being very charitable.' he said, forcing a smiling, not wanting to appear churlish.

'Well, Clive,' she sighed, 'I've learned since coming to live here I've had to be. Gossip is rife in the village and as you've probably gathered already, totally different to city life. What I mean particularly is the way people have this insatiable appetite to learn as much as they possibly can about everyone else and it's not healthy.'

'I quite agree; I don't know how you stand it, Sylvia. Don't you find it claustrophobic?'

'At times, yes, I do, but when that happens I usually go away for a few days and then when I return everything seems so much better somehow.'

'You must miss London though?'

'Only the shopping!' she laughed.

By mutual consent they kept their conversation light. He didn't mention Glenda Nicholson's name and neither did she and from her silence on the subject, he took the hint. Although he had enjoyed seeing her again, he found they didn't have a great deal in common. For a relatively short period of time their paths had crossed, it wasn't only that their backgrounds were different, but they lived in totally different worlds; Sylvia's somewhat privileged background bore no resemblance to his own humble beginnings and he had never quite managed to lose the leech-like chip he'd been saddled with probably since his teens. Although he would never admit it, but Clive Robinson was ashamed of his upbringing, ashamed that his father had only been a shop-floor worker in the steel company close to where they had lived on a council estate in Sheffield and his mother had worn herself out cleaning for the local doctor and dentist. The undisputed fact that she pushed herself to the physical limit had been for his benefit didn't enter his head. He was proud of what he'd achieved, and never for one moment did he consider both his parents had given him the best possible start in life. There was no room in Clive's make-up for sentimentality; in his opinion it was a waste of energy, an attitude which had undoubtedly contributed in him often experiencing difficulty in finding any woman sufficiently attracted to him to see beyond the impenetrable barrier he'd spent years creating and on the rare occasions when there had been, they had been quick to back off, once they realised his reluctance to commit himself to anything as long term as marriage, and that afternoon, as he looked across at Sylvia, he was finding it difficult to recall with any real clarity those earlier years. He could hardly remember Patsy, wondering now, how they had managed to stay together for as long as they had. He literally cringed when he remembered the exaggerated theatrical gestures of her crowd and once, when unable to contain his embarrassment, he'd asked her why they felt they had to purport themselves in such a flamboyant and artificial way, she had only laughed at him, telling him to lighten up. "You don't understand, Clive, my sweet," she'd said, pursing her lips teasingly, "we simply *have* to! It is *the* way, and the *only* way to be noticed and, to be noticed is to be recognised!" Naturally, he couldn't understand, and he hadn't pursued it.

Sylvia didn't have another drink, and he wasn't sorry; he was anxious to carry on with what he'd set out to do, regretting now the decision to call into the pub instead of driving along to where Claire was living, sure from the directions he'd been given he would have no trouble finding Tulip Cottage. As though sensing his impatience, she quickly finished her wine and standing up, kissed him on both cheeks.

'I've enjoyed talking to you, Clive,' she said, before leaving, 'and taking a short trip down memory lane. It's seldom,' she added, 'I get the opportunity since leaving London.'

He watched her as she walked over to the door, pausing a couple of times to shake hands with people she knew at the further end of the bar. An attractive woman, he thought. He'd heard, from Patsy probably, but he couldn't remember, she had re-married, some remote half-cousin on her mother's side of the family, but he hadn't thought to ask her and it had never occurred to him to see if she was wearing a wedding ring. Not that it mattered, he decided, and almost immediately dismissing her from his mind as he concentrated on what sort of approach he should make if he was able to see Claire Walters.

***

Seven o'clock was chiming from St. Paul's church, the sound of the eight-hundred-year-old bells drifting lazily across the heathland, as Gerry approached the open gates of the Grange, the tyres crunching on the gravel as he continued up the drive to pull up outside the front door. As he'd expected, Johnnie was in the lounge, his fingers strumming lightly on his guitar, the final chords of "No Reason to Cry" fading forlornly into the warm stillness of the early evening.

'Hi, Gerry.'

'Hi,' Gerry replied, stepping into the room through the French windows, 'I expect you've been wondering where I'd got to.'

'Frankly, Gerry,' he said, propping up the guitar beside his chair, 'I was, especially when you didn't give me a call to tell me you were going to be out all day.'

'I tried, but I'd forgotten to re-charge my mobile and when I eventually found a phone, the line was engaged; that was earlier this afternoon, and I must admit, I gave up after that.'

'So,' making it plain he didn't believe a word of what he'd said, 'where have you been; or is it another secret which is being kept from me.'

'No secret, Johnnie,' taken aback by his tone, and deciding on a different tack than the one he'd already planned, 'after I'd finished the shopping, and as I knew you wouldn't be needing me this afternoon, I decided to drive along the coast to Bournemouth and visit the new fitness centre.'

'Was it you who left a copy of the local rag in the hall?' throwing him with the rapid switch.

' "The Gazette?" ' stalling.

' That is what Upper Nettles weekly newspaper is called.'

'I know that, Johnnie and yes, I did leave it there.'

'For me to see as soon as I came downstairs?'

'Not particularly.' lying and speculating as to where he was going to come from next, realising with Johnnie as he appeared to be at that moment, completely sober, he would have to tread carefully.

'You've obviously read about Glenda.'

'I read about her, yes.'

'For Christ's sake, Gerry, quit this prevaricating; have you got nothing else to say?'

'There's nothing I can say, Johnnie, nothing at all.'

'Do I have to spell it out to you, man; she was murdered on Saturday night. She had been here, and you took her home!'

'You remember that?'

'It's about all I do bloody remember!'

'You don't remember anything else then, about when she became hysterical and started thumping you?'

'Only vaguely.'

'Well, that's alright then, Johnnie; if I were you I would just forget the incident.'

'Forget the incident?'

'Yes, that's what I meant, forget she was here on Saturday. Nobody else except you and I know.'

'Just what are you implying?'

'I'm not implying anything, Johnnie. Okay, she was hysterical and as she was obviously not fit to drive I took her back to Lyndhurst.'

'To her house?'

'No, she'd rallied round by that time, so I stopped the car and told her she could drive the last hundred yards or so back to where she lives.'

'Then what?'

What do you mean?'

'Then what happened?'

'I came back here.'

'You walked back?'

'Yes, of course, thought the walk would do me good.'

'And did it?'

'Yes, Johnnie, it did me the world of good.' matching his sarcasm and not caring whether he believed him or not. If it came to the crunch and he had been seen by anyone that night and the police came sniffing round, Johnnie wouldn't have a bloody leg to stand on. By his own admission, he couldn't fully remember what happened which suited him fine. Talented though Johnnie was, he was a drug addict, while he had never touched the stuff. During his chequered career and, by some miracle, he had always succeeded in steering clear of the law and he intended it to remain like that. He was getting a bit more than pissed off with living in this outlandish place, even although as far as jobs went, working for Johnnie was a cushy number, but he missed the city life. He missed London, the clubs and pubs, in fact the whole gamut. Also, he was tired of being treated as a general dogsbody; it was time he moved on, but not yet. For the first time in his life, Gerry was discovering he would have to think seriously. He would have to carefully consider every move he made until this murder business was done and dusted.

***

Richard was thoughtful as he left Tulip Cottage, deciding in view of what Claire Walters had told him, to delay calling at The Grange until the following day. The interview with Johnnie Wall required skilful handling and for that he had to remain impartial until such time he had something more substantial than circumstantial evidence to support any suspicions he may have of whether he had been responsible, either directly or indirectly, for Glenda Nicholson's death. There was also Claire Walter's situation to consider. She was his nearest neighbour and even if he avoided actually mentioning her name, he would immediately realise the information would have come from her.

He didn't see Peter's car outside the Station and as he passed the front desk on the way to his office, Sergeant Baker handed him a slip of paper.

'Miss Blakeman from the hairdressers brought this in, sir; she said she had forgotten about it until this morning.'

'Thank you, Sergeant.' he said, recognising the post office's logo and printed format for undelivered registered mail. According to the almost indecipherable scribble, the postman had attempted to deliver a package to Glenda Nicholson at the salon on Tuesday morning at eleven-thirty and, according to the printing at the bottom of the form, it could be collected from Lymington Head Post Office between their normal business hours. Bureaucracy gone mad, he muttered to himself, opening the door to his office; obviously the post office in Upper Nettles was not considered to be sufficiently adequate to hold on to mail for the short length of time a person was given to claim it.

There were two reports on his desk; the profile on Glenda Nicholson and this morning's search of her property in Lyndhurst, and after going through the ritual of opening the window to relieve the build-up of stuffiness in the room, he sat down to read them:

Career & Personal profile on Glenda Nicholson

Born on 7th August 1970 in Shrewsbury, Shropshire

Education: 1975 - 1981: Market Drayton Junior School

1981 - 1986: Grove Secondary School, Market Drayton

1986 - 1990: Served apprenticeship with Lewis', Shrewsbury

1990 - 1991: Hair Stylist with Debenhams, Oxford Street, London

1991 - Opened "The Cutting Edge" Hairdressing Salon, Russell Square in partnership with Lilian Grahame)

1993 - 15th August, married Ted Warren, owner of "Ted's Revue Bar" London

1995 - 23rd November, Ted Warren killed in nightclub brawl

2000 - 3rd February, married Nicholas Wade-Brown, Impresario

2001 - Divorced (Wade-Brown citing her affair with rock star, Johnnie Wall as grounds for divorce)

2004 - Sold business and moved to Lyndhurst, Hampshire, purchasing Number Six Willow Crescent

Opened "Scissors" Hairdressing Salon in High Street, Upper Nettles

Richard had just finished reading the reports when Peter walked past the open door on the way to his own office and called out to him.

'Can you spare a few moments, Peter,' he said when he came in, 'I'd like you to have a look at these, in particular the profile on Glenda Nicholson.'

'Of course,' he said, 'anything interesting.'

'I believe there could be.' passing the report to him.

'So,' he commented when he reached the last line, 'she did know Johnnie Wall. Do you think she had been on her way to his place, then?'

'It seems more than likely.' going on to tell him about his meeting with Claire Walters.

'Well, that could clear up one aspect of this case; it's going to be tricky moving forward on that though.'

'That's exactly what I've been thinking and I'm glad now I didn't try and see him after I'd finished at Tulip Cottage. I had intended to, but thought it best to wait until tomorrow, Peter and now we have this,' tapping the report, 'it does give us a little more ammunition. It is going to be very interesting to see whether he admits knowing her, far less that she was visiting him that night.'

'There was something else which caught my eye, sir,' Peter said, picking up the profile once more, 'what I mean is this mention of her partner's name.'

'My goodness, you could be right, and I must say that had missed me.'

'I could be wrong, sir, although Lilian isn't all that usual a name.'

'True, and we could be stretching credibility a bit too far in supposing she's the same woman who visited her house on the Sunday.'

'I spoke to Barbara Freeman's husband this afternoon and although he couldn't give me the registration number of the couple's car, he did remember the name of the company where they purchased it, because they had one of those showroom stickers in the rear window. Knights of Kensington they're called, so it shouldn't be too late to give them a ring and hopefully they'll be able to give us their name. Bob Freeman,' he added, 'was quite certain about it being the very latest model.'

'Use this one, Peter,' he suggested, pushing the phone towards him, 'the sooner we know the better.'

'Right,' picking up the receiver, 'first, I'll get the number through Directory of Enquiries. Incidentally,' he said, 'there was another interesting twist to our enquiry.'

'Yes?'

'Glenda Nicholson's male friend; one of her other neighbours told me she recognised him, and she was adamant she wasn't wrong, but it would seem he's called Bernie Croft and that he used to be with "The Bandanas".'

***

When the Chief Inspector had gone, Claire had stood on the front doorstep for several seconds until she could no longer hear his car as it reached the last bend in the road before reaching the town.

'Claire;' Jack said quietly from behind her, 'you mustn't concern yourself so much about all of this, let the police get on with what they're trained to do.'

'I know,' she sighed, turning round to face him, 'but I can't help thinking about that poor woman. She was asking for help, Jack and I didn't do anything!'

'What *could* you have done, Claire. Listen, my love,' taking both of her hands in his, 'it isn't that I don't understand how you're feeling, but think about yourself. Please. Whether she met her death from one of those men you saw her with or not, she felt sufficiently threatened by them to come running to your front door. If you had reached the door before she was dragged away, you would have put yourself in a vulnerable position.'

'You're right, of course you are,' not taking her hands away, reassured by the concern in his expression that she wasn't on her own, 'but it's all so ghastly. Ironic when you think about it,' she smiled ruefully, 'I write crime thrillers, but almost coming face to face with the real thing, well that's something else.'

'The harsh reality of the world we live in, eh?'

'You can say that again! And then,' she went on, 'there's still the problem of that computer disc to sort out. I could always destroy the thing I suppose.'

'Will you?'

'I have too curious a nature to do that,' she smiled again, 'what do you think I should do with it, Jack?'

'I'm not sure,' he said, leading her back into the kitchen, 'but, as I said before, its presence here worries me, Claire.'

'You think that was why Tom was so anxious to find where I was, so that he could come and collect it?'

'I would say that was more than likely,' he nodded, 'but I'm more concerned about the relevance of the contents, what I mean is, they could be equally as important to someone else.'

'Not a pleasant thought.'

'No, not pleasant.'

'I could always just send it off to Tom.' she suggested, but not with any real conviction.

'That's true, you could; it might be simpler if you did.'

'You say *might* be?'

'You've sensed my doubt, haven't you?' he grinned, 'I thought you would. But seriously,' he went on, leaning his back against the worktop, 'there is the possibility that if you did return the disc to him, he would automatically assume you were aware of what had been written on it, which may or may not concern him, although I would say it would concern him a great deal. He could do either one or two things; he could choose to ignore any knowledge you may have picked up, or he could put an end to whatever he's been up to. Sorry, I'm taking a long time to reach my point, Claire.'

'No, that's alright.'

'Some people would argue that the disc was none of your business, but

I would say that the fact Tom had deliberately concealed it inside one of your possessions without your knowledge, he has theoretically implicated you and, honestly, my dear, Claire, that makes me angry.'

'I feel pretty angry myself, but it still doesn't solve the problem, does it?'

'No,' he agreed slowly, 'it doesn't; I think,' he continued, 'what we need is some professional and unbiased advice in order to safeguard your interests.'

'You believe he's involved in something quite big?'

'I think he could be, they were substantial amounts of cash and it looks as though he's not working entirely on his own.'

'You mentioned us getting some advice, Jack; had you anyone in mind.'

'I did, actually. He's an old friend of the family and I've known him for years; Adam Brookfield, he's called and recently retired, he was a corporate lawyer and had spent most of his career working for one of the 'big boys' in the City. With your permission, of course, I could have a word with him, show him the disc and see what he comes up with. What do you think?'

'It would be a relief to share what is fast becoming the proverbial pain in the neck.'

'Okay, I'll give him a ring and hopefully I'll be able to see him tomorrow.'

'Where does your friend live?'

'He has a delightful house in Swiss Cottage.'

'And you would make the trip especially up to London.'

'Of course, Claire, unless you're free and we could both see him, I'll try and make it for some time during the afternoon as I've some work I must do in the morning; what do you say, can you spare the time?'

'I was planning on having an easy day tomorrow; Sylvia Crossman has invited me for coffee in the morning and I was going to start preparing the plot of a sequel to one of my older books, Dan has asked for, but I can easily do that over the weekend.'

'That's settled then.'

'I'll open a bottle of wine, shall I, that is unless you have other plans for this evening?' she suggested.

'The only plans I have,' the schoolboy grin re-appearing, 'are to spend them with you; there's a new restaurant in Beaulieu I've been meaning to try; I thought it would be a chance for you to see a little bit more of the New Forest.'

'That sounds lovely, I'll just go upstairs to freshen up, it won't take long.'

'And while you're doing that I'll give Adam a ring.'

***

The drive across the forest to Beaulieu at seven o'clock in the evening had been breathtakingly beautiful, the sun still high in the sky, filtering through the thick foliage of sturdy oaks bordering either side of the road, and casting dappling shadows on the surface of the winding streams alongside narrow stony footpaths; now and again the greenery dramatically highlighted by clumps of flowering shrubs and, tropical-like, a riot of glorious shades of scarlet through to palest pink merging naturally to form a solid mass of colour. Claire had loved the small picturesque village of Beaulieu nestling on the bank of the Beaulieu River, Jack informing her that it was where in the early eleventh century King John had given the area, known as Bellus Locus, to the Cistercian monks and adding another historical note that further up the river was where King Rufus met his death from an arrow.

The restaurant, "The Rufus Restaurant", was delightful; they had taken their drinks outside into the walled garden, sitting under the shade of a dark green parasol, and for the first time that day Claire felt totally relaxed, Jack's undemanding company and strong presence comforting, the warmth of the sun on her arms and the calmness of the surroundings erasing the troubled thoughts which had been with her practically from the first moment she had arrived at Tulip Cottage.

Dusk was beginning to fall as she opened the front door of the cottage, turning to wave goodnight to Jack before going inside. It wasn't yet dark enough to switch on any of the lights, and she walked through the lounge to the kitchen, noticing as she reached the window, the tall figure of Jack as he opened his own door. As though sensing she was there, he waved again before going in.

Finding it stuffy, she walked over to open the door on to the terrace, her fingers going automatically to where the key should have been, but it wasn't there. Puzzled, she bent down to see whether it had dislodged itself from the lock and fallen on the floor, but she couldn't see it. Straightening up, she looked around the kitchen as if miraculously it would turn up, but the worktop was exactly as she'd left it, and then she saw it, half-hidden under the lower edge of one of the worktops and, thinking it must have slid along the tiles after falling from the lock, she picked up the key and unlocked the back door.

Walking back to the lounge, she switched on the small lamp on the top shelf of the bookcase, and as she did so, the breath catching at the back of her throat, saw that the books had been moved. They were in a different order; her collection of travel books had been filed alphabetically, but not now. Also, on the middle shelf, the end book which she had laid flat to act as a temporary book-end was not the same one. She took a deep breath and slowly looked round the room; the cushions on the sofa and the two armchairs were undisturbed, also the ornaments; she checked the position of each of the paintings; the first being the one where they'd found the disc, but it was straight, but then the picture on the opposite wall, above the fireplace, wasn't. It was tilting slightly to the right. Someone had been in the cottage! Feelings of repugnance replaced her former apprehension. She went upstairs, going straight to the study and opened the drawer where she kept her supply of paper, replacement ink cartridges and boxes of computer discs. There were two boxes, one of them unopened, the seal still intact and knowing there should be eight discs in the other box, she opened it. They were all there, including the one they'd found. As she went back downstairs, she didn't know whether to be relieved or not that whoever had broken in had not been able to find what they were looking for. She was positive the disc she'd just seen was the same one because she had already noticed when Jack had first handed it to her, there was a slight, miniscule, tear at the side of the packet.

Thoughtfully, she went back downstairs and tried to apply some logic to what she was thinking. She was reluctant to believe that Tom would have gone behind her back in going so far as to break-in to retrieve something which presumably was his own property. Surely, he had only to ask her and reluctant though she would have been, she would have given it back to him. If it had been Tom, there would have been no necessity for him to check the other pictures; he would have quite simply gone to the one where he'd concealed it. Even if he had discovered it was no longer there, he wouldn't have believed she would have found a similar hiding place. Then there were the books; he could have searched through them, but again, wouldn't that have been far too obvious a place to find it? Jack's words came back to her, and as their possible meaning sunk into her brain, she felt the first chill of fear.

"….. I'm more concerned about the contents," he had said, "they could be equally as important to someone else apart from Tom….. "

Chapter Nine

It was shortly after eleven the following morning when Tom pulled up outside Tulip Cottage. Claire's car wasn't there, but undeterred, he walked up the path to the front door and rang the bell. A short dumpy woman, wearing a pale blue overall hesitatingly opened the door a fraction.

'Good morning,' giving her one of his well-practised smiles he reserved for any woman over the age of fifty and as so often before it appeared to work, as she smiled in return, although a trifle nervously, obviously at a loss for words, 'I'm a friend of Claire's,' he explained quickly, 'is she at home?'

'I'm afraid she's not, sir.'

'Oh, that's too bad; have you any idea when she'll be back? You see I've driven all the way from London especially to see her.'

'Miss Walters didn't actually say when she would be back, perhaps around midday, but I don't know for certain. If you'd like to give me your name, I'll tell her you called.' she added, but he could see by her expression she was unbending, but not discouraged, he adopted another tactic of ingratiating himself with older women, 'My name's Tom; Claire and I were close friends at one time, and I'm sure she will be sorry she's missed me, but would you mind terribly if I waited for her, until midday, I mean. I really would like to see her again.'

'Well - ' the last vestige of any wariness she may have had about a complete stranger turning up on the doorstep, evaporating, ' - I suppose that will be alright,' opening the door further and gesturing for him to come in, 'just after twelve, so you can stay until then.'

'Thank you, Mrs -?' noticing she was wearing a wedding ring.

'- Green,' she said, 'Maud Green.'

'Maud, an unusual name.'

'I suppose so. A bit old-fashioned now; nobody calls their children Maud these days.'

He noticed the picture straight away; it was directly facing him as he stepped into the lounge. So near and yet so far, he muttered under his breath, dragging his eyes away from it, feigning an interest in another part of the room. She offered to make him a coffee and he was quick to accept, although he didn't really want one, but while she was in the kitchen it should be long enough to give him the time he needed.

He waited until she had reached the kitchen at the far end of the lounge before casually moving over to the picture and stretching up removed it from the wall. Fortunately, it wasn't large, simplifying the handling of it, and turning it over, peeled back the tape securing the backing, but only half-way, with just sufficient space for him to place his hand underneath, but in less than a minute, he came to the grim conclusion his disc wasn't in there. Someone had beaten him to it! Such was the twisted and suspicious way in which his mind worked, he didn't consider it would have been Claire. He couldn't recall the type of tape he'd seen before, only that it looked the same, therefore concluding it probably was, and securing the loosened tape, replaced the picture, making sure he'd left it exactly as it had been.

'Pretty picture, isn't it?' the woman said quietly from behind him, startling him for a moment; he hadn't heard her coming back, wondering how long she had been standing there and whether she'd seen him with the picture in his hand.

'I've always admired it,' he answered, turning to face her, 'and that's why I couldn't resist the temptation to examine it more closely.' giving her another contrived smile, but not altogether convinced this time whether she was taken in by him. He hadn't been fooled by her bland, slightly subservient manner, reckoning that those black button eyes didn't miss much. If, he thought, glancing at his watch, Claire should return now, it was questionable whether he would get the opportunity to tell her about the disc with the woman within earshot, not that he wanted to mention it to her now anyway, having by now convinced himself she hadn't been the one who had removed it. It must have been either Clive or David; he couldn't think of anyone else. He didn't believe David Waterman would have had the nerve or be sufficiently devious to carry out anything so underhand as to break into someone's property, never mind the wit to work out where he'd put the disc, but Clive Robinson on the other hand, Tom was sure, would have. He had nothing to substantiate this, only that he recognised a ruthless character when he saw one, and from his experience Clive possessed all the signs. The bottom line could simply be they didn't trust each other, although the slightly disturbing fact remained and one which had been bothering him for some weeks; there was a definite coolness in Clive's manner towards him and it would not have surprised him if Clive decided to put an end to his involvement with them and it went without saying that David Waterman would go along with any decision his partner wanted to implement, therefore Tom concluded all the more reason he had the disc back, the contents of which were, as far as he was concerned, his insurance in the event there were any unpleasant shocks.

He drank most of his coffee quickly, wanting to leave before Claire returned, having in a matter of minutes reached the decision not to say anything to her about the disc. If the woman took it upon herself to tell her, well so be it, he shrugged, there was nothing he could do about that, replacing the cup and saucer on the coffee table and making the excuse that as time was getting on he would have to get back to London. She hadn't made any comment, but stolidly watched him as he walked across the room to the door and let himself out. He didn't look round when he reached the car, certain she would be at the window making sure he really did leave the premises.

It was almost twelve and, reversing the car in the open gateway of the house across the road, he headed back in the direction of the main road and as much as he would have liked to have stopped for a beer and something to eat, decided to wait until he reached Lyndhurst, not wanting to bump into Claire. He wasn't impressed by Upper Nettles; to Tom it epitomised genteel living, expecting to see Miss Marples cycling through the village on her old bone-shaker of a bike with a loaf of freshly baked bread protruding from the basket on the front of the handlebars! He'd die if he had to live in a place like this, wondering how Claire could stand the sheer parochialism: one long street, one pub pretending to be an ancient hostelry, a handful of cafés and tea rooms and about half a dozen gift shops! One place, though, did catch his attention, standing out incongruously from all the other businesses, as he slowly progressed, constantly hampered by a series of speed humps, a sneaky attempt to catch the unwary. "The Gallery" looked totally out of place, he couldn't imagine for one minute any of the people he'd seen so far, venturing inside, far less actually buying one of their paintings, which no doubt would be ridiculously over-priced, wondering what sort of person could have even considered such a venture and then as if to answer his question a man emerged from inside the gallery, leaving the door open as he walked to the edge of the pavement and head on one side, critically viewed the window display. He had to be the proprietor, Tom decided, indeed who else? A tall lanky guy, well on in his fifties, he reckoned, with one of those old-fashioned goatee beards, incongruously wearing a pair of tight-fitting jeans and a red and white checked shirt, the whole ensemble more suitable for a country and western gig than representing what presumably could be described as a collection of fine arts, not that he knew much about the subject; he could recognise an Old Master but that was about the extent of his artistic knowledge.

By now, well past the gallery and nearing the end of the High Street, he noticed the "Nettles Hotel" on his left-hand side; he'd seen it earlier but hadn't given it more than a glance, his one aim being to reach Tulip Cottage and retrieve his disc, but liking the look of the place, he decided it was bound to be better than anywhere else he was likely to find around here and turned into the driveway, following the sign directing him to their car park.

***

Richard Cavendish had intended to drive along to the Grange earlier in the morning, but a series of telephone calls, including an impromptu request from his supervisor, Brian Burrows, to ask what progress had been made in solving the Nicholson case, meant it was approaching midday before he was able to leave the office. He hadn't needed to be reminded that it was now over three days since the body of Glenda Nicholson had been found, not overlooking the fact that the murder had taken place almost a week ago, and no report of any real significance had been made. Brian Burrows was not an unreasonable man, but his patience only stretched so far and as with anyone in his position, he expected results. Richard still remembered when he had only been in the Force for a very short time, his superior, an old die-hard and long retired, had repeatedly told him that everyone had a boss. It had been good advice. Brian Burrows, even in his elevated status, was answerable to someone of a higher rank than himself and when, as he was this morning, more acerbic than usual, Richard understood why, but it didn't change the status quo; they knew how the victim met her death, but they had no proof where this had taken place; they had an approximate time of death, but no knowledge of where the victim had been prior to her death; they had no motive, neither did they have any suspects. Up to now, no-one had been brought in for questioning and as far as his supervisor's gripe went, they had made no arrests. As far as the last two elements were concerned, it was very much the chicken and the egg syndrome; what came first, the motive or the suspect? The irony of this being, Richard had sighed when he finally emerged from Brian Burrow's office, if they had a strong suspect, this should lead them to the motive, alternatively, if they had a credible motive, they should have a suspect. What a conundrum, he sighed, going out to his car.

He was on the Lymington Road and a few yards from the entrance to the Grange when he noticed the light flashing on his mobile and pulling into the grass verge, switched off the engine. Peter's number was on the display monitor and knowing it must be important and may even by relevant to what he hoped would be an interview with Johnnie Wall; he hadn't phoned in advance, deciding to treat this visit as being a routine one, no different to his call the previous afternoon when he'd spoken to Claire Walters.

'Thought you should know at once, sir,' Peter was saying, 'but a report has come in from Lymington police headquarters to say that a car has been discovered partly-submerged in one of the creeks which by the description they've been able to give so far, suggests it could have been Glenda Nicholson's.'

'You say so far, Peter.'

'Yes, that's right, they're in the process of bringing it to the surface and then once they're able to see the registration number, we'll know for sure. Also,' he added, 'there's a man's body inside slumped over the steering wheel.'

'Jamie Green.'

'Could be, sir; they reckon he's young. Do you want to make your way down there, or shall I?'

'I'd prefer if you would, Peter. I'm at Johnnie Wall's place now and I'm anxious to get some answers from him apropos of what we've learned from Claire Walters before any more time is lost. You won't be surprised to hear that Brian Burrows is starting to get impatient.'

'I thought he might be, but I suppose he has a point, sir; this case has been very sluggish.'

'I know, Peter, but perhaps there might be an increase in tempo, especially if it turns out that it is Jamie Green's body in the car.'

Saying he was on his way to Lymington and would be in touch as soon as he had something definite to report, Peter rang off. As he drove on to the Grange, Richard considered the possible implications if it transpired that the car had belonged to Glenda Nicholson and that the body inside was Jamie Green. They would then have a possible pattern which already was beginning to hang together, albeit somewhat tentatively and only triggered off by what Claire Walters had told him, which in essence was no more than circumstantial evidence; the disturbance she witnessed could have been what is now described as a domestic incident involving the people who lived across the road from her and had nothing to do with Glenda Nicholson, similarly, the light she had seen, although possibly from a bike's lamp, may not have been Jamie Green returning home from a night out in Brockenhurst with his friends. All the more reason, he decided, pulling up outside the property, to clarify whether there was any feasible reason why he should consider the person he hoped to see as a possible suspect in their enquiry.

The front door was open and as Richard approached, Johnnie Wall was walking across the hall, stopping half-way when he saw him, his eyebrows raised in surprise, his expression remaining unchanged when Richard introduced himself.

'Chief Inspector Richard Cavendish,' reading from the identity card, 'and how can I help you, Chief Inspector?' a trace of mockery in his voice as he continued his appraisal.

'This is a purely a routine call, sir.' Richard said, going on to explain.

'And you want to know whether I heard anything unusual, anything out of the ordinary,' correcting himself, 'such as what, exactly, Chief Inspector; I'm not quite sure I follow you?'

'As the victim's body was discovered less than a mile away from here, it would indicate she was murdered in close vicinity to where she was found. We know she was in Upper Nettles during the evening, after which, instead of returning to Lyndhurst where she lived, she came the other way which presumably would have taken her past your property and any other one between Upper Nettles and Brockenhurst.'

'Why Brockenhurst?'

'We have reason to believe she must have either been waylaid as she was heading in that direction or was visiting someone who lived nearby, in other words, sir, she didn't reach as far as Brockenhurst.'

'I see, well to answer your question, last Saturday night was like most other nights when I'm at home and if I did hear anything, I've forgotten, therefore it couldn't have been important.'

It was no answer and he knew it! The man was stalling for time, time to arrange how he intended to respond to any further questions. Richard wasn't prone to making rash judgements of anyone he had met for the first time, preferring to wait, to conserve those first impressions and analyse them later, but there was something about Johnnie Wall he didn't like. Whether it was because he was obviously a smart-arse, presumably accustomed to being centre stage, both literally and metaphorically, he wasn't sure. He had never been a great fan of "The Bandanas", although he had to admit, having listened to their music over the years, Johnnie Wall was a gifted guitarist. He remembered seeing them on television a few times years ago and although superficially he looked the same; the tall lean frame, the flopping blonde hair and the rather startling blue eyes, but his face was now heavily lined which made him look considerably older than he probably was.

'Were you here on your own on Saturday night, sir?'

'Why should you want to know that?'

'Because if you had visitors I would like to ask them the same question as I asked you.'

'Oh, I see; well, apart from Gerry, there was no-one else here.'

'Gerry?'

'Gerry Steele, my assistant; he lives here, Chief Inspector.'

'And is he in at the moment?'

'As far as I know. He's been around for most of the morning, but he may have gone into the village. I'll just go and ask my housekeeper, she will know, and before you ask, she doesn't live here and only works weekdays.'

Obviously he wasn't going to invite him in, but Richard wasn't too bothered, he could say everything he wanted to say just as well outside, standing on the man's doorstep. He was only away for seconds, returning with a heavily-built man with short crinkly grey hair and a disgruntled expression, reminding him of a larger edition of Dennis Waterman in the television series. Even although assistants came in many different guises, minder was the one he'd choose for Gerry Steele.

The man's response was expected, therefore not disappointing. He could have been telling the truth in that he'd spent a quiet evening watching television, but on the other hand, Johnnie Wall had had sufficient time to prime him. Dissatisfied though he was by the man's monosyllable answers, he didn't think anything would be achieved by persisting with him. Richard had met his type before and invariably they fell into the same mould: taciturn, exuding undisguised animosity towards authority, plus the ability to display resentment at being asked the simplest of questions, meaning they didn't trust anyone and he didn't think Gerry Steele was any different. He watched as, from a slight nod from Johnnie Wall who had remained silent throughout the limited exchange, he turned round and went back inside the house.

'You're not having much luck, Chief Inspector, with your *routine* enquiries, are you?' he drawled, leaning against the door frame.

'Perhaps not, sir,' Richard admitted, choosing to ignore the jibe, 'but these are questions we have to ask in the event they may be of some help to us, especially in a crime of this nature when it is not clear where the murder took place.'

'What a gruesome task you do have.'

'Did you know the victim, sir?'

'Should I have known her?'

'I would remind you, Mr Wall,' tired with his habit of repeating a question by one of his own, 'that I am the one asking the questions and I'd be grateful if you would give me a straight answer.'

'I do apologise,' he answered unconvincingly, 'I hadn't realised, but no, I didn't know the woman.'

'You knew her name?'

'Only from what was in the local rag, Chief Inspector; she was apparently called Glenda – something, I can't remember the surname.'

'Nicholson, sir; she was called Glenda Nicholson,' Johnnie Wall's attempt to stall floundering slightly and encouraged, he pressed on, 'she had her home in Lyndhurst, but owned a hairdressing business in Upper Nettles and according to our information spent much of her leisure time in and around the town;' expanding the truth somewhat, but if any interview needed a nudge this one certainly did, 'I've already mentioned she was in Upper Nettles on the night of her death and before ten that evening when she was in "The Hunters' Arms" she took a call on her mobile and shortly afterwards, left the pub and drove in this direction.'

'You say *this* direction, I hope you're not implying she was driving here, to The Grange, Chief Inspector, because if you are -'

'- I'm not implying anything, Mr Wall, I am merely conveying to you what direction she took when she left "The Hunters' Arms"; she may not in fact have reached as far as your property, or she may have driven past and on towards Brockenhurst; this is something which remains unclear, however, we have strong reason to believe she may very well have intended to come here, but this is not substantiated, at least not yet.'

'I don't know where you get your ideas from,' he commented in the same tone of voice he'd been using since the start of the interview, 'but I've already told you I didn't know this woman, therefore why on earth should she have come here?'

'You have told me you didn't know Glenda Nicholson, but it is possible she knew you.'

'Well -' he drawled, 'as you say it is possible, but many people know who I am, Chief Inspector and that I live here, but, as far as I know, there haven't been any uninvited guests ringing my front door bell!'

'I see,' Richard nodded, deciding to take the interview one step further, a move which might unsettle the man further, at the least, wipe off that smug sardonic expression from his haggard face, 'we have already spoken to your neighbour who has recently moved into Tulip Cottage and asked her whether she had been disturbed in any way on Saturday night.'

'Really; conducting your routine questions, I presume.'

'You presume correctly, sir and she informed us that she had been disturbed that night by someone knocking repeatedly at her front door.'

'There you are, then, Chief Inspector! This Nicholson woman must have been visiting her!'

'Glenda Nicholson left "The Hunters' Arms" before ten that night; it would only have taken her at the very most fifteen minutes to reach Tulip Cottage. The lady I spoke to told me this disturbance took place around midnight.'

'She's probably mistaken; about the time I mean.'

'I don't think so; as you're aware, it is still quite light around ten, but by midnight it was too dark for her to see who was at the door.'

'If she had opened the door to her she would have seen her.' obviously the best he could come up with and, noticing an imperceptible narrowing of his eyes which could signify nervousness, wondered what was going to be said next.

'Ladies living on their own,' Richard said sharply, 'are not in the habit of opening the door to anyone they are not expecting, whether they know them or not, especially in the middle of the night.'

'Very wise.'

'I would say it was a natural reaction; nevertheless,' Richard went on relentlessly, 'the undisputed fact remains that there was something happening around this area on Saturday night and whether the unknown person who had been trying to attract the attention of your neighbour had anything to do with the murder enquiry we are conducting, remains to be seen.'

'Well, Chief Inspector,' his response by this time predictable, 'all of this has nothing to do with yours truly.'

'There's also the question of the car, sir.' experiencing a certain satisfaction in the way he reacted to the sudden switch.

'Car?' frowning, 'What car?'

'Glenda Nicholson's car; your neighbour was certain there was no car outside her property, either in the driveway or at the side of the road.'

'How did she know if it was dark?'

'A car, Mr Wall, is considerably larger than a person and even on a night as dark as it was on Saturday, the shape of one would be recognised immediately. If it had been Glenda Nicholson at her door, she must have walked there, meaning she must have left her car somewhere; the question is where?'

'You're talking in riddles; this detective stuff is beyond me. Utterly beyond me, Chief Inspector.'

'Perhaps the riddles will become clearer once the car bearing a close resemblance to the one owned by Miss Nicholson, is dredged from the sea off the Lymington coast.'

This time he refrained from saying anything, but by the flicker of alarm which crossed his features, Richard could see this had shaken him, and taking advantage of his obvious discomfort made no further comment; instead, for the second time during what was proving a fairly unsatisfactory interview, he moved swiftly on to something else.

'We've been trying to locate a friend of yours, sir, and we were hoping you may be able to help us.'

'What friend?' gratified to see that at last, he was beginning to lose his air of detachment.

'Bernie Croft.'

'Oh, Bernie.' the name seeming to take him by surprise, as though he knew a number of men called Bernie, or perhaps expecting him to name someone else.

'Yes,' Richard nodded, 'he was with your group for a while, we understand?'

'God! That was years ago, Chief Inspector; we've since lost touch.'

'Yet, he was also in the music industry and presumably continued after you'd parted company, I'm surprised your paths never crossed.'

'Well, they didn't. I vaguely remember hearing he'd gone to France, bought a villa there, in the south I think. Quite frankly, I wasn't interested. Bernie is history. One must move on in this business.' returning to his former nonchalance, but Richard wasn't taken in; the man was nervous, although concealing it well. He hadn't shown any interest in why they were asking about Bernie Croft; that struck Richard as odd. Did he genuinely not want to know or, the idea suddenly occurring to him, did he know already? Either way, it didn't alter the fact that from the moment he had mentioned Bernie Croft's name, his manner had changed significantly. Bernie is history, he'd said, but whatever happened in the past can have a strong bearing on the present. Rosemary Coleman had told Peter that Bernie had left the group in 2000, ten years ago; was that the period they should be concentrating on? He had certainly been lying when he'd denied knowing Glenda Nicholson, this was probably instinctive, but he'd also been lying when he'd said there had been no visitors, but according to what Claire Walters had told him, there had been a woman at the Grange on Saturday, apparently in considerable distress, and she'd been joined by two men and taken back to the house against her will. It was stretching coincidence and logic to suggest there were two women in the vicinity at more or less the same time and the one Claire had seen had not been Glenda Nicholson. All very well in theory, he knew, but trying to prove it was another matter, but Richard was confident they would.

Now that they knew Johnnie Wall had known Glenda Nicholson, the next step would be to trawl back to that time. Wade-Brown had divorced her in 2001, but how long before then should they go; to when Bernie Croft was with the group? If so, it was logical to presume she would have also known him then. Was this the reason behind why Johnnie was reluctant to discuss him, also for his nervousness?

Making no further reference to Bernie Croft, Richard thanked him for sparing the time to talk to him and walked back down the steps to the car. As he reversed to face the gateway, he glanced in the wing mirror, not displeased to see a look of bewilderment on Johnnie Wall's face; this could have been because of his somewhat abrupt departure or because he had expected to be asked more about his relationship with Bernie.

***

They had time for a coffee before meeting Jack's friend. They'd driven to London in Jack's car, rather than taking the train, agreeing that Swiss Cottage was relatively easy to reach and, unlike most of London, finding a parking place less hopeless. On the drive up, Claire had told him about the cottage being broken into during the time they'd been in Beaulieu the evening before, but they didn't talk about it in any depth, with Jack needing his concentration on the driving and she intentionally left what Maud Green had told her when she got back from her coffee with Sylvia. She hadn't even had time yet to think properly about Tom's visit, except that he'd had a damned nerve and despite still having the possession of the disc which was rapidly taking the form of something alien and definitely not welcome, she was relieved he had not been able to get his hands on it.

Adam Brookfield lived in one of the streets opposite Swiss Cottage's Central Park, and after finding somewhere to park the car, they walked along to a coffee shop on the main street with tables and chairs outside on the pavement, the gingham tablecloths and matching parasols a colourful additive for somewhere pleasant to spend half an hour and as they waited for their coffees, idly watched the never-ending stream of pedestrians walking past their table.

'Does it make you nostalgic?' he asked her.

'For London, you mean?' she smiled.

'Yes, I can tell by your expression you're enjoying yourself.'

'Okay,' she laughed, 'I own up; it does make me nostalgic. Upper Nettles seems another world away, but I know that one day I'll come back here. What about you, Jack, how do you feel?'

'Apart from being idyllically happy this moment sitting beside you and enjoying the warm July sunshine, I feel the same. It is where our roots are, after all.'

'I know and with everything that's being going on recently, I have to admit there have been times when I've wished I was anywhere but in Upper Nettles, although I do love living in Tulip Cottage; so far, that hasn't lost any of its magic.'

'Going back to last night,' he said, 'whoever broke in must have been pretty anxious to get their hands on that disc. I didn't ask you, but was there any damage to the lock?'

'No, it seems to be alright. It's actually quite a simple one; perhaps I should have another one fitted. I suppose anyone with the necessary skill, once they'd pushed the key out and fiddled around with a piece of wire or something, could have managed to open the door.'

'He must have known what he was doing though.'

'Someone with criminal tendencies, you mean?'

'I would be more inclined to say he had considerable skill; have you ever tried to unlock a door without using the key, Claire?'

'No.' giving him a wry smile, knowing she wouldn't be able to.

'By all means have the lock changed,' he said, looking at her with concern, 'but at the risk of making you more nervous than you probably are, I don't think that additional security measure would have deterred this character. I would dearly like to know who it was; I would be seething if someone broke their way into my place.'

'That was exactly how I felt, you know, but as it happened he was wasting his efforts. A couple of other things have happened since last night which I haven't mentioned yet.'

'I had a feeling there might be, you've been looking very thoughtful ever since I picked you up this afternoon.'

'I hadn't realised I was making it so obvious, but I didn't want to distract you while you were driving and thought it best to wait until we had a chance to talk properly and preferably before we see your friend.'

'This sounds ominous.'

'I don't know whether it is or not, but I don't think so. Anyway,' pausing while the waitress brought their coffees out to them, 'it's something Sylvia said to me this morning. She was telling me how yesterday she bumped into someone she hadn't seen for years, over twenty years she said; this had been in "The Hunters' Arms". Apparently, before then he'd been in "The Gallery" and had asked Trevor Wheatley's partner whether he knew where I lived.'

'What! Did he tell Sylvia this?'

'No, Trevor had joined them at the bar and mentioned it; apparently, he'd overheard Maurice talking to him.'

'He would have!'

'He is a bit of an old busybody, isn't he?' Claire shrugged resignedly; after only a week she had quickly learned it was impossible to do anything in Upper Nettles without someone noticing.

'That's an understatement; those two, Trevor and Maurice, thrive on the tiniest morsel they pick up during their day.

'Sad.'

'Very. Did Sylvia give you the name of her friend?'

'Yes, I was just coming to that,' she smiled, anticipating his reaction, 'he's called Clive Robinson.'

'Clive Robinson,' Jack repeated, his jaw dropping, 'of Robinson & Waterman!'

'I would think so; it would be too much of a coincidence for it not to be. So, Jack,' she added, 'as I had never heard of the man before, what other reason would he have had for asking someone where I lived?'

'I can't think of any, therefore,' he concluded grimly, 'he was your intruder and presumably from what we've able to glean from the disc, one of Tom's business contacts.'

'Tom, yes,' she sighed, taking a sip of her coffee and replacing the cup on the saucer before continuing, 'that brings me to what I was going to tell you next.'

'I don't know how you manage to keep so calm.'

'I don't feel calm really; merely muddled and wondering what's going to happen next.'

'Okay,' he said, lightly covering her hand with his, 'I understand, but don't forget I'm with you and somehow we'll get it all sorted out. So, where does Tom fit into what you quite accurately describe as a muddle?'

'Well,' taking a deep breath, 'when I got back from Sylvia's, this was around midday and Maud Green was just on the point of finishing, she told me that Tom had called at the cottage asking to see me; he didn't give her his surname, only that he was called Tom, but from how she described him, it was Tom alright. Apparently, he'd asked if he could come in and wait for me; she was quite apprehensive about that, worried I suppose that I wouldn't have been pleased, but I assured her it was alright as I did know him. Anyway,' going on, more quickly now, aware that it was almost four and time for them to leave, she offered to make a coffee for him and when she came back into the lounge, he was holding the picture - '

'- *the* picture, I presume?'

'- yes; *the* picture. He said he wanted to take a closer look as he'd always liked it. She felt, I think, that she had to tell me that, especially as she had noticed he wasn't looking at the picture at all, but at the back of the frame.'

'Good God!'

'She said he'd left quickly once he'd put it back and made the excuse he had to return to London. He didn't even finish his coffee; I think she was quite offended by that.'

'Phew! I don't know what to say; obviously he didn't want to see you, especially with Mrs Green being within earshot. He must have got a shock when he discovered the disc wasn't where he left it, no doubt assuming someone had got there before him.'

'This Clive Robinson guy?'

'Yes, exactly; you know what they say: it takes a crook to catch a crook! But when you come to think about it, there is a certain twisted irony in this; Clive Robinson, if it had been him, will believe Tom has retrieved his disc while Tom will believe he has it.'

***

Adam's house was one of six elegant Georgian town-houses in

Madison Terrace; a two-storey building with high sash windows, a short flight of steps leading directly up from the pavement to the front door. A clock in the hall was striking four as Jack leaned over to press the bell and almost immediately the door opened.

'Jack, my boy, how splendid to see you again;' Adam Brookfield, a square-shaped man with white bushy eyebrows and thinning white hair, a pair of rimless spectacles suspended from a slim gold chain round his neck, greeted him, shaking his hand vigorously, 'and you must be Claire.' turning to her and smiling expansively, 'Do come in.' gesturing them inside.

They followed him across the hall; wood panelling, parquet flooring, a Chinese fringed rug in the centre of which there was a low mahogany table, the polished surface reflecting an arrangement of scarlet and yellow roses and as a perfect backdrop, a sweeping staircase with shining brass banisters. With a flourish, he flung open a door on the right-hand side.

'Jack will tell you, Claire,' he said, 'that this room has always been my special domain. You remember, don't you, Jack,' he turned to him, 'when you and your parents were visiting us, how you children had strict instructions not to disturb me if you found the door closed?'

'I certainly do;' Jack grinned, 'we kids were very much in awe of you, even your own children.'

'I suppose they were,' he laughed, 'must have lost the knack though; my grandchildren are definitely not in any awe!'

Looking round the room, Claire could well understand why he regarded it as his own private domain: books lined the walls, so many of them, several leather-bound and much-faded, more were piled on one side of a massive oak desk, alongside his computer, the blue light of the monitor flickering silently, the window at the far end of the study looked out on to a walled garden, climbing wisteria, a riot of blue and purple, covering the brickwork, and edging the narrow path down to a wooden bench at the bottom of the garden, rose bushes, their branches heavy with blossom.

Once they were seated, Claire took the disc from her bag and handed it across the desk to him.

'Ah, yes;' he said, taking it from her, 'Jack told me on the phone where you both found it. Extraordinary, but I'll just run through it, shall I?'

'Please, I would be grateful if you would, Mr Brookfield -'

'Call me Adam, Claire,' he smiled, 'and I can well imagine how you must have felt realising that someone had taken it upon themselves to use your property to hide what must, at least to him, be of some importance.'

'Annoyed, actually.'

'And I would have felt the same.' inserting the disc into the hard disc. Nobody said anything during the time it took him to scroll down and run through to the end, and although she hadn't made any attempt to print it out, she reckoned it wouldn't have covered more than two sheets of A4 paper. She watched him as he worked and noticing, it must have been half-way through the text, when he frowned and looked as though he was going to say something, but perhaps changing his mind, his expression more thoughtful now, he continued to the end. All the time, she was conscious of Jack's presence beside her, the soft fabric of his shirt brushing lightly against her arm; a gentle breeze, as soft as a caress, from the open window was, apart from when Adam moved the cursor, the only other movement in the room. Anxious now for him to finish and to say something. Anything. She had no idea of what to expect; she hadn't fully realised until this moment just how much the sheer furtiveness of Tom's actions had affected her. As though sensing her unease, Jack smiled reassuringly at her.

'Well,' Adam said, pushing his laptop to one side, 'I believe you were both right to be concerned.'

'It's a scheme, isn't it, Adam,' Jack asked, 'something to do with inside dealing, but way above my head, I'm afraid.'

'I believe you're right, it sounds very much as though it is a scheme someone has devised and normally I may have been inclined not to put too much importance on it, but I don't think this can be dismissed so lightly.'

'Why do you say that?' Claire asked, out of her depth, but it didn't prevent her experiencing a feeling of foreboding, although if asked to explain, knew she would be unable to do so. Her forte was to write books; when it came to figures, while she managed to cope with her own financial affairs, anything of a more complicated nature was bordering on the incomprehensible to her.

'Because, Claire,' he answered slowly, placing his hands palm-down on the desk in front of him, 'of one of the names mentioned on the disc, which was towards the end, where a note had been inserted of a meeting which was going to take place to discuss the Clarkson case. You may remember?'

'Yes, I do.' she nodded.

'It is possible I may be wrong and it isn't the same Clarkson I knew, but given what I learned only the other day, I firmly believe we should try to find out. I'll explain,' he went on, smiling at them both apologetically, 'without boring you to tears, but last week I attended the funeral of a very old friend of mine; he was called Henry Clarkson. After the service, and when we were having lunch, Henry's son pulled me to one side. Gary is a few years older than you, Jack,' he went on and I've known him since he was a child. Why I'm mentioning this is because I know without a shadow of a doubt that what he told me was not out of any avarice, or resentment. He is wealthy in his own right and has done well within the banking profession; he also has a strong sense of, shall we say, fair play, and when he'd been going through his father's papers and documents, he discovered that for several years a considerable amount of money had been systematically siphoned from his investments, most of which had been handled by the merchant bank he had been with since he was a young man. Gary had been concerned about his father's health for some time and although he had offered to help him with any paperwork he didn't feel up to dealing with, Henry had adamantly refused, insisting he was perfectly capable of handling this himself, but sadly, it would appear that he wasn't as meticulous as he might have been and this could have accounted for someone – and he or she must be with the bank – to take advantage of the fact he never raised any queries regarding his investments.'

'That's dreadful, Adam.'

'I know, Jack, but regrettably, this is not an isolated case; there have been rumours circulating for some months which indicate that more and more investors are, not to put too fine a point on it, being fleeced.'

'Adam,' Claire said quietly, almost afraid to ask the question, 'would you mind telling us the name of the bank your friend was with?'

'The WHL Group in Regent Street, Claire.' he told her.

'That's where Tom works.'

'And you're sure he was the one who concealed the disc?'

'There couldn't have been anyone else; it's just not possible. It was Tom alright.'

'You've nothing to worry about, Claire.' Jack said, deep concern in his eyes.

'I know,' she sighed, 'but I can't help feeling the way I do. Do you know, Adam, I feel so terribly angry with him for involving me in this deceitful way.'

'Your reactions are understandable, my dear,' Adam said, 'and Jack's right, you really have nothing to worry about. With both your agreement, I would like to have a talk with someone I know in Scotland Yard, this will be a private talk, you understand, but I suggest we pass the matter over to the authorities. What do you say?'

'Of course,' Claire nodded without any hesitation, 'I think we should.'

'Jack?'

'I agree with Claire.'

'That's fine; I'll have a word with Gary first; I'm sure he'll think the same, and if you can give me Tom's full name, Claire, that should be sufficient.'

'It's Jackson.' and going on to tell him about Tom's visit earlier in the day and how her cleaning lady had seen him with the picture where the disc had been hidden. She also mentioned about someone breaking into the cottage when she was out the night before and as she did, noticed how his expression changed from his previous calm manner to one of concern.

'Incidentally,' Claire put in quickly, 'I believe I might know the man's name.'

'Do you really?'

'Yes, I was having a coffee with a friend this morning and she was telling me how she bumped into someone in Upper Nettles she hadn't seen for years and that he had been asking in the town if anyone knew where I was living now. He was called Clive Robinson,' she added, 'Jack and I wondered if it could be the same Robinson as the one on the disc.'

'My word; you could be right. Robinson & Waterman,' he said without having to check the screen.'

'You've heard of them, Adam?' Jack asked.

'Yes, I have, Jack; they're a firm of Financial Investment Consultants and have been in existence for some considerable time, must be at least fifteen years; their offices are in the West End, not sure exactly where; they are what is termed as hedge fund managers. I don't know whether you know anything about them.'

'Afraid not, only that I understand they probably have more flexibility than the banks.'

'Yes, that's true,' he agreed, 'basically a hedge fund is an investment fund which pools capital from a limited number of accredited individuals or institutional investors, and invests in a variety of assets, often with complex portfolio construction and risk management techniques, which is, I might add, only available to investors with significant assets.'

'Sounds complicated.' Claire smiled, finding it difficult to follow him.

'It can be very complex indeed.' he agreed, 'and of course not without a certain amount of risk, but then that's what they're trained to do.'

'What do you think, Adam;' Jack asked him, 'could there be another attempt, although of course I know you can't possibly answer that, but I'm worried about Claire -'

'- please, Jack,' she placed a hand on his arm, 'there's no need to be; nobody is going to harm me.'

'As you say, Jack, I don't know whether there'll be another attempt, I would say it was unlikely and whoever it was probably doesn't want to risk being seen again in the neighbourhood, especially in such a small town as Upper Nettles. I will, of course, mention both incidents when I speak to David Armstrong at Scotland Yard and see what he has to say.'

Chapter Ten

The body of Jamie Green was brought back to Upper Nettles and taken to the police mortuary, followed about fifteen minutes later by a grim-faced Peter Gale. He had been able to identify the car as having once belonged to Glenda Nicholson. The forensic team, predictably, had been unable to conduct anything approaching a normal inspection, and because of the lapse of time since the vehicle must have been, while not fully immersed, subjected to the intake of a considerable amount of water, they would have to wait at least another twelve hours or so, until the mechanic was able to carry out an inspection to verify perhaps how the car came to end up in the relatively shallow water of the creek. The fact that Jamie Green had been in the driving seat didn't necessarily mean he had been driving the car. At this stage of the proceedings there was no clear evidence to support it was anything else but an accident, either mechanical or otherwise, although until a full post mortem had taken place and they were informed of how Jamie Green had died, including an estimated time of death, they could not say with any authority that foul play was suspected, but given what had transpired so far in their investigation into the murder of Glenda Nicholson, it was becoming clear that both the murder and Jamie Green's death were linked, not only by his bike being found so close to the body of Glenda Nicholson and the corresponding timing of the events on that Saturday night, but by the fact that a silk scarf had been found by forensic in one of the pockets of Jamie Green's denim jacket, although they wouldn't know for certain whether this had been used by the assailant until the fabric was compared with the shreds of silk removed from one of the earrings worn by the victim.

Before leaving Lymington, Peter had called into the Post Office and collected the registered package. The sender, he noticed, had neglected to put his address on the reverse, nor was there any note clipped to the thick bundle of American dollar bills and apart from the Bournemouth post mark that was all they had to give them any hint of whether this package had any connection with Glenda Nicholson's murder. It looked very much as if they had come up against a dead end as far as this latest development, yet another reminder they knew very little about her despite the fairly informative background profile the office had provided; he was rapidly coming round to Richard's view that they should be looking more closely into the woman's past, rather than concentrating too much on the actual night of her murder.

He was on the point of going along to Richard's office to find out whether he'd returned from Johnnie Wall's place, when Joanne, Richard's secretary buzzed through to say they'd been able to locate Bernie Croft's address.

'He's living in Bournemouth, Peter,' she said, 'and I've got the number if you want to phone him.'

'Thanks, Joanne, I'll do that right away; is the Chief Inspector back yet?' he added.

'He came in about five minutes ago.'

He dialled the number Joanne had given him, letting it ring for a few seconds and was about to replace the receiver when he heard a click, followed by the metallic voice, presumably Bernie Croft's, informing him that if he would like to leave his name and number he would phone him back as soon as possible. Reluctant though he was to leave a message, having a dislike for the impersonal and one-sided conversation of the answering machine, he briefly introduced himself saying he would like to talk to him in respect to a friend of his, namely Glenda Nicholson.

The call he made to the number Knights of Knightsbridge had given him yesterday had been equally as frustrating as when he'd been told by a grim-sounding housekeeper that Mr and Mrs Thornton were abroad and wouldn't be back until Monday; he'd left a message with her, but wasn't altogether confident she would pass it on to her employers, meaning he may have no option but to go there himself, which might not be such a bad idea as he could possibly see Bernie Croft at the same time. Bournemouth. Should he be reading something into the fact that both the Thorntons and Bernie Croft lived in the same town? The registered package had been mailed from there. Not too far-fetched to consider that this had been done by one of them, he concluded and taking the package with him went along to Richard's office.

'Ah, Peter, I was just going to call you; were we right about the car having belonged to Glenda Nicholson?'

'Yes, we were, and you won't be surprised to hear that the dead man was Jamie Green, sir.'

'I already knew about him,' Richard said, 'Joanne told me; he was a local lad as you know, Peter, and it didn't take long for the news to reach the town.'

'Upper Nettles' grapevine as efficient as ever, but I did anticipate that happening, so I phoned back here from Lymington and arranged with Sergeant Grainger to get in touch with Mrs Green.'

'Poor woman.'

'I know, but I rather suspect she would have been fearing the worst, but it will still be a shock to her.'

'I see you've picked up the registered package while you were there, Peter.'

'I haven't counted the notes,' Peter told him, passing the package over to him, 'but there are a lot of them; unfortunately, there's nothing to tell us who sent them.'

'A pity.' turning the package over as he'd done earlier, 'presumably Glenda Nicholson would have known; but it is somewhat unorthodox all the same. I see there's a Bournemouth postmark, so why didn't the person simply deliver it to her personally?'

'Perhaps he or she wanted to remain anonymous, not wanting to be seen by anyone.' he suggested.

'Or,' Richard said thoughtfully, 'he did try to and was for some reason or other prevented.'

'It could have been this Thornton guy.'

'The one who turned up at her house on the Sunday; he does live in Bournemouth.'

'So does Bernie Croft, sir. I haven't mentioned yet, but Joanne gave me his address a few moments ago; I've tried to ring him,' he added, 'but had to leave a message on his answering machine.'

'This case is certainly not a straightforward one, is it?' Richard commented dryly, 'Here we have a wodge of bank notes, American dollars at that, being sent to a woman who had already been dead for twenty-hours. It does suggest something though, Peter.'

'Yes?'

'Whoever sent this money couldn't have known she was dead which would immediately indicate he couldn't have been her killer.'

'It would rule out one of the possible suspects.' Peter agreed.

Richard went on to explain how his meeting went with Johnnie Wall and the few words exchanged with Gerry Steele.

'Whether Johnnie Wall is guilty or not, Peter,' he concluded, 'he was lying and what we have to do is try to discover why.'

'About him saying he hadn't known Glenda Nicholson?'

'Yes, there was that, but it was when his so-called assistant, Gerry Steele, insisted they'd had no visitors that night. We believe they did, Peter. Who else but Johnnie Wall and Gerry Steele would have been outside Claire Walter's house; even if it hadn't been those two and it had been a couple of the other group members, it would still prove they'd been lying. There was something else I noticed; as soon as I mentioned Bernie Croft's name, his attitude changed which I would describe as nervousness, or if not as strong as that, certainly apprehension.'

'It's relating to the past again, isn't it, sir?'

'Yes, I think so; I asked Joanne to do her best to get as much as she could on Johnnie Wall, and if possible, those other members of the group.'

As Peter was leaving the office, one of the telephones on Richard's desk rang.

'Alright, Joanne,' Richard said, 'it's Bernie Croft, Peter; do you want to take it in your own office or in here.'

'In here, sir; if that's alright.' Peter said, taking the receiver from him and sitting down again.

'Mr Croft,' Peter said, as soon as Joanne put the call through, 'thank you for getting back to us so quickly.'

'That's alright, Inspector; you mentioned Glenda's name.'

It wasn't a question, neither was there the slightest hint of any surprise in his voice at being asked to return the call from a member of the constabulary. In other words, the man was giving nothing away. A cool customer, Peter decided, but two could play that game.

'We are conducting an enquiry into the murder of Glenda Nicholson, sir,' pausing just long enough for him to interrupt, either to say he knew of her death, or a reaction conveying shock at hearing of her demise, 'it is our understanding she was a friend of yours and we hoped you would be able to help us in filling in parts of her background, in particular, before she moved here from London, which are at the moment somewhat sketchy.'

'I'll try of course, but I don't think I'll be able to tell you much.'

'That remains to be seen, sir,' keeping his tone matter of fact, 'however, to do this we have to meet, preferably as soon as possible.'

'Of course.' a man of few words.

'Would tomorrow be possible; if you prefer, I could see you in Bournemouth.'

'That won't be necessary, Inspector Gale; I can easily drive to Upper Nettles.'

A time was agreed for the following morning at ten-thirty and Peter, without saying anything further, brought the call to a close.

'I take it he wasn't too forthcoming.' Richard smiled ruefully.

'Not the easiest person to talk to, sir.'

'I realise to a certain extent we are going in blind here,' Richard said, 'in knowing next to nothing about him, apart from him having been with the rock group and had known Glenda Nicholson. Has it occurred to you, Peter,' he added thoughtfully, 'that this enquiry keeps returning to the group?'

As if on cue, Joanne brought in the information Richard had asked for in respect of Johnnie Wall.

'Thanks, Joanne,' he said, taking the printed sheet from her, 'that didn't take you long.'

'I'm still working on the backgrounds of Gerry Steele and the other members of the group,' she told him, 'but I've listed their names at the bottom of the sheet and with the exception of Spike Harris, their guitarist, who replaced Bernie Croft in 2001, they've been with "The Bandanas" since they were formed in 1979.'

'That would tie in with what Glenda Nicholson's neighbour told me yesterday.' Peter said when Richard finished reading the report and had passed it over to him.

'And the question remaining; why did he break away from them. If I remember correctly they were doing well around then and had started to make a big name for themselves in Europe.'

'And coincidentally,' Peter remarked, looking at the report, 'that was the same year he began his prison sentence in Germany.'

'2001;' Richard said thoughtfully, 'that was also the same year Wade-Brown divorced Glenda Nicholson. There could be some relevance in all of that, Peter.'

'It's going to be interesting to hear what Bernie Croft is going to tell us.'

'*If* he decides to tell us.' Richard emphasised.

'There's something else, sir,' Peter said, looking up from the report, 'I see that Johnnie Wall was once married to Sylvia Crossman.'

'I noticed that, but the name didn't mean anything to me.'

'Sylvia Crossman, if in fact it's the same woman, lives in Upper Nettles; she's a regular customer in "The Hunters' Arms".'

'Is she now?'

'According to this,' lightly tapping the report, 'the marriage didn't last long, only a couple of years.'

'Neither did his next one,' Richard commented dryly, 'I wonder where she fitted in, although I see the poor woman committed suicide, 1994 wasn't it, Peter?'

'That's right,' checking the report again, 'Penelope Driver she was called, I wonder what went wrong, perhaps it had something to do with the affair he was having with Glenda Nicholson; that's something Bernie Croft may be able to tell me, but returning to Sylvia Crossman, sir, it's likely she would have known Bernie Croft; she could be a useful source for information about the whole set-up.

'The snag is, Peter,' he reminded him, 'from what we've gleaned up to now, she was probably off the scene shortly after she divorced Johnnie Wall.'

'Have you any particular reason, sir, for believing Glenda's murder has some connection with what may have occurred all those years ago?'

'Nothing specific, Peter, except for the fact we still don't have a motive. Here we have a particularly violent death, the circumstances leading up to her murder indicate that it wasn't premeditated, but having said that, there is something else which is concerning me.'

'You mean this money having been mailed to her?'

'Yes, also the man she met earlier on Saturday.'

'Apart from his surname, that's about all we do know about him, sir.'

'True, although the description they gave you at the hotel, plus the type of car he was driving, shouldn't be discounted. With continual probing we might be able to find him. However,' he continued, 'in respect to this cash transaction; I don't believe we should necessarily be treating it as being connected to her murder.'

'Two separate incidents.'

'Yes; it doesn't make sense otherwise. If we're right, and she was involved in something which could be illegal, or at the most, irregular, why would she have met her death in the way she did? After all, there's no law in sending bank notes to someone, although we have to admit the source of those notes could be considered questionable, but I still think this is a separate matter, Peter and could in the end have to be treated separately. Going back to Johnnie Wall, and incidentally those connected with him, and although up to now I've only spoken to him and Gerry Steele, there still remains the other three members and of course Bernie Croft. There seems no doubt that both Johnnie Wall and his assistant were lying, that in itself is suspicious; it now remains to be seen whether any of the others will also be lying.'

'And now we have the second victim.'

'Yes, Jamie Green, but you know, Peter, I'm inclined to keep an open mind for the moment, in not assuming the same person murdered Glenda Nicholson and Jamie Green, although in his case, we need the pathologist's report to substantiate that he was in fact murdered.'

'That hadn't occurred to me.'

'It may turn out not to be as unlikely as it sounds. If it had been Jamie Claire Walters had seen, he would have also noticed those people out on the road and even if he hadn't been close enough to have made out who they were, he may have heard them. If that had been the case, he could have either continued to cycle on home, or, being curious, had stopped to find out more. Unless there was someone else out there that night, we can only conjecture, we'll never know for certain, but we've also got to remember his bike was found close to where the killer had made an attempt to conceal Glenda Nicholson's body.'

'We've only got Johnnie Wall's word for it that there were just the two of them, sir; apart from asking Bernie Croft what he was doing that night, it might be a good idea to find out how the other three members of the group spent the weekend. I believe Pete Carr, that's their saxophonist, spends a fair bit of time here, but I don't know about Eddie Gallagher and Spike Harris.'

'I think you're right; I'll have another word with Claire Walters. I only spoke to her about the Saturday night, I didn't think to mention the following morning. She may have seen something of her neighbours, perhaps noticed if there had been another car parked outside, apart from the one I saw this morning, which presumably belongs to Johnnie Wall; I wouldn't have thought Gerry Steele could afford to own such an expensive model.'

***

Since Saturday night, his brain had been in a constant turmoil; a conflicting mixture of indecision, social consciousness and self-interest which, on receiving the message on his answering machine from Inspector Gale, immediately intensified. Mentally, and regardless of what he'd seen, he had refused to believe that Glenda had been murdered, even when earlier in the day he'd read about it in one of the nationals, he had continued to blot it out from his mind.

Bernie had known of Glenda Nicholson from way back. He supposed she could have been described as a music groupie; at any gig where they were playing she would always be there, mixing with the usual crowd, but it had been a few years later before she met Johnnie. She'd been married to Ted Warren by that time and he could still remember how Johnnie had described her to him. He and Pete had been in Ted's nightclub that night and apparently, she had been in there; ironically it had been Ted who'd introduced her to them; Bernie didn't think he'd really noticed her before then, to him she'd just been one of the many hangers-on, but whether Ted ever knew about their affair, Bernie had no idea. It must have been about a year before Penelope died and when Ted had been killed in the night club brawl, Bernie had fully expected them to get together, Penelope or no Penelope, but surprisingly, although he knew they were still seeing each other, none of that changed, not even after Penelope's suicide. As far as he knew Johnnie had never married again; just as well, he thought cynically, Johnnie lacked any staying power.

He hadn't expected to see Glenda again, although someone, he thought it may have been Eddie Gallagher who'd kept in touch with him after he left, told him that Glenda had continued seeing Johnnie even after she married Nick Wade-Brown, although probably because he hadn't been as long-suffering as Ted, actually divorced her after a couple of years, citing Johnnie. Not that Johnnie was all that bothered as around that time he was serving his prison sentence in Germany. But, then, in a somewhat circuitous way, not long after he'd moved to Bournemouth and had made friends with Greg and Lilian Thornton, it turned out that Glenda and Lilian had been in partnership for some years before she married Greg and then, he reckoned, it was only inevitable that, especially when Lilian told him Glenda was living in the New Forest, they should see each other.

Neither of them had mentioned marriage, or even moving in together. He had wanted to marry her but had always held back; possibly realising she wouldn't have been interested. Theirs had been a good relationship, easy-going, neither making any demands on the other. He had hoped they would have a future together, but again he'd been reluctant to broach the subject. Of course he knew why, deep down he knew; he didn't trust her. It was as simple as that. Although she had insisted she had stopped seeing Johnnie years ago, as much as he had wanted to believe her, he recognised that if he did he would have been fooling himself. Johnnie and Glenda had been two of a kind; basically selfish, inconsistent, money-orientated; he had loved her, but seeing her car outside Johnnie's house on Saturday night had destroyed everything he had felt for her.

They hadn't made any arrangements for seeing each other that night; he had phoned her earlier in the week and she told him she wanted to spend Sunday at the new health spa in Bournemouth, but she would call in on her way back to Lyndhurst and have a drink with him. Of course she didn't turn up, but it still hadn't prevented him from expecting her to come. She would never know that he had, on the spur of the moment on Saturday evening, decided to call and see her. He knew she would be working and allowed her plenty of time to get home before setting off for Lyndhurst. He had been inordinately disappointed not to see her car outside, but deciding she must have been delayed, drove back into the town, pulling up outside "The Mailmans' Arms", a pub they'd been in many times during the past twelve months; not expecting to see her in there, but thinking he could phone her from there and possibly have a drink while he waited for her to get back. He'd dialled her number, wondering why he hadn't done this before leaving Bournemouth, but he'd wanted to surprise her. The line was engaged, but when he tried it again a couple of minutes later, he couldn't get through; for some reason she must have switched off the mobile. On reflection, and some hours later, he realised he should have left it at that and finished his beer and made his way back to Bournemouth, but the more he puzzled over why she would have switched her phone off, the more he was beginning to read something more significant into what was for Glenda an unusual action. Johnnie Wall. She was with Johnnie. As he sat there, at the end of the bar, surrounded by a large crowd of Saturday night customers, he became more and more certain that she'd gone there. She had driven to Johnnie's house after she'd closed the salon. That's where she was.

It was getting late by the time he finally left Lyndhurst, having ordered another drink to give him time, time to think, to work out what he would do if he was proved right, and it was around eleven when he drove through Upper Nettles, but before reaching the house where he knew Johnnie lived, he stopped the car and made a further attempt to call her. The line remained dead. Nothing. His resolve strengthening, he switched on the engine and continued along the road; driving slowly, he'd passed the open gates to the house and looked up the drive. Glenda's car had been there, clearly illuminated from the open French windows. He had driven on for a short distance, pulling on to a grassy area by the side of the road and walked back to the house. Before he reached there, he heard voices, raised voices, and not knowing why, he stepped off the road and on to the grass verge, keeping close to the hedge and stopping only a few feet away from where they were coming from; then, he saw them: Johnnie and Glenda, in the middle of the road. He appeared to have dragged her away from the cottage on the other side of the road and was telling her to calm down; he couldn't hear much of what she was saying, only to let go of her wrist, but he ignored her protests and continued to haul her over towards the open gate. Somebody else was there, standing in the driveway, recognising the burly figure of Gerry Steele and before he had time to take in what was happening, Gerry had grabbed Glenda's other arm and between them they took her back up the drive to the house. He could have stopped them at that point. He could have called out. But he didn't; instead he watched, by now coming closer, until the three of them went inside, not by the front door but by the French window.

He waited until they were inside before walking up the drive, once again keeping to the grass until he reached the bushes outside the window. As he did so, common sense was telling him to go back, return to his car and drive home. And now, almost a week later, he remained uncertain why he hadn't. Perhaps he did have some idea of intervening, but he was still seething at the way she had deceived him. Why should he help her? She had obviously chosen to be with Johnnie, not him. So why had he remained there, like some sad wimp, incapable or unwilling, to either step back or go forward and make his appearance known to them?

***

Keith Armstrong, a senior officer at New Scotland Yard, did not like coincidences. Not only didn't he like them, but he didn't trust them; all too often, as he had discovered, they had an insidious way of overriding the logical process of thought, misleading and in the end time-wasting, but when he heard the name of a virtually unknown village mentioned twice within a matter of hours, he had to, albeit reluctantly, admit this could be described as one. He was later than usual returning home on Friday evening, although just in time to catch the nine o'clock news. Upper Nettles, positioned between Lyndhurst and Lymington, flashed up on to the screen; the newsreader, accompanied by her usual expression of professional indifference, was walking towards the cameras, her high-heels stumbling slightly on the uneven cobbles of the pavement, coming to a standstill outside what appeared, judging by the ancient sign suspended some feet above her head, to be the local inn, instantly confirmed by the handful of customers huddled in the open doorway, all of them clutching pint tankards of ale.

'The grim discovery earlier today of the body of a young local man has stunned the residents of this small New Forest town, especially,' she continued, 'following so soon after the murder of Glenda Nicholson, the owner of the hairdressing salon further along the street from where I'm standing. The victim has been named as Jamie Green, aged twenty-two. I have been unable to talk to his mother as, understandably, she was too distressed, but it would seem when her son didn't return home on Saturday night she had reported this to the police. Chief Inspector Richard Cavendish of the Upper Nettles police force was unavailable for comment but the general consensus of opinion among the people I spoke to this afternoon was that they believe the two tragedies are connected in some way although whether they are correct in their assumption remains to be verified by the authorities. …..'

Keith turned down the volume; he'd heard enough; he wasn't going to learn anything further from the newsreader, it being quite plain to him she was using padding tactics to fill out her report, making a half-hearted attempt to feed any viewer's appetite who was sufficiently interested in what was happening in a part of the country of which they had little or no knowledge, or even interest. An insular attitude, he sighed wearily, but only one which was endemic among his fellow men, opening the fridge door and taking out a can of beer.

He'd eat later, he decided, pulling out one of the kitchen chairs and sitting down. He wanted to mull over what Adam Brookfield had told him earlier. He took a deep gulp of the ice-cold beer before looking at the scribbled notes he'd made during the long conversation he'd had with him. He'd known Adam for several years and although he was a good ten or twelve years older, they had always had a good rapport; the older man had a keen brain and he respected his judgement, wondering what his reaction must have been when he heard tonight's news.

The gist of what Adam had told him was sufficient to give him more ammunition to fill in some of the gaps in an ongoing case they'd been involved in for some weeks now on their growing concern of what could turn out to be a massive case of fraud within the confines of insider dealing in that genuine investors' funds were being systematically siphoned off by either individual dealers or, as they were becoming to believe, by an organised consortium. Up to now, they hadn't been successful in coming up with any positive trail or link, or with actual names, apart from those investors who had discovered discrepancies in their accounts, but it could be that at last they may be making a breakthrough.

Bringing his briefcase over towards him from where he'd left it by the hall table, he took out his pad, turning to a clean sheet and began to jot down a few relevant points. First, the computer disc; Adam had promised to drop it into the Yard first thing in the morning. From what he was saying there were a number of names listed, he'd get someone to sift their way through those, then there was the management firm, Robinson & Waterman. It shouldn't be too difficult to get them sussed out, and then this chap, Tom Jackson, who had apparently put the disc together and had for reasons best known to himself decided to conceal it the way he had. Adam had said he worked for the WHL Group in Regent Street, making a note to arrange to see them, hopefully tomorrow, although being a Saturday it might not be easy. But then, Keith thought cynically, finishing off his beer, they probably wouldn't be too keen to talk about one of their employees, but too bad; if it transpired that this Tom Jackson was involved in something which would ultimately affect them anyway, it would be pointless to be obstructive. Last, but not least, there was the name Robinson cropping up again if Claire Walters was right in her belief that the person who broke into her house had been him. Chances were, Keith decided, that she was right.

There was another call he would make in the morning, too late now, and that was to the Chief Inspector in Upper Nettles, Richard Cavendish. In fact, the idea just occurring to him, it might not be a bad idea to drive down there and see for himself just what this place was like, the scene apparently of two very recent murders and where there could be a link to what he wanted to know about the fraud case.

Chapter Eleven

Bernie arrived punctually at ten-thirty on Saturday morning, the desk sergeant escorting him along the corridor to Inspector Gale's office. He'd had no preconceived ideas of what to expect, only a vague one, mostly gleaned from watching police movies that it would be a stark and clinical sort of place, but he'd been quite wrong. The office he was being shown into was neither, noting the various touches which had been made to make it, if not exactly inviting, reasonably comfortable: cream slatted blinds at the window showing slices of the High Street; a red and green fringed rug in the centre of the wood-block flooring; an occasional table with a copy of the local "Gazette" and in the event he needed to be reminded, Glenda's name in bold print on the front page, and facing the door, a plain pale wood desk, virtually paper-free, a flat-screened monitor at the left-hand side, and at the other, three filing trays labelled simply *In*, *Pending* and *Out;* an A4 spiral notepad, a mini-calculator and a balsa-wood pen and pencil tray with a scrolled inscription somewhat incongruously proclaiming it had been carved in South America.

'Good morning, Mr Croft,' the blond-haired man seated behind the desk greeted him as he stepped into the office, 'I appreciate you taking the trouble to come in, especially at the weekend.' gesturing for him to take one of the seats in front of him.

'No problem, Inspector; it was a pleasant drive.'

'Indeed.' dismissively, he thought, not taken in for a moment by his polite expression, noticing the smile didn't quite reach his eyes. He must be at least in his late thirties, Bernie thought, to have reached the position of inspector, but he appeared younger.

'As I mentioned when I phoned you yesterday we are conducting an enquiry into the murder of Glenda Nicholson and require to learn more about her background; this has meant talking to as many people who knew her, while not necessarily from before the time she came to live here, but in the hope that she may have mentioned to any of these people something about her past.'

'I see, and you think I can help you?'

'We hope so, sir.'

'Well, I'm not sure whether I can. It's true I had known Glenda for a while, but not terribly well. This was in the days before we formed "The Bandanas" - I presume you know I was with them, Inspector?' knowing damn well he would know, but he needed the time to plan out just how much he should tell him, sensing already he wouldn't be satisfied with half-truths or a cobbled together précis of what he actually knew about Glenda. Somehow, he decided, he had to find the middle road and at that precise moment as he sat facing him, he was unsure of where he should start.

'We know about the group, yes and that you were with them until, as we understand it, 2001.'

'That's right.'

'You say you knew the deceased before the group was formed. Where was this?'

'Sorry?' not knowing where he was coming from; what the hell did it matter where he saw Glenda; she'd just been around, but what sort of answer was that?

'What I meant was those times when you saw her, were they arranged meetings, just the two of you, I mean, or were they more public?'

'Oh, I see; I was never alone with her and mostly, although she would be in the clubs where we were playing, very often I never even spoke to her. She wasn't my girlfriend, Inspector.'

'Whose girlfriend was she?'

'Johnnie's.' without thinking the name came out, instantly regretting the admission.

'Johnnie Wall?'

'Yes.' of course he bloody knew that!

'She was married during this time.'

It wasn't a question, he knew that also, realising with a jolt, he would have to tread warily with him. He reminded him of a cat, Bernie thought: watching, waiting and ready to pounce should he make a wrong move.

'Yes, to Ted Warren.'

'And Johnnie Wall was also married.'

'Yes, he was.'

'Although two years later after they'd met, Johnnie's wife committed suicide.'

'This is history, Inspector,' Bernie said, 'and you obviously know all this.'

'We're merely verifying the number of facts we've able to glean, sir.'

'I suppose so.' grudgingly, but not convinced; the cat and mouse game continued.

'Did you know Penelope Driver?'

'Not well; I didn't see her very often, probably because of her career.'

'In what way?'

'She was a professional dancer, Inspector which meant that she and Johnnie would be working unsocial hours and naturally at different venues.'

'That wouldn't be the reason for her committing suicide.'

He had this disarming way of avoiding the actually asking of a question, although the inference strongly suggested he expected his affirmation. Inspector Gale certainly worked in what was in Bernie's jaundiced opinion a convoluted and disconnected way. What the hell could Penelope have to do with what happened to Glenda?

'Apparently,' Bernie supplied grudgingly, 'she was on medication for depression.'

'It's our understanding,' he was continuing, 'that Glenda Nicholson re-married after the death of her first husband, Ted Warren, but it would appear the marriage only lasted a year, the divorce being in 2001. What we would like to know, Mr Croft, is whether she was still continuing her relationship with Johnnie Wall.'

He had been waiting for just such a question, realising that cleverly and manipulatively, the Inspector had been working up to this point; a verbal crossroads had been reached, he had two choices; either he feigned ignorance of what he'd asked, or admit he had been aware Johnnie had continued their affair. Although there was no love lost between Johnnie and himself, Bernie was uncomfortable with the stark reality that if he chose the latter, it would strengthen any possible case they were building up against him. Was he prepared to take the responsibility? But, if he pleaded ignorance he could very well be placing himself in the situation where they would switch their suspicions on to him.

'I think so,' he said slowly, 'but as I'm sure you know, Johnnie was away for two years serving a prison sentence in Germany, therefore I would say it was doubtful he and Glenda would have picked up the threads of their relationship when he returned to England.'

'And of course you were no longer with the group then.'

Another bloody statement; the man was beginning to get on his nerves. Bernie was sure by this time the Inspector was leading up to something, another crucial turning point in this so-called interview, which was sounding more of an interrogation.

'I left in 2001, Inspector.' as you well know, he added under his breath.

'What was your reason?'

'Did I have to have one?' deliberately being obtuse; anything to stall him, to give him some time to think.

'I'm sure you did.'

Cat and mouse game again.

'The reason was quite simple, Inspector; I felt jaded, needed a complete change; Johnnie and I had been working together for over twenty-five years.'

'Have you heard the name, Nicholas Wade-Brown?'

'Yes, he was Glenda's second husband.'

As soon as he uttered the words, he realised he'd made a mistake and the way the Inspector's eyes narrowed he knew his slip-up had been noted, but then, Bernie thought cynically, he was probably expecting just such an answer. He had been too quick for him, mentally kicking himself.

'You would know then, sir, that Nicholas Wade-Brown divorced her one year later, citing Johnnie Wall as co-respondent?'

'I did hear, yes, but I'd already left the scene by that time, so I think someone must have told me; I can't remember who it was.'

'Although you did keep in touch with Miss Nicholson?'

'No, I didn't actually;' he didn't have a choice; it was obvious they must have found out somehow that he had been seen with her, probably one of her nosy neighbours, 'we met up quite by chance about a couple of years ago through mutual friends.'

'Mr & Mrs Thornton?'

This time it was a question, which only went to prove he didn't know for certain; he was guessing, but once again he had no choice; he'd been placed in the proverbial corner.

'Yes, that's right, Lilian and Gregory Thornton.'

'When did you last see Miss Nicholson, sir?'

Here it comes, sighing with the sheer inevitability of it all. This wasn't merely the mouse in a trap, but a rabbit in a snare!

'A week past Saturday, a week before she was killed.' he added unnecessarily.

'Did you see her most weekends?'

'Usually, yes.'

'But not last weekend?'

'No, not last weekend; she told me she wanted to spend some time at Bournemouth's new Health Spa on the Sunday, but that she'd call in for a drink before going back home in the evening.'

'Were you concerned when she didn't arrive?'

'I wouldn't say concerned, but I suppose I just presumed she'd been too tired and had gone straight home.'

'How long have you known Mr & Mrs Thornton?'

'Two or three years.'

'And Miss Nicholson,' he persisted doggedly, 'how long had she known them?'

'I don't really know, but Glenda told me that she and Lilian used to be in partnership together; this was when she had her hairdressing business in London.'

'Was she married to Gregory Thornton then?'

'No, she wasn't; apparently, the business partnership broke up when Lilian married him.'

'I see.'

Well, it was more than he could; he was rapidly losing track of where the conversation was going and to Bernie, it didn't seem to be going anywhere. And why this interest in the Thorntons?

'How did you spend last Saturday evening, Mr Croft?'

Although he'd been expecting it, the way he threw the question in without any preamble, caught him unawares.

'Quietly.'

'Yes?'

'I'd been in London for most of the week and as I hadn't made any plans for the weekend, all I wanted to do was relax over a couple of drinks, nothing special.'

'Did you stay at home or did you go out for a drink?'

'I drove into Lyndhurst and had a drink in "The Mailman's Arms.'

'Why Lyndhurst; rather a long way to drive for a couple of beers?'

'I didn't think so, Inspector; I've lost count of the times I've driven up there from Bournemouth.'

'Did you hope to see Glenda Nicholson that evening?'

'I did, as a matter of fact, but when I tried to phone her, I couldn't get through.'

'As you were already in Lyndhurst, didn't you decide to find out whether she was at home?'

'Why should I have, Inspector? The relationship I had with Glenda was I guess what could be described as a fairly open-ended one, neither of us made any demands on each other, we each had our lives, separate lives, and we never encroached on each other's space.' and that was the best he could do and although only partially true, it might just fob him off. He knew he didn't have to mention he'd been in Lyndhurst that night, he reckoned the odds were high in them not finding out, but the last Bernie wanted to do was place himself in the vulnerable position of having to lie. He knew he had nothing to do with Glenda's death, but he was also prosaic enough to realise that the police would very well think differently; to them, until they were convinced otherwise, he would remain one of their potential suspects.

'Can you remember what time it was when you tried to call her, sir?'

'About nine-thirty, I think.'

'And the line was dead?'

'Not that time; it was engaged and then when I tried again, no more than ten minutes later, she must have either switched her mobile off or the battery could have run out.'

'We knew she had taken a call on her mobile around that time, but as we haven't been able to locate the mobile, we have no way of knowing who had called her.' surprising him by proffering something, rather than the bombardment of questions. 'However,' he went on steadily, his eyes never leaving Bernie's face, 'it is from that moment we lose track of her movements that night although we do have a witness who believes she was within reasonably close vicinity to where her body was found. What we're trying to do, sir, is to re-create as far as possible that time between, shall we say, eleven at night and one o'clock the following morning.'

'I understand what you're saying, Inspector, but as I said at the beginning of this interview, I didn't see how I could be any help.'

'On the contrary,' he emphasised, leaning slightly forward, 'we think it is quite feasible to suggest that you may be able to.'

It was a trap; it had to be. Immediately following on from that thought, he made his decision, based primarily on his inbuilt dislike of being placed in such a position. Why the hell couldn't he come out with what he wanted. Ask him a direct question.

'I'll be interested, Inspector, to know why you should think that, also I'm finding it a trifle difficult to know where you're coming from. Perhaps you could be more explicit.'

'You have told me, Mr Croft,' he carried on talking as if Bernie hadn't spoken, 'that you had hoped to see Miss Nicholson when you drove to Lyndhurst that Saturday, but I am somewhat surprised you didn't follow up on your efforts in trying to get in touch with her. You said you made two attempts to call her and by that I have to assume you did nothing further, a statement which surprised me somewhat; you said you weren't unduly concerned, but weren't you curious?'

'Curious?'

'Yes, sir, curious, didn't you wonder where she could have been or with whom? Also, didn't you wonder why, after hearing the engaged tone on her mobile and within minutes discovering there was no connection, why.'

'Not particularly.'

'I would suggest, given you apparently had an ongoing relationship with Miss Nicholson you would have had a natural interest in her welfare.'

'I didn't consider for one minute there could be anything wrong.'

'Perhaps not, but you knew she'd had a previous affair with Johnnie Wall, wasn't there a smallest element of doubt in your mind that she may still be seeing with him.'

'She assured me she'd finished with him.'

'You say, *assured* you;' he emphasised, 'did you feel you needed that reassurance?'

'Possibly.'

'And you believed her?'

'Of course.'

'Were you aware that Johnnie Wall is living in Upper Nettles and had been for a number of years?'

'I did know, yes.' Again, he could have lied, but he hadn't. There was always the possibility he'd been seen outside Johnnie's place, remembering the vague mention of a witness who 'believed' she'd seen Glenda close to where her body was later found. Reasonably close, the Inspector had said. What did he mean by *reasonably*? Had this witness seen him also? Perhaps this was something else he was ready to fling at him if he'd said he didn't know Johnnie was living at the Grange and he wasn't prepared to take that risk.

'I see.' he nodded.

And that was all he said, nothing else. Either he had suspicions about Johnnie being involved or it was his devious way of accusing him; suggesting that he'd been so consumed with the conviction that she had gone to Johnnie's that night, that he'd driven to The Grange, seen her there with him and in a jealous rage, had strangled her, hiding her body half a mile up the road. Was that the line he was taking?

***

Richard had been in his office reading through the pathologist's report on Jamie Green's death, including the report from Forensic on the silk scarf, when Joanne put through the call from New Scotland Yard. Keith Armstrong hadn't wasted any time in introducing himself and explaining that the reason why he wanted to meet him was to discuss certain developments in the financial fraud case they were currently investigating. He hadn't gone into any detail over the phone, only to say there could possibly be some link-up with recent events in Upper Nettles. Intrigued, Richard had been quick to agree, Keith saying he should be with him by midday.

The way Richard was feeling, once they'd brought the call to a close, was one of inevitability in that there was considerably more to the murder of Glenda Nicholson and to a lesser degree, Jamie Green's death. Perhaps they had been wrong in treating the appearance of a particularly large sum of cash as a separate issue. Bournemouth head post office hadn't been able to tell him a great deal when he'd phoned them. Apparently, the sender hadn't included his or her address, only a surname. How many Bennets were living in the Bournemouth area, he wondered cynically. There had been no initials even, therefore not much to go on. For the moment they were stymied; it wasn't as though he had entertained any hope that it would have been either Thornton or Croft, but all the same he couldn't help feeling disappointed. This murder enquiry is resembling one big rollercoaster; just as a breakthrough was made, almost immediately they were transported back down again almost from where they started, but then, he thought philosophically, that's what this job is all about; one long challenge and invariably with the strong conviction that they would reach a satisfactory conclusion, but it took time. A fact of which he was constantly being made aware by the background presence of Brian Burrows. Richard reckoned he had until Tuesday at the latest before he could expect another summons to his supervisor's office.

He glanced down at the report, under-lining the salient points: the time of death, which had been estimated at between midnight and two the following morning, and equally important, how Jamie Green had died.

The post mortem had revealed no internal injury and although there was bruising at the back of the skull, it had been established this had not been fatal, the cause of death being by drowning. Whether Jamie Green would have known how to drive had yet to be checked. How he gained access to the vehicle could only be conjecture at this stage, but Richard considered it feasible, given Claire Walter's evidence, it had been Jamie she'd seen cycling back to Upper Nettles from Brockenhurst and had witnessed what had been going on in the road in front of him, his curiosity getting the better of him, he'd held back, perhaps until Glenda Nicholson's car left the Grange, before carrying on. The distance from the Grange to where her body had been found was well under a mile and by the time Jamie would have reached the car, which presumably by then would have been at a standstill during the time it would have taken for the driver to conceal the body, he couldn't have failed to see the vehicle. With Nettles Hollow being a few yards off from the road and where it would have been impossible to drive, he may, assuming there would be no-one around at that time of night, have left the car door open, even to leaving the key in the ignition, while he walked over to the make-shift grave, and either Jamie had taken advantage of the situation, driven, not into Upper Nettles, but back the other way, beyond Brockenhurst to Lymington or, and probably more feasible, the driver of Glenda Nicholson's car spotted him, rendered him unconscious by a blow to the back of the head, hence the bruising, and bundling him into the car, proceeded to Lymington to dispose of both the car and Jamie Green.

Forensic had completed their examination of the scarf and this proved beyond any doubt by the comparison of the threads of silk found on the body, to have been used to strangle her. It may never be possible to learn how the scarf came to be in Jamie Green's pocket; either by finding it in the car he'd pushed into his jacket pocket or this had been done by the person who'd brought Glenda Nicholson's body to Nettles Hollow. They were still in the same position, Richard concluded, placing the reports in the file, of not knowing whether they had one murder or two to solve, although it didn't alter the fact that even if Jamie's death turned out to have been an accident it remained a crucial part of their investigation.

He would have time to drive along to Tulip Cottage and have another word with Claire Walters before Keith Armstrong turned up. He hadn't given her a call, working on the premise he didn't want to alarm her by making the visit sound in the least official. Richard's years of experience dealing with witnesses had taught him that most people had an inbuilt wariness towards officialdom of any kind and making appointments beforehand invariably worried them. He had often wondered about this, having come to the conclusion it was probably quite normal and if he hadn't been in the force, probably he would have felt the same.

He parked outside Tulip Cottage and walked up the path to the front door. Although surprised to see him again, she assured him she didn't mind and as soon as he'd followed her through the lounge and into the kitchen she offered him a coffee.

'I always have one at this time in the morning, Chief Inspector,' she smiled, pulling out a chair for him, 'it must be a throwback to the days when I was conditioned to office routine.'

'How do you feel making the transition from London?' he asked her, accepting the mug of freshly made coffee.

'I'm not sure,' smiling again, a little ruefully this time, 'but of course it's early days yet. I've only been here for just over a week, but in many respects, it seems much longer.'

'Would you say that the recent events have something to do with that?'

'Possibly.' sitting down opposite to him at the table.

'I don't suppose you are the only person in Upper Nettles to be experiencing a certain unease at the moment, but all I can say, Miss Walters, we are doing our utmost to solve these crimes and this is why people like yourself are invaluable to us in an enquiry of this nature.'

'I realise that, Chief Inspector.' she said, taking a sip of her coffee.

'What I would like you to do is to think back again to last weekend. You've already given me a good description of what you saw on the Saturday night Glenda Nicholson was murdered, but because of the lack of light it was impossible for you to make out the features of either of the three people we're unable to establish whether the woman you saw was the victim or not. You've probably worked out for yourself that for her not to be the same person must be unlikely, but as I'm sure you will agree, this can only be considered as circumstantial evidence; it's really no more than that and it isn't sufficient.'

'I know what you mean; you need proof, something considerably more substantial.'

'How right you are, and conversely,' he went on, 'even if the woman had been Glenda Nicholson we can't assume one of the men you saw with her could have been responsible for her death, therefore my task is to either prove beyond any doubt that either they were responsible for what happened to her or are entirely innocent.'

'Not easy.'

'No, it isn't, but we've got to persist, delve a little deeper and this is why, as I said, witnesses like yourself, Miss Walters, are important to us. You will have heard about the death of the young man, Jamie Green?'

'Yes,' she answered slowly, 'he was my cleaning lady's son. I knew he had been missing for several days before they found his body, it's terribly sad.'

'It is,' he nodded, his expression grim, 'and as the time of death has now been officially confirmed as having been around midnight on the same night Glenda Nicholson was murdered, we are treating both deaths as being connected.' To believe otherwise would be stretching credibility too far.'

'That flickering light I saw,' she said quietly as though the idea had only occurred to her, 'could that have been from a bike, Jamie's bike, I mean?'

'Yes, it must have been; his bike was found abandoned very close to where the killer had attempted to conceal Glenda Nicholson's body.'

'How macabre!'

'A fair description,' he agreed, 'and from that evidence we can safely assume that Jamie had either heard or seen what was going on as he approached along the road, but unfortunately for him, and from here it is no more than conjecture, his curiosity may have got the better of him and, because of where his bike was found, he followed the vehicle which the killer had used to drive to where he disposed of her body. Again, unfortunately for Jamie, being a local lad, he may have recognised Glenda

Nicholson's killer.'

'Poor boy, and he was no more than a boy, wasn't he?'

'Early twenties.'

'So young.' she murmured sadly.

'So, Miss Walters, I intend to work on the premise that there may have been a third witness.'

'Why do you say that? Sorry,' she added apologetically, 'perhaps I shouldn't have asked you that.'

'That's alright,' he smiled, 'you're quite entitled to; let's say that over the last couple of days there have been developments indicating that someone had been in the area around the same time that night and had been trying to get in touch with Miss Nicholson and it would not be unreasonable to assume he may have found out where she had gone. This is only supposition, you understand, but obviously needs to be investigated.'

'I understand what you're saying, but I'm still certain there was no-one else out there.'

'I wasn't meaning someone you saw, but possibly you heard someone. If my theory is right, they would have been driving, possibly past the entrance to the Grange, stopping further up the road and walking back, this could have been at the same time when you saw the couple outside your window, he may have watched and even heard what they were saying and when they left to walk back up the drive, he followed them. Even if he is guilty or not of being responsible for her murder, either way it is unlikely he will admit he was there, to do so would be to compromise his situation when being questioned. But,' he went on, 'if a vehicle, not necessarily his, you understand, had been heard on the road around the time we're talking about, it could weaken his resolve to remain quiet about any visit he may or may not have made.'

'Oh, dear,' she sighed.

'I apologise for lumbering you will all of this.'

'No, I'm interested in what you've been saying and if I can help in any way by thinking back to that night I will, if only for Jamie's sake or I should say his mother's. I feel so sorry for the woman, Chief Inspector, I hardly know her yet, but already I've come to the conclusion she must have had a hard life.'

'Raising a child single-handedly is never easy, I'm sure,' he agreed.

'I've been thinking again about that night,' she said, taking her time as she remembered, 'but I'd actually forgotten about this until now; when I returned to bed after I'd seen those people walk up the drive to the house, it took me ages to get back to sleep and it must have been about ten minutes later, I'm not sure exactly, but not much more than that, when a car pulled out from their drive and turned towards the town, this was because the lights were shining through the curtains for a couple of seconds, and then very soon afterwards, only minutes, there was another car which passed going in the same direction.'

'I see,' he said encouragingly; Claire Walters, he decided, was an excellent witness, wishing more people he interviewed could be the same, 'and when you heard the second vehicle, how far away was it before you heard it?'

'Oh,' she said, 'I see what you mean; I should have heard it approaching, shouldn't I? But I didn't, Chief Inspector. I think I may have heard the engine starting up, although I'm not completely sure about that, but certainly it appeared to start from only yards further up the road, the road to Lymington, I mean.' she added.

'This could be what we're looking for.'

'So many cars.' she remarked.

'You're right,' he smiled, 'which brings me to what perhaps I should have asked you on Thursday, but it occurred to me that as the driveway up to the Grange is directly opposite, you may have noticed any cars parked outside over that weekend.'

'Well, as you know I only arrived on the Friday and everything was very new to me, in fact when I was first shown round here, I scarcely noticed the house across the road to me, but once I moved in I began to get my bearings and I can remember there were a couple of cars parked outside the Grange.'

'Were you able to see the makes of them?'

'Yes, a Porsche and I think a BMW, in fact I'm fairly sure it was; the

Porsche was dark red and the other, a metallic blue.'

'And this, you said was on the Friday; were they there the following day?'

'I don't know about the Saturday, I don't believe I even looked across then, but they were on Sunday morning, in fact there was another one, a VW open-top and bright yellow.'

'Were they there all day, do you know, Miss Walters?'

'I saw two of them leave around midday, but the BMW was still there.'

Johnnie Wall's car. She really was an excellent witness, he thought.

'Chief Inspector?' she said as he made to leave.

'Yes.'

'There's something I feel I should tell you, and the reason I haven't before is because I felt, and still feel actually, that it had nothing to do with these murders. You see,' she started to explain and he could hear the hesitancy in her voice, but he didn't prompt her, feeling sure she would enlighten him once she got her thoughts in order, 'but the other day, the same afternoon you called here as a matter of fact, Jack had been helping me to hang the pictures I'd brought with me from London and he discovered that a computer disc had been concealed in the back of one of them.'

'My goodness.'

'Yes,' she smiled in spite of the obvious seriousness of what she was explaining, 'my reaction entirely. However, we ran it through my computer and it appeared to relate to various stock market transactions, several names had been included, but quite frankly, as neither Jack nor I are terribly *au fait* with the financial world, we decided to seek professional help. Jack has an old family friend who was a corporate lawyer in London before his retirement a few years ago and we went along to see him yesterday, taking the disc with us. He immediately recognised the seriousness of the content and offered to approach someone he knew in New Scotland Yard, primarily for an unofficial talk, you understand.'

'Thank you for confiding in me, Miss Walters. You'll be interested to learn that I received a call from one of New Scotland Yard's officers this morning and will in fact be meeting him at midday to discuss presumably what you've just told me, so once again I'll say thank you.'

'I didn't want you to think I'd been going behind your back as I honestly didn't believe it could possibly have anything to do with the recent events in Upper Nettles.'

'And now you're not so certain?' he smiled at her, trying to put her at her ease.

'It's another I'm not sure.' returning his smile, 'There is one other thing, although I expect Keith Armstrong, that was name we were given of the officer,' she explained, 'will tell you, but the only way that disc could have found its way behind the picture was by being put there by someone I used to live with called Tom Jackson. I ended the relationship two months ago and haven't seen him since, also I didn't tell him I intended to leave London and although I know he's been trying to find where I am, up to now he doesn't have my address, which means of course if he wanted to retrieve the disk he wouldn't be able to.'

He didn't ask her any further questions, feeling she had reached saturation point and it had been apparent she had found the whole subject unpalatable. She opened the front door for him and as he stepped outside he asked her if she had met her neighbours yet, glancing as he did so at Johnnie Wall's house across the road.

'I've seen a few of them from the window, but so far not to speak to. I did try actually; this was on the Sunday morning, but,' she gave a rueful smile and a slight shrug of her shoulders, 'it wasn't too pleasant.'

'Really?'

'I didn't think to mention this to you when you first came here, Chief Inspector, because quite frankly I didn't put too much importance on the incident. You see, what I'd heard and seen the night before had upset me; I realised the woman was in considerable distress and just standing there, at my bedroom window, I felt so helpless. I suppose it prayed on my mind, so I decided to go across on the pretext of introducing myself, when really I was hoping to find out whether the woman was alright; because,' she added, 'I had naturally assumed she must live there, but it would seem from what you've been saying, I was quite wrong.'

'As you say, it was a natural assumption, but did you speak to anyone?'

'I did, yes, and when I explained why I had called, he made it perfectly plain I wouldn't be welcome, so I left.'

'Do you think this was Johnnie Wall?'

'At first I had no idea whether he was or not, but I mentioned this to Jack later in the day and he said that by the description I gave him, it sounded like Gerry Steele; apparently,' she added, 'people in the village call him Johnnie Wall's minder.'

'They're probably not far wrong,' Richard smiled at the description, 'I, too, have met him, Miss Walters, and yes, he's somewhat lacking in charm. It's a pity there hadn't been someone else there, they may have been more welcoming, but perhaps Johnnie Wall wasn't in and he had the place to himself.'

'I'm not sure whether there hadn't been anyone else inside the house, on the other hand he could have been in one of the cars which I saw leaving at midday; this was not long before I walked across there.'

'I would say you're probably right, especially as you mentioned that the BMW was still there when they went off and I believe that does belong to him.'

'I expect you're thinking I'm an extremely inquisitive person, Chief Inspector, but I have to admit it's quite a novelty for me to have neighbours who are actually visible; I've always lived in London, in an apartment where one can go for weeks, sometimes even months, without seeing one of the other residents. Country life,' she smiled, 'or perhaps it would be more apt to say, Upper Nettles' life is extremely interesting.'

An understatement, Richard thought as he left Tulip Cottage to drive back in time for his meeting with Keith Armstrong, and what she'd been saying was interesting. Who were these two other people? Pete Carr and Eddie Gallagher? And, more importantly, had they been staying the night at the Grange on the night Glenda Nicholson met her death.

***

Claire had already put in a couple of hours expanding on the plot for her current book before the Chief Inspector had turned up and afterwards when she had the cottage to herself again, she felt unsettled; it wasn't only having to talk about last Saturday night again and accept the strong possibility that the woman she'd seen had been Glenda Nicholson and that only a matter of hours later she had met her death, it was more than that, something else was niggling at the back of her mind, but the more she tried to rationalise the more confused she became. Real life bore absolutely no relation to the one she created on paper; her plots held together, even if it meant spending hours perfecting the credibility which was expected by readers of any work of fiction, and her characters hand-picked and manipulated by her, only she, the writer, knew what they were thinking, why they reacted in a certain way and what would happen to them at the end of the book, but none of these crafting techniques could be applied to flesh and blood human beings and actual situations and events. Perhaps the way she was feeling now was frustration, the utter frustration of never having known Glenda Nicholson or Maud Green's son, neither had she any idea of, in the case of Glenda Nicholson, the reason why she'd been murdered, but the other thing which was bugging her and if she was honest, causing her more concern was the possibility, however obscure, that the business with Tom and that damned computer disc could be connected. There was no doubt it was being considered as a matter of some importance, although she couldn't help wondering why New Scotland Yard had wasted no time in contacting the Upper Nettles Police Force. That wasn't making any sense and the only interpretation she could think of was there must be considerably more than the contents of the disc at issue here. As far as she could see, she was the only link New Scotland Yard had, merely because the disc had been found among her possessions. They would of course have Tom's name, but he didn't live in this area and neither did Sylvia's friend, Clive Robinson; again, only she had been the link to both Tom and him. Even trying to apply straightforward logic didn't give her any sensible answers; she would have to resign herself to possibly never learning the full facts.

What she needed, Claire decided, was some company, deciding to drive into the town and call in at "The Hunters"; even having a chat with the outrageous Trevor would be light relief to her at the moment she thought, picking up her handbag and car keys from the hall table and letting herself out of the cottage. Ideally, she would have liked to have seen Jack, but hadn't wanted to disturb him as it was likely he would be working.

Deja vu, she thought fifteen minutes later, pulling up outside "The Hunters" and, as she had done last Saturday, Deidre served her.

'Hello, Claire,' she smiled, looking genuinely pleased to see her, 'a Chardonnay?'

'Yes, please, Deidre.' feeling herself relax and feeling for the first time since arriving in Upper Nettles, that she was really being accepted and discovering, in spite of her previous doubts, she quite liked the experience; a tiny remonstrative voice in her head telling her to give it time, and as she'd said to the Chief Inspector, it was still early days, remembering her first impressions of the town, Tulip Cottage, the splendid view across the terrace and the tranquillity of the countryside.

'Well,' Deidre said, placing her wine in front of her, 'that's your first week over. How do you feel?'

'Tricky question;' she laughed, paying for her drink, 'I suppose bemused could more aptly describe how I'm feeling.'

'It has been a strange week, hasn't it?' she sympathised, 'I expect you're wondering what you've let yourself in for coming to live here, but all I can say, Claire, it isn't always as eventful as it has been lately. Everything will settle down once all this awful business is cleared up.' she promised.

'Good morning one and all!' Trevor Wheatley called out to them as he tip-toed towards them, pausing for a couple of seconds to wave theatrically in the direction of an ethnic-looking couple huddled closely together at the end of the bar, 'Don't be put off by the way they're dressed, Claire,' he stage-whispered to her, 'they are truly very nice people, just a trifle over-the-top in their choice of fashion.'

'What would you like to drink, Trevor, your usual?' Deidre asked him and by the flicker of a smile hovering on her lips, Claire knew what she was thinking, meanwhile Trevor, completely impervious of the effect he was having on his immediate audience, continued, regaling them with a wickedly exaggerated description of a couple of Scottish holidaymakers who'd spent over an hour in the Gallery that morning deliberating over whether to purchase, in his opinion, a particularly attractive piece of work by a local artist.

'Honestly,' he said, 'you should have seen them; they weren't *really* interested in the *actual* painting; it was whether it would blend in with their newly decorated lounge! I ask you!'

'And did they buy the picture in the end, Trevor?' Claire asked him.

'Of course not, Claire! Poor Maurice; I really felt for him. Honestly, I don't know why some of these people even bother coming into our Gallery; I really don't!'

'It sounds as though you and Maurice have had a rather frustrating morning.' Deidre commented lightly.

'Well - ' he drawled, 'not *really*, Deidre. We did make a few sales, but what was interesting, intriguing *really*, I was looking out of the window during a quiet moment and who should I see but Bernie Croft.'

'Who's Bernie Croft?' Claire and Deidre asked him in unison.

'Bernie Croft, dear ladies,' he answered, taking full advantage of being centre-stage, especially as they weren't the only two people within easy earshot, 'is a professional guitar player of some note, pardon the pun,' he added, 'but Bernie used to be with "The Bandanas" years ago; you'll remember, Claire,' he added turning to look at her, 'Sylvia and I were telling you last Saturday about them, also that Maurice and I actually went to one of their concerts when we were living in Australia and that was when Bernie was still with them.'

'You did, yes.' she agreed, wondering why he was getting so excited.

'Perhaps he'd been visiting Johnnie Wall.' Deidre suggested.

'I don't think so, Deidre. You see,' he went on when neither of them said anything, 'when I saw him, he was walking up the steps of the police station!'

'Oh,' Deidre said, 'well, it's none of our business is it, Trevor?'

'Probably not,' obviously choosing to ignore her polite attempt to reprimand him, 'but it does make you wonder though. Probably something to do with this murder case.'

Deidre was spared making any reply by more customers coming in and, giving Claire a sympathetic smile, moved over to serve them.

What on earth can one possibly say to a person like Trevor Wheatley, Claire thought; he was obviously on a roll and making no attempt to disguise his insatiable appetite for what in his mind was high drama practically taking place on his doorstep. In some respects, she couldn't entirely blame him, but the last Claire wanted was to enter into any sort of discussion which was only based on conjecture. The irony of what he was saying could very well turn out to be true and although he was only jumping to conclusions she could imagine how easy it would be for the more sensational-seekers of Upper Nettles to believe him.

Her mobile rang at that moment and, excusing herself, walked over to the open doorway to take the call.

'Hello, Claire, Jack here; I hope I haven't disturb you.'

'No, of course not,' quick to reassure him, 'I'm in "The Hunters" actually, trying to avoid talking about 'you know what'.'

'Oh, dear, that bad?'

'It could be; I was being collared by Trevor.'

'You sound as if you need rescuing.'

'I might be.' she laughed; it was good to hear his voice, just talking to him made her realise she was taking this whole business far too seriously, wishing she could be more matter of fact, but recognising she would never be able to.

'Do you like curries?' he asked, changing the subject.

'I love them, why?'

'Well,' he explained, and she could tell by his voice he was smiling, imagining the quirky lop-sided grin, 'as it's about the only meal I can cook with any degree of success I thought you'd like to sample one of my renditions; this evening,' he added, 'if you've nothing else planned?'

'I'd like that very much, Jack.'

'Great, come early and we can have a couple of drinks first, but I warn you once you start eating one of my curries you're going to need loads of water!'

'I've been warned;' she laughed, her flagging spirits immediately uplifted, 'I can get to your house by walking across the bridge, can't I; there's no need for me to drive round?'

'That's right; you'll see a small white gate at the other side of the stream; it's at the right-hand side, then all you have to do is walk up the path to where the conservatory is, but I'll see you coming anyway, you can't get lost.'

Chapter Twelve

Jilly Waterman spent Saturday morning shopping, Bond Street being her favourite haunt; for her, never browsing, it was the real thing. She spent money and sometimes a great deal. It wasn't as though she actually needed another Stella McCartney exorbitantly-priced design or a pair of Jimmy Choo's glittering spiky-heeled summer sandals or had any specific occasion for wearing them. It certainly wasn't because she wanted to look alluring for her husband or anyone else if it came to that. Even Tom, who, although he never failed to compliment her on the way she looked, wouldn't recognise one designer label from another. She bought these creations to please only one person and that was herself. She enjoyed the sensual feel of silk against her skin and the knowledge that she could afford to indulge in what pleased her most, with the result that at the end of each shopping spree, she felt euphoric, light-headed with the satisfaction of doing whatever she wanted without any censure. At least, she thought for the hundredth time, David wasn't mean, not like many of her friends' husbands.

She was later than usual returning home, having bumped into an old college friend she hadn't seen for ages and they had spent a while drinking far too much coffee catching up with each other's news. Clive's car was parked outside the house when she got back which took her by surprise; David hadn't said anything at breakfast about him coming, and not particularly wanting to talk to him went straight through to the kitchen, dumping the half dozen glossy carrier bags on the table and opening a can of lager to quench her thirst, beginning to regret the excessive intake of caffeine.

She could hear their voices coming from the dining room, David's low and deliberate, and the lighter, quicker tones of Clive, distinctive by the emphatic way he clipped the end of each phrase or sentence as though determined to make his point. She was pouring the Carlsberg into a glass when she began to wonder why she should be hearing them so clearly and then she realised; the serving hatch through to the dining room was slightly open and she moved over to close it, having no wish to hear what they were saying, sure it would be something tedious about the business and way above her head, as David had often reminded her. She had her hand on the metal handle when she heard Tom's name mentioned. She knew Tom worked for them on a freelance basis, although had never been sure what it was he exactly contributed and hadn't been sufficiently interested to ask either David or Tom.

'So, David,' Clive was saying, 'it would appear that our worst fears have been realised; come Monday morning as soon as he turns up at the bank, Tom will be issued with the ultimatum; my contact was present at the meeting yesterday and apparently the board's decision is final, and because of the seriousness of, shall we say Tom's indiscretions, there will be no preliminaries, no official letter of warning, also he won't be given the opportunity to defend himself. In other words, he's for the high jump.'

'And where does that leave us exactly?' David asked him.

'We're in a shaky position, there's no denying that,' Clive went on, and even if she wanted to, Jilly was incapable of closing the hatch or even to walk out of the kitchen and pretend she hadn't heard, 'but somehow, David, we'll weather this one; we have to. When all's said and done, Tom Jackson is small fry and quite frankly I wouldn't like to be in his shoes. WHL, apparently, are prepared to make up the shortfall in the Clarkson account; as I said the other day, they want to avoid any adverse publicity which could ultimately and drastically affect the market.'

'You've already mentioned about the bank having certain reservations about Tom's handling with his other clients; let's hope the Clarkson fiasco doesn't act as a precedent.'

'No point looking on the gloomy side, David, old chap.'

'I suppose you're right,' but Jilly could tell by the despondency in his voice he wasn't of the same opinion, 'and what about Tom's contract with us; have you ideas on how best to handle that?'

'I suggest we let things ride for the moment; wait for him to tell us he is no longer one of WHL's employees. He could continue 'feeding' us even if he was no longer with them, I'm pretty sure he has quite a formidable list of contacts. He'll make sure he doesn't starve, so it's the old adage, David, I think; give the man enough rope, and all that!'

'Meanwhile,' David said, 'we should make every effort to erase from our records any tangible links with him; that is if we can, although his own records continue to concern me considerably.'

'I suppose you mean that elusive disc?'

'That's if it ever existed.'

'It *must* exist, David. Everybody needs back-up, even smart-arse Tom Jackson!'

'But where the hell is he keeping it?'

'If I'd known that old chap, I'm certain we would have got our hands on it by this time; I must admit that foray to the New Forest the other day was a total waste of time.'

Jilly had heard enough, and leaving the hatch open, she picked up her shopping and took it upstairs. The first thing she had to do was warn Tom. That was the very least she could do. She may not have understood what was behind the seriousness of what David and Clive had been discussing, but she knew one thing; Tom would soon be out of a job and if, as they'd been saying, there was something shady about his forthcoming dismissal, she didn't want to have anything to do with it. Jilly was sufficiently realistic to realise that within the relatively small community in which she and her friends circulated, word would soon reach them and Tom's presence in their midst would not be welcome. In other words, in the insular, materialistic and name-dropping world in which many of them lived, he would be ostracised. She would have no alternative but to bring their affair to an end; to Jilly, her own position was paramount. She had always been aware that as far as she was concerned their relationship wouldn't have lasted indefinitely; it had been fun, for a while, but she wouldn't permit herself to have a choice. It suited her to remain married to David and she didn't intend to do anything which would jeopardise that.

***

'I must apologise for not elaborating more when I phoned, Chief Inspector,' Keith Armstrong said as soon as he was shown into Richard

Cavendish's office shortly after midday, 'but I'm a great believer, where possible, in face to face communication, although you must have been somewhat puzzled why I should have wanted to talk to you.'

'At first, yes,' Richard smiled, grateful to Claire Walters for supplying the possible reason, 'but after your call, I had another discussion with a witness we have in respect to the recent murders in Upper Nettles, during which she mentioned your name in respect to a computer disc she and her friend found among her possessions.'

'Ah, Miss Walters.'

'Yes, that's right; she was quite apologetic actually, for not telling me when I first spoke to her, the reason being she didn't think it would have any bearing on our murder enquiry.'

'That's understandable,' he nodded, 'but by a strange, and so far unexplained, quirk of circumstances, we believe that it could very well be connected in some tenuous sort of way and which means both you and I respectively must try to unravel.'

'I will of course give you copies of reports we've made since we started our enquiries; they may be of some help.'

'I'm sure they will,' going on to explain the backbones of New Scotland Yard's investigation into a case of insider dealer fraud in the city, 'we believe this to be organised, what I mean by that, not one person siphoning off from investors' funds singlehandedly. There are a number of people involved, but up to now we've been lacking any possible contact name.'

'I take it the disc did contain something possible in that direction?'

'Yes, Chief Inspector,' he answered, 'it did, these still require to be sifted through and they will be, but there was one name which we found particularly interesting.'

'Yes?'

'A firm of financial investment consultants based in London's West End; they're called Robinson & Waterman; Clive Robinson and David Waterman,' he qualified. At first glance on reading through the disc they may not sound suspect, although given the significance of the contents, the question would need to be asked why they have been included, until you come to Tom Jackson.'

'Claire Walters mentioned him, Inspector Armstrong; she was quite certain he was the only person who could have concealed the disc behind one of her pictures.'

'I'm sure she's right. Tom Jackson,' he went on, 'is employed by the WHL Group; merchant bankers with their headquarters in Regent Street, the same bank where both Clive Robinson and David Waterman worked until they resigned fifteen years ago to set up their consultancy business. It appears likely that Jackson is supplying them with details of selected bank customers, presumably investors and included in his official portfolio although this has yet to be verified. I should explain that Robinson & Waterman are chiefly involved in administering hedge funds, and by the very nature of this type of business they can be considerably more flexible in selecting the type of shares, where, apart from investing in what is described as long positions, meaning buying stocks, they also invest in short positions, which means selling stocks with borrowed money and then buying them back later when their price has fallen. Risky, especially when it is someone else's money and when that person is unaware of what is happening with his or her investment.'

'Complicated.'

'It is, I agree. As a possible first step we need to consult with WHL, followed by a meeting with Tom Jackson; it was impossible to make any appointment today, but I have made arrangements to see the bank on Monday morning; at this stage I have no idea what the outcome will be, except to say I fully expect to come up against the proverbial brick wall when talking to them; banks, I have found, dislike outside interference in their affairs.'

'True.' Richard agreed, 'I think I may be able to add a couple of significant points to what you've been saying, Inspector, but first I'd like to ask why you believe there could be a connection between the financial fraud in London and the murder of two people in Upper Nettles.'

'Sounds bizarre, doesn't it?' Keith smiled, 'but then I'm sure you'll agree with me, Chief Inspector, many police investigations can turn out that way, but I'll answer your question. As you're aware, I haven't spoken to Miss Walters or Mr Andrews, but only to Mr Andrews' friend, whom I've known for many years. He's called Adam Brookfield, and when we were talking about this case yesterday, he told me that on Thursday evening while Miss Walters and Mr Andrews were out, someone had broken into her house. It sounded as though he had been searching for this disc which is causing so much trouble, but more importantly, she believes the intruder was Clive Robinson.'

'Goodness! Why did she think that?'

'Because, and this I suppose could be called chance, her friend, Sylvia Crossman, who also lives in Upper Nettles, had told her that she'd bumped into an old friend of hers on Thursday who had been asking around the town if anyone knew where Claire Walters lived.'

'And this had been Clive Robinson.'

'Yes, exactly.'

'Presumably, your friend Adam Brookfield would have told you that Tom Watson had arrived unannounced at her house yesterday morning while she'd been out.'

'Oh, yes.'

'Well, Inspector, it's my turn to supply some additives.'

'Fire ahead.' he smiled.

'What I'm going to say relates to the murder of Glenda Nicholson; on the day she was killed, during the early evening, she met someone in The Nettles Hotel; we haven't been able to find out much about him, except from the name on his credit card which he used later to pay for his meal after she'd left, which was D. Waterman, and the type of car he'd been driving, unfortunately not the registration number. Not much, I'm afraid.'

'It could be.'

'On Sunday, around midday, a couple called Gregory and Lilian Thornton arrived at Glenda Nicholson's house. According to her neighbours, they told her they'd been invited for lunch. The Thorntons, who live in Bournemouth, are currently in Hong Kong, but will be returning on Monday when we hope to interview them. A further twist to these, possibly related events, was that on Tuesday morning a registered package arrived at Glenda Nicholson's hairdressing salon. We now have the package which incidentally had no name of the sender, only the Bournemouth postmark; it contained fifty thousand American dollars.'

'Very interesting indeed.'

'It becomes more so.' Richard promised.

'I thought it might.'

'On checking with the Bournemouth post office we've learned that the sender was a Miss Bennett. Lilian Thornton's maiden name was Bennett, Inspector, also before her marriage she was in partnership with Miss Nicholson.'

'I see, again interesting, and Gregory Thornton; what's his line of business, Chief Inspector?'

'Gaming clubs apparently; our background of him is somewhat sketchy to say the least. We are not particularly lacking in suspects, Inspector, although Gregory Thornton at the moment is not being considered as one; until we've spoken to him and his wife, we know virtually little about him, but if we are to believe the couple genuinely expected to see Glenda Nicholson last Sunday, it does seem to rule him out for the time being.'

'If you're agreeable,' Keith suggested, 'we could get him sussed out, but I don't want to encroach.'

'Not at all, I'd be grateful in fact and certainly with this development, it does somewhat expand on what started out as a relatively straightforward murder enquiry.'

'Fifty thousand dollars is a considerable amount, which does indicate this could have something to do with what's going on in London, although it must raise a question in your mind, Chief Inspector; in what way was Glenda Nicholson involved?'

'Hence the connection you were talking about earlier.'

***

'Pete, I've been trying to ring you for the last couple of days; is there something wrong with your mobile?'

'You've got through now, haven't you, Eddie, so what's the panic?'

'It's Johnnie; have you spoken to him lately?'

'Not since the beginning of the week, why?'

'I called him yesterday afternoon as soon as I got back from Amsterdam and quite frankly he just wasn't making any sense. Kept going on about Glenda, saying the police are going to pin her murder on to him, that he was being used as a scapegoat.'

'Sounds as though he was drunk, or something.'

'I don't think he was, more confused than anything else. Says he can't remember anything about last Saturday night, that Gerry was no help, and there was a conspiracy against him.'

'He's being paranoid, Eddie. In fact, he more or less said the same to me on Sunday; he must have been in a pretty bad state on Saturday, but it's not been the first time. He passed out Eddie; you must have seen him when you got back; flaked out on the sofa; I shouldn't worry about him, he'll snap out of it, he has done before.'

'I think it's different this time, Pete.'

'You're a worry-guts, you know that? Keep cool; you don't want to give yourself a heart attack, do you? Stress is a killer, Eddie.'

'I know; there are times when I honestly marvel that we've managed to stick together for as long as we have.'

'Well, we have.' Pete answered, affecting a casualness he was far from feeling. He didn't blame Eddie for how he was thinking; Johnnie had always been a problem, but in spite of his escalating dependence on drugs, miraculously his talent as one of the best guitarists of their generation remained unimpaired. He was gifted, no-one in the music world would say differently, but like many naturally talented people, he wasn't stretched; there was too much time between the adrenalin-filled atmospheres of a live concert and those periods when there were no pressures or demands made on any of them. In his particular case, apart from the women in his life, he did have other business interests, but he had to admit they fell far short of standing up in front of an audience who were there for the sole purpose of listening and applauding to their music. As soon as he'd heard about Glenda's death, he had instantly remembered Eddie telling him about seeing Gerry walking back to the house in the early hours. Oh, he'd done his best to make light of it when he knew as well as Eddie that Gerry never walked anywhere. Eddie hadn't been fooled, and neither had Johnnie when he'd asked them what was up the following day, if the caustic expression on his face was anything to go by. Johnnie knew Gerry probably better than any of them, even Spike who'd only been with them since Bernie had stormed off in a temper.

'He said he'd had a visit from Upper Nettles' Chief Inspector yesterday morning.' Eddie said, interrupting his thoughts.

'Routine I expect, Eddie.' He was at it again; making light of what could potentially be bloody disastrous. 'Sorry,' immediately apologising, 'but presumably he told Johnnie why he turned up.'

'Something about the police having a bee in their bonnet that Glenda was at The Grange that night, but Johnnie thought they were probably only guessing, except, and here's the puzzling bit, Pete, that the woman living in the house across the road had told them someone had been knocking at her door around midnight.'

'And they're saying it had been Glenda?' appalled at what he was hearing.

'Not in so many words, but Johnnie got the message loud and clear and when you think about it Pete, who else could it have been?'

'Hell!'

'Not good, eh?'

'As you say, Eddie, not good, but what do you think; was Glenda there on Saturday?'

'I don't know what to think,' he answered flatly, 'she could have been I suppose, but I didn't ask him, I thought he was wound up enough already. It's damn difficult over the phone.' he added.

'You're telling me! And what about Gerry; where did he go that night?'

'That's anyone's guess, but I tell you this, Pete, I don't like the way I'm thinking one little bit.'

'There's another thing,' Pete went on doggedly, doing his best to rationalise, 'if Glenda had gone to The Grange, she would have taken her car, so where is it?'

'It sounds from what Johnnie was saying that it might have been her car which had been found yesterday morning off the Lymington coast.'

'Lymington?'

'Yep, that's what he said.'

'It's a long walk from Lymington to Upper Nettles, Eddie.'

***

Sylvia Crossman lived in one of the single-storeyed Georgian properties in the High Street which in more recent years had become known by a new breed of estate agents eager to entice prospective and status-seeking buyers, as town houses. Looking at the identical wrought-iron window boxes, there was very little to differentiate one from the other. A pity, Peter Gale thought, these old houses, while continuing to retain their historical appearance, seemed to have lost their individuality. He rang the doorbell of number twenty-two, intrigued despite his cynicism to see what the interior of what he knew to be extremely highly-priced properties.

Sylvia Crossman didn't take long to come to the door and although he had never spoken to her before he recognised her from seeing her in "The Hunters". She was an attractive woman; slim, shiny blonde hair cut in what possibly would be considered by younger women to be somewhat dated, but it suited her; he could only hazard a guess as to how old she was, but remembering she had, more than thirty years ago, been married to Johnnie Wall, she must be in her early fifties.

'Inspector Gale.' she smiled, before he had a chance to introduce himself. Although she had sounded surprised when he'd phoned her earlier after Bernie Croft had left his office, she hadn't raised any objection to seeing him.

'I appreciate you taking the time to talk to me, Mrs Crossman.' showing her his card.

'That's alright, Inspector;' barely giving the card a glance, 'come in, won't you? Ever since you rang I've been trying to puzzle out why you should want to see me;' she said, leading him across the parquet-floored hall to the lounge; a generous proportioned and high-ceilinged room, with high sash windows facing out towards the main street; a mass of geraniums filled the window boxes, their heavy blooms acting as a scarlet screen and shielding her from the steady stream of pedestrians walking along the pavement immediately in front of the building, 'you said it was something to do with what's been happening here recently.'

'First of all,' Peter answered, 'I want to reassure you these are only routine questions and in particular they are in respect to the murder of Miss Nicholson.'

'Yes? Please sit down,' she added, gesturing towards one of the sofas, 'you make me nervous towering above me.'

'Sorry,' unable to suppress a grin; there was something infectious about the way she would suddenly smile, not a practised smile, there was nothing remotely contrived about it; perhaps she just had a happy disposition, he decided, 'it's not my intention. Did you know Glenda Nicholson, Mrs Crossman?' he asked, deciding on a slightly different approach than he had planned, with the idea of leading up to bringing in Johnnie Wall's name. He wanted to avoid leaving her with the impression they may be considering him as a possible suspect.

'Only because she was my hairdresser and had been since she opened her salon here.'

'Which was in 2004.'

'Was it? I couldn't have told you that, but all I do know is when I came to live in Upper Nettles in 1993, she didn't have the business then and I had to drive into Lyndhurst if I wanted to have my hair done.'

'Did she ever mention about the time before she was here?'

'Only that she owned a hairdressing business in London, somewhere in Bloomsbury I believe she said.'

'The reason I'm asking you,' Peter explained, 'is that there have been a number of developments since we began our investigation suggesting Glenda Nicholson's past could have some bearing on her death.'

'May I ask why, Inspector?'

'Of course; up to now there has been an absence of any motive for what happened to her; we can't even be certain whether it was premeditated or not. We know how she was murdered, and the approximate time, but we don't know why and once we have the answer to that, we hope to be closer to finding the person responsible.'

'And you think this relates to how she lived in the past?'

'Not how she lived perhaps, Mrs Crossman, but the person or persons with whom she associated at some point in her life before she left London.'

'That's certainly very logical, but it does sound rather complicated, Inspector.'

'I agree,' he smiled at her, having already recognised her intelligence; Sylvia Crossman was not just a pretty face, remembering his mother saying a few years ago when he'd taken one of his girlfriends to visit her and when during the course of conversation, or in his mother's case, an interrogation of the girl she'd convinced herself her son was intent on marrying, she had learned that the girl, who had been exceptionally pretty, was a trainee lawyer, 'but somehow,' he continued, 'we have to do our utmost to unravel it all, discard anything which proves to be irrelevant, in order to reach the core of what I suppose you could describe as a mystery surrounding not only Glenda Nicholson's death, but that of the young man, Jamie Green.'

'Yes, I read about him and that was really dreadful, shocking in fact, but I've been listening to what you've been saying, Inspector, and I still can't help wondering why you should be so intent on finding out about how Glenda lived her life before she came here.'

'We've spoken to quite a number of people in Lyndhurst where she lived and in Upper Nettles and while they may have known her, none of them seemed to have known her very well, the implication being it sounded as though she had been reluctant to discuss her past with them, this has made us curious, and as our enquiries continued we discover that there are a number of people living locally who knew her very well indeed and had done for several years. Does this make it any clearer to you, Mrs Crossman?'

'A little, yes,' but sensing by the quizzical raising of an eyebrow, she knew where he was heading, 'but it still doesn't explain why you should want to talk to me, when after all I only fall into the category of those people who barely knew her.'

No, he reminded himself, she was not just a pretty face; Sylvia

Crossman was an extremely clever woman, also she was giving nothing away, deciding it was now time to move the interview forward, appreciating he would have to exercise a certain amount of guile here to unearth what was no more than a hunch, nothing substantial, but he considered it worth pursuing.

'As you've told me, you only knew her as your hairdresser and I accept that, but I would suggest, Mrs Crossman, that you knew of her.' leaving it at that, waiting to hear what her reaction would be.

'Inspector Gale,' she said slowly, looking at him directly, and as she spoke her eyes never leaving his face, 'you're quite right, I did, but first of all, to try and explain why I was reluctant to mention this; it was because I have an ingrained dislike for gossip of any kind and this includes passing on anything which could be detrimental to a person, whether he or she deserves it or not. When you phoned me this afternoon, the first question I asked myself was why, out of I'm sure many other people whom you haven't interviewed, did you elect to talk to me. I could only come up with one credible answer. I apologise for being somewhat long-winded, but I want to keep the record straight, I don't want to create any misunderstandings and the last thing I want to do is to cast aspersions at anyone, whether I know them or not.'

'I understand completely, and I appreciate your frankness, Mrs Crossman.'

'Thank you, Inspector;' the smile making another brief appearance, 'I concluded that in the course of your enquiries somehow you learned that once, years ago, I was married to the guitarist, Johnnie Wall; the marriage only lasted two years, we were divorced in 1979. At that time, and right up to 1988, I was a dancer with the Felicity Boardman Dance Studios in London. Although I never kept in touch with him, I suppose, as I was also in the entertainment business, it was only natural most of us heard when he'd been convicted in Germany for drug offences, the group had been touring there when this happened; anyway,' she went on, 'around the same time, word leaked out that he had been cited in a divorce petition when Nicholas Wade-Brown, an impresario, decided to divorce his wife for infidelity, that woman was Glenda Nicholson. This happened in 2001, but apparently she and Johnnie had been having an affair for years, as far back as 1993 when she had been married to her first husband, Ted Warren. You see, Inspector,' she admitted wryly, 'just because I dislike gossip and go out of my way to avoid it, there are times when it continues to encroach, and old memories are inclined to stick.'

'How true; once again, thank you, you've been very frank.'

'There's no reason not to be, unpleasant though it is.' she shrugged.

'Much of what you've told me, Mrs Crossman, we did know already, but it is helpful to have it corroborated. Presumably you were aware Johnnie Wall is living in Upper Nettles.'

'Of course,' she smiled, 'who doesn't here? Yes, I knew Inspector and while I won't say I was all that pleased, what could I do about the situation. It was over twenty-eight years ago after all. It's history and isn't something I talk about. If anybody should take it upon themselves to ask me, then I would tell them; it isn't a secret, just something that happened a long time ago.'

'Did you know Penelope Driver?'

'Yes, Inspector, I knew Penelope;' taking several seconds to answer, 'she and I were with the same dance studios and as you've mentioned her name, am I right in assuming you know that she was married to Johnnie?'

'Yes, we knew that, also that she committed suicide.'

'Poor Penelope; we were friends, you know, at least I thought we were; you see, she married Johnnie three months after we were divorced.'

'Do you know why she committed suicide?' The question he'd been leading up to ask almost from the start of the interview, intrigued to see how she would respond.

'I don't know, Inspector.' taking longer to answer this time, her expression sad, presumably remembering those years when she could have only been in her twenties, 'does anyone really know why a person should want to end their life; certainly, one reads of many people attempting to commit suicide, but for one reason or another, not succeeding, which always makes me think it must be a way of crying for help. But what Penelope did was sad, very sad, in fact. I believe she'd been suffering from depression and I suppose you would ask why. The obvious answer of course is that she wasn't happy.'

'Did she continue with her dancing after she'd married him?'

'Yes, she did, and strangely enough we did pick up the threads of our friendship again, although naturally it was never the same. I guess I felt sorry for her, she was a very nervous sort of person; highly strung, always looking on the black side of things.'

'It sounds as though she wasn't happy in her marriage.'

'She wasn't.'

'Did she tell you?'

'She didn't have to, Inspector. I wasn't the only one who noticed how she'd changed, and some of us did try to get her to open-up, share whatever was bothering her, but she never did.'

'Did you, yourself I mean, have an inkling of what was wrong?'

'Because I'd been married to Johnnie?'

'Perhaps.'

'She was afraid of him, Inspector.' she said quietly, her expression remaining the same.

'Did she say in what way?'

'No, that was all she said, just that she was afraid of him. Nothing more, but I didn't take her seriously. I had never found Johnnie in the least bit frightening. He had one passion, Inspector.'

'Yes?'

'His music. I knew this, anyone who knew Johnnie knew it, but I don't think Penelope did, but on reflection, perhaps she did after all; perhaps she was jealous of the time he spent playing and it was actually his music which frightened her. I don't know and we'll never know now, will we, Inspector?'

***

Tom joined the long line of vehicles waiting to board 'The Normandie', one of the Brittany ferries sailing from Portsmouth to Ouistreham in northern France, the embarkation time being eleven forty-five. His decision to leave had been instantaneous. Immediately Jilly had broken the news to him, a plan of how he could extricate himself from his present predicament was being formulated. It wasn't only the loss of his job which concerned him, but the inevitable aftermath. The scale of his manipulations was such that with the close scrutiny and inspection of every account for which he'd been responsible since joining the bank would reveal the discrepancies which up to now he had skilfully and methodically camouflaged, resulting in, he was certain, the charge of fraud and no doubt a prison sentence. He had always been aware of the possible consequences but had been prepared to take the risk and certainly, when he considered how his own personal savings had grown over the years, he considered the risk worth taking.

And, then there was Jilly. He had been over-confident there; also, he had under-estimated just how ruthless she was. She wasn't only a good-time girl, she had proved earlier this evening as she had sat opposite to him in the lounge bar of the Hilton, she was also a hard-headed business woman. Honestly, he had thought cynically, as he'd driven down to Portsmouth, Robinson & Waterman should have taken her into partnership with them; she would have been an asset.

Even when he'd asked her to come with him, he knew before the words left his mouth, he was wasting his breath and the contemptuous way she had looked at him, the blonde head to one side and her hazel eyes which he'd once thought attractive, told him everything.

'I don't think so, Tom, darling.' was all she'd said and without finishing her drink, had stood up, brushed her lips lightly across his cheek, and left the bar without looking back.

So that was that, he'd thought cynically, watching her as she walked across the hotel lobby to the main door, the end of a beautiful friendship.

The cars in front of him were moving at last and he needed all his concentration to negotiate on board and follow the directions to park. Switching off the engine and making sure the windows were closed, he picked up his travel bag and briefcase containing his laptop, the only pieces of luggage he'd allowed himself, and walked up the steps and into the reception area. By the time he'd found a seat by the window and bought a beer, they began to slide away from the dockside and within minutes only the lights of Portsmouth and neighbouring Southsea were a reminder he was leaving England, possibly for an indefinite length of time.

He had booked a cabin, determined to have a comfortable night's sleep as he had a long drive the next day and wanted to reach the south of France by the evening. Tom had no wish to spend any time in Normandy, a part of France he wasn't particularly fond of, much preferring the south where it was considerably warmer, and he reckoned the lifestyle would suit him fine for a few weeks before moving on to somewhere new and to a country where he had never been before where he could start the next phase in his life which was turning out a little differently from what he'd expected.

As he sat there, talking to no-one and appreciating his beer, he allowed his mind to wander; already, as rapidly as the boat was forging ahead across the channel, memories were beginning to blur, lose their former importance. Even Jilly, or perhaps especially Jilly, didn't seem real, and what he had considered as important as the disc with all his data which could or could not be used against him, so what. Catch me if you can, the words dancing in his brain.

Chapter Thirteen

Keith Armstrong was shown into Clarence Fountain's office at ten on Monday morning. Clarence was one of WHL's senior executives; he was also Tom Jackson's immediate superior and the person, regardless of the number of years Tom had worked for the merchant bank, who acted as the impregnable barrier to the board of directors. Aware of the protocol, Keith was employing as much diplomacy as he thought necessary, in explaining the reason for his visit. As soon as he mentioned Tom Jackson's name he knew he had hit upon a nerve in the way the man's eyes narrowed behind the steel-framed spectacles and by the stiffening of his shoulders.

'This is all most unfortunate Inspector Armstrong,' he said after remaining silent for some seconds, 'when my secretary informed me that an officer from New Scotland Yard wished to see me, I naturally had no idea of the reason. Now you have explained, I must make it clear that our policy at WHL is to handle indiscretions or misdemeanours by any member of staff internally. It is true we have, over the past two or three months become increasingly concerned with complaints we've been receiving from one or two of our clients, these have not been made officially you understand, but recently they have intensified to such an extent that, knowing the person responsible, a meeting of our board of directors was held last Friday to discuss the matter when, as a matter of course, Tom Jackson's name was mentioned; a vote was taken and it was unanimously decided he should be dismissed; the shortfall in the investments handled by Mr Jackson would be rectified by the bank. In other words, we did not intend to prosecute, the reason being, to avoid any adverse publicity which would without a doubt be harmful to WHL.'

'I understand what you're saying, Mr Fountain,' Keith said quietly, 'but unfortunately there appears to be a much wider and possibly more serious aspect involved here. While there is strong evidence against Tom Jackson in his handling of certain accounts, we believe there are a number of other people involved, not only Tom Jackson and in respect to the funds being misappropriated, they appear to fall into two categories, private individuals and those who have elected banks, other than WHL, to handle their portfolio of stocks and shares.'

'I see.' he nodded, removing his glasses to rub his eyes, 'not a straightforward matter, Inspector.'

'I'm afraid not, sir. However, we will proceed as circumspectly as possible, also as speedily as we can to reach the core of what would seem to be a systematic and organised scheme. I would, with your agreement, like to talk to Mr Jackson while I'm here as there are a number of questions I want to ask him and, if you wish, I would have no objection to you being present.'

'Very well, Inspector; I'll buzz through to his office, but before I do, I should inform you that it's our intention to call him into the conference room at eleven-thirty this morning when one of my directors will be there to formally dismiss him, together with a full explanation for the board's decision.' he said, glancing pointedly at his watch.

'That's alright, sir,' Keith assured him, 'I don't intend this meeting to last more than thirty minutes.'

Keith watched him as he leant forward and pressed one of the buttons on his internal phone, waiting for a few moments before looking across the desk at him.

'Odd,' he murmured, 'he doesn't seem to be there, I'll get my secretary to have a look for him; he may be with one of the other consultants.' pressing another button. 'Julie would you mind having a scout round to see where Tom is; I've just tried his office, but he's not in there?'

Minutes later, there was a light tap on the door and she came in. 'Tom hasn't arrived yet, Mr Fountain.'

'Really; no call from him?'

'No, and I've just checked and he hasn't booked any time off, but he could be sick.'

'Perhaps, thanks, Julie; will you let me know as soon as he comes in?'

Poor man, Keith thought, and it wasn't too difficult to read what must be going through his mind.

'He could have been taken ill, I suppose.' he said as soon as the girl had gone.

There seemed little point in prolonging his visit, but first he needed to have Tom Jackson's address and telephone number. As he wrote them down on one of the bank's compliment slips, he mentioned that as far as he understood Tom Jackson was only living there as a temporary measure, adding he was sharing with one of his colleagues.

'Any idea why, Mr Fountain?'

'He didn't actually explain in any detail, Inspector, and I didn't press him. I suppose I just assumed he may have sold his previous property and was still waiting to move into a new one; I didn't consider it all that important.'

Keith had a very good idea how this had come about, remembering what Adam Brookfield had told him. Tom Jackson probably hadn't much of an option if, as he suspected, for some reason or other Claire Walters and he had recently ended their relationship. Adam had said she'd only moved to the New Forest a week ago and it would seem more probable he would have been living with her at the time he concealed the disc; this could also explain why he'd taken it upon himself to drive down to Upper Nettles the other day. A trip which fortunately for them had been a waste of time and looking at what Clarence Fountain had written.

'Care of J. Rivers,' he read out, 'he's the colleague you mentioned?'

'Yes, that's right,' recognising the reluctance in his voice, 'Jeffrey Rivers, he's in our foreign investment section.'

'I'd like to have a word with him, if that's possible.'

'Inspector Armstrong,' a look of panic crossed his features, 'I really am not happy about involving anyone else in this matter, my directors - '

' - Mr Fountain,' Keith said slowly, but firmly; treading on sensitive toes of directors did not unduly concern him. Tom Jackson may be sick, but on the other hand he could have learned what was going to face him when he reported for work this morning, he couldn't afford to take the risk of letting the man literally slip through his fingers especially before having the opportunity to talk to him, ' - I am more than prepared to explain to your directors the importance of acting as speedily as possible, even if Tom Jackson should arrive at any moment; surely,' he added, 'any employee of the bank would realise the folly of talking indiscriminately.'

Within minutes, there was another tap on the door and Jeffrey Rivers came into the office.

'Ah, Jeffrey, there you are;' Clarence Fountain, adopting what he presumably considered a bracing tone, 'apparently Tom hasn't arrived for work this morning and as there a few questions Inspector Armstrong wishes to ask him,' gesturing towards Keith as a means of introduction, 'this is posing something of a drawback for the Inspector.'

'I understand Mr Jackson is currently staying with you,' Keith said, considering it was time he stepped in having noticed the puzzled look on the younger man's face, 'and presumably you would know whether he had been taken ill, or there was any other reason for him being absent.'

'Normally,' Jeffrey Rivers said slowly, 'I would have, Inspector, but I've not been at home this weekend.'

'When did you last see Mr Jackson?'

'Not since Thursday night; Tom had a day's leave on Friday and I went straight to my girlfriend's flat when I finished work that day.'

'I see, and have you tried to phone him at any time over the weekend, or perhaps he's called you.'

'No, I didn't expect him to, there was no need; he has a key to my apartment.'

'Have you any idea of how he was planning to spend his day off on Friday?'

'He didn't say. He isn't what I would call a close friend, we're work colleagues, Inspector and when he and his girlfriend split up about four or five weeks ago, he asked me whether I would mind putting him up for a few weeks until he got himself organized and as I had a spare room I agreed.'

'Did he bring much with him when he moved in?'

'Surprisingly little actually, but as it was only going to be as a temporary measure he probably thought there was no point.'

'So, what did he bring with him, apart from clothes, I mean?'

Keith didn't miss Clarence Fountain's sharp intake of breath, fully expecting him to intervene, but he didn't; he remained in the same position he'd adopted when he'd first spoken to him. Jeffrey Rivers' bewildered expression remained which may or may not indicate he was fully aware of the situation. As the secretary hadn't buzzed through to say Jackson had arrived, Keith was becoming more and more convinced he must have had some advance warning, not that he was going to be questioned by an officer from New Scotland Yard, but about the board's decision to fire him.

'I think he only had his laptop, I don't remember seeing anything else.'

A man of few personal possessions, Keith thought cynically; in itself that could be considered unusual, doubtful about anyone who'd reached maturity could manage to go through life without accumulating anything more than presumably an adequate supply of clothing and a personal computer, unless he had anticipated he may have to make a quick exit at some time. It was sounding very much as though he'd had to leave rather rapidly from when he'd been living with Claire Walters, a property either owned or rented by her, which had placed him in the predicament, according to what Jeffrey Rivers had just said, of finding somewhere to go, even if only temporary and wondering what could have promulgated the end of the relationship. Another woman? It did seem to be the most obvious reason.

'You mentioned, Mr Rivers that he and his girlfriend split up about five weeks ago, did he tell you why?'

'No, he didn't.' taking a few seconds to answer, looking uncomfortable and Keith couldn't help noticing him glancing at the silent Clarence Fountain; a strong indication he was reluctant to say anything further in front of his superior, but suddenly it seemed important to find out more.

'But perhaps you had a good idea of why?'

'Well – it is very much like telling tales out of school, Inspector, but,' he went on reluctantly when getting no response, 'most of us knew he had another girlfriend, so we assumed I suppose that Claire must have found out.'

'You only discussed this amongst yourselves; you didn't say anything to him?'

'That's right, it wasn't really any of our business; it wasn't as if Claire and he had been married.'

'Did you meet this other girl, then?'

'Not really, no, but a few weeks ago he started meeting her on a Friday night in the pub we often go to when we finish work, but he never actually introduced her.'

'Which pub is this, Mr Rivers?'

'The Masons Arms in Devonshire Street.'

'Do you know the girl's name?'

'Not her surname, but I heard someone say she was called Jilly.'

'Would you say it is a serious relationship?' Keith asked him, interested to hear what he would have to say.

'It seemed like it.'

'Am I right in saying you don't know anything more about her; where she worked, where she lived, that sort of thing?'

'Sorry.'

'What is puzzling me slightly, Mr Rivers is that instead of maybe moving in with this girl he approached you, his colleague.'

'It could have been because she's married.'

'What makes you say that?'

'Because she was wearing a wedding ring.'

As simple as that. Although not conclusive; she may be married, but not necessarily living with her husband, he thought, but even without a surname, it could be useful information. After thanking him for his time, Keith brought the interview to an end and with obvious signs of relief, and with only a nod from Clarence Fountain, he left the office.

'Inspector,' he said as soon as the door had closed behind Jeffrey Rivers, 'I am at a complete loss to understand why you should have been asking him about Tom's personal life. Can it possibly have any bearing on what we've been discussing?'

'I believe it could have, sir; if, as I believe we are both of the same opinion, Mr Jackson has elected not to turn up for work today is because he had learned that he would, not only be dismissed, but be asked pertinent questions about his handling of those accounts in his portfolio with the bank, the logical explanation is that someone told him.'

'Oh. Of course. That hadn't occurred to me, Inspector, but surely this girlfriend Jeffrey Rivers was telling you about could have nothing to do with any of this.'

'At this moment that is something we don't know, but I intend to find out. It's unfortunate Mr Rivers was unable to supply us with her surname, but that shouldn't be insurmountable. However,' Keith went on, anticipating his reaction, 'if it turns out that he has been warned, we have to consider who is responsible for passing this information on to either Tom Jackson directly or through a third party.'

'I understand that, Inspector, but I'm finding the – the whole business extremely difficult to accept and to even think of the consequences, to WHL I mean, is extremely worrying.'

'All the more reason,' Keith stressed, 'for us to proceed as quickly as we can in trying to locate Mr Jackson; evidence has transpired to support our belief that he could be instrumental in assisting us in flushing out the key figures of what has every appearance of being a syndicate formed exclusively to acquire funds illegally in order to swell their own investments, in other words, Mr Fountain, Tom Jackson is a crucial link.'

'I understand.'

'I hoped you would, sir. I realise you will be conferring with your directors whether Mr Jackson makes any appearance today or not, and all attempts to contact him have failed, but in the event there is every indication that he has gone, I will require a list of names of everyone present at the meeting held here on Friday, including anyone else who would have been privy to what had been discussed.'

'Is that really necessary?'

'It will be, yes; I am not suggesting any specific person, you understand, for being responsible for leaking what would have been in essence confidential information, but he or she must exist and therefore has to be found.

The "Masons Arms" was only a short distance away from the bank and were just opening their doors when Keith reached Devonshire Street. He was their first customer and after ordering a lager, showed the barman his warrant card and, to pre-empt any unnecessary alarm, explained he was trying to locate someone whom he understood was one of their regular customers.

'This is merely a matter of routine,' Keith added, 'but we're anxious to talk to her in connection with an investigation we're currently conducting.'

'Well -' he hesitated, clearly uncomfortable at being asked questions by an officer from New Scotland Yard, but then Keith was well used to this sort of reaction from members of the public, wondering, and not for the first time, why quite innocent people should regard the police with such trepidation, 'we do get a lot of customers, but – but you say she comes in here regularly.'

'I believe so, yes; you see, we don't have her surname, only her Christian name, which is Jilly.'

'Jilly.' he repeated, 'I don't think so, 'it's short for Gillian, isn't it?'

'Probably; she would have been with one of the banking crowd, the WHL Group, in fact.'

'I see, well,' he repeated, obviously trying to remember whether he'd ever heard her name mentioned, 'I know two or three of them by name; would she have been with anyone in particular?'

'She was as a matter of fact, he's called Tom Jackson and I've been told she's his new girlfriend.'

'Oh, I know Tom alright; he's been coming in here for years, and you're right, he has got a new girlfriend, but I don't know her name. Sorry.'

A crowd of lunchtime customers came in at that moment and he had to move away to serve them, but not prepared to give up yet, Keith decided to stay where he was until he came back. While he waited, he dialled the number Clarence Fountain had given him of Tom Jackson's mobile, but the line was dead which only further convinced him he'd been right in suspecting he had made himself scarce, although it was anyone's guess where he'd gone. Jeffrey Rivers had said he hadn't seen him since Thursday, although he had been seen by the cleaning lady in Upper Nettles the following day. It depended on when he'd learned of the impending dismissal; this could have been when he returned to London that day, if in fact he had returned, or at some time over the weekend. He could be anywhere. Considering the potential seriousness of what he was involved in, he could very well have decided to make a clean break and left the country. They would find him, of course, but it would take time. A stumbling block, Keith admitted, and perhaps he should have anticipated this, but he hadn't. Perhaps Jackson hadn't been so smart after all; by making his quick exit had to be an admission of guilt, although whichever way he looked at the man's situation, whether he did turn up at the bank with a valid reason for his absence, or whether he had left with the sole intention of not being found, he would still be facing criminal charges, with or without WHL's agreement or intervention.

'I've just had a word with Allan, Inspector,' the barman said, pointing over to one of his colleagues at the far end of the bar, 'and he told me that Tom Jackson's girlfriend was in here on Friday evening with a crowd, but he hadn't been with her,' he explained, 'some special do, Allan thought, anyway, she's called Jilly Waterman.'

'Well, that's a help, you'll thank him for me won't you.' Keith said, finishing off the rest of his beer.

'Of course, sir.'

Jilly Waterman. David Waterman's wife? Jeffrey Rivers had mentioned her wedding ring; this, he thought, was something which could soon be verified as he had intended to see both the partners sometime this afternoon, but there was certain logic in the way various factors appeared to be slipping into place. Tom Jackson's connection with Robinson & Waterman, according to the computer disc; his relationship with the wife of one of them; Clive Robinson's abortive attempt to find the disc last Thursday and the meeting a certain D. Waterman had with Glenda Nicholson, the woman who had been murdered only a matter of hours afterwards. Apart from the tenuous link between the frauds and the recent murders in Upper Nettles, it was, as he'd told Clarence Fountain, crucial to find the person in WHL who had leaked boardroom information. On reflection, Keith decided, as he made his way back to headquarters, it might be best to try and see the woman before going along to the offices of Robinson & Waterman.

When he arrived back at Headquarters, the reports on the backgrounds of Gregory and Lilian Thornton were on his desk. The one on Gregory Thornton was reasonably straightforward, although with certain ambiguities which would require clarifying, while the profile on his wife revealed an intriguing twist and should, he thought, be of some interest to Richard Cavendish, dialling the number he'd given him on Saturday.

'Keith Armstrong here, Chief Inspector,' he said, once he'd been put through to him, 'I've just returned from a meeting with one of the executives at WHL; apparently Tom Jackson didn't turn up for work this morning.'

'Sounds as though he may have had a tip off.'

'I would say so; quite frankly, I'm finding it difficult to believe otherwise, the bank has had no call from him.'

'They won't be too happy about that.'

'You're right; Clarence Fountain, that's Tom's immediate superior, is certainly in a bit of a quandary, but then, not meaning to be entirely without sympathy, that's their problem. However,' Keith went on quickly, I was able to speak to the young man Jackson has been staying with for the last five weeks or so, but unfortunately he was away for the whole weekend and the last time he saw Jackson was on Thursday.'

'Of course, Tom Jackson must have taken the Friday off.'

'Yes, I would say so. I sounded this chap out about whether he knew why Tom had finished with his girlfriend as suddenly as he must have done and although he was reluctant to tell me, which was understandable I suppose given that he had his boss practically breathing down his neck at the time, but it would seem Tom had another girlfriend and this could have been the reason.'

'It would make sense though, wouldn't it? Wherever they lived in London must have been hers and no doubt the break-up of their relationship precipitated her making a complete change in her life by moving down here.'

'I think that's the way it must have been.'

'Were you able to get the name of the new girlfriend?'

'He was only able to tell me her Christian name which is Jilly, but I've since been able to find out she's called Jilly Waterman; that's only because he told me he'd seen Tom with her in "The Masons Arms", where apparently a number of the WHL staff frequent.'

'Could she be David Waterman's wife, do you think?'

'I think it's very likely; he told me she'd been wearing a wedding ring.'

'One of life's few coincidences.'

'I agree; you don't get many of them.' Keith commented dryly.

'The eternal triangle.'

'What's new?'

'Not a lot.'

'There's something else and I know you're going to find this bit interesting; I have the background reports on the Thorntons, I'll send them through to you as soon as I come off the line, but Lilian Thornton was once married to Pete Carr.'

'That's a find; I take it he's Pete Carr of "The Bandanas"?'

'Yes, I would say he's the same alright.'

'When was this?'

'Between 1994 and 1998, and then in 2004 she married Gregory Thornton.'

'Odd the way we keep coming back to Johnnie Wall. Incidentally, we were unable to see the Thorntons today; according to their housekeeper, who isn't one of the most helpful of characters, they won't be back until later this evening, she couldn't or wouldn't tell us whether either of them would be at home tomorrow. Gregory Thornton has a mobile, but she informed us that she didn't have his permission to pass the number on to anyone, so we're a bit stymied there, although one of us will go along to their house tomorrow morning and see what's going on. There is something about that couple which worries me slightly, but quite frankly, I can't quite put my finger on it.'

'I know exactly what you mean; you have an extremely tricky case on your hands, Chief Inspector.'

'With certain complications.'

'You're not wrong,' he agreed, 'the connection between this fraud business and the murders is too strong to dismiss, there are too many links now and as you say, we keep returning to "The Bandanas", namely,

Johnnie Wall. What are your views about him being involved in the killings?'

'He's certainly involved,' Richard answered, 'but as to whether he was the one who strangled Glenda Nicholson and was directly responsible for Jamie Green's death, I'm unable to say. We have no real evidence, what we do have is only circumstantial, and I'm sure you'll agree that isn't sufficient to arrest him on suspicion of murder. Also,' he went on, 'we have to consider the possibility of someone else being equally as guilty and it would now appear we have more than a couple of likely suspects.'

'I was going to suggest you might find it helpful to be present when I question David Waterman and Clive Robinson.'

'I think that's a good idea; when are you planning to see them.'

'I had intended to get in touch with them today, but I feel it would be best if I try to speak to Jilly Waterman first, so it looks as though it's going to be tomorrow; would that suit you alright?'

'That would be fine; I'm as anxious as you are, Inspector, to move this investigation forward.'

***

Before Keith Armstrong's call, Richard and Peter had been discussing the pathologist's report on Jamie Green which had confirmed that the cause of death had been by drowning although heavy bruising at the base of the skull suggested that possibly the victim may have been rendered unconscious prior to the car entering the water. The fact he had been buckled into the driver's seat further suggested his death had been contrived. Previous police records held at the Station confirmed that he had never learned to drive, therefore would not have had the ability to have driven from Nettles Hollow to Lymington. The silk scarf had since been analysed and, as they had suspected, had been used to strangle Glenda Nicholson; the logical theory agreed by them both was that Jamie Green had possibly witnessed what happened that night at the Grange, had cycled behind Glenda Nicholson's car and by the time he had turned off the main road into the one which led to Nettles Hollow and to where he lived on the council estate, whoever had been driving would presumably be in the process of concealing the body in the undergrowth, this being further back from where he would have had to leave the car. The bicycle had been found a couple of feet away from the makeshift grave. Jamie had presumably been seen, taken unawares as indicated by the position of the injury to his skull, dragged into the car by the assailant who, once arriving at the creek at Lymington, moved him over to the driver's seat and fastened the seat belt. He'd put the scarf into his pocket before releasing the handbrake and pushing the vehicle into the water. Possibly, he had the idea that when the body was discovered Jamie Green would be posthumously charged for the murder of Glenda Nicholson.

As far as the mechanic's findings were concerned, they were as they'd expected; the car had been mechanically sound with no evidence of any tampering with the controls; the key was still in the ignition and the engine in first gear at the time of the incident. Glenda's handbag had been on the floor in front of the passenger seat, the contents disappointingly of no real significance: a wallet, containing two credit cards, twenty-five pounds in notes and a purse containing a handful of coins, a make-up bag and her mobile; the latter, because of the water damage, proving useless to them. As Peter had remarked, rather like the results of the search carried out on her property in Lyndhurst. It had given them no further insight into Glenda Nicholson's life; bank statements had shown healthy balances, with no questionably large deposits or withdrawals, household bills, also were all in order.

'Well,' Richard said, replacing the receiver, 'you were probably able to get the gist of that, Peter?'

'Tom Watson's done a disappearing act.'

'Sounds like it, and here's the interesting bit; Watson's new girlfriend is called Jilly Waterman.'

'David Waterman's wife?'

'Keith is fairly sure she's one and the same.'

'And if she is, sir,' Peter suggested, 'it's possible that somehow she found out through them in some way and promptly passed the word on to Jackson.'

'Yes,' he agreed, 'which points to WHL having a 'mole', yet another facet to the fraud business.'

'And, of course, whether she was aware of what was going on, Glenda Nicholson's involvement also.'

'Yes, no matter how much we try to separate the two cases, the possible connection continues to reappear.'

'Anything of note from the Inspector's background search into the Thorntons, sir?'

'Yes, there was; Lilian Thornton was once married to Pete Carr.'

' "The Bandanas" again.'

'Quite; apparently, as with Johnnie Wall's marriages, his didn't last very long either; four years, from 1994 to 1998.'

'1994 to 1998,' Peter repeated thoughtfully, 'Bernie Croft was with them then; he would have been bound to have known they were married.'

'Exactly, but given how you've described him, I suppose it's understandable why he chose not to say anything.'

'I would say he went out of his way not to, sir, when I asked him on Saturday how long he'd known the Thorntons he told me a couple of years and it was Glenda who'd told him she'd been in partnership with Lilian Thornton, or Lilian Bennett, as she was called then.'

'Not too clever.'

***

Monday nights in "The Hunters" were normally quiet; the build-up from about Thursday onwards having reached saturation point by the time Chris Portman finally closed the door behind the last customers on Sundays, but the appetite of those regulars whose daily lives had for years run along predictable lines had been stimulated by recent events and this Monday, although there had been no further developments since the body of Jamie Green had been brought back to Upper Nettles, there were many who couldn't let the subject drop even when it should have been obvious to them there was really nothing more to say especially as the shocked aftermath of both murders had lessened considerably and they had even exhausted their spate of earlier suggestions of who the murderer could have been and why they had been committed.

'They just don't let up, do they, Chris?' Deidre said to him as she rang up another round of drinks.

'Human nature, love, but who are we to complain; there's even more locals in here tonight than holidaymakers.' he added, smiling ruefully at her, 'Mind you,' he went on, 'I should have realised we would likely be run off our feet tonight and asked Christine to come in, but no doubt we'll cope.'

'She may not have been all that keen.'

'Why do you say that?'

'I bumped into Steve when I was out this afternoon, he only arrived back from the Gulf this morning and please don't look like that, Chris, you're wearing your cynical hat, but I'm sure in spite of what you've told me about her friendship with Pete Carr, she'd never do anything to hurt Steve.'

'My sweet wife, don't you be so sure. Ah.'

'What do you mean, ah?'

'Look who's just pulled up outside.'

'Who?' looking over towards the open doorway, 'Oh, Pete Carr.'

'Talk of the devil.' Chris muttered under his breath, moving along the bar to serve him.

After he'd finished talking to Eddie on Saturday, Pete had given Johnnie a ring. He and Johnnie went back a very long way, even before he'd married Sylvia. In those early days, they'd both still been in their teens, and shared the same passion for music, wanting to make a name for themselves in the highly competitive business. Looking back, he couldn't remember when Johnnie had switched from soft drugs to the hard stuff; it must have been a gradual process, but he'd been so completely absorbed by then in the group, he hadn't noticed, but when he did, he'd been shocked. He'd tackled Johnnie, conversationally, not wanting to make him mad, only to warn him off, concerned he would reach the stage in his addiction where he wouldn't be able to retract, but soon realising he was wasting his breath; Johnnie simply refused to listen and, yes, he did get mad, resulting in him going on a real 'bender' when none of them saw him for more than a month. They all believed that would be the end of "The Bandanas", but, miraculously, they'd held together. Now, with what Eddie had been saying it sounded he was going down the same spiral as when Penelope had died when he became paranoid he would be blamed for her death, convinced that his arrest was imminent. No matter how the three of them had attempted to convince him that the authorities were satisfied with the suicide verdict, it had made no difference to what was going on in his brain. There were, Pete realised, certain parallels in the two deaths, but only that they had both been sudden and as far as what had happened to Glenda, there was no doubt whatsoever that she'd been murdered. There had been times over the years when he'd seriously believed Johnnie had a death wish; self-flagellation at its very worse; namely, he blamed himself for Penelope dying and in some sort of sick way, he was also blaming himself for Glenda's. The fact that he could scarcely remember anything about that night and didn't even know whether Glenda had been at the Grange, certainly wasn't helping. Gerry would know of course, but Gerry Steele had his own agenda; if he didn't want to tell you anything, then that was it, you might as well forget it! They had another concert booked in Amsterdam in three weeks' time and it looked as if it was going to be up to him to keep Johnnie on an even keel and the only way to do that was to be in his company as much as possible up until then. It wouldn't be the first time, and he didn't need a crystal ball to tell him it wouldn't be the last.

'Hi, Chris,' putting his front of house face into gear, 'how are you?'

'Fine, Pete,' Chris grinned, 'how about yourself?'

'Okay, thought I'd call in and have a drink before driving on to Johnnie's.'

'What would you like, a beer?'

'No, I'll have something different, Chris; a scotch and soda, please.'

Chris had moved to the Johnnie Walker optic at the same time as Christine and her husband came in. She'd seen him, and he was on the point of saying hello to them both when he caught her expression. Oops, he thought, she's obviously going to take that line. Pretty stupid though;

she should know better than that in a small town like this, that sort of reaction was a waste of time. Pete had been coming into "The Hunters Arms" fairly regularly since Johnnie moved down to Hampshire and it hadn't taken him long to learn that practically everyone took a keen interest in what everyone else was saying or doing. Village gossip. A forest fire has nothing on this lot! And here was Christine who was their part-time barmaid and who had always acknowledged him publicly, treating him as though he was some sort of pariah!

Okay, he admitted he'd asked for that; he had been a fool to have become so involved with her, mentally cringing as he recalled how unreasonably possessive she had become; the fact she was married had made no difference to her. Yes, he had made one big mistake and when she had turned up unexpectedly at the Grange the other Friday night and had started making demands, he'd flipped. Having an affair was one thing in his book but putting their relationship on a more permanent level was something else; apart from avoiding any commitment of that kind, he wasn't in love with her and after that night, he didn't even like her very much. Christine, he had discovered from the first moment he'd met her, was for Christine, almost sorry for that poor guy she was married to and wondering if he had any idea of what she got up to while he was away. Probably not, he decided, looking over to where they were both standing, as far away as possible from him as they could be in a crowded pub of this size.

*

Christine knew she wasn't handling the situation well, but this was the first time she'd seen Pete since the night he had told her in no uncertain terms that he wanted an end to their relationship, and the rejection still hurt. She wasn't the type of woman to ever admit that it was her pride which had been hurt, but she'd had it all worked out and had, wrongly as it turned out, thought that Pete would be as eager as she was for her to move in with him. Of course she hadn't believed him when he'd said he didn't love her; all he needed was time to come round to the idea of sharing his life with someone else. The fact he'd said right at the beginning of their relationship that he would never marry again was something else she hadn't believed. But now, over a week later, she wasn't so certain. He hadn't been in touch, also he hadn't returned the message she'd left on Johnnie's answering machine and from that she had to accept that whatever they'd had was well and truly over. Christine wasn't accustomed to being turned down, also she wasn't accustomed to losing and she was not enjoying the experience. She hadn't expected him to be in the pub this evening, although she realised it was only inevitable she would see him in there at some point and was therefore annoyed with herself for the way she was re-acting.

There was something else bothering her, apart from Pete's rejection, and had been since last Thursday when everyone was talking about Glenda Nicholson having been murdered, but ostrich-like, she'd pushed it to the back of her mind, almost succeeding in dismissing it as either unimportant or none of her business. She had hardly known Glenda, possibly if she had lived in Upper Nettles, they may have become friends; there were only a few years between them and she'd been an outgoing sort of person, likeable, not bitchy like many of the women she knew in the town, but apart from serving her when she came in, that was about the extent of any exchange of words they'd had.

Steve had remarked on how abstracted she appeared and was there something on her mind, and this was only within an hour of him getting back that morning, but of course she couldn't tell him, Steve of all people. To do so, would mean she would have to mention Pete, but merely by his comment, the half-buried worry came scurrying back to the forefront of her brain, forcing her to think again and decide whether she should say anything to someone in authority. In authority? That meant the police and quite frankly that prospect frightened her.

Allowing her thoughts full reign at the same time as going through the motions of sipping her wine and appearing to listen to Steve's anecdotes about people he knew in Bahrain, she thought back to the Saturday, the day that Glenda was murdered; she had been on duty although she hadn't served her, Chris had, but when Glenda's mobile rang she'd just taken the glasses out of the dishwasher, and had been close enough to hear what she'd said, which hadn't been much, but perhaps sufficient, sufficient to prove to the police who the caller may have been: "I didn't expect to hear from you so soon …......." she had said, and then, "…….. a party, Johnnie?", followed by, "…. okay, I'm on my way." That was all; somebody she called Johnnie had asked her to a party, and after finishing her drink she left. She'd seen her driving away from the pub, along the road which led towards Johnnie's place. It may not be the same Johnnie and the party may not have been at the Grange, but Christine instinctively knew they were. Of course, the police, if she ever plucked up the courage to mention it to them, would say she was only assuming, but she wasn't, and it was for this reason she had up to now been withholding what could be considered as firm evidence, because she had seen Glenda's car parked outside the Grange. It wasn't as if she hadn't had the opportunity to say something to Peter Gale on the Tuesday when he'd asked her about the call Glenda had taken and the only explanation she could give for not doing so, was because Glenda was at that time being treated as a missing person. Poor excuse, she knew, and not exactly true.

Much later on the Saturday night, when she finally got home, she couldn't understand why she'd driven along to Johnnie's after she had finished work, it may have been only curiosity, to see whether Pete was there; it wasn't as if she had any intention of subjecting herself to another confrontation with him, but perhaps it was just curiosity, tinged with what she recognised as a spark of jealousy. It was the word party which had done it; if Johnnie was holding a party it was more than likely Pete would be there and, knowing him as well as she once thought she did, she didn't think he would have been unaccompanied. Christine had never had any illusions about Pete Carr and although he was almost fifteen years older than her, women were attracted to him, not particularly for his looks which were in her opinion, pretty average, but because of the so-called glamour which surrounded him; the concerts, the fans, the general buzz of the world of show business; that was his appeal and she hadn't missed the way he reacted to the adoration of those female groupies. For a short time she had been taken in by his laid-back charm, really believing she was the only one in his life who mattered to him, but after what he'd said to her the night before had changed all that, but all the same, she felt irresistibly drawn to him, a form of self-flagellation perhaps, but she couldn't help the way she was feeling and as soon as the last customers had gone and she'd helped Deidre to clear up, she went out to where she'd parked the car, and switching on the engine, pulled away from the kerb in the direction of The Grange.

The street lamps ended at the "Nettles Hotel", the trees of the forest dark shapes along each side of that stretch of road leading out of the town; she hadn't passed any cars, aware only of the enveloping blackness of a night without stars, even the moon which should have been directly ahead of her was obscured by cloud. In the distance, she could hear the plaintive call of an owl setting off on his nocturnal foraging and for a moment she'd been distracted by a fluttering line of bats flying low in the sky, their tiny bodies uneven shadows as they passed in front of the windscreen. Involuntary, despite the warmth, she'd shivered, almost changing her mind, but she hadn't; instead she drove on, slowing down as she approached Johnnie's house. Lights were on in some of the ground floor rooms, noticing both French windows of the lounge were wide open, but she couldn't see anyone; there was no loud music, or the sound of voices which she would have expected to hear, in fact there didn't appear to be any party at all. Pete's car wasn't outside; she recognised Johnnie's, also the one parked next to it. So, she'd thought, she'd been right; Glenda Nicholson had been going there. Accelerating, she continued along the Lymington Road, only because, apart from the gateway of the Grange there wasn't a convenient place to reverse. She could only have been a few yards away when she noticed a flash of white in her rear-view mirror; someone was running across the road from the Grange to what she knew to be Tulip Cottage. Although she had eased the pressure on the accelerator, she was too far away to make out much more, also it was too dark, although she'd been fairly certain the figure she'd seen had been a woman.

She had driven on almost as far as Brockenhurst, continuing to have the road to herself, except for a cyclist who'd passed her on his way towards Upper Nettles, and using the roundabout as her turning point, made her way back home. This time, she didn't slow down when she reached the Grange and, as before, there was no-one around; the same lights were on in the house and Tulip Cottage continued to be in darkness. There was no sign of whatever had occurred no more than fifteen minutes earlier, dismissing the incident as probably nothing important and certainly no concern of hers.

It wasn't until last Thursday when she'd read about Glenda in "The Gazette", she was reminded with a sickening jolt of what she had seen, but she'd continued to say nothing. And then, this Saturday, when she'd been on duty in "The Hunters" she had heard someone, she thought it may have been Charlie Oakes, saying that Jamie Green's bike had been found practically in the spot where Glenda's body had been; that had really got to her, especially when the news had leaked out the following day of his body being discovered inside Glenda's car in one of Lymington's creeks. But, still, she had remained silent. What did it all mean? Had Glenda been murdered when she'd been at Johnnie's that night and had she been the woman running across to Tulip Cottage? So many questions and deep-down Christine wasn't sure whether she wanted to know the answers. And seeing Pete again this evening, only served to remind her of what she was keeping to herself. Who the hell was she trying to protect, she wondered angrily. Pete, but he wasn't even there! Johnnie? And then there was that creep, Gerry Steele.

'Come back, Christine;' Steve smiled at her, 'you were miles away.'

'Sorry, Steve.' she apologised, immediately feeling guilty; Steve didn't deserve the way she was treating him, he really didn't, but sadly, she no longer loved him, not the way she loved the guy standing only yards away from her at that precise moment and she didn't know what to do.

Chapter Fourteen

Peter Gale was ringing the front door bell of Gregory and Lilian Thornton's house at ten the following morning; it wasn't difficult to work out that the woman who came to the door was their housekeeper, her severe appearance matching perfectly her manner on the phone; forbidding wasn't in it, he thought, showing her his warrant card and saying he would like to talk to Mr and Mrs Thornton; after peering short-sightedly at the card, her thin lips becoming even thinner as she glared up at him.

'I'm not sure whether it will be convenient.'

'Madam,' he said quietly, keeping his voice level, 'I would be grateful if you would find out whether it will be convenient.'

She didn't say anything further, but leaving him standing on the doorstep, turned abruptly on the low heels of her lace-up shoes and walked across the hall towards one of the doors on the right-hand side. How anyone could employ such a gorgon of a woman was completely beyond him; he'd seen thick-skulled bouncers with more manners than she had, wondering how long she would keep him waiting. At least she hadn't said the Thorntons weren't in, which meant unless the pair of them were ill, they would have to see him.

'Come this way, Inspector.' she instructed him exactly five minutes later, the flat vowels giving no indication of what part of the country she came from before taking up such inappropriate employment.

The couple standing waiting for him in the centre of the room he was shown into matched the description Barbara Freeman had given him last week reasonably well, except perhaps for the husband's age; Peter reckoned he was nearer fifty than what she'd said. Gregory Thornton, not only oozed prosperity, but he was full of a self-confidence which Peter had learned to distrust; the man, he was certain, was acting a part, but quite what part, he didn't at that precise moment know.

'Good morning, Inspector Gale,' he greeted him, striding forward to shake his hand, 'and to what we do owe this unexpected visit from the constabulary?'

'I didn't explain to your housekeeper when I spoke to her, deciding it would be best to wait until I could meet both you and your wife.'

'Just as well, probably a wise decision,' he laughed loudly, the sudden noise sounding incongruous in the luxurious surroundings of a dining-room which wouldn't have looked out of place on the front cover of 'House Beautiful': perfectly proportioned, high-ceilinged, tall sash windows framed by dark red velvet curtains, ornately carved coving and highly polished wood-block flooring with the only splash of vibrant colour, a thick-piled oriental carpet, swirls of tropical reds, blues and yellows catching the light from the sparkling crystal chandeliers which even at that time of the day had been switched on, 'however,' he continued, waving his arm expansively, 'do sit down, Inspector; you would like some refreshment, perhaps; a cold drink, coffee, tea?'

Neither of them appeared to be particularly concerned when he declined; his expression remaining in the same mould of the perfect host, while Lilian Thornton, who up to now hadn't spoken, merely looked at him appraisingly, an unfathomable smile on her face. She was an attractive woman, reminded again of how Glenda Nicholson's neighbour had described her; very sophisticated she'd said, and she had been right. In fact, summing them both up, as far as their appearances went, everything about them appeared to him to be contrived, elegant without any doubt, but not quite real.

'I'd like to say that this visit is a purely routine one,' he said, 'but I'm hoping you will, both of you perhaps, be able to assist us in our enquiries into the recent murder of a woman called Glenda Nicholson.'

'We know about Glenda's death, Inspector, although we only heard last night when we arrived back and were utterly stunned, shocked in fact.'

'You must have been, sir,' Peter nodded, 'and this is why we are trying our utmost to find out who was responsible, also,' he added, 'we are treating the matter as a double murder enquiry.'

'There have been two murders, Inspector Gale!' Lilian Thornton spoke for the first time, her eyes widening in shocked surprise, 'We didn't realise; Bernie never mentioned another murder, did he, Greg?'

'No, darling, he didn't;' his expression softening as he looked at her, 'how do you believe we can help you, Inspector?'

'Through your friendship with the deceased mainly, Mr Thornton; you see,' he went on, 'as Glenda Nicholson had only been living in this area for six years, we need to know what she was doing before then, who her friends were, the places she used to frequent and whether she kept in touch with any of those people.'

'Why?'

Just the one word; nothing else, but it did convey something; Gregory Thornton either had no idea of why they should be searching through Glenda Nicholson's past, which he thought was extremely unlikely, or he knew perfectly well and was using the one syllable question for the sole purpose of trying to find out just how much was known about her; he was stalling, possibly preparing to select his response to suit himself.

'Because as yet we have no motive for her killing; we know how the murder was committed and approximately the time of her death, but we don't know why, therefore we have no alternative but to trawl back some years until we're satisfied we've exhausted each separate line of enquiry.'

'Complicated.'

'Murder enquiries invariably are, sir.'

'Well,' shrugging his shoulders almost dismissively as though he was finding the whole conversation boring, 'Lilian and I have both known Glenda for a few years -' pausing as though stuck for words, but Peter thought differently; he was stalling, conscious of perhaps saying too much, or more than he needed to.

' - we'll talk about your friendship with her first, shall we and then your wife can fill in with how well she knew her and for how long.'

'Very well;' he said, moving slightly forward in the chair and leaning one elbow on the table, 'I first met her when she was married to Ted Warren, he had the Revue Bar in Leicester Square, but I expect you knew she'd been married to him, Inspector?'

'Yes, we did.'

'Ted introduced us actually, she was often in the club during that time, but I wasn't always in her company and then it wasn't until Lilian and I were married, or shortly before, when I saw her again. We weren't what you would call *friends,*' he emphasised, whether for his benefit or for his wife's, Peter couldn't say, 'anyway, quite a few years went by and I never saw her again; it wasn't until she moved to Lyndhurst and bought the business in Upper Nettles that we started meeting fairly often, dinner parties, that sort of thing, you understand.'

'A few moments ago, Mrs Thornton, you mentioned someone called Bernie, would that be Bernie Croft?'

'Yes, that's right; Bernie is a neighbour of ours.'

'Mr Thornton,' Peter asked, turning to face him, 'did you visit 'Ted's Revue Bar' regularly?'

'You could say that, yes.'

'Do you know Johnnie Wall, the guitarist?'

'Oh, Johnnie, of course, we all knew Johnnie; he was good company and is a brilliant guitarist.'

'Did you also know Nicholas Wade-Brown, Glenda's second husband?'

'I knew of him, but I don't think I was ever in his company.'

'You may consider these questions somewhat irrelevant, sir, but I assure you they're not; we are through this persistence beginning to form a picture of those years when it would seem there were a number of people all mixing or meeting in the same venues around London, this has been helpful.' he added.

'It is all somewhat tedious, though.' the first hint of a complaint in his voice.

'I apologise for that, but as I've said, necessary. However,' ignoring the quick frown, but not altogether displeased, 'I would now like to return to this year, to the weekend when Glenda Nicholson met her death.'

'Yes, Inspector.' resignedly, leaning back and folding his arms.

'Not to the Saturday night, but to the following day when, according to witnesses, you and Mrs Thornton called at Glenda Nicholson's house.'

'Neighbours! But we've nothing to hide, Inspector,' he smiled, 'Lilian and I had been invited for lunch and of course by then poor Glenda was no longer with us.'

'Were you surprised when you found she wasn't there?'

'Yes, we were as a matter of fact, very, but what could we do? Of course we had absolutely no idea of what had happened the night before. None at all; not until as I've said, Bernie told us last night.'

'Did you try to phone her?'

'A couple of times, yes, but we couldn't get through. We were leaving the following day in any case, so we decided to wait until we returned to get in touch with her.'

'You weren't worried?'

'No, why should we have been.'

'Although you said you were surprised; does that mean you considered it out of character for her after inviting you for lunch to find she wasn't at home?'

'Well, put like that, yes, but we weren't unduly worried; we even thought she may have got the dates mixed up.'

'That's possible, of course.'

'We all lead such busy lives these days, don't we, Inspector; too much to think about, trying to cram as much as we can into each day of the week.'

'That's true. You didn't think of sending her a note, an email perhaps; after all you were going to be out of the country for several days?'

'I have to admit it just didn't occur to us, Inspector.'

'And yet when she didn't turn up for work on the Monday, her assistant was worried.'

'Really?'

'So much so, she reported her as missing, although her body wasn't discovered until the Wednesday.'

'Yes, I know, Inspector, but if I may point out, this was only a lunch appointment, quite different from not arriving for work, especially when the business is your own.'

'You knew she had been reported missing?'

'Yes, Bernie told us.'

'I see.' and he did see, he saw very clearly. Bernie Croft would not have known that Sara Blakeman had called at the station on the Monday and reported her as missing; therefore, the logical conclusion was that he already knew about Glenda Nicholson's death before last night.

'Mrs Thornton,' he said, looking towards where she was sitting next to her husband, a silent figure, patient, with only the odd fleeting glance in his direction to indicate she was interested in what was being discussed, 'we are aware that you and Glenda Nicholson were in partnership back in the early nineteen-nineties -'

' - are you really, Inspector?' she interrupted, 'I hadn't realised.'

'All part of our routine questioning,' he smiled encouragingly at her, hoping she would be more natural and therefore more forthcoming than her husband, 'and that this had been before your marriage to Mr Thornton?'

'Oh, yes, Greg and I were married on the 1st April 2004 and Glenda and I were already making arrangements by then to close the business, shortly after that, she moved out of London and bought her house in Lyndhurst.' she added.

'And during the time you were in partnership together your name would have been -?

' - Lilian Bennett.'

'Not Carr?'

'Just a minute, Inspector!' sitting upright with a jerk, 'I object to the way you're questioning my wife; what on earth does it matter what her name was?'

'Mr Thornton,' putting up a restraining hand in his direction, 'I am merely trying to put everything into some semblance of order.'

'It's alright, Greg,' Lilian Thornton said quietly, putting a hand on his arm, 'it doesn't matter. My husband believes I could be upset by you mentioning a period of my life I would rather forget, but I was married before and he was called Pete Carr; but, Inspector Gale, the marriage wasn't a happy one and after four years we divorced, quite amicably as it happens.' she added, with another of her secretive little smiles. Was she a very clever woman or was she really as guileless as she was purporting; Peter couldn't make up his mind.

'Thank you, Mrs Thornton, for being so frank.'

'That's alright, Inspector; I understand you have your job to do.'

accompanied by another smile which meant all or nothing.

'When you were married to Pete Carr, Mrs Thornton,' he asked, ignoring the darkening expression on Gregory Thornton's face, 'presumably you would have known Johnnie Wall?'

'Yes, of course.'

'It would seem that after his second wife, Penelope Driver, died he has never re-married.'

'It used to surprise me, but you're right, as far as I know he hasn't.'

'No serious attachments, then?'

'Apart from Glenda of course, but then their relationship was really common knowledge to us all at the time.'

'Did you expect them to marry after Penelope's death?

'We all did, actually, well, I didn't.'

'May I ask why?'

'It was something Glenda said to me, actually. This is all rather embarrassing, Inspector.'

'Take your time.' he encouraged, fully expecting a second intervention from Gregory, but this time he remained silent.

'She confided in me, Inspector, but I suppose now that she's no longer alive, it doesn't matter all that much. You see,' she started to explain, 'by this time and probably even before, he was heavily into taking drugs, the hard stuff, I mean, and I honestly believe it was affecting him - '

'In what way?' gently prompting.

'Sexually; he'd started making extraordinary demands which she found unacceptable. She didn't go into any detail, but it was just the way she said it; she even looked - '

' - yes?'

'Afraid; I think there were times she was afraid of him; she never said as much, but I always thought she was.'

'Do you think, although she had reservations about him, she continued seeing him?'

'I honestly don't know and of course I never asked her, but I don't think so, because certainly from about three or four years ago, I don't exactly know when, she started going with Bernie and they seemed to have a steady relationship.'

'Again, I'm grateful, Mrs Thornton for you telling me this and you have my assurance this knowledge will be treated with discretion.'

'Thank goodness for that!' Gregory Thornton said, obviously unable to remain quiet.

As Peter was leaving, aware of the almost tangible air of relief from both of them, he paused at the opened front door: You have told me, Mr Thornton that it didn't occur to you to contact Glenda Nicholson either by sending her an email or a letter, but what about you Mrs Thornton,' but before giving her a chance to answer, he added casually, 'because a registered package arrived last Tuesday morning addressed to Miss Nicholson at her salon in Upper Nettles; there was no name of the sender, only from where it was mailed, which was Bournemouth and on enquiring there were informed that the name of the sender was a Miss Bennett.'

'Miss Bennett;' and on cue, the smile made another appearance, 'what a coincidence, but no, Inspector, I didn't send that package; why should I have, my name is now and has been for six years, Mrs Thornton, Lilian Thornton.'

Yes, Peter thought to himself as he returned to the car, the lady is a very good actress; she hadn't even flinched when he'd asked her, and not by one tiny flicker of those unnaturally long eyelashes had she shown any surprise. She had anticipated the question.

***

Keith waited until he reckoned David Waterman would have left for work, and at exactly the same time as Peter, sixty-odd miles away in Bournemouth was waiting for someone to come to the door of the Thorntons' house in Melbourne Crescent, he was introducing himself to Jilly Waterman.

'Inspector Keith Armstrong, New Scotland Yard;' she read out loud from the card he'd shown her, 'and you want to talk to *me?*' she emphasised, a look of disbelief on her face, 'Surely there's some mistake.'

'You are Mrs David Waterman?'

'Yes, of course I am.'

'Could you spare a few minutes, Mrs Waterman; I'd like to ask you about your friend, Tom Jackson.'

'Tom! You want to ask about Tom?' she repeated, but there was something about her eyes which alerted him; she wasn't as surprised as she was making out to be. They were rather unusual eyes: brown, but with a tinge of gold; cat's eyes, round and unblinking as she looked at him, 'Oh,' she sighed, 'I suppose you'd better come in, although it's terribly inconvenient, I'm meeting some friends for coffee at eleven.'

'What I have to ask you shouldn't take long.' he said, stepping into their hall and following her into the kitchen.

'Alright,' she said, not bothering to ask him if he'd like to sit down, 'what do you want to ask me, Inspector?'

'When did you last see Mr Jackson?'

'Saturday evening, we had a drink; in the Hilton.' she added, 'Why do you want to know?'

'What time was this?' he asked, ignoring her question.

'Oh, early, just before seven, actually. We only had the one drink and then I left.'

'Any particular reason?'

'Sorry?'

'Was there any particular reason why you left so early?'

'Not really; we hadn't made any plans to spend the whole evening together.'

'Whose idea was it to meet for a drink, Mrs Waterman?'

'It was my idea, Inspector.' she had taken so long to answer, he was beginning to think she wasn't going to, but it was clear to him that she'd needed the time to decide what she was going to say.

'Mr Jackson didn't turn up for work either yesterday or this morning, his flatmate has confirmed that he hadn't seen him since Thursday, he hasn't phoned his bank to explain his absence, also it appears that he is non-contactable. And,' Keith went on, 'as you are the only person we have spoken to who has not only seen him recently, but has been in his company, it is possible he may have told you where he was going.'

'Why should you think he's gone anywhere?'

She was prevaricating.

'We believe he has gone somewhere, and it is a matter of some importance that we find out where.'

'I honestly don't understand why there's all this fuss, Inspector, I really don't.'

'Tom Jackson holds a position of considerable trust with his bank, Mrs Waterman; his role as senior executive, is to handle clients' investments where substantial funds are involved, therefore when someone of his standing goes absent without leave, naturally the bank have to be concerned.'

'New Scotland Yard, though! That's a bit over the top, surely!'

'I am conducting an enquiry which contains highly confidential information where discretion is paramount. All I am asking you, Mrs Waterman, is to tell me as much as you may know about your friend Tom Jackson's intentions to possibly, not only to abandon his position with the bank, together with the inevitable consequences, but to leave England.'

'I've told you all I know.'

'I don't believe you have.' Keith said, keeping his tone level; he recognised stubbornness when he saw it, but he didn't think she would be able to maintain it for much longer, 'Let's start again, shall we?' disregarding the sigh, heavy with ill-disguised exasperation, 'You've told me it was your suggestion to meet for a drink on Saturday evening; did you have any special reason for wanting to see him?'

He spotted immediately that what had been no more than a calculated guess on his part, had been right. He had nothing definite or even tangible to support his idea that she could have told him about the bank's decision to dismiss him, except for the fact that she was married to David Waterman who was in partnership with Clive Robinson and that they were somehow involved in this fraud business, also that WHL had a 'mole', suggesting that he or she could be supplying Robinson & Waterman with inside information. Jilly Waterman may have heard about the dismissal plans. How? What was now considered to be old fashioned, pillow talk or had she overheard them discussing Jackson or had someone else told her? Take your pick.

'Not really, I hadn't seen him for a few days, that's all.'

'I suggest you did have something to tell him, and that something instigated his decision to leave Britain; in other words, Mrs Waterman, to make himself scarce.'

'I had nothing to do with Tom leaving the country.'

'How do you know he was leaving the country; did he tell you?'

'He may have done.'

'I would remind you that this is a serious matter and one which should not be dismissed by yourself, I would appreciate therefore if you would give me a straight answer to a straight forward question. I'll repeat, did Tom Jackson tell you on Saturday evening that he intended to leave this country.'

'He did, yes, but it was no concern of mine, Inspector.'

'Were you sorry to hear about his decision?'

'Not particularly.'

'Was he sorry to be leaving you and personally never seeing you again?'

'He didn't say he would be.'

'Had you made any plans to meet up later?'

'No, why should we have?'

'Because you and Tom Jackson were in a relationship, Mrs Waterman; I don't believe your friendship was a platonic one.'

'Oh, alright, we were sleeping together, but I would never have gone off with him.'

'Did he ask you to on Saturday?'

This time she took longer to answer, but he was confident she would.

'Yes, he did.'

'And you refused; was this the reason you spent so little time with him on Saturday evening; you only had one drink you've told me.'

'That was perfectly true; I had nothing more to say to him, so I left; it was as simple as that.'

'Did he tell you where he intended to go, Mrs Waterman?'

'Why should he have?'

'I would have thought it was extremely likely he would have told you where he was heading, especially if he wanted you to accompany him.'

'France.'

'He was going to France; did he specify where?'

'No specific town; he just said the Côte d'Azur.'

'He didn't try and persuade you to change your mind?'

'No, he didn't. He probably knew he would be wasting his time. Anyway, I like living in London and I *am* married.' attempting, but failing, to adopt the pious look.

***

On their way to the offices of Robinson & Waterman, Keith was able to give Richard the outcome of his earlier meeting with Jilly Waterman and her admission about Tom Jackson telling her he was making for the South of France, both agreeing to say nothing of this when they spoke to the two partners.

They were shown into Robinson & Waterman's conference room where Clive Robinson and David Waterman were waiting for them.

After the introductions were made, Keith lost no time in explaining that in the course of the murder enquiry being conducted by Chief Inspector Cavendish, certain evidence had come to light which encroached on New Scotland Yard's investigations into a fraud case of some significance, and further explaining that this evidence was being considered as a crucial element in compiling the dossier which would ultimately bring the perpetrators to justice.

Neither Clive Robinson nor David Waterman displayed any visible signs of emotion, no sideways' glances at each other, no reaction whatsoever, which could be because they'd been forewarned, if that was the case, Keith decided, it was more than likely they would know of Jackson's desertion.

'You will have noticed,' Keith continued, 'of my use of the plural, the reason being there is no doubt that a fraud of this scale is not being carried out singlehandedly, although as with all plans, illegal or otherwise, there has to be a key figure.'

'This is all very well, Inspector,' Clive put in quickly, while David Waterman remained silent, leaning forward in his chair, an unfathomable expression on his somewhat bland features, 'but you haven't explained exactly why you are here.'

'I was coming to that, Mr Robinson, but first I believe it is important that you are made aware, firstly of the seriousness of this case and secondly,' hesitating for a fraction of a second, 'your own positions.'

'Our own positions?'

'Yes, your own positions,' Keith repeated, his tone level, 'in that your name and Mr Waterman's have occurred in this evidence which I suggest you consider carefully before dismissing out of hand.'

'No doubt you intend to enlighten us as to the content of this evidence.'

'Certainly; it is a computer disc containing the names of several individuals of considerable financial standing, all of whom have either willingly or unwillingly permitted their investments to be handled by financial institutions, although several of them had previously raised, not necessarily complaints, but had voiced their concern in respect to how their investments were being looked after. Aside from the data on the disc, both your names were mentioned -'

'- that means, nothing, Inspector,' he interrupted, 'and if your visit here this afternoon is based on only that, well, all I can say is, you have wasted your time.'

'Your names were mentioned,' Keith went on, ignoring the interruption, 'in respect to a meeting to be held in your office on the 10th of April this year.'

'We have many meetings in the office, don't we, David,' he asked him, obviously attempting to bring his partner into the conversation, 'scarcely a day goes by when we're not seeing clients.'

Keith waited, giving David Waterman the opportunity to reply, but he only nodded, presumably in agreement to what Clive Robinson had said. Up to now, he had shown every reluctance to contribute, leaving it to his partner, but Keith wasn't fooled; the pair of them were an act, reminding himself they had been working together for a long time and therefore had

had plenty of practice.

'I'll return to what you said a couple of minutes ago,' Keith said, 'and you were right, reading your names on the disc didn't motivate our visit; it did act as a link though in that your names had come up separately during the Chief Inspector's enquiries into Glenda Nicholson's death.'

'What on earth do you mean?' almost spluttering, again glancing towards his partner, presumably expecting some sort of verbal support. Keith took the opportunity to give Richard a nod indicating he might wish to take-over.

'Mr Waterman,' Richard said, focusing his attention on him and pointedly ignoring Clive Robinson's outburst, 'it is our understanding you were in Upper Nettles on Saturday, the 12th June, the day Miss Nicholson met her death and did in fact have a drink with her in the lounge bar of the Nettles Hotel. Is this correct?'

'Er – well, yes.'

'I would just like to recap, sir,' he said, proceeding to extract from him just how well he had known Glenda Nicholson to have actually gone out of his way to meet her for only a drink before returning to London, but the answers he received were brief and unhelpful, obviously exercising considerable care in how much he intended to divulge. Altogether not an entirely satisfactory exchange of words, except it went a long way to reinforce their beliefs that he was hiding something, his ultra-cautious manner more difficult to penetrate than that of his more volatile and short-tempered partner. Richard hadn't included Clive Robinson, having agreed with Richard earlier that Robinson's activities would be in the province of New Scotland Yard, working on the premise that there was nothing to support he had, even indirectly, been involved with Glenda Nicholson. Whether he had known her was feasible and remained to be seen, but all the evidence suggested so far that his visit to Upper Nettles had been to locate the computer disc, which did further suggest both partners had known of its existence, or if not actually known about it, they had assumed that Tom Jackson would have kept a record of the various transactions, especially if any of them could be linked to Robinson & Waterman.

Keith, watching the expressions of both partners closely, considered it was now time to metaphorically 'go for the jugular', intrigued to find out what their reactions were going to be; even although they were expecting Jackson's name to be mentioned at some point, and had formulated a plan on how they would react, the outcome would be interesting and, hopefully, assist them further in the labyrinth of information they had put together to crack what had escalated into wide-spread fraud of investors' funds.

'I would like one of you to explain what the relationship is between yourselves and Tom Jackson.' Keith said, gratified to notice the brief flash of what could be described as apprehension on their faces, Clive being the first to say anything, but not before taking a deep breath; whether to control his annoyance, Keith wasn't certain.

'I don't quite understand what you mean by a relationship, Inspector.'

'I was referring to a business relationship, Mr Robinson.'

'Ah, well, the answer is simple; we don't have a business relationship with him.'

'Are you saying you are only friends and any meeting you may have with him could be classed as social?'

'It's one way of putting it; what would you say, David?' this time giving him no chance to avoid any attempt to opt out from participating, also, Keith thought, this wasn't part of their act. It should have been of course, but then they'd only had a matter of hours from when he'd phoned their office, to concoct a joint strategy.

'Tom Jackson,' David Waterman answered, slowly and selecting each phrase with deliberation, 'is an ex-colleague of ours, not a close friend.'

'You're talking from when you were with the WHL merchant bank?'

'Yes, that's right, the WHL Group, they're in Regent Street.'

'I know where they are, Mr Waterman.' The man was unbelievably pedantic, although in some respects that could be contrived; he'd learned that in certain situations such people used this trait as a ploy, one which would give them more time to select what they were going to say next, also to work out where the questioning was leading and David Waterman, he thought, was no different. 'How long have you been in partnership with Mr Robinson?'

'Since 1995.'

'Fifteen years; that's a long time.'

'Yes, it is.'

'Especially when you consider you have both kept in touch with Tom Jackson since then and you've just told us you were not friends.'

'I believe I said we were not close friends.' he emphasised.

Touché.

'You did, yes, so do we take it that Tom Jackson is a friend of yours?'

'Yes.'

'Mr Waterman,' Keith went on, 'I would like to remind you that the Chief Inspector and I are conducting two extremely serious investigations, one of murder and the other of fraud, and neither of us will tolerate any prevarication; not only is it time-wasting, but it is obstructive. What I'm trying to establish,' he persisted, 'is the extent of the relationship you have with Tom Jackson. For instance, when you meet, is this for social or business reasons?'

'We usually have a drink together, so I suppose that means they were social.'

'The meeting I referred to earlier was to be held here, rather than in a pub or a restaurant.'

This time he didn't say anything, only by a shrug of his shoulders which Keith read to mean he was attempting to dismiss the statement as insignifcant.

'Mr Robinson,' he said, choosing to ignore what was tantamount to impertinence, 'it is our understanding that last Thursday you were in Upper Nettles with the intention of looking up a friend of yours who had apparently recently moved there.'

'That's true,' his answer came quickly, too quickly, 'I was, but I wasn't able to see her.'

'You went to her house?'

'I did, but she wasn't in.'

'What time of day was this?'

'Early evening; I can't remember the time exactly.'

'According to one of the people you spoke to before then, you arrived in the town around midday; is that correct?'

'If you say so, I can't remember.'

'I'm surprised as you had the whole afternoon there you didn't try and see your friend earlier.'

'Well, I didn't.'

'And your friend's name, Mr Robinson?'

'I'm sure you are already aware of that, Inspector.'

'I would like the name of your friend, please.'

'Claire Walters.'

'And if I were to inform you that Miss Walters had never heard of you until your name was mentioned to her the other day?'

'She'd probably forgotten about me.'

'I would say that was extremely unlikely, Mr Robinson,' for the first time permitting an edge to creep into his voice, 'in fact, I would go so far as to say you've never seen the lady in your life before.'

'That's a ridiculous statement.'

'Is it?' increasing the tempo, 'Tom Jackson, Mr Robinson, is an ex-boyfriend of Claire Walters; he had been living with her for a few years until about six weeks ago when, for personal reasons, she told him to leave. I would suggest you were aware of this and having found out where she was living, you decided to take the opportunity to find out whether by any chance Tom Jackson had, in his haste to vacate her previous property, left behind evidence of his dealings with yourselves, but your plan failed.'

'You've got absolutely nothing to substantiate what you've just said.'

'I will leave my questioning there for the time being,' Keith said, standing up and pushing his chair back, 'but I have to inform you that any further meeting between ourselves will be conducted at New Scotland Yard Headquarters. As this will be recorded and conducted along formal lines, you may decide to have your solicitor present, to which you are entitled. I am, of course,' he added, 'referring to the fraud investigation; should the Chief Inspector require to speak to you further, Mr Waterman with reference to the murder of Glenda Nicholson, he will be contacting you personally.'

'It appears to me, Inspector Armstrong,' David Waterman obviously sufficiently motivated to make his first spontaneous remark since the start of the meeting; 'you are deliberately involving me in both investigations which quite frankly I find unacceptable.'

'I have no intention of discussing any aspect of the murder enquiry with you, Mr Robinson; that as I've explained is the province of the Upper Nettles Police Force, the murder investigation being led by Chief Inspector Cavendish, but as far as the New Scotland Yard investigation is concerned, you and Mr Robinson are being considered as important figures - '

' - you mean suspects!' Clive Robinson protested loudly, jumping up from his chair.

'No, sir, I don't mean that.' Keith answered smoothly, 'We have considerably more work to do before reaching that stage, but we have to satisfy ourselves whether there is any significance in your names being included on the disc compiled by Tom Jackson, the contents of which concerns questionable investment transactions. There is the added aspect of your visit to Upper Nettles, ostensibly you say to visit a friend of yours, who until very recently had no knowledge of your existence; this also requires clarification.'

He had the sense this time to remain silent, the sullen expression on his face indicative of his indignation, and possibly his impotence of being unable to extricate himself from a situation of his own making; he should have realised they would be aware of Tom Jackson's previous relationship with Claire Walters as by now he must have worked out that only she would have handed it over to the authorities. He'd slipped up there and if he had retracted from he'd said, he would only have pushed himself further into the mire. At least, Keith thought cynically, if he'd achieved nothing else from this interview, he would have succeeded in upsetting Clive Robinson's equilibrium.

***

On the way back to Upper Nettles later that afternoon, Richard reflected on the meeting he and Keith Armstrong had had with Clive Robinson and David Waterman. The final outcome hadn't been particularly satisfactory; the manner of their responses to Keith's questions had been identical, leaving no doubt in both his and Keith's mind, they had planned beforehand exactly how much they were prepared to say. It wasn't as if they had been obstructive in any way; they had merely answered as succinctly, but as frugally, as was necessary, but it hadn't been enough. As far as New Scotland Yard's fraud case was concerned, there remained a considerable amount of work to be done before they reached a conclusion, a task made considerably more difficult by the fact that ultimately major banks and financial institutions would be involved and it remained to be seen exactly how much they were legally prepared to divulge in respect to their clients' investments, but then, Richard thought with some relief, he was conducting a murder enquiry, a double murder enquiry, and as far as he was concerned, after listening to what had been said, he didn't consider either Clive Robinson or David Waterman as having been involved.

The explanation, although a weak one, given by David Waterman for meeting Glenda Nicholson on the evening of her death, was credible and, if necessary, could be checked out to make sure he had in fact returned home at the time he'd told them.

"I would just like to recap, Mr Waterman," recalling now what he'd said to him, "you say you had been with a client in Winchester on that Saturday afternoon and, Glenda being a friend of yours, you thought as you were in the area you would have a drink with her on your way back to London. Is that correct?"

"Quite correct." he'd nodded.

"The drive from Winchester to Upper Nettles would have taken you, what; thirty, thirty-five minutes?"

"About that, yes."

"It would have still been out of your way, though; I wouldn't say that Winchester is exactly in this area."

"Perhaps not."

"How well did you know Miss Nicholson?"

"I'd known her a while."

"How long is a while, Mr Waterman?"

"Ten or fifteen years."

"And did you see her often?"

"No, not really."

"And yet you decided to meet her and have a drink before returning to London."

"Yes, it was a spur of the moment decision. There was no rush for me to get back that evening, that's why I had a meal in the hotel; this was after Glenda had left."

"I see." and he did; David Waterman did not strike him as being a spur-of-the-moment sort of person. He had mentioned this to Keith when they were leaving Robinson & Waterman's office.

"You haven't met his wife." Keith had chuckled, "whatever she saw in him I can't imagine."

"From how you've described the lady, I would say it was money, a comfortable no-questions asked life with a husband too busy to care what she was getting up to."

"And she wasn't prepared to take the risk of leaving him and going off with Jackson."

"Too risky a proposition for her, presumably she was well aware he was a shady character and there was always the fear of the ominous ring of the front doorbell."

"That's true," Richard had agreed, "but whichever wait you look at it, the way things are turning out for her husband and his partner, her future with him doesn't appear to be particularly promising."

By the time Richard had reached the junction for the A337, he had turned his thoughts to the progress he and Peter had made over the last couple of days, in particular to the outcome of Peter's meeting with the Thorntons. The trouble with this murder enquiry, Richard thought, was they were being continually hampered by issues concerning the fraud case, although there had been something Lilian Thornton had said to Peter this morning which could be applied to their investigation into the murder of Glenda Nicholson. It had been when Penelope Driver's name had been mentioned and how everyone in their crowd, except for herself, had expected Johnnie Wall to marry Glenda. The thread of thought which this had triggered off in his mind had been elusively tenuous and it was only now, when he'd separated the two cases, a pattern was evolving and one he hadn't been able to pick up on previously; two women in his life had died suddenly, one, his wife and the other, Glenda Nicholson, his lover, and both had confided they had been afraid of him. According to Lilian Thornton, Glenda had complained about him making unacceptable sexual demands. Her death was a violent one and there was no doubt she'd been strangled, but as far as Penelope Driver was concerned, all they knew was that she committed suicide by taking an overdose on the drugs prescribed to her for depression. Until they had seen the results of the pathologist's findings, together with the circumstances immediately leading up to her death, he was unable to take his hypothesis any further.

He was now approaching the outskirts of Upper Nettles and negotiating the late afternoon traffic in the High Street, pulled up in front of the Station, alongside Peter's car. There wasn't much more he could do today, except meet up with Peter to give him the gist of the afternoon's meeting and then he intended to relax for the remainder of the evening over a couple of beers and one of "The Hunters"' renowned steak and kidney pies. He needed to give his brain a rest, suddenly weary of spending too many hours literally going round in circles.

***

Claire had spent most of the day working, not dissatisfied with what she'd done; she had fine-tuned the plot of her new book, including the draft of the first two chapters, also, she had made time to read through her old notes on "Tomorrow Never Comes", going so far as to jot down some ideas for the sequel. Dan would be pleased, she smiled to herself, switching off her computer; she would have something positive to tell him when she saw him at the end of the week. She was half-way downstairs when her mobile rang and, continuing to walk through to the kitchen, pressed the button.

'Claire?'

'Hi, Sophie, this is a nice surprise. How are things?'

'It depends what you mean by *things*, but I'm fine, working hard as usual trying to achieve the impossible with deadlines, but then I don't need to tell you that.'

'Come on Sophie,' Claire prompted, 'don't be so cryptic.'

'Sorry, but I'm phoning about Tom.'

'Tom?'

'You sound as though you'd forgotten who he is.'

'I suppose I have, but what's happened?'

'It would seem he's disappeared.'

'What?'

'Just that, but from what I've been hearing, it sounds more as though he's done a bunk.'

'Good grief!'

'Is that all you can say, Claire; your ex-boyfriend has scarpered and apparently nobody has a clue where he's gone. Mind you,' she went on in her usual rapid way, scarcely pausing to take a breath, 'if you're as laid back as that it's a good thing, just thought you might be interested.'

'Oh, I am I suppose, Sophie, but it all sounds so – well, so dramatic.'

'It *is* dramatic.'

'So how did you hear about this?'

'From a couple of his colleagues at WHL; I was in the "The Masons Arms" this lunchtime and got chatting to them. Apparently, their boss had a visit from an officer from New Scotland Yard yesterday morning, asking to speak to Tom, and that's when they discovered he hadn't turned up for work, he wasn't in today either.' she added.

'Sounds serious.' knowing she shouldn't say too much, having a good idea why the bank had been contacted by New Scotland Yard.

'Presumably they've tried to get hold of him?'

'Yes, they've only got his mobile phone number of course, and Jeffrey Rivers, he's the guy Tom's been sharing with, says he's not seen him since last Thursday.'

'Sounds as though he's got himself into something of a fix.'

'You've had a lucky escape there, Claire, you really have. You know I never liked him, and I'm not going to say I told you so.'

'I should hope not!' Claire laughed.

'You sound happy.'

'I am happy, Sophie.'

'What about Jack; is he happy?'

'Sophie!'

She was incorrigible and just for a few seconds there Claire wished she was back in London, but that was all it lasted, although realising she did miss the place where she'd lived all her life and the friends she'd made, Sophie being her only real friend, her confidante; she'd meant it when she'd said to her that she was happy and of course she guessed why, but once again she was right in her mystic Meg predictions. It was true, Sophie hadn't liked Tom; she'd never explained why and naturally enough she didn't ask her and now, it would seem, without any warning he'd decided not only to give up his job with the bank, but presumably to leave London. It was such a drastic and ultimate decision and she wouldn't have thought he was the type of man to run away, but perhaps she had never known him, the salutary implication being that during those six years spent with him had no meaning.

She would phone Jack in a moment, but first she poured herself a glass of chilled white wine, something which had in so short a time become something of a ritual when she'd finished work for the day.

'Claire,' he said, as soon as he heard her voice, 'I was on the point of calling you, you beat me to it; what sort of a day have you had?'

'Busy,' she smiled, 'but finished now. I've just had a call from Sophie,' she told him, 'by all accounts Tom hasn't turned up for work this week, I know it's only Tuesday but from what she was saying the bank hasn't been able to get hold of him.'

'News certainly travels fast,' he said, 'and it sounds as if Sophie is right; Adam phoned me a few minutes ago to give me an update on what's been happening and his friend at New Scotland Yard went along to the bank yesterday morning asking to speak to Tom, only to be told he hadn't come in; as you can probably imagine his absence, together with what they've been told about their suspicions about Tom's activities, is causing something of a panic.'

'Certainly not good for business once this leaks out.'

'Too true.'

'What about his girlfriend; did Adam mention whether they've been in touch with her?'

'He did, yes; in a nutshell, she didn't want to know, although she did tell them he was going to France.'

'That wasn't very clever of him.'

'It wasn't, was it; according to Adam, she told the officer Tom had expected her to go with him and she gave him the big heave-ho.'

'Oh, dear.' but not really meaning it; as far as she was concerned, considering what Tom had been up to, he deserved everything he got; 'Now, of course,' she added, unable to keep the cynicism from her voice, 'he'll have a police record, whether they manage to find him or not.'

'They'll find him, Claire and when you consider the seriousness of what they're investigating, if he has left the country, New Scotland Yard will no doubt pass the matter over to Interpol.'

'What a mess.'

'You're right, it is a mess and thank goodness not our concern.'

'When the time comes, Jack, and there's a court case, do you think I'm going to be called to give evidence; evidence of having the disk in my possession I mean, and not forgetting the attempt the other night to try and find where Tom had hidden it; I'd almost forgotten about the break-in.'

'I wouldn't think you would have to appear in court; you're not worried about all of this, are you, Claire?'

'Not worried exactly, just finding it so very unpleasant and then, of course, there's all this business over what's been happening here.'

'The authorities certainly have their hands full, but I believe we have an excellent police team in Upper Nettles, I'm sure they'll find out who's responsible. Anyway, on a more cheerful note, have you any plans for this evening?'

'To relax; I'd just opened a bottle of wine before I rang you, would you like to come over and share it with me.'

'I can think of nothing better and then, perhaps we can drive into the village and have a meal in "The Hunters", unless you would prefer the more salubrious surroundings of the "Nettles Hotel"?'

'I've yet to visit the hotel, but I think I would prefer a pub meal; Deidre is really a brilliant cook.'

The bar of "The Hunters" was packed by the time they got there; the evening was still warm, with a few more hours of daylight left. Many of the customers were seated outside, one or two of whom she recognised from when she'd been in before, including, she noticed, the over-the-top Trevor Wheatley, even more colourful this evening in a canary yellow shirt with the same blue and white cravat he'd been wearing the first time she'd met him. He gave them a wave as soon as he saw them, but giving every appearance of being engrossed in talking to the young man standing next to him who, judging by his bemused expression, was finding it difficult to extricate himself from what appeared to be a one-sided conversation, but only grateful to be spared from being subjected to Trevor's monologues.

'He's on good form.' Jack grinned, leading the way to the bar.

'Isn't he just.' she laughed.

'Hello, Jack.'

'Steve! When did you get back?'

'Yesterday morning, but I've got until the end of the week.'

'Not long, eh; Steve,' Jack went on, turning to include Claire, 'I'd like you to meet a friend of mine, Claire Walters.'

'Hello, Claire.' he smiled, giving her a warm handshake.

'Claire has very recently moved here, Steve,' Jack told him.

'Really; well, I hope you'll be very happy here; Upper Nettles isn't too bad a place, can be somewhat claustrophobic, that is if you let it.'

'I'll take your advice.' she laughed. She liked him; he had one of those open faces, also there was nothing pretentious about him and he didn't ask the inevitable questions of where she was living or where she'd lived before coming to Upper Nettles as many of the others she'd met since coming here.

'Claire and I have actually known each other for years and to learn she had chosen to move here was, as you can imagine, Steve, a remarkable coincidence.'

'I'm sure it was;' he agreed, 'life moves in a very strange way at times, doesn't it.'

'You're not wrong.'

'Look, Jack, I would have loved to have had a longer chat with you both, but I have to rush off as I'm expecting a phone call; from my boss.' he added, 'but we must get together before I go back, how about Thursday, around this time and if Christine isn't working she'll be able to join us.'

After Steve had gone, having quickly finished off his beer, and Deidre had served them, they found a free table out on the back-terrace Deidre had told her about; she had been right, it was a suntrap, even at that time of the evening.

'He sounds a nice guy.'

'He is; he was one of the first people I met when I arrived here and although he spends more time overseas, we always manage to have a drink together when he gets any leave.'

'Jack?'

'There's something on your mind isn't there.'

'You're very observant.'

'I believe I am, at least where you're concerned, Claire, so are you going to tell me?'

'It's about Christine, but first of all, I take it we are talking about the woman who works here part-time?'

'Yes, that's right; you've met her?'

'Deidre introduced her to me the other evening. You remember I told you about being woken up on my first night here?'

'Yes.'

'Well, I believe I know who had caused it.'

'Really?'

'On the Saturday afternoon; I had just returned back from the village and there was a message on my answering machine which was strange because I hadn't given the number to anyone; and of course when I listened to the message, I had no idea who it could have been; after that, I really did forget all about it, merely assuming it was some sort of mix-up with the lines, but I didn't bother to report it. Then, on the Tuesday evening I was having a drink with Sylvia in here and that was when I was introduced to Christine; her voice was identical to the one I'd heard, Jack.'

'How odd.'

'It was, especially when one of the customers, he must have been a regular because he seemed to know her, he commented on the broken rear light on her car which she said had been caused by someone in the car park outside Waitrose.'

'Can you remember what the message was on your phone?' he asked, his expression serious.

'Yes, I can actually; she seemed to believe she was phoning Johnnie Wall's number, at least I think it must have been Johnnie Wall, but she said: Johnnie, I need to talk to Pete, he's not answering his mobile, so will you please tell him to call me?'

'Oh, dear.'

'You think I'm right?'

'I'm sure you are, Claire. All I can say is, poor Steve.'

Chapter Fifteen

Richard's evening didn't turn out exactly as he'd planned. Immediately he pushed open the glass swing doors and stepped inside the Station, the burly figure of Superintendent Brian Burrows came striding towards him.

'Chief Inspector, I've been waiting for you; I'd like a word if you don't mind.' he ordered and not waiting for any response, quickly turned on his heels and walked back along the corridor to his office. Richard, aware of the desk sergeant's nervous reaction, gave him a brief nod of acknowledgment and followed his superior.

'Close the door, if you will.' he growled, without even glancing at Richard as he stomped heavily round his desk and sat down.

'Sir?' bracing himself for the onslaught, mentally writing the script for him. At least he was predictable in his repetitive tirade when a case was taking so long to solve and with nothing specific to report.

'I have had a complaint.' surprising him; he hadn't expected that, running through in his mind who it could have been; he had virtually lost count of the people he'd spoken to since the start of this murder enquiry, but whoever he or she was, the complaint must have been sufficiently strong to have caused such a furore.

'Yes, sir.' Not unfamiliar with being the direct recipient of Brian Burrow's wrath, Richard had learned to keep his responses as brief and succinct as possible, working on the premise of "least said, soonest mended", although this time he had a sinking feeling he was going to be forced to use different tactics in dealing with 'the old man', a nickname Brian Burrows had been given long before he had even reached his forties.

'I received a telephone call this afternoon, Chief Inspector,' he began, looking at him directly for the first time since he came into the room, the pale blue eyes peering short-sightedly through the thick lens of his spectacles, 'from a most irate member of Bournemouth Council to complain about being subjected to what in his opinion was tantamount to an interrogation from one of my officers, a certain Gregory Eliot Thornton.' he added, emphasising each syllable of the name.

'Inspector Gale has given me a detailed report of his meeting this morning with Mr Thornton and his wife, and I was satisfied with the way he handled his questioning.'

'I have no doubt you're right, Chief Inspector, but the unsavoury fact remains, Mr Thornton felt he was being intimidated; he particularly stressed that he took extreme exception to the reference the Inspector made in respect to his wife's previous marriage; this he told me had considerably upset her.'

'According to the transcript of the conversation regarding the mention being made to Mrs Thornton's ex-husband, she had assured him that although that period in her life had not been a happy one, any mention being made did not upset her in the least.'

'I trust I will be receiving a copy of the report.'

'Of course, sir.'

'May I ask why Inspector Gale considered it necessary to the murder enquiry to say anything about a man she was married to over ten years ago?'

'His name, sir, is Pete Carr; he's a saxophonist with the group, "The Bandanas" and has been with them since they were first formed in 1979. As you will have read in our initial reports on this investigation, the leader of the group is called Johnnie Wall. Johnnie Wall and Pete Carr have known and worked with each for several years, long before "The Bandanas" came into existence. Johnnie Wall is one of our main suspects, possibly directly responsible for the murder of Glenda Nicholson, but before we can reach the stage of formerly charging him, there are a number of anomalies which require to be cleared up, and we feel that Pete Carr could be a link to what we're looking for; namely, a further insight into the character and background of Johnnie Wall.'

'And did this interview with the Thorntons achieve that for you?' he asked, his former antagonism dissipating, exactly as Richard had hoped.

'To a large degree it did, sir.'

'Alright, Chief Inspector, we'll leave it there. I won't argue that this isn't a difficult case you're handling, and the final conclusion is taking considerably longer than I had hoped, but nevertheless it doesn't mean we should ignore the sensitivities of those we interview. Mr Thornton is a councillor of some standing; his manner may be arrogant and unreasonable, but money talks, Richard and by all accounts he has a great deal of it. We must avoid standing on any political toes.'

Not an easy meeting, but then, Richard thought, as he left his office, there was no reason to expect anything else. The 'old man' had had his say, and the message had been understood loud and clear. Richard had never supported the 'soft pedalling' approach; how else would they ever get down to the bare bones of an enquiry as convoluted as this one, and certainly Peter's meeting this morning had proved fruitful: there was more to unearth on Johnnie Wall, but before tackling him, there was still more to be done; first and foremost, obtain full details of the post mortem and accompanying reports on the death of Penelope Driver, find out for example where Johnnie Wall had been on the night she died and the one person, apart from asking the man himself, was to talk to Pete Carr. It might also be a good idea to learn where he was when Glenda Nicholson was murdered. Richard couldn't help but feel there was something here they were overlooking, something which should be glaringly obvious, but so far, hadn't revealed itself.

The door to Peter's office was open, and although it was after seven, he was still at his desk. Who would be a police officer, he thought, cynically, although not really meaning it; he could think of no other career which would have suited him better and he was certain Peter felt the same.

'It's been a long day, Peter.' he said, standing in the open doorway.

'I know,' he smiled ruefully, looking up from what he was doing, 'I was just about to pack up, sir, that is unless you want us to discuss this afternoon's developments.'

'I do, as a matter of fact, but I think we should call it a day. Have you any plans for this evening, because if not perhaps we should call in to "The Nettles" for some light refreshments?'

'There's no-one at home,' he explained, 'Sally's away for a few days visiting her parents, and I wasn't looking forward to heating something up in the microwave.'

'That's alright, then; we need to give our brains a rest anyway.'

***

Within minutes of the two officers leaving the office, Pippa called through to say that Mr Thornton was on the line, asking to speak to David. Passing the receiver to him, Clive walked over to the window in time to see them emerging from the building and walking in the direction of Oxford Circus. He was doing his utmost to calm down, reign in the rising panic, while mentally backing away from facing the possible consequences of what had been said, regretting now, when it was too late, the way he'd handled the interview, but it would be like asking a bloody leopard to change its spots! If only he and David had had more time to prepare, and the fact they should have anticipated, either sooner or later, they would receive a visit from the authorities only added to his frustration. Where the hell do we go from here, he thought, only half aware of what David was saying to Gregory Thornton. Not that there would be any surprises there; they had fully expected Gregory to call when he got back from his trip and neither of them could be blamed for what happened to Glenda. It was unfortunate for Gregory that he had this paranoia of conducting his business affairs as though he was some sort of undercover agent; he should have realised there was always the possibility of the package not turning up at its proper destination; not murder perhaps, Clive conceded, albeit reluctantly; nobody could have foreseen that, but all the same, Gregory needn't think they could solve his problem, conjure up the missing money merely by a snap of their fingers! Let's face it, he concluded, Gregory Thornton was the least of their problems at this present time and, hearing David replacing the receiver he turned round to face him.

'Well?'

'Apparently he and Lilian had a visit this morning from an Inspector Gale from Upper Nettles police station.'

'I suppose it was about his registered package turning up, although I'm surprised he hadn't taken the precaution of making sure in the event it didn't reach Glenda that no-one would be able to trace it back to him.'

'Somewhat more than that, Clive, they were more interested in his friendship with Glenda, gave him quite a grilling he was saying.'

'But how did they find out he knew her?'

'He wasn't quite sure, but he thought it must have been through one of Glenda's neighbours; the husband had made a mental note of the firm where he bought his car and the police had taken it from there.'

'Big Brother is watching you; or in Gregory's case, a nosy neighbour.'

'I expect this neighbourhood watch scheme is normal practice in a parochial town such as Lyndhurst.'

'You're probably right; probably no different in Upper Nettles, from what I saw of the place I would say if you so much as sneezed you'd read about it in the local rag by the end of the week. Anyway,' Clive went on losing interest in Gregory Thornton's dilemma, wanting only to get back to what was all-important to them, 'what do you make of this afternoon's meeting?'

'Not good, Clive.'

'I know it's not, but is that all you can say; do we merely just sit here, carry on with our business as though we didn't have a care in the bloody world. Surely there is something we should be doing to keep them off our backs?'

'Unless we know what's on that disc, I would say it's unlikely.'

'You think we should let events take their course and when the time comes, as it very much looks as if it will, and we're in the dock, we take what is coming to us? Is that what you mean?'

'Don't you think you're over dramatizing the situation?'

'No, I do not! I'm beginning to think Tom's had the right idea.'

'You don't mean that, surely; I would say it's only a matter of time before they catch up with him.'

'I suppose the police *are* aware he's buzzed off.'

'Bound to, Clive. Oh, I know they never mentioned it, but when you think about it, they didn't have to, did they? For all we know, they may already have caught up with him.'

'They're not that damn smart!'

'Don't you believe it; you heard what the Inspector was saying, he kept stressing the seriousness of this fraud business, wouldn't be surprised if Interpol aren't also involved.'

'Wonder how they got their hands on the disc.'

'Does it matter, Clive; they've got it, that's the main thing.'

'Don't remind me. I hope they fling the bloody book at him!'

'He's not the only one who'll be in the firing line. And,' David added, 'what about WHL?'

'What about them?'

'I was thinking about your contact, whether he's been in touch again to say whether they're likely to prosecute?'

'It's a she,' Clive said abstractedly, forgetting for a moment he had never told David who had been supplying him with inside information, working on the premise that the less he knew in that respect, the better, 'and the last time I spoke to her all she said was that they seemed to have clammed up somewhat since yesterday.'

'What, because of Tom not turning up for work, you mean?'

'She wasn't sure, but she thought it was because of the visit they had from New Scotland Yard; apparently, the officer was with Clarence Fountain when they learned Tom hadn't arrived.'

'Oh, you didn't say.'

'That's because I didn't know until last night and haven't had much of a chance to tell you.'

'You're obviously reluctant to tell me who she is Clive, but I think perhaps it's time you did.'

'Okay, okay; it's Julie.'

'Julie Webster, Clarence's secretary?'

'You sound surprised.'

'I suppose I am.'

'I'm not in the habit of discussing my private life, as you well know, David.'

'Sorry, didn't mean to pry.'

'It's okay.' he repeated, hoping that would be an end to it. It had always been an unwritten rule between them to keep their personal and business lives separate, all the same, he knew he was reacting unreasonably with him, but the meeting this morning had shaken him, far more than he was openly admitting and recognised that soon, very soon, he was going to be forced to make a decision and one which would inevitably affect David. Clive Robinson was a realist, also he didn't relish the idea of merely hanging around, waiting for the inevitable summons to police headquarters and to face a further barrage of questions, the final outcome of which could result in having to face charges. That particular scenario just didn't bear thinking of, although he wouldn't be on his own; David, as an equal partner in the business would share the same fate. Small comfort, cursing Tom Jackson under his breath for putting them in this predicament. Clive reckoned that before any of that happened New Scotland Yard would be sending in their investigating team to scrutinize their records and there just wasn't sufficient time to either eliminate certain data or to even fudge the figures.

'Incidentally,' David said, breaking into his thoughts, 'Gregory made a complaint to the superintendent of police after the Inspector left this morning.'

'What the hell for?'

'You may well ask; apparently he took exception to the way he was questioning Lilian.'

'From what you've told me about Lilian Thornton, she sounds as though she was perfectly capable of standing up for herself.'

'I'm sure she is, but the Inspector wanted to know about the time she was married to her first husband; he's with the rock group, "The Bandanas", you may have heard of them?'

'Of course I have; go on, I still don't see why Gregory should have been so irate.'

'Neither do I and he didn't elaborate, also,' David went on, 'before the Inspector left he made the comment about the registered package having been sent by someone with the surname of Bennett, which was Lilian's maiden name.'

'Of which, presumably, he was aware?'

'Gregory got that impression, yes.'

'It doesn't sound all that important to me; there must be hundreds of

Bennetts in the Bournemouth area; I take it the package would have had a Bournemouth post mark.'

'I would say so, yes.'

'All in all, not a very sensible thing to do, especially when you consider the circumstances, but perhaps Gregory's not too concerned about the police asking him about sending such a large amount of money through the post, which they may very well have done when they saw him this morning.'

'He didn't say.'

'So, to get back to Tom,' Clive persisted, 'someone from WHL must have given him the tip-off about the board's decision.'

'One of his colleagues, you mean?'

'Could have been.'

'Christ!'

'What is it?'

'I believe I know how he could have known; Jilly; she may have told him.'

'But surely you wouldn't have said anything to her.'

'I didn't, but on Saturday, when you came to the house and we were talking about Tom and the outcome of WHL's meeting the day before, that's when she may have overheard and promptly passed it on him'

'But she wasn't at home; you said she was shopping.'

'I know, and she was; and it wasn't until later, after you'd left when I realised she must have come back during the time we were in the dining room because when I went upstairs a pile of carrier bags were on the bed, she hadn't even taken the time to unpack them. I didn't think much of it then; Jilly's like that, I never know where she's going and she never bothers to tell me unless I make a point of asking.'

'I suppose you could be right, David, but there's no point us worrying; I think we've got quite enough to concern ourselves with at the moment.'

'There's no point dwelling on it, stress is a killer.'

'No point on dwelling on it! I *am* dwelling on it, David! You can't tell me you're not worried?'

'Of course I am, but I think we should do our best to keep all of this business in perspective.'

'How?'

'Well, it would appear the police are focusing their attentions on Tom and until such time he's brought back here, we should look on this as a respite, brief though it may be.'

'And what do you propose we do during this indeterminate period of respite?' finding it increasingly difficult to keep the sarcasm out of his voice. He had always recognised his partner's pragmatism and in many respects, compared to his more volatile and impulsive nature, to be an asset, but there were times, such as right this minute, when he dearly wished he would just let rip.

'I can see you don't agree with the approach I'm trying to make,' he went on, half apologetically, 'Tom is the main offender here, Clive; he is the one who's been extracting funds from what has every appearance of being his inexhaustible sources. He's the one taking the risks. Alright, we are involved, but not to such a large degree and the fees we've deducted are quite legitimately calculated, percentage-wise they are spot on, as you know, all of which have been declared to the Inland Revenue. Not so, Tom. He has quite literally been creaming off undeclared income which, as you are aware, is a punishable offence. And,' he added, 'I'm not forgetting what he's been up to in respect to siphoning off from us more than he should in what he's been somewhat nebulously describing as commission. He is the one who should be stressed out, Clive, not us.'

'Okay,' raising his hands, palm upwards, 'I'll go along with that, David; for the moment.' he added.

***

'Have you had a chance yet, Peter to read the notes which came through from Notting Hill Gate on the outcome of the inquest on Penelope Driver?' Richard asked him the next morning.

'I have, yes, but there wasn't a great deal in them, was there, sir?'

'Perhaps not, except for one interesting aspect which struck me, at the same time solving something which has been niggling me ever since I spoke to Johnnie Wall last week.'

'Yes?'

'It should have occurred to me sooner, but it's the way he seems to be permanently cocooned from a world most of the rest of us have to face on our own, if you know what I mean.'

'I think I do, mainly, ever since you mentioned this guy, Gerry Steele, but then I suppose I just thought that was the way all these high-profile celebrities behave.'

'Except that Johnnie Wall is no longer in that particular category. He probably was, around the time Penelope Driver died; always with one person or another, not necessarily to protect him, but to boost his ego, remind him he was still famous. What I'm trying to get at Peter, is this; having met the man, I think you can rule out any necessity for an ego-booster, he's got more than enough self-confidence to last him a lifetime, and as far as any protection is concerned, unless we can be convinced he's living in fear for his own safety, receiving hate-mail, that sort of thing, why should he need a bodyguard. No, I'm coming round to believing something quite different, and remembering again what we've been told by two of the women we've interviewed, it could be those other members of the group, rather than Gerry Steele, who are acting as self-appointed protectors.'

'You mean because of the sex angle?'

'Yes, that's exactly what I mean, Peter; so, you've spotted it then.'

'I have to admit, sir, I haven't followed it through as far as you have, but I think you could be right. Are you considering the possibility that Penelope Driver may not have committed suicide?'

'Well, I am; put it this way, I don't think any more of his explanation of where and how he spent the evening she died than I do of what he's told us about the night Glenda Nicholson was murdered. We already know he's a liar, which does make me wonder what else he's lied about. It's almost seventeen years since Penelope died, therefore we are somewhat restricted in who we should be talking to. According to this report, he spent the whole evening in "Benny's Bar" in Baker Street in the company of Pete Carr and didn't return home until 1 a.m. and by then she'd been dead for at least four hours; certainly as far as anyone in the pub are concerned, it would be next to impossible, to have this corroborated which means the only course we have is to concentrate on those few people who were regularly in his company back then and to some degree still are today.'

'Going off at a slight tangent, I'm not happy about Bernie Croft's alibi, sir.'

'Neither am I, Peter; I think we should make a point of seeing him again before we call in Johnnie Wall, also Pete Carr. For instance, how did he spend the other weekend? We know where Gerry Steele *said* he was on the Saturday, but how do we know whether he left the Grange later that night; if Glenda had been there, and we're fairly sure she was the same woman Claire Walters had seen, if only because it's stretching credibility to believe there were two females within a radius of not more than a mile in distress on the same night, how did she reach as far as she did?'

'Which brings us back to Bernie Croft, doesn't it, sir?'

'You're right, it does; let's put ourselves in his shoes, Peter; here we have a man who was in a relationship with Glenda Nicholson and, although he told you he'd hoped to see her that evening and had actually tried to phone her, and when he couldn't get through he meekly let the matter rest, finished his drink in Lyndhurst and drove back home to Bournemouth.'

'Especially knowing Johnnie Wall was living in the area and needing Glenda's reassurance she was no longer seeing him, I would say that any man in a similar situation would have immediately jumped to the conclusion she could have been with him and that was the reason why he couldn't get through on her mobile because pre-empting a call from him, she'd switched it off.'

'And,' Richard following on from him, 'only being a few miles from Upper Nettles decided to find out whether he was right or not, remembering what Claire Walters told me about the other car she heard.'

'That could be the lever we need to get him to open up.'

'Yes, and if necessary, we'll make use of it, therefore at the risk of further exacerbating 'the old man' I suggest we not only see Bernie Croft again but have a word with the other two in the group, Spike Harris and Eddie Gallagher, before tackling Johnnie Marr; in that way, we should have more to fling at him. Unfortunately, we've no idea where they live; you don't happen to know the name of their agent, do you, Peter?'

'Afraid not, sir.'

'I'll ask Joanne to try and find out; he's bound to have contact numbers for them.'

Half-way through the morning, Joanne came into Richard's office with the mobile numbers for Pete Carr, Eddie Gallagher and Spike Harris, and by midday, Pete Carr who fortuitously happened to be staying with Johnnie Wall, was bounding up the steps of the Station and introducing himself to the desk sergeant.

Why is it, Richard grumbled to himself, as Pete Carr was shown into his office, that some people had the knack of literally rubbing you up the wrong way, even before they have uttered a single word; there was nothing pretentious or even remotely theatrical about the way he was dressed: light-weight grey cords, soft leather loafers and a short-sleeved red and white check shirt; his hair, only slightly longer than the regulation short back and sides, no sign of any tattoos or ear-piercing, his only jewellery, a thin gold chain with a St. Christopher cross, not a large cross and scarcely noticeable, certainly not statement-making in any patronising way. Perhaps, Richard concluded, standing up to shake hands with him, the reason for his immediate impression was simply his well-developed mistrust for anyone who in his somewhat jaundiced opinion was playing a part. Where Johnnie Wall's manner was one of over-confidence with more than a dash of supercilious arrogance, Pete Carr's manner, while lacking the arrogance, affected a detachment as though he considered this visit of no real interest.

'Thank you for coming in so promptly,' Richard said, gesturing to the chair in front of his desk, 'as no doubt you are probably aware we are conducting an investigation into the recent murder of a woman called Glenda Nicholson. We have reason to believe she was visiting the area on the outskirts of Upper Nettles, very close to where her body was found.'

'I know this, Chief Inspector,' he said, making no attempt to conceal his boredom, 'I read about it in the local paper; also,' he went on, leaning back slightly in his chair and languidly crossing one leg over the other, 'that you've spoken to Johnnie, who incidentally was more than a little put-out at your suggestion that this woman had been visiting him that night.'

'I haven't asked you in, Mr Carr to discuss Mr Wall; I would however like you to tell me how you spent the evening and the night of Saturday, the 12th June.'

'I was with Eddie Gallagher, he's the drummer for our group, "The Bandanas", we were at my flat, in London,' he added, 'and spent all evening going over the details for our forthcoming concert.'

'And your address in London, sir.'

'The Penthouse, George Court, Southampton Row, Bloomsbury.'

'Thank you, and how often do you come to Upper Nettles?'

'Fairly often; we always rehearse at the Grange; can't disturb any neighbours there.'

'You've already told me you're staying there at the moment.'

'That's correct.'

'When did you arrive?'

'What on earth has that to do with your murder investigation, Chief Inspector?' a look of disdain skimming across his features.

'I'd like to know, Mr Carr.'

'Monday evening.'

'I see, and when was the last time you were here?'

'This really is so very tedious.'

'Tedious it may be to you, but necessary in order for us to build-up as much as possible of the period before and after Miss Nicholson met her death.'

'I drove down early on the Sunday morning.'

'Sunday, the 13th of this month.'

'Yes, Chief Inspector,' sighing, 'the day after she was murdered.'

'Were you on your own?'

'Of course, why shouldn't I have been?'

'I was just wondering as Eddie Gallagher had been with you the previous evening and you'd been discussing your forthcoming concert, he may have come down with you.'

'Well, he did, but he left London after me because he went back to his apartment first.'

'And you would therefore have been at the Grange before him?'

'Of course.'

'Did you see him when he arrived?'

'No; I went straight to bed.'

'Did you know the deceased, Mr Carr?'

'No, I didn't.'

'You had never heard her name mentioned prior to reading about her murder?'

'I've just said I didn't know the woman.'

'You haven't answered my question, sir.'

'Good God, how pedantic,' he drawled, 'and the answer is still no, no I'd never heard her name mentioned before.'

'You were married at one time to Lilian Bennett.'

'My word, Chief Inspector, you have been doing your research, my marriage to Lilian really is ancient history.'

'It may seem like that to you, sir,' Richard remarked and wondering how long it would take to break through his calculated indifference, 'however, the fact that during the time you were married, your wife was in partnership with Glenda Nicholson, therefore I'm finding it surprising, even if you hadn't met her, that her name had never cropped up at any time.'

'Well, it hadn't.'

'I see.' and he saw very clearly; by Pete Carr's very attitude and his stubborn refusal to admit he had no knowledge of Glenda Nicholson, went a long way to support what Peter and he had been saying earlier, 'Returning, sir, to the weekend when Glenda Nicholson was murdered,' not missing the sigh of exasperation, 'you've told me you arrived at the Grange on the Sunday morning, also how you spent the Saturday evening, but what I would like to know is when did you visit prior to then.'

'Prior to then?' accompanied by the first genuine expression he'd shown since coming into the office.

'Yes, when was the last time you came to Upper Nettles?'

'Oh, I see; probably the week before, I'd have to check up in my diary to be exact.'

'That may not be necessary, sir.'

'Do explain, Chief Inspector, I'm sure you already know exactly when that was.' his voice heavy with sarcasm.

'It's my understanding,' Richard went on stolidly, watching him closely, 'it could have been the Friday afternoon as you were seen driving through the town in the direction of the Grange.' stretching the truth, but feeling it was the only way to push the case forward. All he had to go on was what Claire Walters had told him about the Porsche being outside Johnnie Wall's house on both the Friday and the Sunday; it may not have been Pete Carr's, although by his own admittance he'd said he was there on the Sunday and, unless the car belonged to someone else and it hadn't been the same Porsche which was unlikely, it was a fairly safe bet to say it belonged to him. He wasn't dismissing the drummer, Eddie Gallagher, but he couldn't help feeling that as apparently Pete Carr was a regular visitor, the Porsche was his.

'I don't know where you're getting your information from, Chief Inspector; no doubt from one of the many good people who reside in Upper Nettles who enjoy indulging in tittle-tattle, and of course they're wrong.'

'Very well, sir, if you say so.' reluctant though he was to let it drop, but he didn't want another complaint making its way to Brian Burrows.

Richard decided to bring the interview to a close; it was all too apparent he and Johnnie had worked out their joint alibis, also he didn't want to prematurely alert him; the less time Johnnie Wall had for preparing some slick answers all the better, and as he walked over to open the door for him, gratified to read from the puzzled look on his face the unspoken question, sorely tempted to voice his reply; that yes, the interview was over - for the time being.

Richard watched him as he left with only a curt nod and the remains of bewilderment in his expression. Unsurprisingly, the last thirty minutes hadn't achieved a great deal, except reinforcing his view that "The Bandanas" saxophonist came from the same mould as Johnnie Wall. Who was supporting who, he wondered. Eddie Gallagher was probably of the same mould, Gerry Steele being the exception, but then he wasn't part of the group; he was an ex-bouncer and as Claire Walters had said, Johnnie Wall's minder. At least he was playing a part; he even *looked* like a bouncer, as in his cynical view, bouncers should look like. Richard had seen enough Gerry Steeles in his career to recognise a thug when he saw one, but it didn't mean he was a murderer. He was certain there was a lot more to the murder of Glenda Nicholson than having met her end at the hands of a surly and ill-educated character of Gerry Steele's ilk; for the first time since the start of their investigation he was beginning to see a breakthrough, a slotting into place of each convoluted jigsaw piece through which Peter and he had been painstakingly sifting. Presumably, Pete Carr would be on his way back to the Grange to report to Johnnie on this morning's interview, but there would be nothing new to tell him, all of which may or may not cause a ripple in Wall's nonchalance.

Richard reckoned he had enough time to get something to eat before he and Peter left for Bournemouth and was half-way to the door when Joanne buzzed through to say Eddie Gallagher, was on the line.

This better be worth it, waiting for her to put him through; eating at regular meal-times had recently become something of a luxury, he grumbled.

'I've only just got your message on my answering machine, Chief Inspector; I've been away for a couple of days.'

'That's alright, sir, but thanks for calling. I take it you've heard about the recent murder of Glenda Nicholson?'

'Yes, I was talking to Johnnie Wall the other day and he told me.'

'Right; there's a few questions I'd like to ask you regarding that night, purely routine, although since I left that message I've had a meeting with Pete Carr asking him more or less the same, therefore your confirmation would be a help to us.'

'Yes?'

'We understand you spent the Saturday evening in Pete Carr's company; is that correct?'

'Certainly.'

'And later that night you drove down to Upper Nettles?'

'Yes, that's right.'

So far, his manner was pleasant enough, especially compared to the reception he'd received from Johnnie Wall and Pete Carr.

'What I would like you to tell me is the time you arrived here?'

'Oh, it was around three.'

'And yet, I understand Pete Carr arrived here much earlier.'

'That's correct, I had a couple of things to attend to first and I wanted to go home and freshen up, that sort of thing.'

'I see, and when you reached the Grange, was there anyone about at that time of the morning?'

'Er – only Gerry.' detecting the slight hesitation in his voice.

'Gerry Steele?'

'Yes, he was just coming in, said he couldn't sleep and had been out for a walk.'

'And you didn't see or speak to anyone else.'

'Well, Johnnie was in the lounge, but he was sound asleep, but I didn't disturb him, I went straight up to the room I usually have when I'm there.'

'And Pete's car was parked outside?'

'Yes, it was, and Johnnie's of course.'

'Well, I think that's all I need to know for the present, sir, although it's possible I may need to talk to you again.'

'That's alright, Chief Inspector; I'll be here in London for the next couple of weeks and then we're all off on tour.'

***

It was precisely three in the afternoon when Richard and Peter drew up outside Bernie Croft's house. They'd still not had any response from Mike Harris' number when they tried earlier, but Richard felt they couldn't afford to delay their meeting with Johnnie Wall until such time as either he or Peter could speak to him, bearing in mind that by this time it was probable that either Johnnie Wall or Pete Carr had brought him up to-date which made talking to him a waste of time.

'It would seem they're all in cahoots together, Peter,' Richard said to him on their way to Bournemouth, 'and not forgetting Gerry Steele of course, so it now remains to be seen whether Bernie is part of this conspiracy, that is if we're thinking along the right lines.'

'I got the impression when I spoke to him on Saturday that there was no love lost between him and Johnnie Wall, meaning it would be unlikely he would want to get involved.'

'I think you could be right there,' Richard agreed, 'because if he was, Johnnie Wall would have told him of my visit the day before.'

'Also, sir,' Peter added, 'he'd been quick enough to mention the fact that Johnnie Wall and Glenda Nicholson's relationship was common knowledge among their crowd -'

' - while both Johnnie and Pete had been equally speedy in denying any knowledge of her, which was not clever, not clever at all.'

'From how you've described them, I can't help get the impression they consider themselves to exist in a totally different world to the rest of us.'

'Show biz, eh?'

'Too much money, I expect.' Peter commented dryly.

'As you say, Peter, another world.'

'We're almost there, sir,' Peter said, turning into Melbourne Crescent, 'that's the Thorntons' property,' nodding in the direction of the two-storey mock-Georgian house on the right-hand side; 'Bernie Croft's must be a bit further along,' looking out for the number Bernie had given him, 'here we are.' he said, pulling into the side of the kerb.

Bernie Croft was waiting for them, standing in the open glass porch, silently watching as they stepped out on to the pavement and walked up the red gravel drive towards him.

Another arrogant bastard, Richard muttered under his breath. If Bernie Croft was surprised to find that Peter wasn't on his own, only a miniscule raising of his eyebrows indicated this.

'Mr Croft,' Richard said, once they had been taken into the kitchen;

sliding glass doors leading to a gazebo-style conservatory and overlooking a walled garden at the rear of the property, 'I would like to ask you some further questions relating to the murder of Miss Nicholson.'

'I can't imagine what I could possibly add to what I've told Inspector Gale.' he answered, glancing towards Peter as he turned back the pages of his notebook to last Saturday's interview.

'Before I do,' Richard went on, determined not to let the man's parsimonious manner wrangle him, 'I'll just go over the main points of that interview.'

'If you must.'

'On the evening of Saturday, the 12th of June, you attempted to call Miss Nicholson twice on her mobile; the first time you found the line was engaged, this was around nine-thirty and the second time, about ten minutes later, there wasn't any tone.'

'That's right.'

'And you didn't try again later.'

'I've already said so; I gave up and when the pub closed I drove back here.'

'Both Inspector Gale and I are finding it difficult to understand why you made no further attempt to get in touch with her, either later that night when you returned home or the following morning.'

'I didn't see any point,' he answered, 'I was expecting to see her on the Sunday evening.'

'But you didn't and by then she had been dead for several hours.'

'I had no way of knowing that had I?' an edge of irritation in his voice.

'When you first knew the deceased she was married to Ted Warren.'

'Yes, that's right.'

'And she would have been called Glenda Warren.'

'She kept her maiden name and everyone knew her as Glenda Nicholson.'

'Since Inspector Gale spoke to you on Saturday, further evidence has come to light to substantiate our belief that on the night Miss Nicholson was murdered, she had called at the Grange, the property owned by Johnnie Wall, and this had been between nine-thirty and ten. Less than a couple of hours later her car was seen leaving the Grange and being driven away in the direction of Lyndhurst, but it only got as far as Nettles Hollow where four days later her body was found. We also know that the same car must then have gone in the other direction where it was discovered last Friday morning half-submerged in the sea off the coast of Lymington. There was a body of a young man called Jamie Green, inside the vehicle. On the Saturday night, and shortly before Glenda Nicholson's car left the Grange, he was cycling along the same stretch of road from Brockenhurst back to where he lived in Upper Nettles. We shall never know what he witnessed that night, but we believe there was someone else there around the same time who can.'

'Very interesting, Chief Inspector.'

As much as Richard would have liked to retaliate to his sarcasm, sarcasm which he was making no pretence to conceal, he didn't; instead, he continued, mentally preparing himself for the inevitable outburst, and one which Bernie Croft would be unable to prevent. Peter had been making notes, filling out on the previous ones from Saturday, and knowing from experience, having worked with him for several years, that if he felt at any time during the interview there was anything he wanted to add, he would do so.

'When Glenda Nicholson's car left the driveway of Johnnie Wall's property, Mr Croft,' picking up from where he'd left off, 'within a matter of minutes it was followed by not only Jamie Green on his bike, but a second car, one which had been parked further back along the road with, I might add, its headlights switched off.'

'Surely you're not implying, Chief Inspector,' he answered, a narrowing of his eyes his only reaction which up to that point, had been zero, 'that *I* was in that car, which somehow you've miraculously conjured up since I spoke to your Inspector!'

'Were you, sir?'

'No, I bloody well wasn't!'

On cue. He was rattled, and for the first time Richard felt he had him exactly where he wanted; Bernie Croft was very soon going to have to make a decision and without even looking at Peter, he could sense his heightened awareness.

'I suggest,' Richard pressed on, 'that when you left the pub in Lyndhurst that night, instead of taking the A35 which would bring you back to Bournemouth, you took the Lymington Road; after driving through Upper Nettles and reaching the Grange, you saw Glenda Nicholson's car parked outside. That may have been sufficient for you to assume that she was, despite assuring you to the contrary, continuing to see Johnnie Wall; you then decided to return home, the quickest route from there would have been to reverse and drive back to the roundabout outside Lyndhurst and re-join the A335 -'

' - this is fabrication, and you know it!

'I would prefer to describe it as a credible hypothesis;' Richard corrected, 'however, I'll continue; this is concerning timing, Mr Croft; it takes approximately half an hour to reach the Grange from the "Mailman's Arms" in Lyndhurst and anyone who was approaching the property would have been bound to have seen a man and a woman arguing in the middle of the road, alternatively, if the car I've mentioned had approached the Grange a few minutes earlier, the driver would have noticed the figure of a woman running from the driveway of the Grange to the house across the road;' Richard paused there for a fraction of a second, fully expecting another interruption, but Bernie Croft remained silent, but not discouraged he carried on, 'only minutes later someone had dragged her away from the house and out into the road where they had their altercation. This altercation, Mr Croft, was, we believe, witnessed by you and after the woman was led away you either drove on, or curiosity got the better of you, and you left the car at the side of the verge and followed - '

'- I did not!'

'You didn't what?'

'What the hell are you talking about; this is outrageous! Don't think I don't know what you're trying to do, the pair of you,' glaring over at Peter who, wisely, continued with his notes, 'you can't find out who murdered Glenda, so I'm obviously your number one suspect.'

'Did you drive on, return here to Bournemouth or did you try and find out what was going on?'

'I did bloody neither! I wasn't there!'

'Who are you protecting, sir?'

'Protecting?' a look of genuine puzzlement replacing the anger.

'It was late at night and there weren't many people about,' Richard explained, 'but with further, intense questioning in and around Lyndhurst and Upper Nettles, including in your own neighbourhood, there is a good chance someone may remember seeing you, and your car of course, but it all takes time and we're trying to avoid, if at all possible, any further delay in solving this murder case. You have two choices, sir,' deliberately taking his time to spell it out to him, 'one, you confirm to us that you were a witness to part or all of what transpired that night, or two, you continue to deny you know nothing about it; if you decide on the latter, we will have no alternative, but to increase our search to obtain the truth. I hope I've made myself clear.'

'Perfectly.'

'Good.'

'Okay, Chief Inspector,' allowing several seconds to elapse before saying anything, 'you're right, but only partly; I did drive along to the Grange after I'd left "The Mailmans" and I did see Glenda's car parked outside, also when I'd reversed and was about to drive back, I saw her running across the road and as you've said, a few minutes later Johnnie came dashing out and dragged her away, but that's all I saw. I wasn't in the least curious as to what was going on; why should I have been, she'd lied to me, that was enough, so I came back home.'

'Just like that.'

'Yes, Chief Inspector, just like that.'

'If, as you've said, you saw what was going on outside Johnnie Wall's property and had no interest in what might have transpired, why didn't you merely carry on driving?'

'But I did.'

'While he and Glenda Nicholson were still there?'

'Yes.'

'Nobody drove, or cycled, along there at that time, Mr Croft.'

'Okay, I waited until they went back to the Grange; I didn't want either of them to recognise me I suppose.'

'You waited, yes, but not until they were no longer there; it was a good ten or fifteen before you moved off, it wasn't until you saw Glenda Nicholson's car leave the Grange.'

'That's not true.'

'I believe it is very close to the truth, Mr Croft; I suggest you think again about the accuracy of the sequence of events that night.'

'I've already told you -'

'- I am well aware of what you've told me,' Richard persisted, his voice hardening, 'but I'm more interested in what you haven't told me.'

'I've nothing else to add.'

'I believe you have, Mr Croft. There are possibly two scenarios here; one, you left your car parked as I've said, further back from the Grange, and when Johnnie Wall led Glenda back there, you followed them and witnessed exactly what happened that night, you also witnessed Glenda Nicholson being taken away in her car and for reasons best known to yourself you did not intervene.'

'You said there were two scenarios.' a slight sneer in his voice.

'I believe you know what that is, but I'll spell it out for you to make sure there is no misunderstanding; instead of acting as a mere disinterested onlooker, you *did* intervene -'

'- I bloody did not!'

'Allow me to finish, please; when I used the word 'intervene' I was implying that because of the intensity of your anger towards a woman whom you believed had deceived you and one with whom you'd been in a close relationship for some time, you lost control, to such an extent perhaps that you grabbed her away from Johnnie Wall, naturally she would have struggled, using all her strength to push you away, but you got hold of the scarf she was wearing and strangled her. Because of your previous association with Johnnie Wall through the years you were with the group, he protected you, by either assisting you in taking Glenda Nicholson's body to Nettles Hollow, or he got someone else to do the dirty work for him.'

There was complete silence in the room; Peter continued writing his notes, but for several seconds there was no other movement. Richard leaned back in his chair, his eyes never leaving Bernie Croft's face. It wasn't too difficult to read his expression, he was in a state of inner turmoil, but he was, Richard was certain, fully aware of the position in which he'd placed himself.

'I didn't kill her.' his voice flat, devoid of any expression, but Richard believed him.

'Alright, Mr Croft, you didn't kill her, but who did?'

'I don't know.'

'I believe you can do better than that.'

'It's true; I can't say with any certainty, there was someone else in the room with them.'

'Who?'

'Gerry Steele, he works for Johnnie.'

'Yes, we were aware of that, Mr Croft, so are you saying that he was the person who strangled her?'

'I don't know, he and Johnnie were both trying to calm her down, it was difficult to make out from where I was what actually happened.'

'You say they were trying to calm her; was she hysterical.'

'More angry than anything else I would say.'

'With whom; Johnnie Wall or Gerry Steele?'

'Both of them I guess.'

It was no answer, but somehow Richard didn't think he was going to extract anything further from him. He'd provided them with another angle for when they next tackled Johnnie Wall.

'Finally, Mr Croft,' Richard asked, 'when you left the Grange, who was driving Glenda's car?'

'Johnnie was in no fit state to drive anywhere that night.'

'Why, was he drunk?'

'Possibly, or it could have been he was on something else; he was very unsteady on his feet.'

'I see, so who drove her car?'

'Gerry did.'

'Was there anyone with him?'

'I only saw him.'

'Very well, sir,' Richard said, 'I'd like you to come into Upper Nettles tomorrow; we'll have a statement prepared for your signature. Inspector,' he said turning to Peter, 'have you anything you wish to add?'

'Just a couple of points I'd like clarified, Chief Inspector; Mr Croft,' Peter said, pulling his chair to a position where he was directly facing him, 'Penelope Driver.'

'What about her?' frowning, obviously wondering where Peter was coming from.

'Where were you on the night she died?'

'How the hell do you expect me to remember; it was years ago?'

'When you heard what had happened to her, it must have made some sort of impression on you.'

'Of course.'

'Normally, when an event as unexpected as hearing of a sudden death of someone you knew, when you think back to when you heard about it, you would also recall what you yourself had been doing that night, where you had been for instance. You were still with the group at the time, weren't you?'

'Of course; I told you the other day when I left and in case you've forgotten, it was in 2001.'

'Am I right in saying you would have constantly been in each other's company?'

'Yes, we had to be; when we weren't rehearsing, we would be touring.'

'And those times, when you were doing neither, did you meet socially?'

'Yes, I suppose we did.'

'It was Easter Saturday when Penelope Driver died, Mr Croft and it is our understanding that at least two members of the group were in London, where were you?'

'What is this? Penelope committed suicide, nothing can alter that.'

'The cause of death, sir was an overdose of prescribed drugs and as there was no evidence at the time to prove otherwise, it was decided that these were administered by Penelope herself, and as they were taken at the same time by her consuming a large amount of whisky, the resultant verdict was that she took her own life.'

'So, what are you suggesting now, that she was murdered?'

'I'm not suggesting anything, sir; merely giving you the actual findings at the time of the event. So, I'll ask you again, having hopefully jogged your memory, how did you spend that evening?'

'Where we usually went to when we weren't working, "Benny's Bar".'

'In Baker Street?'

'I only know of one pub in London called "Benny's Bar".'

'Were you on your own?'

'I spoke to a few people I knew; we always used it as our local.'

'Was it busy that night?'

'"Benny's" is always busy and as it was a Saturday, particularly so.'

'Can you remember those people you've just mentioned, their names, I mean?'

'Not really, I probably didn't even know their names.'

'Had you expected to see any of the others from the group?'

'Probably.' shrugging.

'But they didn't come in?'

'No.'

'I see;' Peter nodded, 'returning to the night of Glenda Nicholson's murder, sir -'

'My God! Don't you people ever let up? How many more times do I have to repeat myself?'

'When you were on the road close to the Grange did you pass or see any other vehicle?

'No, I don't remember any.'

'Jamie Green would have been around there at that time of the night.'

'Well I didn't see anyone on a bike.'

'Perhaps not on his bike, sir.'

'What do you mean; he was cycling, wasn't he?'

'Yes, he was, but we have a witness to say he was approaching on his bike at the same time as the couple were arguing, also that he didn't cycle past them while they were still there.'

'If so, I didn't see him.'

'It is possible that he'd been sufficiently curious to find out what was happening, he had got off his bike, perhaps leaving it by the hedge and going into the grounds and, like yourself, saw what was happening.'

'As I said I didn't see him.'

'You mean, you didn't see him in the grounds.'

'He wasn't in the grounds.'

'How do you know?'

'Because I didn't see him; I've just told you!'

'But he may have seen you, sir, but sadly, for Jamie Green, he'll never be able to tell us.'

'What the hell do you mean by that remark;' firing up again, 'are you trying to pin his murder on me as well?'

'We have no proof as yet that Jamie Green was murdered, sir.'

'What!'

'Jamie Green died by drowning.'

Chapter Sixteen

By Thursday evening, Tom Jackson was being personally escorted back to Britain, having been arrested by a senior officer from Interpol that afternoon while enjoying a chilled glass of *Picpoul de Pinet* in the terraced garden of the Hotel d'Or in a village outside Monaco.

From the moment he drove down the ramp of 'The Normandie' and on to the quayside at Ouistreham early on Sunday morning and heading south, Tom experienced the first stirrings of euphoria of actually breaking free from the conformity and predictability of what had been his way of life for as long as he could remember. Freedom. It felt wonderful.

He made good time and by late afternoon he was on the coast road, relieved to leave the monotonous tedium of the toll roads behind, passing easily through Cannes, Antibes, Nice and Villefranche-sur-Mer, until finally driving through the trellised entrance to the hotel. He had phoned them before leaving Portsmouth and being relatively early in the season was able to reserve a room. He was in no particular hurry to proceed on the next stage of the plan he had only recently put together; he wanted to savour these first few days of being answerable to no-one, with nothing more taxing than where he should eat in the evenings and it hadn't taken long for the days to form themselves into a self-indulgent pattern: the mornings; driving into nearby Monaco, choosing a pavement café facing the harbour, ordering coffee and croissants but resisting the impulse to buy an English newspaper, content to sit there watching the stream of tourists sauntering by, particular the women; to Tom they all looked young, beautiful, short flimsy dresses with swinging skirts, as they expertly negotiated the cobbled streets in incredibly high-heels and above all, oozing with confidence; they appeared absolutely carefree and by the way many of them glanced provocatively in his direction, decidedly available, but so far he hadn't made any sign of encouragement, but knew soon he would. The afternoons were spent lying on a sun bed around the hotel's swimming pool, absorbing the early summer warmth and learning the art of emptying his mind of the clutter he'd been carrying for too long. But Tom, if nothing else, was a pragmatist and although for some considerable time, money would not be a problem, the time would come when he'd start to seriously consider what he was going to do with the rest of his life. He had already decided he would try his luck in Hong Kong; he had a number of contacts there, clients he had assisted in various financial dealings and once he arrived there, he wouldn't hesitate to take advantage of this, but for the moment all he wanted to do was chill out.

***

Immediately Keith Armstrong had returned to police headquarters on Tuesday morning, he contacted Interpol in Paris, asking to speak to Stephan le Breton and within seconds had been put through to him and wasting no time in informing him of the latest development in the fraud case with which Stephan in his position of senior investigator was already *au fait*. From then onwards, the wheels to locate Tom Jackson's whereabouts were set in motion.

The first step was relatively simple. Working on the assumption he had indeed be heading for the south of France, it was an educated guess to assume he would at some stage be driving, the chances were he would have taken his own car, crossing the Channel from one of the ferry ports, and a check with the immigration authorities proved this had been the case; Thomas Jackson, British Citizen, date of birth: 14th July 1970, boarded Brittany Ferries' vessel, 'The Normandie' on Saturday 19th June, arrival in Ouistreham, Sunday 20th June at 06.45 hours. Immigration had also included the make and registration number of his car which enabled them to alert selected service stations on the direct route down to the south coast of France, although not anticipating much in the way of any feedback as most of them were self-service, but it was considered worth trying.

The ease with which Interpol had traced him even as far as Ouistreham, demonstrated to them that Tom Jackson had not worked out any kind of strategy. If he had, instead of following the easy option of crossing the English Channel to Europe and taken a flight further afield, not only would it have possibly given him more of a head start, he could have made a far better job in making himself incognito, but he hadn't. He had panicked, and in doing so, had lost more time in widening the gap between apprehension by the British authorities and Interpol.

Stephan Le Breton assigned Pierre Provost to the case; Pierre, around the same age as Jackson, although attached to their Paris office, had spent some years on the Cote d'Azur and knew it well. Not only was he an accomplished and diligent officer, but his suave appearance, together with the ability to blend in unobtrusively with the Cote d'Azur's affluent society, were as effective as any smokescreen. He also had the knack of spotting any imposter among them, a skill which had brought many an unsuspecting law-breaker to justice in the past. If Tom Jackson had chosen this part of France, Pierre was, in Stephan's opinion, the man to find him.

Once it was established that Tom Jackson had arrived in the country, Stephan had put out an alert to all French air and sea ports in the event Jackson was only using France as a starting point; at least now, should he make any attempt to leave the country he would immediately be detained by Immigration. Pierre Provost took over from thereon and by three on the Tuesday afternoon, he was boarding an Air France flight to Nice. An open-top Peugeot sports model had been pre-booked by Stephan and was waiting for him on the tarmac outside Arrivals when he arrived and tossing his travel bag on to the back seat, and familiarising himself with the gears, he switched on the engine and gently eased out into the road.

Before leaving Paris, Stephan had given him a print-out of Tom Jackson's passport photograph and he'd spent several minutes on the plane absorbing to memory the man's features, especially the eyes which he noted were unusual, certainly for a Caucasian, mainly in the way they turned downwards, and by the time he returned it to his wallet he was certain he wouldn't need to refer to it again, he would recognise Jackson as soon as he saw him.

Pierre had no idea how long it was going to take him, but he was reasonably confident he would. As Stephan had said, they really had very little to go on in respect to the man himself, which meant to a certain extent he would have to, not assume exactly, but calculate; balance the odds, one of them being the guy's fluency in the French language, going over again what Stephan had said: Jackson was English, born and brought up in London, middle class background, attended a comprehensive school, spent a couple of years studying at the London School of Economics and started his career as a teller with Lloyds bank in Oxford Street, joining the merchant bank, the WHL Group, sixteen years ago and working for them continuously ever since, all of which did indicate in him having no more than, at the most, an adequate knowledge of French, certainly not sufficient for him to find employment in the country. Also, the longer he stayed in the same place, it was inevitable he would be become a familiar figure among the locals, especially if he held on to the same car; vehicles with foreign number plates were conspicuous, plus the added problem of driving a foreign registered car for any length of time. It was questionable whether Jackson had thought through how, with official checking, his time here was extremely limited. Stephan had stressed the importance of locating him as quickly as possible before the search became more widespread should Jackson decide to move on. They could put an alert out to the hotels along the coast, but Pierre, at least for the next forty-eight hours, preferred to use different tactics, and ones which wouldn't pre-warn Jackson.

Driving along Nice's *Promenade des Anglaise*, the long stretch of sandy beach and the brilliant blue of the Mediterranean on his right-hand side and the luxury hotels on the other, Pierre continued for several kilometres until he reached Villefranche-sur-Mer. He'd reserved a room at *La Villa Patricia*, a lovely hotel on the outskirts of the town and where he'd stayed many times over the years, deciding to book in before driving further along the coast road towards Monaco. He planned to make the principality his starting point, working on the premise that Jackson may have had a romantic notion of selecting one of the most glamorous spots in Europe for his hideaway, the casinos of Monte Carlo perhaps appealing to the gambling side of his nature.

An hour later he was seated outside *Le Bistro* in the centre of Monaco, cafés and restaurants on either side of him were bustling with customers, the atmosphere as it always was at that time in the early evening tingling with excited anticipation as they settled down to enjoy their pre-dinner aperitifs, the rise and fall of the different languages merging with the chink of glass and the popping of champagne corks. Pierre, for the moment content to relax and feel his way back into the flow of the slower pace of life, so very different from Paris, slowly sipped his Campari and soda and without looking directly at anyone in particular, listened to the various accents; he reckoned mainly they were either French or Italian, with a number of Germans, the distinctive guttural tones instantly recognisable and only a smattering of English. It was still too early in the season for the annual influx of holidaymakers from Britain which should theoretically make his task easier. There weren't many people sitting on their own; two or three women and only one other man, well into middle-age, stout, balding and reading a guidebook on Monaco.

Pierre caught the attention of one of the waiters, realising as he came closer to his table that he had seen him several times before, remembering he was called Michel.

'*Bon soir, Michel.*'

'*Monsieur Provost!* You have returned, that is good; *bon soir!*'

'*Comment allez vous, Michel.*'

'*Bon;* I am well, *Monsieur,* and now,' he said, 'as you can see we are becoming busy now the summer season is beginning.'

Pierre had known him for years, long before he left to work in Paris. Michel knew he was in the police force and although he'd never mentioned it, he rather suspected Michel had worked it out for himself that he was with Interpol, but he was far too professional and polite to ever say so.

'There are not too many British tourists here yet though.'

'A few, but they will be coming next month and then we will be, as the English say, rushed off our feet.'

'I know,' Pierre smiled, regretting he was unable to show him Tom Jackson's photograph; there were too many people around, but he would come back the following morning and speak to him again when it was quieter, 'I'd like another Campari and soda please, Michel.'

'*Certainement, Monsieur.*'

Later, after he'd eaten at a little Italian restaurant a couple of streets away from the centre and where it was considerably quieter, and the food was as delicious as it always had been, he drove along to the casino, spending a couple of hours in the area around the main bar, choosing a position from where he could see people arriving and leaving; occasionally he walked around the gaming tables, but there was no-one in there that night who resembled Tom Jackson. Not disheartened, he went back to *La Villa Patrica*, had a final drink in the lounge bar and went up to his room.

He rose early the following morning, ate breakfast in the restaurant and by ten-thirty he was on his way back once more to Monaco. Before calling into *Le Bistro*, he visited half a dozen hotels in the area where tourists usually stayed, and after introducing himself, had a word with the managers, showing them Jackson's photograph, but not only did they not recognise him, which considering the size of the hotels was understandable, but on checking at reception he was told that they had no guests of that name, nor any reservations. Asking each of the managers if they could let him know if they should receive any reservation from a Mr Tom Jackson, he carried on to *Le Bistro*, but before he reached there and found a parking space, he walked the short distance to the only newsagents he knew of in that part of the town who sold English newspapers. Once again, he took the photograph out of his wallet, but the man wasn't able to help. It's possible, Pierre thought as he left the shop, that Tom Jackson, if he was in the area may have chosen not to learn what was going on internationally, and in particular if he was expecting to see his name on the front page, or any other page if it came to that, and deciding as he hadn't had any luck with the hotels he'd been to here, he'd try some of the most likely ones in Cap d'Ail on his way back to *La Villa Patricia*, Cap d'Ail being virtually on Monaco's doorstep.

There were customers sitting outside the café, recognising one of the women he'd seen the evening before, but Pierre was the only one inside and going over to the bar he ordered a cappuccino. Michel was on duty as he'd hoped and showed no surprise when he was shown the photograph and asked whether he'd seen the man before. He took a while to answer, screwing up his eyes as he looked closely at the print.

'*Oui, Monsieur,*' he said slowly, 'I have seen him, I am sure it is the same person; three times, in fact, Monday and Tuesday morning, about this time.'

'And the third time?'

'Yesterday, *Monsieur*, after you had left, no more than five or six minutes it would have been.'

So, Pierre thought, my hunch has paid off; he has made for Monaco!

'Each time you saw him, Michel,' he asked him, 'was he on his own?'

'Yes, although last evening he got into conversation with one of our customers. I thought he may have known the lady, but I am not sure.'

'She would have been English.'

'Oh, yes, but she speaks our language very well, although with an English accent.' he smiled.

'He may have known her, Michel,' keeping his tone casual, 'and seeing her here was perhaps one of life's little coincidences.' but not altogether meaning what he'd just said. She could be the woman who was sitting outside now; he only had to ask Michel but decided not to. Working on the premise, that Michel had been right and his customer was Tom Jackson, if Jackson had arranged to meet her when he reached the Cote d'Azur, she could be one of his contacts and the last he wanted was to display any undue interest in her presence, although not dismissing the fact that she could be the means for him to discover where he was staying.

Thanking Michel for his help, he picked up his coffee and took it outside with him. More people were walking along the pavement in front of *Le Bistro* by now, many of them stopping to read the food and drinks menu on the wooden chalk boards propped up on either side of the entrance. Very soon the tables would be taken, but before they did Pierre had a choice of where he could sit, selecting the one nearest to the woman Michel had mentioned.

She looked up briefly from the copy of "The Times" she'd been reading, but only to acknowledge his presence, and then returned to the paper. Pouring sugar from the tiny sachet, he slowly stirred his coffee, meanwhile mentally absorbing every detail of her appearance, exactly as he'd been trained to do. She was in her early thirties; thirty-two, thirty-three, slim, attractive, in a gamine sort of way, small features, dark hair, glossy, parted in the centre and clipped loosely back from her face. There was an air of fragility about her, which the green, cat-like eyes, belied; she was expensively dressed, stylish and understated; cream linen trousers, short-sleeved royal blue shirt and matching blue pumps. In spite of Michel believing her to be English, that is, if she was the same woman, Pierre wasn't sure. Her colouring suggested she could be Italian, although there was a calmness about her which he wouldn't normally attribute to the Latin temperament. She appeared totally at ease in her own company, not self-conscious as many other women he'd known. She wasn't wearing any wedding ring, which didn't necessarily mean she wasn't married, wondering what she did for a living. Realising he'd allowed his coffee to go cold, he brought his stealthy scrutiny to an end, still unsure how he was going to approach her without making himself appear as though he was making a pass.

He'd noticed the cigarettes and lighter on the table beside her coffee cup and taking out his own packet from his jacket pocket, he made to find his lighter, patting each pocket in turn, then with a sigh replaced the cigarette he'd already taken out.

'Would you like to use my lighter?' she asked, passing hers over to him.

The ruse, corny though it was, had worked and smiling he took it from her, lit his cigarette, and handed it back.

'Thank you; I've been trying to give up the habit, but it's not easy.'

'So have I, but I'm not sure why really; it could be because now in England it's considered extremely unsocial.'

'We, French,' he said, 'strongly protested against this non-smoking ban in public places, but we were wasting our breath.'

'I know you did; I was here then and I remember the posters -'

' - *ne pas prendre de suite notre liberté.*'

'You're right, but all of us value our freedom, wouldn't you agree?'

'Of course.'

'You're from Paris, I think.'

'You are familiar with the different French dialects.'

'Some of them, yes, but I spent a number of years working in Paris, that's probably why.'

A polite, inconsequential exchange between two people who had just met, but why was it he wondered, finishing his coffee which by this time was ice cold, he was getting the impression there was more behind her words.

'But obviously you prefer to spend time here rather than in Paris?' Two can play at that game.

'If I want to relax, yes, but the real reason I'm here is to visit my mother and I wanted to be here before the holiday season gets into full swing.' she added.

She was giving nothing away. Okay, she'd just told him her mother lived here, indicating he could have been right thinking she may not be English although the tiny flicker of unease about her persisted, unable to attach any explanation for it, but by the very nature of his training he had developed a sixth sense, a keener perception, and it had seldom let him down. It could be because of his idea earlier that she might be involved with Jackson, but he wasn't sure.

'But you live in England?'

'Oh, yes, in London.'

And that's all you're going to get Pierre; the lady's told you all she wants you to know and short of asking her outright what she did for a living which, even if she did tell him, would still not provide him with what he really wanted to know. What she and Jackson had been talking about last evening could quite simply be a facsimile of today's brief exchange of words. He was no further forward than he was ten or fifteen minutes ago. He couldn't afford the time to sit outside street cafés all day in the hope his quarry would appear, and making his excuses, accompanied by the social niceties of saying he had enjoyed talking to her, went inside to pay for his coffee.

***

Laura Kendal waited until he had gone before taking her mobile out of her bag and dialling her editor's number in London.

'Martin,' she said as soon as she was put through to him, 'Laura here, I believe I could be on to something, but I wanted to pass it by you first.'

'Laura; I thought you were in France.' the gravelly voice of Martin Webster crackling with static.

'I am, but at the moment I'm here in Monaco.'

'Okay, fire ahead; I'm listening.'

'It's about a guy called Tom Jackson; I saw him for the first time when I was in Upper Nettles last week covering the Nicholson murder, although I didn't know his name then, but he's turned up here. This was last evening; I was in one of the pavement cafés, the same one I'm in now actually, and we got into conversation, nothing much, you know the sort of things people say to each other when they meet as casually as that, anyway, he mentioned his name and naturally I remembered it.'

'Naturally.'

'And that was that, or so I thought; I merely put seeing him again, okay in an entirely different setting, as being a coincidence and I didn't think any more about it until a few moments ago.'

'This is beginning to sound interesting.'

'I think it is because I overheard a customer, a handsome Frenchman incidentally, discussing someone he was trying to find. I couldn't hear what he was saying as they were standing inside the café, not all that far away from where I am now, but the owner's voice was considerably louder and he was looking out towards where I was sitting and said – I'll try to be exact as I can, Martin: "last evening", he said, "he got into conversation with one of our customers. I thought he may have known her -" that's more or less right I think.'

'What makes you think your handsome Frenchman was looking for this guy, Laura?'

'Because he'd handed the owner a photograph, that's why; it wasn't glossy, more like a print-out.'

'You could be right; then what?'

'A couple of minutes later, my handsome Frenchman as you so

eloquently describe him, came outside with his coffee and although there were quite a number of tables unoccupied, he chose the one next to me and using one of the oldest introductory gambits by not being able to find his lighter and, of course, being a polite woman, I asked if he would like to borrow mine.'

'Police.'

'I would say so.'

'And as he's French, I would suggest Interpol.'

'He must be Martin, so what I'm asking you is this; can I follow it up, see if there is a story here?'

'Just a minute, Laura, hold your horses;' he chuckled, but she could tell he shared her excitement, controlled, but nevertheless that's what it was, excitement of being ahead of the pack, front page news, in other words, a scoop. 'Tom Jackson's a fairly common name, I suppose, but it might, just might mind you, be the same one. Did he tell you anything about himself?'

'He had a London accent, a bit affected, you know, but he said he worked in Hong Kong in the financial consultancy business; that was all, he didn't elaborate.'

'It could be true, but if he is the same Tom Jackson I heard about the other day, I don't think so. Also, Laura you may indeed have struck lucky and if the man you're telling me about is Jackson, well, we could have something big here.'

'So, what have you heard about him, then?'

'Apparently, although the merchant bank he's been working for are doing their damnedest to keep it to themselves, word has been going round in the City that as he hasn't turned up for work this week and nobody's been able to contact him, he's left the country and it sounds from what you've been saying, Laura, that could be the case.'

'Wow!'

'Exactly;' another chuckle, 'There have been rumours circulating in the City for several months about misplaced funds, private investors being short-changed, talk of a massive fraud scam and this Tom Jackson was handling investments, that was his special forte.'

'I bet.'

'So, Laura, you have your story; I suggest you try and glean as much more as you can out there and then follow it up at this end when you get back. By the way,' he added, 'how is your mother?'

'She's fine, thanks, Martin. Her villa is beautiful and she's made a number of friends; they've even formed a bridge club amongst them.'

'That's great.'

For all his gruff exterior her editor had a soft centre; a family man, three grown-up daughters, none of them following a career in journalism and above all, he was generous in any praise he meted out. She'd been working for him for ten years since returning to London after her five years with Paris Match and couldn't imagine ever coming back to France, except for holidays and to spend a little time with her mother.

Going over once more what Martin and she had been talking about, she was reminded of the other good-looking police officer she'd seen the week before in Upper Nettles; this had been the day before Tom Jackson had come into the restaurant of the "Nettles Hotel" where she'd been staying, but this time she'd been in the bar having a drink, when exactly as today, she'd overheard his conversation with the hotel's head barman. It's true she hadn't heard Tom Jackson's name mentioned, only the name of the murdered woman, but now seeing him again she was beginning to wonder whether there was anything significant in Tom Jackson being in Upper Nettles at that time. It seemed unlikely, but then, she didn't trust coincidences, determined, now that Martin had given her the go ahead, to find out more. She knew from experience events had a habit of moving in an unlikely and even mysterious way, and the more she puzzled over what had been happening, the more she wondered whether there could be any possible link. Between the murder of a woman in the New Forest and the investigation of what, according to Martin, sounded like a fraud case of some magnitude. Perhaps she was letting her imagination take hold. Equally bizarre though was another undisputed fact; why should a man who lived and worked in London in an environment so alien to the majority of the folk who resided in Upper Nettles, turn up there around the time the Nicholson woman was murdered and now here, in the south of France and sitting outside a café in Monaco. The big question is, she concluded, why had he been in Upper Nettles? It didn't make sense.

***

The remainder of the day turned out to be considerably more productive than Pierre had expected. Driving away from the Port, he headed back in the direction of Villefranche-sur-Mer, and thought about the woman he'd been speaking to. She bothered him; in fact, she bothered him a great deal, making up his mind to return to *Le Bistro* after lunch and have another word with Michel. Chances were that she may be a fairly frequent visitor to Monaco, not necessarily to *Le Bistro*, but to the other cafés along the pavement in front of the port. If she was, Michel would have learned something about her, and if not, he could probably find out, knowing that despite the keen competitiveness there always remained a generous degree of camaraderie among the waiters.

La Villa Patricia's restaurant was half-full, but only wanting something light to eat, went instead into their lounge bar where he'd remembered seeing a snack menu when he'd been in the night before. Ordering a *salade tomate* and *une assiette de fromages* he took his glass of lager over to one of the tables outside on the terrace but made a point of half-facing the bar in the event, remote though it might be, of Tom Jackson making an appearance. *La Villa Patricia* was on a raised piece of ground and from where he was sitting he had a perfect uninterrupted view of the Mediterranean, the shimmering blue of the sea merging with a cloudless blue sky; there were peacock-blue glazed pots of geraniums arranged along the front ledge of the terrace, the crimson, pink and white flowers a riot of colour. A flawless setting and for a time idling with the thought of how good it would be to share the moment of pure idleness with someone; Veronique would have been in her element here he thought sadly, but although she had died almost ten years ago, he often felt her presence, especially when he was in an ideal setting such as this. Not healthy. It wasn't as if he hadn't met other women, some of whom he had been attracted to, but he always held back from making that final commitment. Marriage had suited him, he'd never strayed, not as many of his friends and colleagues had. Veronique had been all he wanted, but it wasn't to be, and losing her had scared him, he couldn't bring himself to face up to even the thought of having his happiness severed a second time.

Giving himself a mental shrug, he returned to the present. Tom Jackson. He knew precious little about the man, so what did he know? He was British, lived in London all his life, will be forty next month, he knew what he looked like from the photograph, knew the make and registration number of his car, that he came over to France on one of the Brittany Ferries' vessels, arriving in Ouistreham early on Sunday morning and probably the most important, he was staying in either the south of France or in Monaco and up to last evening was still in the area. To have visited *Le Bistro* three days running signified that whichever hotel he was in it must be in close proximity to the principality

His food arrived at that point, interrupting his appraisal, incomplete and unsatisfactory as it was, and ordering another lager from the waitress, he settled down to enjoy his lunch. He had reached the cheese stage when his mobile rang, Stephan le Breton's name appearing on the display panel.

'Hello, Pierre; it's early days I know,' he said, 'so of course I'm not calling to ask how you're progressing, but Keith Armstrong has just phoned to say the press have latched on to Tom Jackson's sudden departure from London. Don't ask me how they've found out and, as Keith said, it was probably only a matter of time before they did. He's of the opinion and, from what he's been saying I'm inclined to agree with him, which is that the WHL Group have a mole.'

'In tipping Jackson off about their decision to fire him?'

'Not that so much, and while he doesn't discount it entirely, there's a stronger indication that particular piece of information had been passed on to him by the woman he'd been having an affair with for some time, who,' he explained, 'happens to be married to one of the partners of the financial consultancy firm who, to quote Keith, appear to be up to their necks in this fraud business.'

'A can of worms.'

'Very much so.'

'I'll stop you there, Stephan, if I may,' Pierre said, 'but I'm ninety-nine per cent certain Jackson is here; I haven't seen him myself, but according to the waiter who works at one of the cafés down by the port in Monaco is sure after looking at the print-out that he'd seen him, not just once this week, but three times. Incidentally, I've known Michel for years and I'd vouch for his reliability.'

'That's encouraging.'

'I think so; I'm going back this afternoon to have another word with him, because if he's right about it being Jackson when he saw him outside his café last evening, he spent some time talking to one of their other customers.'

'Man or woman?'

'A woman, Stephan, and I have a hunch she may have been there again this morning and was able to get into conversation with her; quite frankly I can't make up my mind about her.'

'And you think this chap Michel will be able to tell you something about her?'

'I'm hoping he will; you see,' he went on, 'she's British, and told me she lives in London, although she comes over here fairly regularly, mentioning that her mother lives here, so the café world being what it is, chances are there will be many who know her, at least her name.'

'We can then run a check on her.'

'That's what I thought.'

'What's your gut feeling about her, Pierre?'

'Well, until we find out more about her, I'm not ruling out that she could be in cahoots with Jackson, or on the other hand which does sound more likely, she could be a journalist.'

'Ah! Makes sense, doesn't it?'

'Yes, it does; I realise she could have been phoning anyone, Stephan, but immediately I left the café, I caught her reflection in the window of a car which was parked alongside the pavement as she picked up her mobile.'

'As you say, she could have been phoning anyone, but whichever way you view it, Pierre although people seem to be permanently attached to their mobile phones these days, and unless she was receiving a call, it does seem somewhat suspicious.'

'I was only a few yards away and I'm sure I would have heard it, even above any noise from the traffic; you know how individually piercing these phones are, Stephan.'

'Don't I just; an intrusion! Anyway, Pierre, I'll ring off now and wait with interest to hear what transpires this afternoon.'

'I'll give you a call later; hopefully with something positive to report.'

Le Bistro was busy, but there were two other waiters now which meant Michel was free to spare the time to talk to him and what he had to say was considerably more informative than Pierre had hoped for; it transpired that he not only knew the woman's name, but the area in London where she lived. She was called Laura Kendal and owned her own apartment in Tavistock Square in Bloomsbury and had done for years. Her parents, up until the time her father died about eighteen months ago, had owned a property in Villefranche-sur-Mer; afterwards her mother moved to Monaco, purchasing a villa there. Asking him whether she was married although he'd seen no sign of any wedding ring, Michel had told him that she had been engaged to a French boy some years ago, but sadly, he had been killed in a car accident, but no, she hadn't married. Such a wealth of information, but at the end of it all, Michel didn't know what her profession was; her mother had never mentioned on the many times she'd been in and he hadn't liked to ask her, however, Pierre had sufficient for Stephan to implement a more detailed search into her background. Informative though Michel had been, he was still no further forward in locating Jackson, but at least when the report came through he should be in a better position to either eliminate Laura Kendal from having any connection with Tom Jackson or consider her as being a further link in the fraud case.

He didn't have long to wait, within an hour of relaying to Stephan the facts Michel had provided, the results had been emailed through to him.

Laura Kendal, thirty-six years of age, unmarried, residing at Apartment 3C, Baird House, Tavistock Gardens, Bloomsbury, profession, investigative journalist, employed by one of the nationals for the past ten years. Stephan had added an extremely interesting note at the end of the report; apparently, she had been covering the Nicholson murder case and had spent most of the previous week in Upper Nettles, returning to London on Friday afternoon, her piece appearing in the following day's edition of her paper.

Speaking to Stephan later, Pierre further learned that he'd had another talk with Keith Armstrong and according to New Scotland Yard's case notes, Tom Jackson had been in Upper Nettles on Friday with the intention it was believed of trying to retrieve the computer disc he had previously compiled, listing data which was being used as valuable evidence of his involvement in the fraud, together with names of other participants. The disc had been discovered by his ex-girlfriend amongst her possessions during her recent move from London to where she was now living in Upper Nettles, from there it was duly handed over to the authorities, finally ending up on Keith Armstrong's desk. In an effort to attempt to establish whether Laura Kendal had been the woman Jackson had been talking to the other evening, Stephan had asked Keith if New Scotland Yard could possibly find out where she had been staying during her time in Upper Nettles and whether in their opinion there was any possibility she could have seen him there. Again, they had been quick to get back to Stephan, and while not conclusive proof Laura had seen him, it shouldn't be ruled out, but she had been staying at The Nettles hotel in the town and on checking with the hotel they confirmed that a Mr Thomas Jackson had eaten in their restaurant, having paid for the meal by credit card; the day being last Friday and the last day of Laura Kendal's stay.

Some story, Pierre thought when they'd brought the call to a close, but decided, once he'd fitted the pieces together, credible. Had Laura Kendal, by some quirk of fate, recognised Tom Jackson when he'd been in *Le Bistro* last evening as the same man she remembered seeing during the time she was in Upper Nettles? She wouldn't have known his name though, not unless he'd told her, but considering how simple it had been to trace him as far as here, it did indicate he was making no attempt to hide himself away, therefore, the logical conclusion could be that he had told her and even if she was taking a few days off, primarily to visit her mother, being a journalist he reckoned her instincts to recognise anything untoward would be on permanent alert. She may have considered his own behaviour as questionable; he had brought his coffee outside, chosen a table next to hers, although there were others he could have gone to, and finally, the rather lame excuse to get into conversation with her. Hence the call she'd made on her mobile as soon as he'd left the café.

There was no sign of Laura Kendal outside *Le Bistro* the following morning. Michel was standing in the open doorway and gave him a wave as he walked past, Pierre's idea being to try one of the other cafés further along. He'd left his mobile number with Michel the last time he'd spoken to him in the event Jackson should make a return visit, this giving him more scope at a time of the day when traditionally the locals, along with the tourists, gathered to enjoy *un petit café et un croissant* while indulging in people-watching or, as far as the males were concerned, girl-watching.

It was well into the afternoon when he began to realise he was wasting precious time looking out for a man who may or may not turn up, but before finally returning to Villefranche, he called in at the few remaining hotels he'd listed, but again drew a blank; Tom Jackson hadn't booked into any of them. He'd by no means covered all of them in Monaco, only selecting those he considered the most likely, bearing in mind Jackson wasn't behaving furtively while he was here. Conscious of time passing and making little headway, he considered the next step should be to alter his tactics, but for a more intense and wider cover he would need assistance, deciding to speak to the chief of police in Nice. It wouldn't be the first time, Pierre thought wryly, when he was out of Paris on a case such as this, when he'd had to call for reinforcements, but he couldn't help experiencing a stab of disappointment. So near and yet so far, his instincts telling him that Jackson was still in the area. Any escape route he might decide to take would be closed to him and the fact there'd been no word from immigration at any of the outlets in France, reinforced his belief. Up to now, he'd had a head start in that as far as he knew, Jackson was unaware of his situation in respect to the authorities, but once the news of his desertion reached the media's attention, that would immediately change. And now, when he thought of the media, he thought of the woman he'd met the day before. If she had sussed out there was something newsworthy about Jackson, she would be bound to use it. She was a journalist after all and that was what she was paid to do, which ultimately sold newspapers, thereby increasing the industry's coffers.

Back in *La Villa Patricia,* and walking through reception, Pierre noticed some colour brochures of a hotel in Cap d'Ail had been inserted in their stand displaying picture post cards of Villefranche and neighbouring Monaco. Surprised to find one hotel promoting another one within a matter of only a few kilometres away, he took a closer look; "*Hotel d'Or*", reading the caption below the photograph and the glowing description; not one he was familiar with, but he'd call in later.

'The *Hotel d'Or is* another of our hotels, sir,' the girl behind the desk told him, 'and only opened this April.'

'I hadn't realised,' Pierre smiled, '*tres picturesque, Mademoiselle* and should attract many tourists this summer.'

'The bookings are going well,' she told him, 'especially as we now use the internet for our promotion, not only the *Hotel d'Or,* but this one as well.'

'And very close to Monaco.'

'Yes,' returning his smile, 'very close to Monaco and of course the casinos.'

Worth a try, he decided, going into the lounge bar taking the brochure with him. Could this be the one? Saving itself until the last, but if it wasn't, well, he really had no alternative; he'd have to make that call to Nice.

At six-thirty, Pierre was driving through the gateway of the *Hotel d'Or* and up the steep incline to the main entrance. There were no other cars in sight, but a discreet notice on the right-hand side directed the way to the hotel's private car park, but preferring to leave the car where it was, climbed out and walked up the wide steps to the double glass doors, the surrounding stonework screened by trailing wisteria. He introduced himself to the woman at reception, showing her his warrant card and asking, as he had done in all the other hotels, whether they had an English guest called Thomas Jackson staying.

'*Oui Monsieur,*' she said nervously, looking at the register in front of her, '*Monsieur* Thomas Jackson booked in last Sunday.'

His hunch had paid off and once he'd reassured her there was no need for her to be concerned about there being any disruption in the smooth-running of the hotel, she began to look more at ease and directed him out towards their terrace where she told him he would find *Monsieur* Jackson. And there he was. The man he had been assigned to find. Pierre recognised him instantly from the print-out and Michel at *Le Bistro* had been right in the way he described him; the way his eyes sloped downwards definitely did not look western. Before walking over to him, he paused for a couple of seconds in the open doorway considering the best approach; the last he wanted was to cause any disturbance among the other guests enjoying their pre-dinner drinks, but having no knowledge of Jackson's temperament, he had to take the chance of him realising there would be no point in making any voluble outburst. He didn't think Jackson would simply assume he was making the arrest single-handedly and without any back-up, but if he should be impulsive enough to make a run for it, he wouldn't get far. Yes, Pierre concluded, moving away from the doorway, the man would know there was no escape, certainly not for long.

As Pierre reached his table, Jackson was about to re-fill his glass from the carafe of wine when he became aware of him, and shading his eyes from the sun's glare, he looked up.

'Mr Jackson.'

'Yes?' There was no sign of alarm, only polite puzzlement.

Silently, remaining where he was, directly in front of him, Pierre showed him his warrant card.

'Interpol? I don't understand; there must be some mistake.'

Briefly, Pierre explained, but there was very little change in Jackson's expression, perhaps a tightening of the jaw line, but that was the only visible indication of his reaction to learning his attempt to escape justice had come to an abrupt end.

Events moved quickly then. He made no protest when Pierre asked him to leave and accompany him to Nice airport from where they would be leaving for the first available flight for Heathrow. Even when asked to surrender his passport, he didn't object, merely, again without saying anything, handing it to him. Within fifteen minutes they had arrived at the airport, Pierre with his silent passenger sitting beside him. He was well aware he was taking a risk of being in what could be described as a vulnerable position by not having any cover in case Jackson took it into his head to overpower him when he was driving, but it was a calculated risk; Jackson was no fool and if he had taken advantage, he would have placed himself in a far worse situation than he was in already; all the same Pierre had to admit as he pulled into the official area in front of the building to a feeling of relief. The authorities didn't waste any time in allocating them two seats in Business Class and with only thirty minutes wait until they could board, Pierre, moving slightly to one side, but never taking his eyes from him, phoned Juan to give him a quick update. Keith Armstrong in London, acted swiftly on hearing from Juan ensuring there would be a car and driver waiting at Heathrow.

Pierre, with Jackson beside him, were the first to board the aircraft and it wasn't until they were outside Arrivals at Heathrow and walking towards the car, that he noticed Laura Kendal. She had just joined the taxi queue and, although she didn't acknowledge him, for a fraction of a second their eyes met. Well, he thought cynically, no doubt she'll make the most of what she would have had no difficulty in putting together, remembering what Juan had said about the press being on to Jackson's involvement in the fraud case, wondering when the news of his arrest would hit the headlines. Laura Kendal may have placed herself ahead of the media pack.

Chapter Seventeen

Sara Blakeman was opening the shutters of Glenda Nicholson's hairdressing salon when Peter arrived on Thursday morning. He'd learned she was continuing to look after the business until the lawyers had finalised the winding up of Glenda's affairs and fully appreciated she would be finding it difficult to take much time off between clients, but there were some questions which he needed to ask her apropos to what Richard and he had been discussing the day before. Once inside the salon, she was quick to re-assure him she had half an hour before her first client arrived.

'How are you managing?' he asked her.

'Not too badly, Inspector; people have been very understanding when I've had to re-arrange some of their appointments. Also,' nodding over towards the young girl taking a pile of towels from a drier, 'I couldn't have done so without Pru.'

'What I have to ask you,' Peter explained, 'won't take long, Miss Blakeman, only a few questions.'

'Yes?'

'It's in respect to the time from last Monday morning when Miss Nicholson hadn't arrived here to when the news of her death had been made public on the Thursday. Did anyone call asking to speak to her?'

'There were a couple of people.'

'Yes?'

'Glenda's friend came here on Tuesday; it was after six and I was on the point of closing.'

'Her friend?'

'Well, yes; you see, he'd been here before, that's why I recognised him.'

'Do you know his name?'

'Only his first name because I heard her calling him Bernie.'

'And this was on Tuesday?'

'Yes, he sounded surprised not to find her here, so I felt I had to mention she hadn't been at the salon the day before either and that I'd reported this to the police.'

'And you mentioned we were treating her as a missing person?'

'Yes, I did; I hope that was alright, Inspector?'

'Of course it was, Miss Blakeman, indeed what else could you have said to him. You said there had been a couple of people.' prompting her.

'Yes, the other person phoned up last Thursday morning, about ten-thirty, I think it was; he didn't give his name but told me he was an old friend of hers and that he wanted to speak to her quite urgently.'

'And by Thursday the news had already reached the media.'

'That's right, but obviously he had no idea, so I had to tell him.'

'That can't have been easy for you.'

'It was a bit upsetting, but someone had to tell him, Inspector.'

'Of course.'

Walking back along the High Street to the station, he thought over what she'd told him. Why had Bernie Croft waited until the Tuesday before making any attempt to see her, why hadn't he done so on the Monday? Perhaps there was a simple explanation; he had admitted he'd seen Glenda being taken back to the Grange by Johnnie Wall that night and not knowing the outcome wanted to find out for himself, and because of his anger over her continuing friendship with Wall, had delayed doing this, but it had prayed on his mind. Possibly. It did indicate, though that he hadn't known she was dead.

As for that phone call on the Thursday, that did need to be checked up on. British Telecom would be able to provide them with the number, although Peter was starting to get a fair idea of whom it might have been. The news of the discovery of Glenda Nicholson's murder first reached the media on the Wednesday, but at that time the body had not been identified; the second time had been in the "The Gazette" on Thursday morning, followed later in the day on the television news, which made him believe that whoever had called the salon didn't live locally. Glenda Nicholson had met someone called D. Waterman on the Saturday evening. The Thorntons turned up at her house on the Sunday. On the Tuesday a registered package arrived for her, from someone called Bennett. If for instance the contents of that package were to be handed over to David Waterman, she would have had an appointment to meet him and when she didn't turn up he phoned to find out why. Piece by piece, it was beginning to come together. If he was thinking along the right lines, and Glenda Nicholson had been acting as an intermediary for Robinson & Waterman, he considered it feasible that instead of David Waterman returning to Upper Nettles, they had arranged for her to meet him in London; this would explain why David Waterman hadn't been aware of what had happened to her and to further corroborate his reasonings and to explain why such a meeting hadn't been arranged for earlier in the week, Wednesdays being half-days in Upper Nettles, meant she would have been free to meet him elsewhere, presumably in London.

As soon as he reached his office, Peter made the call to British Telecom and within fifteen minutes they rang back to say there had been three calls received by the number of the hairdressing salon on Thursday morning, the 17th of June, two of them local and the third a London number, the name of the subscribers being Robinson & Waterman Financial Investment Consultants.

***

'Isn't that the barmaid from "The Hunters"?'

'Where?'

'Walking up the steps of the police station - '

'- Ooh, yes, so it is;' moving quickly over to the window eager to see for himself, 'well, well, Maurice, I wonder what possible reason Christine Tomlinson could have for visiting our local constabulary.'

'More scandal, do you think, Trevor?' he commented archly.

'Mmm.'

'What does that mean?'

'It means, Maurice, that you may very well have hit the nail on its proverbial head. Mind you,' he went on quickly, eager to share the latest juicy titbit with him, 'just lately with the pace of life in this quiet little backwater speeding up somewhat, I must confess I am rather enjoying myself. In fact,' he grinned, 'Agatha Christie couldn't have created so many twists and turns in one of her plots!'

'I take it you know something about the unapproachable Mrs

Tomlinson.'

'How well you do know me, Maurice!'

'I should, Trevor, after all these years; so,' sounding impatient, 'are you going to spill the dirty, or do you intend to keep it all to yourself?'

'I don't know about dirty exactly,' he replied, pondering for a moment over his partner's choice of words, 'but it was about something I just happened to overhear -'

'- in "The Hunters" presumably?'

'Where else, my friend, where else!'

'The suspense is killing me.'

'I am prevaricating, aren't I, sorry Maurice; that was naughty of me. Anyway, to continue; apparently, Christine has been enjoying extra-marital activities and you'll never guess the lucky, or the unlucky man is?'

'Charlie Oakes.'

'Now you're being silly; of course it wasn't Upper Nettles' indiscreet postman; no, it was Pete Carr no less!'

' "The Bandanas"' saxophonist?'

'You look surprised.'

'I think I'm confused more than anything.'

'Why?'

'Well, I don't see what the state of Christine's love life has to do with her walking into the police station a couple of minutes ago.'

'Do you remember the other day when I told you I saw Bernie Croft going in there; Saturday I think it was?'

'Y – yes, but I'm still in the dark; you'll have to spell it for me.'

'Well, she came into "The Hunters" on Monday evening with her husband and it so happened Pete Carr was in there and, she was definitely not pleased to see him. Honestly, Maurice, you should have seen her expression; I thought at the time if looks could kill, Pete Carr would have dropped dead on the spot!'

'Perhaps she was worried in case her husband got suspicious if she was over-familiar towards him.'

'I don't think so;' shaking his head, 'it wasn't the first time Pete and Chris Tomlinson have been in at the same time and, remember, she is a bar maid after all and would have known him, but there's more.'

'I thought there might be.' Maurice grinned, obviously enjoying himself, nothing brightened up his day more than a juicy bit of gossip as Trevor well knew.

'Their *passionate love affair*,' he emphasised dramatically, raising his eyes heavenwards, 'has, according to what I've been hearing, been going on for months. No, Maurice, there is definitely no flicker of any *rapport* between those two now and to return to your question, I think her visit to the police station *has* got something to do with these murders!'

'In what way?'

'Oh, I know you think I'm imagining things, but it is something I *feel*, Maurice. I don't know *exactly*, but perhaps she knows something detrimental about The Bandanas", Pete Carr in particular, and has decided to *spill the beans*!'

'You are really incorrigible, Trevor. You could be right though; we'll just have to wait and see.'

***

As soon as Christine placed her foot on the bottom step of the police station she began to have second thoughts; seeing those two peering out of the Gallery's window and watching her every movement had unnerved her, for a second shaking her resolve, but she'd spent too many sleepless nights recently to waver now. She and Steve had only lived in Upper Nettles for about five years, but during that time she'd learned to more or less ignore the blatant interest the locals openly and unashamedly showed in other people's affairs, although working in "The Hunters" had made it impossible not to hear what they were saying about others, all too often this would be derogatory, totally uncalled for, but Christine had decided, in her ignorance of living in a relatively small community, that this was normal.

Taking a deep breath, she pushed open the double glass doors and walked inside. As with many people, her only experience of a police station had been founded on watching television movies, although the reception area of Upper Nettles police station bore little resemblance to any she'd seen on the small screen. In fact, she thought, noting the tubs of chrysanthemums and the old sepia-coloured prints of the New Forest lining the walls, there was nothing in the least official or off-putting about the place; even the uniformed sergeant behind the desk didn't detract from her immediate impressions.

She didn't have long to wait before she was taken along the passage to the Inspector's office. Peter Gale didn't appear surprised to see her again and perhaps sensing her unease didn't bombard her with questions, but merely waited patiently for her to explain why she wanted to see him.

'I have an apology to make, Inspector.' she said, deciding to come straight to the point, rather than skirt round what she wanted to say, and she had meant what she had just said, she did have an apology to make to him.

'You have something to add to what you told me last week, Mrs Tomlinson?'

'Yes, I did overhear what Glenda Nicholson said on her mobile, only a few words -'

' - which were?'

'She mentioned the name of the person who'd phoned her, he was called Johnnie and must have been asking her to a party because she repeated the word 'party', followed by saying she was on her way; after that she finished her drink and went.'

'Yes?'

'I suppose you could say that I assumed that the Johnnie she was talking to was - ' hesitating for a second, aware that this was the difficult part, unsure how much she needed to tell him, ' - someone I know. He's Johnnie Wall, but as I've said, Inspector, at that point I was really only guessing.'

'But you learned you were right?'

'Yes, because – I'm really finding this rather awkward for personal reasons, nothing to do with Johnnie but later, after the pub closed, I drove along to Johnnie's house; I didn't stop, but carried on and as I passed the entrance, I saw Glenda's car outside the front door.'

'You're certain it was hers?'

'Oh, yes, I've seen it often enough; when she could get a space she always parked outside "The Hunters" and, although I couldn't have told you the registration number, there are not many sports cars of that type and colour in the area.'

'You could make out the colour?'

'Yes, the light from the porch was shining directly down on it.'

'Did you see anyone?'

'Not then, but when I reached the end of the property, I glanced in my rear-view mirror and saw someone running across the road.'

'You say someone?' prompting her.

'I'm sure it was a woman, she was wearing something white, but I was too far away to make out any more than that.'

'Do you live in Upper Nettles, Mrs Tomlinson?'

'Yes, in the High Street.'

'And when did you finally get home that night?'

'I'm not sure exactly what time it was, but no later than a quarter past twelve.'

'So, presumably you would have reversed along the Lymington Road, rather than take the longer route back here?'

'Yes, I did, but I had to drive on for a couple of miles and the first convenient place for turning was the roundabout before you reach Brockenhurst.'

'Passing Johnnie Wall's house again.'

'That's right.' It hadn't been a question, trying to fathom out what his next one would be.

'Before you reached the house, did you pass any vehicles?'

'Only a cyclist; he was heading in this direction.'

'You would have then been ahead of him when you started your drive back?'

'Oh, yes.'

'When you passed the house, was there anyone around then?'

'No-one, Inspector.'

'I see, well, I appreciate you coming in this morning, Mrs Tomlinson. All I would ask you now is whether you would be prepared to sign a statement confirming what's been discussed; tomorrow, if possible.'

And that was that, she thought coming out of his office. She had fully anticipated having to explain why she'd decided to make a special journey as far as Johnnie's house at that time of the night, but considerably relieved he hadn't asked. She wasn't exactly proud of her behaviour and the last she wanted was to be reminded.

***

'I thought you would be interested, Chief Inspector,' Keith Armstrong said to him when he phoned first thing on Friday morning, 'to hear Tom Jackson is now back on English soil.'

'That was quick work.'

'It certainly was, but Jackson made it comparatively easy for the officer from Interpol who was assigned to the task; he'd done nothing to cover his tracks, was behaving like any other tourist in fact.'

'What's the next step, Inspector?'

'He'll be appearing at eleven this morning at the City of London Magistrates' Court, which will only be a matter of form of course; it's expected he'll be granted bail to allow us the necessary time to collect more information to build up a substantial case against him before the final sentence is passed and depending on the full extent of the embezzlement, the length and type this will be.'

'Have WHL decided to prosecute; I know they hadn't been too keen?'

'They have, yes,' Keith said, 'probably when they realised they weren't the only bank harbouring someone of Jackson's particular so-called talents.'

'The press are going to have a field day.'

'They will, and I wouldn't be surprised if that doesn't happen sooner rather than later.'

'Why do you say that?'

'Because apparently when Jackson was in Monaco; that's as far as he got by the way, he caught the attention of an English journalist and they were seen together outside one of the street cafés; the officer who escorted him back here heard this from the waiter whom he's known for

324

years and vouches for his reliability. He knew the woman's name which is Laura Kendal and that she lives in London, which made it comparatively simple for us to check up on her; she works for one of the nationals and has done for the past ten years; she's respected amongst her peers, isn't pushy which unfortunately is so often the case, and although she may be somewhat unorthodox in the way she operates, she doesn't fabricate to get ahead of the pack, if you know what I mean, but invariably she comes up with the goods, all of which makes me think she won't let go until she has her story.'

'It's inevitable, I suppose,' Richard commented, 'especially where such a large scale of misappropriation of funds is concerned.'

'You're right. Also, and this is interesting, but I did some further checking before I rang you and learned that she covered the Glenda Nicholson murder and spent some time in Upper Nettles last week.'

'That *is* interesting; as you know, Jackson was here on the Friday, she may have seen him then.'

'If that's the case,' Keith said, 'she may be trying to puzzle out why he'd been there when somewhat coincidentally, sees him again, this time in Monaco. Incidentally,' he added, 'she was on the same flight back from Nice last evening as Jackson; Pierre Provost, that's the name of the officer who was with him, told me there was no doubt she'd spotted them on arrival at Heathrow.'

'If she's as tenacious as you say, Inspector, she'll make the most of that. Before you ring off,' Richard went on, 'I should tell you that someone from Robinson & Waterman telephoned Glenda Nicholson's hairdressing salon last Thursday morning asking to speak to her; although the news of her murder had reached the media by then it appears he wasn't aware of this.'

'Thursday morning, you say?'

'Yes, British Telecom confirmed it was made at ten thirty-five.'

'It couldn't have been Clive Robinson; he would have been on his way to Upper Nettles around that time.'

'The question is, why did he want to speak to her.'

'To find out why she hadn't turned up with the package?

'It would certainly tie up that particular loose end.'

'I don't know about you, Chief Inspector,' Keith sighed, 'but there seems to be too many loose ends altogether in these investigations.'

***

There were no vehicles parked outside the Grange when Richard and Peter arrived there shortly after ten-thirty on Friday morning, although seeing the front door was partially opened reassured them that at least somebody was in, they walked up the steps and rang the bell. They waited a couple of seconds, before trying again, but still without any success.

'We'll try round the back.' Richard suggested.

'There's no-one at home.' a woman's voice called out to them from one of the windows on the first floor, followed by her head and shoulders appearing out over the cill.

'We were hoping to have a word with Mr Gerry Steele, madam.' Richard answered.

'Oh, I thought it was Mr Wall you wanted to see; Gerry's in the conservatory.' she added, abruptly moving away from the window and out of sight.

'There appears to be a distinct lacking in cordiality around here, Peter.' Richard remarked dryly.

'So I've noticed, sir. A bonus though that Johnnie Wall isn't here; it will give us the chance we need to hear what Gerry Steele has to say before we tackle him.'

'That's right;' he agreed, 'and if everything goes according to plan this morning, we should be in a position to pull the pair of them in.'

Walking round the side of the property, passing clumps of rhododendrons, they came to the conservatory the woman had told them about and she'd been right; Gerry Steele was in there, leaning back in one of the wicker chairs, a mug of coffee in one hand and a thick paperback in the other.

'Looks as if he hadn't a care in the word.' Peter murmured.

'We'll soon alter that.' tapping a couple of times on the glass door. They couldn't have had asked for a better reaction; instantly, Gerry Steele sat upright, slapping the book on the table in front of him and swivelling his body, turned round to stare at them both.

'Can we come in, Mr Steele;' Richard said, 'there are a few more questions we'd like to ask you.'

'The door's open.'

Richard introduced Peter to him, but it was impossible to gauge whether he found the presence of a second police officer disconcerting or not; the man's features seemed to be set in a permanent expression of surliness. He made no attempt to offer them seats but remained where he was and as Richard had no intention of addressing the man from the entrance of the conservatory, he pulled the nearest chair towards him and sat down, Peter doing the same.

'When I first spoke to you,' Richard said, 'you said you had spent the evening of Saturday, the 12th of this month, watching television.'

'That's what I told you; that's what I did.'

And when you were further questioned you said there were no visitors that night.'

'That's right.'

'When you had finished watching television, Mr Steele, what did you do next?'

'Went to bed; I was tired.'

'What time was this?'

'Don't know; when the film ended, whenever that was.'

'What film did you watch, sir?'

'What the hell does that matter?'

'Just answer the question please.'

'Can't remember.'

'How did you spend the following morning?'

'Pottered about, Sundays are quiet in the country.' he added sourly.

'Where did you have lunch, here or did you go out?'

'Here.'

'Alone?'

'Yes.'

'Was this usual?'

'What d'you mean?'

'Do you normally eat with Johnnie Wall, or do you have separate mealtimes?'

'*Normally,*' he emphasised, 'at the same time.'

'So, why was that Sunday any different?'

'Johnnie went out for lunch, but I didn't go with them.'

'Why not?'

'I wasn't hungry.'

'But you did have something to eat.'

'I wasn't in the mood for going to any restaurant.'

'A couple of seconds ago you used the word 'them', does this mean someone accompanied Johnnie?'

'Pete did.'

'Pete Carr?'

'Yes.'

'When did he arrive?'

'Don't know; some time during the morning, early.'

'When did you last see Pete Carr; before that Sunday I mean?'

'Can't remember.'

'It's our understanding, sir that Pete Carr is a frequent visitor to Upper Nettles and presumably on these occasions he will stay here, at the Grange?'

'He does, yes, but I still can't remember the last time.'

'I'll jog your memory for you, shall I?' throwing in the first bait, 'Pete Carr was here on Friday, the 11th of June, the day before Glenda Nicholson's murder.'

'Well, I didn't see him.'

'Where were you?'

'Around.'

'I'm sorry, sir, that is not an acceptable answer.'

'It's the best I can do.'

'I don't believe it is; I will put it to you that you did know Pete Carr was at the Grange on the Friday and for some reason you are reluctant to admit this. He lives in London, doesn't he?' he went on when it appeared there was no answer forthcoming.

'As far as I know.' a look of wariness appearing, although Richard would more aptly describe it as shiftiness; Gerry Steele was on the alert, it was possible he felt he was being cornered, which of course he was, but no doubt his brain by now was working overtime on how to extricate himself.

'Unless Pete Carr had a reason for being in the New Forest area, apart from seeing Johnnie Carr, I would have thought it would have been impractical, not to say tiring, to drive down from London on the Friday, leave before the Saturday, and then return here early on Sunday morning. It doesn't seem logical.'

The only answer Richard received was a shrug of his thick shoulders.

'In which part of the house did you watch television on the night Glenda Nicholson was murdered, Mr Steele?'

'In the kitchen.'

'From where you would have heard if there had been any visitors?'

'I told you there weren't.'

'I realise what you've told me, yes, but what I asked was, whether you *would* have heard voices coming from the lounge, the lounge presumably being the room on the ground floor with the French windows; not whether there had been any visitors.'

'Well, put like that, yes, I suppose so.'

'But you didn't.'

'No, because there weren't any.'

'Mr Steele,' Richard said slowly, 'either you had the volume of the television extremely high or you have poor hearing, but I would inform you that we have two independent witnesses who say that Glenda Nicholson's car was parked outside this house on Saturday night, the 12th of June.'

Once again, no response, not even a shrug. As a repetition of Wednesday when they'd interviewed Bernie Croft, Richard signalled for Peter to take over.

'Mr Steele,' Peter said, 'these two witnesses the Chief Inspector has just mentioned are prepared to testify in court, under oath, that Glenda

Nicholson was here on the night she was murdered. You have repeatedly said, insisted in fact, that there were no visitors that night, that only you and Johnnie Wall were here. Glenda Nicholson was here. That is indisputable. She was invited by Johnnie Wall, an invitation she duly accepted. She arrived around ten, just over an hour later she was seen by the same two witnesses running from the Grange towards the house across the road, followed within no more than ten minutes by her being taken back up the drive to the Grange, not by one man, Mr Steele, but by two - '

' - this is nothing to do with me - '

' - that remains to be seen, sir. However, I'll continue; after about ten minutes, her car was seen being driven away from here in the direction of Upper Nettles. Who was driving the car?'

'It must have been her, if she was here.'

'She was not driving the car, Mr Steele; it's more than probable she was already dead by then. Did you strangle her?'

'I did not kill her!'

'Who did?'

'I don't know!'

'Alright,' Peter deliberately waited a couple of seconds, not to give him time to concoct any more lies, Richard realised, but to increase the impact of his further questioning and from where he was standing, he studied Gerry Steele; beads of perspiration had appeared on his forehead and both hands were shaking uncontrollably, 'it's been established that Glenda Nicholson wasn't driving her car away from the Grange, also we know it wasn't Johnnie Wall and, if as you have insisted, there was no-one else in the house that night, the obvious deduction is that you must have been the driver.'

'I didn't kill her.'

'Yes, you've already told us.'

'Okay, I drove her back home.'

'To Lyndhurst?'

'Yes, but not as far as her house; when we left here she hadn't been in any fit state to drive, but she rallied round on the outskirts of Lyndhurst and said she wanted to drive the rest of the way home.'

Good one, Richard thought cynically and but for the various pieces of evidence, almost credible. Gerry Steele may be low on intelligence, but what he lacked in intellect, he certainly compensated for in inventiveness. Richard was certain, unlike the members of the group, including Bernie Croft, in that they were protecting Johnnie Wall, Gerry Steele was trying to save his own skin.

'And then what did you do?' Peter asked him.

'I walked back here.'

'And how long did that take you?'

'About an hour, I reckon.'

'Therefore, it would then have been around one in the morning.'

'Probably, I didn't check the time.'

'We don't believe Glenda Nicholson's car ever reached Lyndhurst that night, Mr Steele.'

' 'course it did.'

'Her car was driven as far as Nettles Hollow, a relatively short distance from here, her body was removed and dragged to a makeshift grave where an attempt was made to conceal it among the shrubbery, but he was interrupted, otherwise he may have made a better job of it. Jamie Green was cycling back from an evening in Brockenhurst, reaching the Grange around eleven-thirty, at the same time as Glenda was seen on the road outside, he not only walked into the grounds to see what transpired after she was taken back to the house, but he followed her car when it left ten minutes or so later. He had to cycle past Nettles Hollow on his way home and unfortunately for him just in time to witness what was going on; he was taken unawares, rendered unconscious by a vicious blow to the back of his head, bundled into the car, which was then driven to Lymington, where his assailant completed the final stages of his death. Was that how it happened, Mr Steele?'

Gerry Steele remained silent and judging by his increasing pallor, Richard thought it unlikely he would have been capable of any speech. By his own admission, he had told them he had driven Glenda Nicholson from the Grange, a complete turn-around from what he'd been saying before, and if they were to believe what Bernie Croft had told them about there having been no sign of any other occupant in the car, it could be safely assumed she had been either unconscious prior to being strangled after leaving the Grange or she had been dead already; either way, it disproved Gerry Steele's explanation of taking her as far as Lyndhurst. Whether he had been the person who strangled her or not, was, to a certain degree, questionable, although given what they'd learned about Johnnie Wall's past, their suspicions of him being her killer certainly seemed more likely. Their theory of how Jamie Green met his death was, Richard believed, sufficiently sound to bring a charge against Gerry Steele of violent assault with murderous intent. Noticeably, Peter had said nothing to him about the other witness who had provided them with the proof they needed to seriously consider him as being solely responsible for Jamie's death, but by establishing from him a few moments ago that he'd returned here around one the following morning, had strengthened their decision. According to Eddie Gallagher, he had seen Gerry Steele walking up the drive towards the Grange at the same time as he arrived there around three a.m. Richard reckoned it would have taken anyone of normal fitness at least three hours to walk from Lymington. It looked very much as if Gerry Steele had played his last card and like many gamblers before him, his luck had finally run out.

***

'Where's Gerry, Mrs Rogers?'

'Oh, Mr Wall -' a flustered Vera Rogers appeared in the open kitchen doorway, ' - he's been arrested!'

'What?' swivelling round to face her, immediately taken aback by her appearance; normally his housekeeper's demeanour was one of brisk efficiency, as it had been earlier when he'd left to drive to Salisbury to collect strings for his guitar which he'd ordered, but not now; whatever had happened had shaken her, although cynically he couldn't help noticing more than a hint of suppressed excitement in her habitual dead-pan expression; no doubt she couldn't wait to finish work and pass on what she'd obviously heard, or more probably overheard.

'The police were here, Mr Wall, two of them there were, they weren't in uniform, but I recognised them both - '

' - yes, Mrs Rogers,' impatiently interrupting her, 'just get to the point – please; why has Gerry been arrested?'

'I didn't hear everything they were saying, but it was something to do with Jamie Green - '

' - Jamie Green?' for a fraction of a second the name not registering with him, so certain she was going to say Glenda's, 'But I thought he drowned?'

'He did, but they were saying Jamie had been attacked first and then driven to Lymington.'

'And they believe Gerry did that?'

'Yes, I think so; it sounded very complicated to me, Mr Wall.'

'There must be some mistake.'

What more could he say to her, wanting to hear more of what had been said, but having no intention of pressing her. He had to think. Why had they arrested Gerry for this Jamie Green's death and not for Glenda's? It didn't make sense and walking across the hall to the lounge, dialled Pete on his mobile.

'What's up, Johnnie?'

'Gerry's been arrested?'

'For Glenda's murder?'

'No, for what happened to Jamie Green. I've just got back from Salisbury and all this happened while I was out; it was Mrs Rogers who told me.'

'Perhaps she's got it wrong.'

'She could have I suppose, but I don't think so. What the hell are they playing at Pete?'

'Don't panic.'

'They'll be back.'

'You don't know that, Johnnie. Try to keep calm.'

'Impossible.'

'I can imagine how you must be feeling, stuck down there, without even Gerry for company, so why not come up to town for the weekend;

give yourself a break Johnnie, otherwise you know what'll happen, don't you.'

'I'll get stoned.'

'That's exactly what I mean and we can't afford that Johnnie, not now.'

Pete was right of course, bringing the call to a close, but it was all very well for him; he didn't have the police breathing down his neck and now there was this business with Gerry to worry about. Should he give the Chief Inspector a call? What was the point? Besides, he didn't really want to know, pouring himself a generous measure of whisky. The way he was feeling right then he wasn't even sure now he was in any mood to meet up with Pete and the others in London, although he'd just told him he'd drive up there after lunch.

The familiar waves of the black depression which had haunted him for so long accompanying him as he walked over to the window in time to see the woman who'd taken over Tulip Cottage coming out. This was the first time he'd seen her, remembering what Gerry had told him the other Sunday. Gerry hadn't liked her, but then there were many people he didn't like, watching as she unlocked her car door and wondering whether they had her to thank for the police turning up here. Apparently, she'd told them about hearing someone knocking at her door on that Saturday night but that she hadn't seen who it had been, although it would seem she had been sufficiently interested to look out of her window and had been quite sure there'd been no car outside in the road. She must then have seen him with Glenda and Gerry of course. She may only have moved in, but it didn't mean she hadn't been able to recognise one of them, especially Gerry as she would have seen him again the following morning when she came over to the house. Was that visit as she'd indicated to Gerry, merely a neighbourly gesture or was she, as Gerry had implied, having a snoop around?

All this speculation was literally doing his head in and refilling his glass took a deep sip and as always when he was stressed, picked up his guitar to find the solace he yearned for and could only find through his music; the sweet haunting chords of John Lennon's "Imagine" filling the unnatural silence.

Chapter Eighteen

Claire had spent over an hour with Dan in the afternoon going over the outline plot she'd prepared for the sequel to "Tomorrow never comes", he'd only made a few suggestions which she'd anticipated, but as always she had agreed, knowing from experience these were never in the form of criticism, but he knew her readership far better than she ever would and as he had once said to her years ago: "Your forte, Claire is to write, and you write damn well, while mine is to nurture and encourage that talent to fit the market." Once she'd given him a time frame of when he could expect the first chapters, he'd brought the meeting to an end.

She had given Sophie a call before leaving Upper Nettles, arranging to meet her in "The London Pub" in Russell Square, and one in which they had both spent many happy hours after finishing work. Sophie was already there when she arrived and waved to her through the window where she'd managed to find seats, no mean feat on a Friday. Once they'd bought their drinks, she wasted no time in telling her about Tom's arrest.

'So, Claire,' Sophie, eyebrows dramatically raised, finally coming to the end of what she'd been saying about him, 'it seems that Tom has, at last, met his comeuppance and,' she went on, wagging her index finger in front of Claire's face, 'if you ask me, which I'm sure you won't, you've had a very lucky escape there; you really should have listened to your Auntie Sophie!'

'Okay, okay,' Claire laughed, 'point taken. I know you never liked him -'

' - that's an understatement!'

'But from what you're saying it does sound so – well, so incredible; I mean with Interpol being involved.'

'I suppose it does,' she agreed, for a moment looking thoughtful, taking another sip of her wine, 'what with the chase across the channel, continuing down to the South of France, to Monaco no less. Sounds very Alfred Hitchcock!'

'Grace Kelly and Cary Grant.'

'Quite, but seriously, Claire, even before his arrest, there had been considerable murmurings in the City; nothing specific, except that the general consensus of opinion is that Tom's exposure is only part of a bigger fraud set-up. In other words, certain people who perhaps haven't been absolutely squeaky clean in their business dealings are becoming a trifle jittery.'

'But I thought you said it was only WHL who were pressing charges?'

'At the moment, yes, but when you think about it,' Sophie explained, obviously warming to her theory, 'somebody's got to start the ball rolling.'

'I suppose so.' remembering how quickly Adam Brookfield had noticed the potential implications of what had been on the disc, and from what Sophie had been saying it sounded as though he'd been right. Presumably by now Tom would know that the disc had been handed over by her to the authorities, unless he was assuming it had been stolen which it very nearly had been, but either way, it should mean he would be making no further attempt to retrieve it.

'Anyway, Claire, you haven't told me, but what's the latest on what's been happening in Upper Nettles?'

'I suppose you mean the murders?'

'Yes, there's been nothing further on the news about them, therefore I'm assuming they haven't found out who was responsible.'

'Not as far as I know; in fact, everything seems to have gone quiet these last few days.'

'Not pleasant though; somehow you don't expect these sort of things to happen practically on your doorstep, do you?'

If only she knew just how close they had been, Claire thought later as she was in the taxi on the way to Waterloo Station; it had been good to meet up with her again, but she'd had a long day and was looking forward to getting back, where even after only a couple of weeks, she was beginning to think of Tulip Cottage as home, in spite of the unanswered questions surrounding her neighbours and she had to admit it was good to know that Jack was living nearby, only a matter of yards away across the stream. Paying off her taxi outside the station entrance she bought a copy of "The London Evening Standard", but it wasn't until she was on the train she had a chance to look at the main headlines, the predominant one being a picture of Tom emerging from the magistrates' court earlier in the day. He was on his own she noticed, wondering what had happened to the girlfriend, obviously not there to give him her moral support. Further down the front page, there was a piece which immediately caught her attention. There was no accompanying picture, only a single column:

"Sudden Death of London Businessman – The body of David Waterman, co-partner of Robinson & Waterman Financial Investment Consultants, was discovered by his wife this morning in their home in St. John's Wood. Jilly Waterman was too distressed to make any comment. The police are not treating his death as suspicious, saying only there was strong evidence he had died of a drug overdose, but were awaiting confirmation from the pathologist's report."

Claire read it once more. What was it Sophie had said? "someone's got to start the ball rolling"; had Tom's arrest acted as the catalyst? Or, perhaps more significantly, had the information on the computer disc been instrumental in putting the frighteners on certain individuals? Certainly Clive Robinson had been sufficiently concerned about its existence to take the risk of breaking into Tulip Cottage to try and find it. It was unlikely she would ever learn the true ins and outs of the whole business, and if she was being honest with herself, she wasn't too interested, grateful she didn't work in the financial world, especially in stocks and shares where the unpredictability of it all quite frankly scared her to death.

Dusk was beginning to fall as her train pulled into Brockenhurst Station and as she walked across to where she'd parked the car the village street lamps were coming on. The stretch of road from the station back to Upper Nettles was quiet and she didn't pass any other vehicle, once again struck by the silence, appearing even more pronounced having spent the last few hours in London. In fact, she thought, there really was no comparison and wondering how many months it would take for her to become used to the contrast. Sophie hadn't asked her whether she had any regrets about making such a radical move and she was grateful, because if she had, the way she'd been thinking these last couple of days she wasn't sure how she would have answered. Perhaps she would feel more settled once the police had found whoever was responsible for these murders, but she was finding it difficult *not* to think about it all and as Sophie had so wisely said, it wasn't pleasant.

The Grange she noticed was in darkness although there was a car parked outside the front door. She was at it again. It would seem she was incapable of not looking across at the place. She really must make an effort to stop what was becoming an obsession. What on earth did it matter what they got up to; it had absolutely nothing to do with her.

She was halfway across the lounge on her way to the kitchen when she was aware of a sweet sickly smell, her nostrils dilating as she tried to make out what it was, but it was something she had never smelt before. She stood where she was, in the centre of the lounge, and looking towards the kitchen, the last of the daylight casting up shadows across the worktops, her eyes accustoming themselves to the dimness, all her senses on alert, she listened, but there were no sounds, but then she felt a slight breath of air on her face; it was coming from the kitchen, but she'd closed all the windows, it wasn't possible. Had she imagined it? She took a few tentative steps forward, followed by two or three more. The back door was wide open! She couldn't have moved if she had wanted to now; her whole body, her legs, felt paralysed, every natural instinct was telling her to scream, but she couldn't. She was sure she could hear her own heartbeat, there was a tightness in her throat, in her chest, but using what strength she had left, she took a deep breath, counting, one – two – three – inhale and slowly – exhale. It worked; she felt steadier, at least her brain was functioning more normally. She had to rationalise; firstly, the obvious, someone had broken in; she may have been robbed or maybe nothing had been taken; the break-in could have taken place hours ago, the intruder long gone, but, the terrifying part, he could still be here and, if so, where was he? And, what was that ghastly smell?

With a tremendous, almost painful effort, she walked the rest of the way into the kitchen, but it looked exactly as she'd left it. She was about to close the door when she heard footsteps; somebody was coming down the stairs. She could have taken advantage of the few seconds she had to run outside; it would only take her minutes to reach Jack's cottage; he had just that second switched on his kitchen light so he was in, but she didn't; the intense fear had again rendered her incapable of making any sudden movement and to run would, she knew, have been impossible. Whoever was there had reached the bottom of the stairs now and had started to walk towards her; at first, because of the failing light, she couldn't make out his features, but as he came closer until he was standing in the kitchen doorway, she realised who he was.

***

There was no answer when Richard had repeatedly tried to phone the Grange and he was on the point of driving along there to see for himself whether there was anyone there, considering if Johnnie Wall had returned he may, having learned from the housekeeper that Gerry had been arrested, taken it upon himself not to answer, when he decided to give Pete Carr a call on the mobile number he'd given them, on the premise that he may have some idea, given that it appeared he was keeping a close eye on Johnnie.

Pete Carr answered immediately, and Richard could tell by the flatness in his tone of voice he was not best pleased to hear from him, reminding him once again of the unconcealed animosity certain members of "The Bandanas" appeared to have towards authority, namely the police.

'He's probably on his way here, Chief Inspector.'

'Do I understand you're expecting him, Mr Carr?'

'That's right.'

'When did you last speak to him?'

'Around midday it would have been.' he answered sparingly.

'You have a mobile number for him, Mr Carr?'

'Of course.'

'Would you give it to me, please?'

'Okay.' reeling off the numbers.

'Thank you; I would be grateful,' Richard added, although not holding out much hope he would comply, 'if you would let me know as soon as he arrives.'

'If and when I see him, Chief Inspector; no problem.'

There was no answer when he dialled the number he'd been given, but not altogether convinced Pete Carr had been telling the truth, he made up his mind to see for himself. It was always possible the housekeeper was still there, bearing in mind her reluctance earlier not to answer when they rang the front door bell.

Johnnie Wall's car was parked outside the Grange and pulling up alongside, Richard climbed out and, a repetition of this morning, walked up the steps to the front door. He only rang the bell once and when there was no response, he retraced his footsteps and walked round to the conservatory. The glass door was open, exactly as it had been when they had left with Gerry Steele, but no sign of the woman. Further along the path, he came to the back door which also was open; no bell, but he knocked loudly in what he was beginning to feel was a wasted effort, although he couldn't believe Johnnie Wall would have gone anywhere on foot, in any case, where could he go? He hadn't struck him as the outdoor type; therefore, the logical conclusion must be he was inside. He tried the door handle, surprised when it turned to reveal what appeared to be the utility room with an archway leading into the kitchen and not all that surprised to see the woman Peter and he had taken to be Johnnie Wall's housekeeper, standing by the sink with her back to him. He didn't step over the threshold, but instead, called out to her.

'Oh, it's you again.' was all she said, turning around from what she was doing.

'I was hoping to see Mr Wall; is he at home, madam?'

'Should be.'

'Would you be kind enough to find out, please?'

With a shrug to her plump shoulders, she dried her hands on a tea towel and walked with slow measured steps out of the kitchen into presumably the main part of the house. Richard couldn't decide whether she was deliberately being obstructive, or whether she normally behaved in this belligerent way and wondering as he waited for her to return how on earth anyone with her manner ever managed to find employment.

Within five or six minutes she was back, pale eyes peering short-sightedly up at him.

'Can't find him.'

'Am I right in saying it's Mr Wall's car parked outside?'

'Yes, that's his.'

'Therefore, he did return home from where he'd been this morning because the car wasn't there earlier when Inspector Gale and I were here?'

'Yes, he came back.'

'And you informed him about Mr Steele being arrested?'

'Of course.'

'Has anyone else been here, madam; why I'm asking you this is,' he explained, very much wanting to take the heavy hand with her but realised it would have been pointless; it would get him no further, 'if there had been, he may have gone out again with that person, leaving his own car where it is at the moment.'

'I didn't hear anyone come.'

'Madam,' Richard said, keeping his voice level, 'it is important I speak to Mr Wall and if you are certain he isn't in the house, to do so is going to prove extremely difficult.'

'It's not my fault if he isn't here.'

'I'm sure it isn't, madam, but if you should see him before you finish work for the day will you please ask him to telephone me, at Upper Nettles police station.' he added.

There was not much else he could do; without a search warrant he would be unable to tell whether the woman was telling the truth or not. Johnnie Wall could very well be in one of the rooms and had ordered her not to tell him. He was forced to accept that for the present he was stymied, returning to his car but before driving back he rang the Station and organised for an officer to come along and position himself as discreetly as possible to enable him to see if Johnnie Wall, or anyone else, should turn up.

***

Laura Kendal was outside the City of London Magistrates Court when Tom emerged, immediately to be swamped by reporters, but she held back to merge with the stream of pedestrians struggling to push through curious onlookers blocking the pavement. Attending that morning's hearing had been purely to find out what the outcome would be and, as Martin had predicted earlier, Tom Jackson had been released on bail until further investigations were carried out to enable the case to be finally brought to the High Courts. Meanwhile, Laura had given herself a time limit to fill out the piece which would appear in Sunday's edition. What she wanted to do was find out as much as she could on Tom Jackson's background; his friends for instance, perhaps a girlfriend, where he was in the habit of drinking, in fact anything; she wasn't entirely sure what she was looking for, except she'd recognise when that little bit of extra presented itself to give her column that extra edge over anyone else covering the same story. She knew where the WHL Group had their offices in Regent Street and she also knew, having been there often enough, where many of the staff socialised after work; the Masons' Arms was, in fact, the closest pub to the bank; admittedly, she may be wasting her time, but she had to start somewhere and the Masons' seemed as likely as anywhere, she decided, walking the few hundred yards to the Blackfriars underground station; she'd have to change at the Embankment for the Bakerloo line for Piccadilly, but it shouldn't take long and the pub was only a short distance from there in Devonshire Street.

The place was buzzing; the length of the bar practically obscured by customers. Weekends in London start earlier and earlier, she thought. A television screen flickered into life, the newsreader's voice scarcely audible above the hubbub, but she didn't need to hear what she was seeing as the picture of Tom Jackson, flashed up superimposed over the one of the studio, a look of bemused surprise on his face, whether caused by recent events culminating in his appearance in court or by being confronted by the media wielding microphones and cameras in front of him, she had no way knowing.

'Well, that's an end to his banking career.' she heard someone say from behind her.

'The grand escape, eh;' another one said, 'he didn't get very far did he?'

'Monaco! I ask you, for a smart guy, he was pretty stupid there.'

'Probably wanted to have a bit of a flutter!'

'Talking about a bit of a flutter, what happened to his girlfriend?'

'Which one?'

'Jilly; Claire chucked him out, I thought you knew that?'

'I suppose I'd forgotten. Anyway, what happened to Jilly, then; surprised she wasn't with him this morning, giving him some moral support.'

'He's going to need more than a bit of moral support, Guy; anyway, as far as Jilly Waterman is concerned, she's hardly going to hang around someone with his record, is she.'

By this time, it was Laura's turn to be served and once she'd moved up to the bar, the two behind her were out of earshot, but what she'd heard couldn't have been more informative. Jilly was an unusual name, also there could surely only be one Jilly Waterman, remembering what she'd heard when she'd arrived in the office that morning. It hadn't taken long for the news to filter through to them that one of the partners of Robinson & Waterman had committed suicide. David Waterman's wife had been called Jilly. And it would seem that she and Tom Jackson had been having an affair. Presumably, being married and apparently living with her husband had been no deterrent. There was some sort of link here, there had to be. Money. Investments. Stocks and shares. Tom Jackson had been employed by one of the leading merchant banks. Robinson & Waterman were joint partners in their financial investment business. Within a matter of minutes, she had arrived quite unexpectedly at what she had scarcely hoped for, although she was sufficiently realistic to realise it could be equally as easy for someone else to make the connection, but she had actually seen and spoken to Tom Jackson probably within hours of him arriving in Monaco. No other journalist had that and she intended to take full advantage of her 'find'.

***

It was well after six when Jack finished for the day; apart from a short break at lunchtime, he'd been working for over seven hours, but feeling his concentration going, decided enough was enough. Taking a can of beer from the fridge he took it with him outside on to the decking area overlooking the stream and towards the back of Tulip Cottage. Claire had told him she would be up in London to meet her agent and afterwards, before she took the train back to Brockenhurst, having a drink with Sophie. Thinking about Claire, as he'd found himself doing often these last few days, he wondered how long she would remain here. Although she hadn't said as much, he couldn't help but get the impression she was beginning to have doubts about moving out of London. He was being selfish in wanting her to stay, but his fear of rejection was too strong to actually come out with it and ask her. It was less than two weeks since he'd learned she was here, but it seemed longer. It could be because they had known each for so long, but somehow, he didn't think so; in those days he'd always been with Caroline and Claire was one of the crowd they would have a drink with after work, but naturally with maturity he and Claire had changed. He enjoyed being with her, talking to her and for the first time since Caroline's death, was beginning to believe there could be a chance for him to think ahead, even to hope there might be a future in them being together, but the last he wanted to do was put any pressure on her; Claire needed time and he recognised that. After the way Tom had treated her she would be bound to feel apprehensive about becoming emotionally involved. Give it time, Jack, he told himself.

Later, he'd just finished listening to the nine o'clock news, when he heard Claire's car turn into her driveway. He didn't know why he should look across at Tulip Cottage again; it could have been because he'd expected to see a window open, but they remained closed as they had been since she left, especially as it was a warm, humid night, with scarcely a breeze to stir the sultriness, but five minutes later, no more than that, when the daylight began to fade, and no lights had been switched on, at least not in the kitchen where he guessed that would be the first room she would go to whenever she came home, he began to be concerned. He went outside, walking to the edge of the decking where he could get a better view of the cottage, but there was no sign of life, except for the swifts as they made their way to the thick clump of trees close to the stream. Trying to still the flickering of unease, he took his mobile from his pocket and dialled her number. It rang, but she wasn't answering it.

He didn't hesitate and disregarding the thought that he could be over-reacting, he stepped down from the decking and on to the path which led to the bridge across the stream. It didn't take him long, almost running for the remainder of the way to the cottage, but as he came closer, only a few yards, he noticed that the back door was open, not just ajar, but wide open. And then he heard voices, at first only one and instantly he knew he'd been right. Keeping close to the stone wall, one step at a time, he made his way to the open doorway. Claire was in there; her back pressed hard against a work top, the man, much taller than her, had both his hands at her throat and then, as though he sensed his presence, he turned round.

Johnnie Wall, his features distorted in rage, peered out into the gathering darkness, his hands involuntarily loosening their grip. He hadn't seen him and taking immediate advantage of what could be the only chance to overpower him, Jack sprung forward, catching him unawares; with the impact Johnnie Wall fell against the table, losing his balance, hitting his head with a crack as he landed on the floor.

'Jack!' Claire sobbed his name, but as though paralysed, she remained where she was, red weals stark evidence of what Johnnie Wall had been trying to do to her.

'It's alright, it's alright.' he whispered to her, taking her in his arms. You're safe now, my darling.'

'He's not dead, is he?'

'I doubt it;' gently releasing her and looking down at the prone figure of Johnnie Wall, 'unconscious. I'm going to phone Chief Inspector Cavendish; the sooner they take him away the better.' taking his mobile out and phoning the number of the police station. Within seconds he was put through to Richard Cavendish, briefly telling him what had happened.

'What an ordeal for Miss Walters; how is she, Mr Andrews?'

'Very badly shaken.'

'That's understandable; I already have an officer outside the Grange, and I'm going to contact him immediately and I'll be with you within ten minutes.'

Sergeant Baker wasted no time in placing handcuffs on Johnnie Wall's wrists, meanwhile, he hadn't stirred, but as the sergeant informed them his breathing was steady. The police ambulance arrived seconds before the Chief Inspector and it wasn't until the stretcher had been removed, not only from the kitchen, but from the cottage, he saw the tension and fear slowly ease from her. He desperately wanted to be on his own with her, to reassure her that her ordeal was well and truly over, but he would have to wait until the Chief Inspector had been.

'I'm not going to bombard you with questions, Miss Walters,' he was quick to reassure her, 'only to ask you whether Johnnie Wall proffered any explanation for attacking you the way he did.'

'Only that he seemed to have convinced himself that I had been outside his house that night, snooping he called it,' trying to smile, but failing, her lips trembling as she tried to explain, 'and that I'd seen what had happened to Glenda Nicholson and promptly reported this to you; it was all terribly garbled actually. I think he must have been drunk, but perhaps it was something stronger than that, I don't know, drugs perhaps. And -, faltering for a second, but he didn't press her, '- and, then he lunged towards me, that was when he put his hands on my neck,' lightly touching where the impression of his fingers remained, 'and, I'm trying to remember his exact words, Chief Inspector.'

'I understand,' he encouraged her, 'take your time.'

'He said - "you are no different from her or the one before her; the three of you considered yourselves better – more powerful than the great Johnnie Wall and you will end up dead – just as they did", and that's when Jack came in.'

'It's enough, Miss Walters. You've had a dreadful ordeal, need I say anymore?'

'Not really, Chief Inspector.' and this time she did manage to smile at him. How incredibly brave she is, Jack thought, after what she's been through, at that moment feeling inordinately proud of the woman he was falling in love with.

The Chief Inspector didn't stay much longer and at last they were alone and, incredibly Jack thought glancing at his watch, it wasn't even ten o'clock.

'How are you feeling now?'" he asked her.

'Much better. Jack?'

'Yes?'

'You saved my life tonight; I want to say thank you; it sounds inadequate, I know, but if you hadn't turned up when you had, well – I don't know what -'

'But I did, Claire. I don't think you should stay here tonight; I'd feel a lot happier if you would come back with me.'

'So would I, Jack, but first I think I should check upstairs; you see, that's where he was when I came in. I just want to make sure everything is alright up there.'

'Of course, I'll come with you.'

'There's that smell again,' she said as they went through to the hall, 'I smelt it as soon as I got back and opened the front door.'

'It's cannabis, Claire.'

'So he was drugged!'

'Yes, he was giving every indication of it, not that I'm any judge, but I have seen people as high as that, not a pleasant sight.'

'I'll have to air the place tomorrow.' she said as they reached the landing.

'I know,' he agreed, 'but you'll find it will have dissipated by then.'

She told him everything appeared to be as she'd left it in both the bedroom and the study, with only a faint indentation on the bed where Johnnie Wall had presumably been lying while he waited for her to return home. What a homecoming, Jack thought, feeling a shiver down his spine as he realised what might have been.

They secured the back door before they left and walked hand in hand across the garden towards the bridge and to where he lived. She leaned her head on his shoulder when they reached the other side and he bent down kissing her lightly on the forehead.

'Here we are,' he said, 'home.'

'Home.' she repeated softly, smiling up at him.

*****

'There we are, then, Peter,' Richard said to him the next morning, 'the outcome of this investigation could have turned out drastically different if Jack Andrews hadn't intervened. I must say Claire Walters is an extremely plucky lady and what she told me last night went a long way in providing what we needed to finally arrest Wall.'

'Bernie Croft surprised us, coming in at the eleventh hour as he did; I wonder why.'

'Guilty conscious, Peter.'

'Probably.'

'He said to me yesterday afternoon when he called in here that after our visit to him on Wednesday he realised he'd been foolish in not admitting he'd actually witnessed what was happening, namely when Johnnie Wall was strangling Glenda Nicholson, but he'd convinced himself we wouldn't have believed him.'

'And that he'd get the blame for her murder.'

'That's right.'

'There's something that's puzzling me though, sir.'

'Yes?'

'Why did he call at the hairdressing salon on the Tuesday asking to see her; wasn't he certain that she was dead?'

'That's about it, yes; I asked him yesterday as a matter of fact. Apparently, when there was no news of her body having been found, he began to have doubts.'

'And of course it wasn't identified until the following day.'

'Strange chap.'

'They're all rather strange, wouldn't you say, sir?'

'You mean "The Bandanas"?'

'Yes, even those associated with them; in some undefined way each of them appear to be dependent upon each other, even their personalities, or what we've seen of them, are indistinct, shadowy.'

'You know, Peter, you're right; the way they don't function properly on their own, and of course in the case of Johnnie Wall, I would say he scarcely functions at all.'

'He sounds a mess.'

'I'm sure he is and whether this is a direct result of his drug addiction or there is something psychologically amiss, will be up to the experts in that particular field to establish.'

'Thankfully, not our problem.'

'No, we have enough of our own to solve, but as you were saying, although we've interviewed several of the group more than once we're no further forward in making them out. You're right with your description of shadowy; they are shadows; now you see them, now you don't.'

'And we've spent the last couple of weeks chasing those shadows.'

'Going back to Penelope Driver's suicide, Peter; I'm referring in particular to the conflicting statements from Johnnie Wall at the time of her death and to what Bernie Croft told us. Bernie Croft was quite adamant that Johnnie Wall and Pete Carr hadn't been in "Benny's Bar" that night and when you consider it, he wouldn't have had any reason to lie.'

'Do you think perhaps Johnnie Wall and Pete Carr hadn't been there then, sir?'

'If they were, Peter, I would say this wasn't at the same time as Bernie Croft. I agree Wall was taking a risk in saying they were, but by all accounts, it's a popular place and being a holiday weekend, probably busier than usual and if, as we've been told, they were regular customers, it's more than likely the staff for instance wouldn't realise if they hadn't been in that night.'

'As you say, risky.'

'Yes, but it's only now that the case has been re-opened we're questioning the evidence, otherwise you could say if he did murder her and we are of the opinion he did, he would have got away with it. There's no doubt we would still be able to build up a strong case against him, given a couple of more days, but meanwhile he'll be held in custody, no bail for him, I trust, to await trial for the murder of Glenda Nicholson.'

***

Laura's column was on an inside page of her paper on Sunday, but the lack of prominence didn't detract from the impact it had on a number of people, each of them reacting on a different level. Clarence Fountain of the WHL Group was not best pleased at the suggestion, veiled it was true, of the possibility of a 'mole' within the bank who had promulgated the swift departure of Tom Jackson from London last Saturday, having informed him of his impending dismissal on the following Monday. Clarence's distress was such he was unable to enjoy his weekly game of golf or join in the convivial atmosphere in the club bar afterwards, such was his concern over what he could expect the following morning from his board of directors.

Clive Robinson, still reeling from the shock of hearing of his partner's decision to bring his life to an abrupt end, suffered another jolt when he read, the name of their firm in print implying, although cleverly phrased to avoid any libellous action being taken, a possible connection between David Waterman's suicide and the charges made against Tom Watson, and from what he could make out from what the journalist had written, arrived at through Tom's friendship with David's wife, Jilly.

Jilly didn't read any of the Sunday newspapers being too preoccupied in trying to fathom out what her financial position would now be in the wake of her husband's untimely death, although a so-called well-meaning girlfriend was quick to enlighten her when they met for a drink at lunchtime.

Jilly's first reaction was annoyance, but this didn't run very deeply; she had merely shrugged her shoulders, saying what did it really matter, that they could say whatever they liked about her. She had far more important things to think about.

Lilian Thornton read Laura's column before Greg and without saying anything passed the paper over to him.

'Well?' she asked impatiently when he continued to make no comment after he'd read it, even passing the paper back to her.

'Don't look like that, darling.'

'Like what?'

'So worried; what's happened to David has nothing to do with us.'

'That isn't what concerning me, Greg; of course what's happened to David is dreadful, but it's the way the article has been written, her mentioning the partnership reminded me of that registered package.'

'What about it; we know the police have it, Lilian -'

' - yes,' she interrupted, exasperated at his apparent inability to understand where she was coming from, 'but it's just that I've been waiting for the police to return and ask us more questions about it.'

'My darling Lilian, there is absolutely nothing to worry about, I assure you. If they convince themselves that we sent the cash to Glenda, at the most, they may question the source and I can easily explain that, so once again, don't worry.'

'Tax avoidance is against the law.' she almost whispered the words, not wanting the housekeeper to hear.

'The clubs' accounts are in perfect order; that money can be accurately – and legally – accounted for. Trust me.'

Although the majority of the customers in "The Hunters" Arms" had by lunchtime read their Sunday newspapers, most of them had little interest in the suicide of a man they'd never heard of and as London wasn't Upper Nettles what went on up there was no concern of theirs. What they were, almost without exception, talking about that morning was the recent arrests for the murders of Glenda Nicholson and Jamie Green. Even with Christine Tomlinson to help them, Deidre and Chris were hard pressed to serve the steady influx of customers.

Trevor Wheatley was in his element. Ever since he had spotted Gerry Steele being escorted into the police station on Friday morning, he'd been unable to talk about anything else. Even Maurice, usually laid-back and accustomed to his partner's effusive dramatizing of anything remotely out of the usual, was beginning to tire of hearing Trevor's sometimes outrageous suggestions of what was going to happen next in what he insisted in calling 'the Upper Nettles murders'.

'Tell me, Trevor,' Charlie Oakes asked him, 'how did you hear about those arrests you've been talking about; I know you've already told us you saw that Gerry Steele being taken into the police station, but how could you have known about the rock star. According to what everyone is saying this morning, this happened on Friday night. Surely you couldn't have seen him as well?'

'Not on Friday, Charlie, but it was yesterday morning; I was on my way along to buy my newspaper and Johnnie Wall, looking somewhat dishevelled I might add, was somewhat hastily being escorted into the back seat of one of their cars.'

'Was he in handcuffs, then?'

'I don't think so; probably.'

And that's how rumours start, Deidre thought, they're all as bad as each other. And how, she wondered for the umpteenth time that lunchtime, did Trevor know that Johnnie Wall had been arrested for Glenda's murder. He couldn't. He really was unstoppable, but then she and Chris were in the hospitality business and should have learned by this time not to believe everything they overheard from their more drama-seeking customers, and Trevor Wheatley certainly fitted into that category!

Other titles by Margaret Alty:

Tangled Web – ISBN: 978 1 84549 422 3
Search for the Lion – ISBN: 978 1 84549 627 2
Sequel to *Tangled Web*

Jenny – ISBN: 978 1 84549 442 1

Camouflage – ISBN: 978 1 84549 478 0

The Last Orange – ISBN: 978 1 84549 560 2

A Reflective Image – ISBN: 978 1 84549 681 4

Carbisdale – ISBN: 978 1 84549 691 3

A Meadowbank Mystery

Murder in Meadowbank –ISBN: 978 1 84549 494 7

Double Act –ISBN: 978 1 84549 537 4

Murder After Hours –ISBN: 978 1 84549 579 4

A Gathering of Crows –ISBN: 978 1 84549 594 7

The Circus Comes To Meadowbank –ISBN: 978 1 84549 701 9

All published by arima Publishing.

www.ingramcontent.com/pod-product-compliance
Lightning Source LLC
Chambersburg PA
CBHW051230260626
47162CB00002B/354